Why had Joss brought me to this lonely place?

A feeling of foreboding came over me. Joss didn't want me. He resented me. It must have occurred to him how much more convenient it would be if I were not here. He wanted to be free and lose nothing by his freedom.

I could hear his voice echoing through my mind: "This is a country where life is cheap." Bushrangers roamed the land. How easy it would be for him to kill me. He could find a hundred excuses for it.

"I went down to the horses. . . ." I could hear his explanations. "When I came back she was lying there dead . . . strangled . . . or shot. There were bushrangers in the neighborhood. . . . Some jewels she was wearing were missing . . . so was some money she had. . . ." Or: "She was not accustomed to riding in rough country. I'd given her lessons in England but this was different. She took a toss. I saw that her neck was broken. . . ."

Nonsense, I told myself, this man is your husband.

Victoria Holt

THE PRIDE
of the
PEACOCK

A FAWCETT CREST BOOK

Fawcett Publications, Inc., Greenwich, Connecticut

THE PRIDE OF THE PEACOCK

THIS BOOK CONTAINS THE COMPLETE TEXT OF
THE ORIGINAL HARDCOVER EDITION.

A Fawcett Crest Book reprinted by arrangement with
Doubleday and Company, Inc.

ISBN 0-449-23198-4

Selection of the Literary Guild—October 1976
Selection of the Doubleday Book Club—January 1977
Selection of the Reader's Digest Condensed Book Club—
November 1976

Printed in the United States of America

10 9 8 7 6 5 4 3 2

Contents

1

The Dower House

I was quite young when I realized that there was something mysterious about me, and a sense of not belonging came to me and stayed with me. I was different from everyone else at the Dower House.

It became a habit of mine to go down to the stream which ran between the Dower House and Oakland Hall, and gaze into its clear waters as though I hoped to find the answer there. That I chose that particular spot was somehow significant. Maddy, who was a general servant and a sort of nurse to me, found me there once and I shall never forget the look of horror in her eyes.

"Now why do you want to come here, Miss Jessica?" she demanded. "If Miss Miriam knew, she'd forbid it."

Mystery again! What was wrong with the pleasant stream and pretty bridge which crossed it? It was especially attractive to me because on the other side of it loomed the magnificent gray walls of Oakland Hall.

"I like it here," I retorted stubbornly; and as forbidden fruit could never have tasted sweeter to anyone than it did to me, having discovered that there was some reason why I should not go to the stream, I went there all the more.

"It's not right for you to go there so much," insisted Maddy.

I wanted to know why. This was characteristic of me and resulted in Maddy's calling me "Miss Why, Where, and What."

"It's morbid, that's what it is," she declared. "I've heard Mr. Xavier and Miss Miriam say so. Morbid!"

"Why?"

"There we go!" said Maddy. "It *is*. That's why, and don't keep going there."

"Is it haunted?" I asked.

"It might well be that."

So thereafter I went often to the stream and sat on its banks and thought of its rising in the hills and meandering through the country, widening as it went into Old Father Thames and, with that mighty companion, finally flowing into the sea.

What danger could there be? I asked myself. Shallow except when there were heavy rains, it was pellucid, and looking down, I could see the pebbles on its brownish bed. A weeping willow drooped on the opposite bank. Weeping for something? I pondered. Something morbid?

So in those early days I would come to the stream and dream mainly about myself, and always the theme of my wonderings was: You don't really belong to the Dower House.

Not that the thought disturbed me. I was different and wanted to be. My name for one thing was different. It was in fact Opal—Opal Jessica—and I often wondered how my mother had come to give me such a frivolous name, because she was a far from frivolous woman. As for my poor, sad father, he would surely have had no say in the matter; a cloud hung over him as sometimes I fancied it hung over me.

I was never called Opal, so when I talked to myself I sometimes used it, and I talked to myself a good deal. This was no doubt due to the fact that I was so much alone; and thus I became conscious of the mystery about me which was like a mist through which I could not see. Maddy occasionally shone a little light through that mist, but it was only the faintest glimmer and often had the effect of making everything more obscure.

In the first place I had this name which nobody used. Why give it to me if they didn't intend to use it? My mother seemed very old; she must have been in her forties when I was born, and my sister Miriam was fifteen years older than I and my brother Xavier nearly twenty; they never seemed like brother and sister to me. Miriam served as my governess, for we were too poor to engage one. In fact our poverty was the remorseless theme of our household. I had heard countless times of what we had had in the past and now had no longer, for we had come sliding down in the world from the utmost luxury to what my mother called penury.

My poor father used to cringe when she talked of "Better Days," that time when they had been surrounded by myriads of servants and there had been brilliant balls and elegant banquets. But there was always enough to eat at the Dower House, and we had poor Jarman to do the garden and Mrs. Cobb to cook and Maddy as maid of all work, so we weren't exactly penniless. As my mother always exaggerated about our poverty, it occurred to me that she did the same about past riches, and I doubted that the balls and banquets had been as grand as she implied.

I was about ten years old when I made a portentous discovery. There was a house party at Oakland Hall, and the grounds on the other side of the stream were noisy with the hearty voices of people. From my window I had seen them riding out to hounds.

I wished they would invite me to call, for I longed to see the inside of the big house. True, I could catch glimpses of it from my side of the stream in winter when the denuded oaks no longer shielded it, but I could see no more than its distant gray stone walls, and they fascinated me. There was a winding drive of about half a mile, so it was impossible to see the house from the road either, but I had promised myself that one day I would cross the stream and, with great daring, approach.

I was in the schoolroom with Miriam, who was not the most inspiring of teachers and was frequently impatient with me. She was a tall, pale woman, and as I was ten years old she must have been twenty-five. She was discontented—they all were because they could never forget those Better Days—and sometimes she looked at me with cold dislike. I could never think of her as my sister.

On this day when the hunting party—guests from Oakland Hall—came riding past I got up and ran to the window.

"Jessica," cried Miriam, "what *are* you doing?"

"I only wanted to see the riders," I replied.

She gripped my arm, none too gently, and dragged me from the window. "They might see you," she hissed, as though that would be the depth of degradation.

"What if they did?" I demanded. "They did see me yesterday. Some of them waved and others said hello."

"Don't dare to speak to them again," she said fiercely.

"Why not?"

"Because Mama would be angry."

"You talk about them as though they're savages. I can't see what harm there is in saying hello to them."

"You don't understand, Jessica."

"How can I, when nobody tells me?"

She hesitated for a moment and then, as though she was considering that a little indiscretion was creditable if it saved me from the mortal sin of being friendly towards the guests from Oakland Hall, she said: "Once Oakland Hall was ours. That can never be forgotten."

"Why isn't it ours now?"

"Because *they* took it from us."

"Took it from us? How?" I immediately visualized a siege, Mama militant and dominating, commanding the family to pour down boiling oil from the battlements upon the wicked enemy who were coming to take our castle, Miriam and Xavier obeying without question and my father trying to understand the other side of the case.

"They *bought* Oakland Hall."

"Why did we sell it then?"

Her mouth hardened. "Because we could no longer afford to live there."

"Oh," I said, "*penury*. So it was there that we had our better days."

"*You* never had them. It all happened before you were born. I lived my childhood at Oakland Hall. I know what it means to come down in the world."

"As I've never had Better Days, I don't. But why did we become so poor?"

She would not answer that. All she said was: "So we had to sell to those . . . barbarians. We did, however, keep the Dower House. It was all that was left to us. So now you see why we do not want you so much as to notice those people who have taken our house."

"Are they really barbarians . . . savages?"

"Not much better."

"They look like ordinary people."

"Oh, Jessica, you are such a child! You don't understand these things and therefore you would be wise to leave them to your elders, but now at least you know that we once lived in Oakland Hall and perhaps you will understand why we do not want you to go about staring like a peasant at the people you see coming from there. Now, it's time for our algebra lessons, and if you are going to have the slightest education you must pay more attention to your books."

But how could one be interested in x plus y squared after such a discovery, and now I was desperately anxious to know something of the barbarians who had taken our house.

That was the beginning of discovery, and in my energetic —and as I thought, subtle—way, I began to probe.

It seemed to me that I might have more success with the servants than the family so I tried Poor Jarman, who came for long days in the summer and short ones in the winter and kept the Dower House garden in good order under

Mama's supervision. Poor Jarman! He was kept poor, he told me, by Nature, who presented his wife with a new baby every year.

"It's Nature what keeps me poor," was a favorite saying of his, which I thought very unfair to Nature. "*Nature is the great provider,*" I used to write out in best copperplate under Miriam's guidance. She had evidently been too beneficent to Poor Jarman. It had made him very humble and he touched his forelock to almost everyone except me with great reverence. To me it would be: "Keep off those dratted flowerbeds, Miss Jessica. If the mistress sees them trod down she'll blame me."

I followed him round for a week hoping to prise information from him. I collected flowerpots, stacked them in the greenhouse, watched him prune and weed. He said: "You're getting interested in orty-culture all of a sudden, Miss Jessica."

I smiled artfully, not telling him that it was the past I was probing.

"You used to work at Oakland Hall," I said.

"Aye. Them was the days."

"Better days, of course," I commented.

"Them lawns!" he said ecstatically. "All that grass. Best turf in the country. Just look at this St.-John's-wort. You only have to turn your back and it's all over the place. It grows while you're watching it."

"Nature's bounty," I said. "She's as generous with St.-John's-wort as she is with you."

He looked at me suspiciously, wondering what I was talking about.

"Why did you leave Oakland Hall?" I wanted to know.

"I came here with your mother. It seemed the faithful sort of thing like." He was looking back to the old days before Nature's bounty had made him Poor Jarman. He leaned on his spade and his eyes were dreamy. "Them was good days. Funny thing. Never thought they'd end. Then suddenly. . . ."

"Yes," I prompted, "suddenly?"

"Mistress sent for me. 'Jarman,' she said, 'we've sold the Hall. We're going to the Dower House.' You could have knocked me down with a dove's feather, though some had said they'd seen it coming. I was took back though. She said: 'If you come with us you could have the cottage on the bit of land we're keeping. You could then marry.' That was the beginning. Before the year was out I was a father."

"You said there was talk. . . ."

"Yes, talk. Them that knew it all was coming after it had happened . . . they was talking. Gambling was in the family. Old Mr. Clavering had been very fond of it, and they said he'd lost quite a tidy sum. There was mortgages for this and that—and that's not good for a house, and what's not good for a house ain't good for them that works there."

"So they sensed the gathering storm."

"Well, we all knew there was money trouble, 'cos sometimes wages wasn't paid for two months. There's some families as makes a habit of this, but Claverings wasn't never that sort. Then this man came. He took the Hall. Miner he'd been. Made a fortune out of something. Came from abroad."

"Why didn't you stay and work for him?"

"I'd always been with gentry, Miss. Besides, there was this cottage."

He had eleven children so it must have been about twelve years ago. One could calculate the years by Jarman's children, and people were never quite sure which was which so that it was like trying to remember which year something had happened.

"It all took place before I was born," I went on, keeping his thoughts flowing in the right direction.

"Yes. 'Tis so. Must have been two years before that."

So it *was* twelve years ago—a lifetime—mine anyway.

All I had learned from Jarman was that my father's gambling had been responsible. No wonder Mama treated him with contempt. Now I understood the meaning behind her bitter remarks. Poor Father, he stayed in his room and spent a lot of time playing patience—a solitary game in which he could not lose to an opponent who would have to be paid, yet at the same time preserving contact with the cards he still loved, although they had apparently been the cause of his family's expulsion from the world of opulence.

Mrs. Cobb could tell me little. Like my family she had been accustomed to Better Days. She had come to us when we went to the Dower House and was never tired of telling any who would listen that she had been used to parlormaids, kitchenmaids, a butler, and two footmen.

It was, therefore, something of a come-down to work in a household like ours; but at least the family, like herself, had known Better Days, and it was not like working for people who had "never been used to nothing."

My father, of course, playing his patience, reading, going for solitary walks, with the heavy weight of guilt on his shoulders, was definitely not the one to approach. He seemed scarcely aware of me in any case. When he did notice me, something of the same expression came into his face as that which I saw when my mother was reminding him that it was his weakness which had brought the family low. To me he was a sort of non-person, which was an odd way to feel about one's own father, but as he expressed no interest in me, I found it hard to feel anything for him—except pity when they reminded him, which they contrived to do on every occasion.

As for Mama, she was even more unapproachable. When I was very young and we sang in church:

> "Can a mother's tender care
> Cease towards the child she bear?"

I had thought of a little female bear cub beloved by its mother bear, but when I had mentioned this to Miriam she had been very shocked and explained the real meaning. I then commented that my mother's tender care towards me had never really ceased because it had never existed. At this Miriam had grown very pink and told me that I was a most ungrateful child and should be thankful for the good home I had. I wondered then why for me it was a "good home," though clearly despised by the others, but I put this down to the fact that they had seen those Better Days which I had missed.

My brother Xavier was a remote and romantic figure of whom I saw very little. He looked after the land we had been able to salvage from the Oakland estate and this contained one farm and several acres of pasture land. When I did see him he was kind to me in a vague sort of way, as though he recognized my right to be in the house but wasn't quite sure how I'd got there and was too polite to ask. I had heard that he was in love with Lady Clara Donningham who lived some twenty miles away, but because he couldn't offer her the luxury to which she was accustomed, he wouldn't ask her to marry him. She apparently was very rich and we were living in what I had heard Mama so often call penury. The fact was that he and Lady Clara remained apart although, according to Mrs. Cobb who had a link through the cook at the Manor, which was Lady Clara's home, her ladyship would not have said no if Mr. Xavier had asked her. But as Xavier was too proud, and convention forbade Lady Clara to ask him, they remained apart. This gave Xavier a very romantic aura in my eyes. He was a chivalrous knight who went through life nursing a secret passion because decorum forbade him to speak. *He* certainly would tell me nothing.

Miriam might be lured into betraying something, but she was not one for confidences. There was an "understanding" between her and the Rev. Jasper Crey's curate, but they couldn't marry until the curate became a vicar, and in view of his retiring nature that seemed unlikely for years to come.

Maddy told me that if we'd still been at Oakland Hall there would have been coming-out dances, people would have been visiting and it wouldn't have been a curate for Miss Miriam. Oh dear no. There would have been Squire This or Sir That—and maybe a lord. They had been the grand days.

So it all came back to the same thing; and as Mrs. Cobb could never be kept from telling of her own Better Days, I couldn't hope to get her interested in those of my family.

As I might have known, Maddy was the only one who could really help. She had actually lived at Oakland Hall. Another point in her favor was that she loved to talk and as long as I could be sworn to secrecy—and I readily promised that—she would at times let out little scraps of information.

Maddy was thirty-five—five years older than Xavier—and she had come to Oakland Hall when she was only eleven years old to work in the nursery.

"It was all very grand then. Lovely nurseries they was."

"Xavier must have been a good baby," I commented.

"He was. *He* wasn't the one to get up to mischief."

"Who then? Miriam?"

"No, not her either."

"Well, why did you say one of them was?"

"I said no such thing. You're like one of them magistrates, you are. What's this? What's that?" She was huffy now, shutting her lips tightly together as though to punish me for asking a question which had disturbed her. It was only later that I realized why it had.

Once I said to Miriam: "Fancy, you were born in Oakland Hall and I was born in the Dower House."

Miriam hesitated and said: "No, you weren't born in the Dower House. Actually . . . it was abroad."

"How interesting! Where?"

Miriam looked embarrassed as though wondering how I could have lured her into this further indiscretion.

"Mama was traveling in Italy when you were born."

My eyes widened with excitement. Venice, I thought. Gondolas. Pisa with its leaning tower. Florence, where Beatrice and Dante had met and loved so chastely—or so Miriam had said.

"Where?" I demanded.

"It was . . . in Rome."

I was ecstatic. "Julius Caesar," I said. " 'Friends, Romans, countrymen, lend me your ears.' But why?"

Miriam looked exasperated. "Because you happened to appear when they were there."

"Father was with her then?" I cried. "Wasn't it costly? Penury and all that?"

She looked pained in the special way Miriam could. She said primly: "Suffice it that they were there."

"It's as though they didn't know I was about to be born. I mean they wouldn't have gone there, would they, if. . . ."

"These things happen sometimes. Now we have chattered enough."

She could be very severe, my sister Miriam. Sometimes I was sorry for the curate, or should be if she ever married him—and for the sad children they would have.

So there was more to brood on. What strange things seemed to happen to me! Perhaps it was because they were in Rome that they had called me Opal. I had tried to discover information about opals. After looking up the dictionary I had mixed feelings about my name. It was not very flattering to be called after "a mineral consisting chiefly of hydrous silica," whatever that was, but it did not sound in the least romantic. I discovered however that it had varying hues of red, green, and blue . . . in fact all the colors of the spectrum and was of a changing iridescence, and that sounded better. How difficult it was though to imagine Mama, in a moment of frivolity inspired by the Italian skies, naming her child Opal, even though the more serviceable Jessica had been added and used.

Soon after that occasion when I had seen the guests riding out from Oakland, I heard the owner had gone away for a while. Only the servants remained, and there were no longer sounds of revelry across the stream, for visitors never came— only those, of course, connected with servants and they were quite different.

Life went on for a while in the old way—my father solitary with his patience and his walks and the ability to shut himself away from his complaining family; my mother dominating the household, busying herself with Church matters, looking after the poor, of which community she was constantly reminding us we had become a part. However, we were at least still sufficiently of the gentry to dispense benefits rather than receive them; Xavier went his quiet way dreaming no doubt of the unattainable Lady Clara (my sympathy was tinged with impatience because had I been Lady Clara, I should have said it was all nonsense to make a barrier of her money, and if I were Xavier, I should have said the same); and Miriam and her curate too. Of course she might be like Poor Jarman and bring a lot of children into the world. Curates did seem to breed rather freely, and the poorer they were the more fecund they seemed to be.

So as the years began to pass the mystery remained, but my curiosity did not diminish. I became more and more certain that there was a reason why the family gave me the impression that I was an intruder.

Prayers were said each morning at the start of the day and every member of the household had to be present for them—even my father was expected to attend. These were said in the drawing room, "since," my mother often commented coldly, "we have no chapel now!" And she would throw a venomous glance towards my father and then turn to Oakland Hall, where for so many years she had knelt in what was meant to be humility. Poor Jarman, Mrs. Cobb, and Maddy would be present. "*All* the staff," my mother would say bitterly. "At Oakland there were so many that one did not know all their names, only those of the ones in higher positions."

It was a solemn ceremony conducted by my mother when she exhorted us all to be humble, grateful, and conduct ourselves with virtue in the station into which God had called us—which always seemed incongruous to me, since she was far from contented with hers. She was inclined to be a little hectoring towards God, I thought. It was: "Look down on this. . . ." and "Don't do that. . . ." as though she were talking to one of the superior servants she must have had at Oakland Hall.

I always found morning prayers irksome, but I did enjoy the church services, though perhaps for the wrong reasons.

The church was a fine one and the stained glass windows, with their beautiful colors, a joy to study. Opal colors, I called them with satisfaction. I loved the singing of the choir and most of all I liked to sing myself. I always thought of the times of the year through hymns. "Christian dost thou see them," used to thrill me; and I would look over my shoulder almost expecting to see the troops of Midian prowling around. Harvest time was lovely. "We plow the fields and scatter. . . ." and "Hark the Herald Angels" at Christmas; but best of all I loved Easter, "Hallelujah. Christ the Lord is risen today." Easter was a lovely time, when the flowers were all delicate colors—whites and yellows, and the spring had come and the summer was on the way. Miriam used to go and decorate the church. I wondered whether the curate helped her and whether they sadly talked of their inability to marry because they were so poor. I always wanted to point out that the people in the cottages had far less and yet seemed happy enough. But at least the church was beautiful, and particularly at Easter time.

We still had the Clavering pew in the church. This consisted of the two front rows with a little door, which had a lock and key, and when we walked in behind my father and mother, I believe she felt that the good old days were back. Perhaps that was the reason why *she* enjoyed going to church.

After luncheon on Easter Sunday we always went to the churchyard, taking flowers, and these we put on the graves of the more recently family dead. Here again, prestige was restored, for the Clavering section was in the most favorable position and the headstones were the most elaborate in the churchyard. I know my mother was constantly irritated by the fact that when she died her memorial would be far less splendid than it would have been if the money to provide a worthy one had not been gambled away.

I was sixteen years old on that particular Easter Sunday. Growing up, I thought, and I should soon no longer be a child. I wondered what the future held for me. I didn't fancy growing old in the Dower House like Miriam, who was now thirty-one years of age and as far from marriage with her curate as ever.

The service was beautiful and the theme interesting. "Be content and thankful with what the Lord has given you." A very good homily for the Claverings, I thought, and I wondered whether the Rev. Jasper Crey had had them in mind when delivering it. Was he reminding them that the Dower House was a comfortable residence and quite grand by standards other than those of Oakland Hall; Miriam and her curate should be thankful and marry; Xavier and Lady Clara should do the same; my father should be allowed to forget that he had brought us to our present state; and my mother should rejoice in what she had? As for myself I was happy enough and if only I could find the answers to certain questions which plagued me I should be quite content. Perhaps somewhere inside me I yearned to be loved, for I had never really enjoyed that blessing. I wanted someone's eyes to light up when I came by. I wanted someone to be a little anxious if I was late coming home—not because unpunctuality was undesirable and ill-mannered but because they were fearful that some ill fortune had come to me.

"Oh God," I prayed, "let someone love me."

Then I laughed at myself, because I was telling Him what to do just as my mother did.

When the time came to visit the graves I took a basket of daffodils and walked with Miriam and Mama from the Dower House to the church. There was a pump in the Clavering section from which we filled the jars which were kept there, and then put the flowers on the graves. There was Grandfather, who had begun to fritter away the family fortunes, and there was Grandmother and the Greats, and my father's brother and sister. We could not, of course, deck out the graves of all the dead. I liked to wander round and look at the shrubs and open books in stone and read the engraved words. There were memorials to John Clavering, who had died at the battle of Preston for his King in 1648. James who had died at Malplaquet. There was another for Harold, who had been killed at Trafalgar. We were a fighting family.

"Do come away, Jessica," said Mama. "I do declare you have a morbid streak."

Called from the guns of Trafalgar, I walked solemnly back to the Dower House, and it was later that afternoon when I wandered out through the gardens to the edge of the stream. I was still thinking of long dead Claverings who had died so valiantly for their country and how John had fought the Roundheads in an unsuccessful attempt to keep his King on the throne, a struggle which had cost the King not only his throne but his head, and James fighting with

Marlborough and Harold with Nelson. We Claverings had taken our part in the making of history, I told myself proudly.

Following the stream I came to the end of the Dower House gardens. There was a stretch of meadow—about an acre in which the grass grew long and unkempt. By the hedge grew archangel or white dead-nettle with its flowers just coming out. They would be there until December, and later the bees would be so busy on them that it wouldn't be possible to get near them. Very few people ever came here and it was called the Waste Land.

As I walked across it I noticed a bunch of dog violets tied up with white cotton, which was wound around their stems. I stooped to pick them up, and as I divided the grass I saw that the spot on which they had been lying was slightly raised. It was a plot of about six feet long.

Like a grave, I thought.

How could it be a grave? Because I had been to the churchyard that afternoon with Easter flowers, my mind was on graves. I knelt down and pushed aside the grass. I felt round the earth. Yes, it was a mound. It must be a grave, and today someone had put a bunch of violets on it.

Who could possibly be buried on the Waste Land? I went and sat thoughtfully by the stream and asked myself what it meant.

The first person I encountered when I went back to the house was Maddy, who, now that I no longer needed a nurse, had become maid of all work. She was at the linen cupboard sorting out sheets.

"Maddy," I said, "I saw a grave today."

"It's Easter Sunday so I reckon you did," she retorted.

"Oh, not in the graveyard. In the Waste Land. I'm sure it was a grave."

She turned away, but not before I had seen that her expression was one of shocked horror. She *knew* there was a grave in the Waste Land.

"Whose was it?" I insisted.

"Now why ask me?"

"Because you know."

"Miss Jessica, it's time you stopped putting people in the witness box. You're too inquisitive by half."

"It's only a natural thirst for knowledge."

"It's what I call having your nose into everything. There's a word for that. Plain nosiness."

"I don't see why I shouldn't know who's buried in the Waste Land."

"Buried in the Waste Land," she mimicked; but she had betrayed herself. She was uneasy.

"There was a little bunch of violets there—as though someone had remembered it was Easter Sunday."

"Oh," she said blankly.

"I thought someone might have buried a pet dog there."

"That's as like as not," she said with some relief.

"But it was too big for a dog's grave. No, I think it was some person there . . . someone buried long ago but still remembered. They must have been remembered, mustn't they, for someone to lay flowers there so carefully."

"Miss Jessica, will you get from under my feet."

She was bustling away with a pile of linen sheets, but her heightened color betrayed her. She knew who was buried in the Waste Land, but, alas, she wasn't telling.

For several days I worried her but could get nothing out of her.

"Oh give over, do," she cried at length in exasperation. "One of these days you might find out something you'd rather not know."

That cryptic remark lingered in my mind and did nothing to curb my curiosity. All that year I brooded on the matter of the secret grave.

When there was activity across the stream at Oakland Hall, I ceased to think about the grave. I was aware that something was happening because suddenly tradesmen called constantly at the house, and from my seat by the stream I could hear the servants shouting to each other. There were regular thwacks as carpets were brought out of the house and beaten. The shrill feminine tones mingled with those of the dignified butler. I had seen him several times, and he always behaved as though he were the owner of Oakland Hall. I was sure *he* was not haunted by the spectre of Better Days.

Then the day came when I saw a carriage arriving and I slipped out of the Dower House to see it turn into Oakland's drive. Then I hurried back, darted across the stream, crept close to the house, and hidden by bushes I was just in time to see a man lifted from the carriage and placed into a wheelchair. He had a very red face, and he shouted in a loud voice to the people around him in a manner to which

I was sure the rafters of Oakland Hall had been unaccustomed during the Better Days.

"Get me in," he shouted. "Come on, Wilmot. Come out and help Banker."

I wished that I could see better, but I had to be careful. I wondered what the red-faced man would say if he saw me. He was clearly a very forceful personality and it was, I felt, very necessary indeed for me to remain hidden.

"Get me up the steps," he said. "Then I can manage. Show 'em, Banker."

The little procession went into the house at last, and as I made my cautious way to the bridge I had a fancy that I was being followed, perhaps because I felt so guilty to be on the wrong side of the stream. I did not look round but ran as fast as I could, and it was only when I had sped across the bridge that I paused to look back. I was sure I saw a movement among the trees, but whether it was a man or woman there I was unsure. I did have the curious sensation that I had been observed. I began to feel uneasy, wondering whether whoever had seen me would complain to Mama. There would certainly be trouble if he—or she—did. That I had stepped onto forbidden territory would be bad enough but to have been seen doing it would bring forth storms of contempt upon my head.

On my way to my room I met Miriam. "The owner of Oakland Hall is back," I told her.

"May God preserve us!" she cried. "Now I suppose there'll be entertaining, eating, and drinking and all kinds of depravity."

I laughed gleefully. "It'll be exciting," I began.

"It'll be disgusting," she retorted.

"I think he's had some sort of accident," I ventured.

"Who?"

"The er . . . the one who took Oakland from us."

"I've no doubt he deserved it," she said with satisfaction.

She turned away. The very thought of them was obnoxious to her; but I was enormously interested.

I asked Maddy about them because she always gave me the impression that she could tell me a good deal if only I could make her break some vow she had made not to, and often, in fact, she did seem secretly as though she wanted to talk.

I said: "Maddy, a man in a Bath chair was taken into Oakland Hall yesterday."

She nodded. "That's *him*," she said.

"The one who bought it from us?"

"He made a fortune. Never been used to such a place before. He's what you call one of them new rich."

"*Nouveau riche*," I informed her grandly.

"Have it your own way," she said, "but that's what he is."

"He's an invalid?"

"Accident," she said. "That's what happens to his sort."

"His sort? What sort?"

"Made a great fortune, he did, and so he buys Oakland Hall and them that has lived in it for generations untold has to give it up."

"The Claverings gambled while he worked," I said. "It's like the ant and the grasshopper. It's no use blaming him. They both got their desserts."

"What's insects got to do with it? You're what I call a hopper yourself, Miss Jessica. You're no sooner on to one thing before you're after another."

"This is all part of the same subject," I protested. "I'd like to get into the Hall. Is he going to stay here?"

"You can't get about all that easy when you've had one of your legs off. Still, he got the fortune, though it did cost him a leg." Maddy shook her head. "It only goes to show that money's not everything . . . though in this house you'd sometimes think it was. Mrs. Bucket says she reckons he's home to stay."

"Who's Mrs. Bucket?"

"She's cook over there."

"What a perfectly glorious name. Bucket! Though that ought to have been the housemaid. The cook should be Mrs. Baker or Mrs. Stewer. So you know Mrs. Bucket, do you, Maddy?"

"Considering that she was at Oakland when I was there it seems natural that I should know her."

"And you see her now and then?"

Maddy pursed her lips. I knew that she was visiting Mrs. Bucket and I was glad. A little careful prodding and I might learn something.

"Well, it ain't for me to stick my nose up in the air when I pass someone I've known for twenty years, just because. . . ."

"It certainly is not. You're an example. . . ."

"It couldn't be laid to Mrs. Bucket's door, nor Mr. Wilmot's neither. It wasn't as though there was a place for them here. To expect them to throw themselves out just because. . . ."

"I understand perfectly. So he lost a leg, did he?"

"You're on your cross-questioning again, Miss. I can see through that sure as eggs is eggs. It's one thing for me to have a word with Mrs. Bucket now and then and it would be another for you to. So you make certain you keep on the right side of the stream and don't go asking so many questions about things that don't concern you."

So in spite of the fact that Maddy had visited Mrs. Bucket I was not going to prise any more information out of her.

It was a sultry July day and I was sitting by the stream looking over Oakland territory when it happened. A chair, with a man sitting in it, came into view. I started up because as the chair came towards me I realized that the occupant was the man I had seen arriving in the carriage. There was a tartan rug over his knees, so I couldn't make out whether or not he had one leg. I watched while the chair seemed to gather speed as it came towards me. Then I realized what had happened. It was because the chair was out of control that it moved so fast and it was gathering momentum as it came down the slight incline towards the stream. In a few moments it would be there and would surely overturn.

I wasted no time. I ran down the slope and waded through the stream. Fortunately we had had a drought and there was not a great deal of water, but willingly I splashed through what there was and ran up the slope on the other side just in time to catch the chair before it went down into the stream.

The man in the chair had been yelling: "Banker! Banker! Where in God's name are you, Banker?" until he caught sight of me. I was clinging to the chair and it took all my strength to hang onto it and at one moment I thought it was going to carry me down with it.

The man was grinning at me; his face was redder than ever.

"Goodo!" he shouted. "You've done it. A little shaver like you and you've done it."

There was a kind of steering bar in front of him; he guided this, and the chair started to move along parallel with the stream.

"There," he said. "That's better. I'm not used to the perishing thing yet. Well, now I've got to say my piece, haven't I?

Do you know I'd have turned over but for you."

"Yes," I said, coming round to the side of the chair. "You would."

"Where were you then?"

"On the other side of the stream . . . our side."

He nodded. "Lucky for me you were just at the right spot at that time."

"I'm often at that spot. I like it."

"Never seen you before. Do you live over there?"

"In the Dower House."

"You're not a Clavering?"

"Yes, I am. What are you?"

"A Henniker."

"You must be the one who bought Oakland from them."

"The very same."

I started to laugh. "What's funny?" he said; he had a rather sharp way of talking.

"Meeting like this after all these years," I said.

He started to laugh too. I don't know why it should have seemed so funny to us both, but it did.

"Nice to meet you, Miss Clavering."

"How do you do, Mr. Henniker?"

"Quite well, thank you, Miss Clavering. I'm going to drive my chair up a bit. It's uncomfortable here. Up under the trees there . . . in the shade. Let's come and get acquainted."

"Don't you want . . . Banker?"

"Not now."

"You were shouting for him."

"That was before I saw you."

I walked beside the chair, thinking what a marvelous adventure this was, and I heartily applauded his suggestion, for I had no wish for us to be seen. He brought the chair to rest in the shade and I sat down on the grass. We studied each other.

"Are you a miner?" I asked.

He nodded.

"Gold, I suppose."

He shook his head.

"Opals."

A sudden shiver of excitement ran through me. "Opals!" I cried. "My name is Opal."

"Well, now is it? Opal Clavering. It sounds very grand to me."

"They never call me by it. I'm always Jessica. That's rather ordinary after Opal, don't you think? I often wonder why they gave me the name if they didn't want to call me by it."

"You couldn't have a prettier name," he said. The reddish tinge in his cheeks deepened, and his eyes were a very bright blue. "There's nothing more beautiful than an opal. Don't start talking to me about diamonds or rubies. . . ."

"I wasn't going to."

"I can see you know better than to do that to an old gouger."

"A what?"

"An opal miner."

"What do you do? Tell me about it."

"You smell out the land and you hope and you dream. Every miner dreams he's going to find the most beautiful stones in the world."

"Where do you find them?"

"Well, there's South Australia—Coober Pedy and Mooka Country, and there's New South Wales and Queensland."

"You're from Australia," I said.

"That's where I found opal, but I started out from the Old Country. Australia's rich in opal. We haven't scratched the surface of the land yet. Who'd have thought there was opal in Australia? You can picture the excitement when they found it was. *Can* you picture it? Some brumbies scratching the land with their hoofs and . . . there's opal. By God, what a find! In those days we thought they had to come from Hungary . . . never thought to look elsewhere. They'd mined them there for hundreds of years. That milky kind. Very pretty . . . but give me the black opals of Australia."

He paused and looked up at the sky. He was scarcely aware of me, I was sure. He was back in time, in space, miles away on the other side of the world, gouging—or whatever he called it—for his black opals.

"Diamonds . . . pah!" he went on. "What's a diamond? Cold fire, that's what. White! Look at an opal. . . ."

How I should have loved to, but the next best thing was to listen to him.

"Australian opals are the best," he went on. "They're harder. They don't splinter as easily as some. They're lucky stones. Long ago people used to believe opals brought *good* fortune. Do you know emperors and nabobs used to wear them because they were said to protect them against attack?

It used to be said that an opal could prevent your being poisoned by your enemies. Another story was that they cured blindness. What more can you ask than that?"

"Nothing," I agreed heartily.

"Oculus Mundi. That's what they're called. Do you know what that means?"

I confessed that my education did not carry me so far.

"The Eye of the World," he told me. "Wear it and you'll never commit suicide."

"I've never had one, but I've never wanted to commit suicide."

"You're too young. And you say Opal's your name? And Jessica too. Do you know, I like that. Jessie. It's friendly."

"At least it doesn't make you think of a cure for blindness and a protection against the poison cup?"

"Exactly," he said, and we both burst into laughter.

"Opals bring the gift of prophecy," he went on. "So they used to say—prophecy and foresight."

He took a ring from his little finger and showed it to me. It was a beautiful stone set in gold. I slipped it on my thumb, but even that was too small for it. I watched the light play on the stone. It was deep blue shot with red, yellow, and green lights. He held out his hand for the ring as though he were impatient that it should be too long out of his possession so I gave it back to him.

"It's beautiful," I said.

"New South Wales . . . that's where it comes from. I tell you this, Miss Jessie, there are going to be some big finds there one day . . . even bigger than we've had already. I won't be in on it though." He tapped the tartan rug. "Hazards of the business. Got to accept them, you know. Think of the rewards. I'll never forget the day this happened. I thought it was the end of me. I was collecting nobbies. Clinging to the roof, they were, like oysters . . . yes, just like oysters. I couldn't believe my luck. Picture me . . . gouging away. It was in a cave and I was deep in, and there they were in this gritty, reddish seam . . . lovely nobbies. Suddenly there was a rumble and down came the roof of this cave. It was three hours before they could get me out. I'd got my opals though, and one of them—well, it was a real beaut, worth losing a leg for, or so I told myself. But between you and me your own limbs shouldn't be bartered for anything . . . not even this little beauty of mine. By God, she's a prize. For a moment I thought I'd found the Green Flash again. Not quite, though . . . still there's a wonderful green in this one . . . a magic sort of green. She was the first thing I saw when I came around . . . because I was in a hospital for a long time while they cut my leg off. Had to. Gangrene and all that. It was a long time before they could get me down to Sydney, and by that time the leg was a goner. And the first thing I said was: 'Show me that green opal.' And there she was, lying in the palm of my hand, and though I knew there was nothing there where my leg used to be, I felt such pride as you wouldn't understand just to look at the lovely thing lying there in my hand."

"It ought to have brought you protection against the falling rock," I commented.

"Well, you see, it wasn't mine until the rock started to crack. I look at it like this: It was the price I had to pay for my nobbies."

"It would have been awful to lose your leg for nothing."

"I knew it was the end of my mining days. Who ever heard of a one-legged gouger? But perhaps I'll get out again when I get used to hobbling around. But first I'll have to educate myself in the way of my wooden leg. I've got to have a long rest, they tell me, so I thought the best place to come to was Oakland. And here I am trying to get used to a crutch and a wooden leg and relying on this old chair to carry me around, and you see what nearly happened to me but for a certain young lady."

"I'm so glad I saw you, not only because. . . ."

"Yes, because what?"

"So that we could meet and I could hear about opals."

"There's been a sort of feud between our families." He laughed aloud, and I laughed with him. It was a certain bond between us, which kept us laughing for not much reason, for it wasn't so much the laughter provoked by amusement as that of sheer pleasure and the unusual nature of our meeting. I thought then—and I became sure of it later —that he liked the idea of snapping his fingers at my family.

"I bought their home, you see," he said, "and it had been in their family for ages. They've got the Clavering arms over the hall fireplace . . . all drawn out on the wall and very pretty too. This one married that one and there'd been Claverings at Oakland Hall since 1507, until this rough Henniker came along and took it from them—not with fire and sword, not with gunpowder and battering rams—but with money!"

"The Claverings should never have let it go if they wanted to keep it so much. As for you, Mr. Henniker, you risked your life to get it and you've got it . . . and I'm *glad*."

"Strange words from a Clavering," he said. "Ah, but this one's an Opal."

"I could never think why they gave me such a name—except that I was born in Italy. I think my mother must have been very different then."

"People change," said Mr. Henniker. "What happens to them can often bring a turnabout. I've got a man calling to see me at half-past four, so I shall have to go now, but listen. We're going to meet again."

"Oh yes, please, Mr. Henniker."

"What about here . . . at this spot . . . tomorrow at this time?"

"I'd love it."

"I reckon we'd have a lot to say to each other. Same time tomorrow then."

I watched him guide his chair towards the house and then, in high spirits, I ran down to the bridge. I stood on it looking back. The trees hid the house—his house now—but I was picturing him in it, shouting for Banker, laughing because one of the Claverings had become his friend.

"He's an adventurer," I thought, "and so am I."

I tried to hide my exuberance, but Maddy noticed it and commented that she couldn't make up her mind what I resembled most—a dog with two tails to wag or a cat who's stolen the cream.

"Very pleased with ourself, I'd say," she added suspiciously.

"It's a lovely day," I answered blithely.

"Thunder in the air," she grumbled.

That made me laugh. Yes indeed, the atmosphere would be decidedly stormy if it was discovered that I had actually spoken to the enemy and arranged another meeting.

I could scarcely wait to see him again.

He was there when I arrived. He talked—how he talked and how I loved to listen! He told me about his life when he had been very poor in his early days in London.

"London!" he cried. "What a city! I never could forget it, no matter wherever I was. But there were some hard memories too. We were poor—not as poor as some others, there being only one child . . . me. My mother couldn't have more, which in some ways was a blessing. I went to a dame school, where I learned my letters, and after that to a ragged school, where I learned the ways of the world, and when I'd done with education at the age of twelve, I was ready to fight my battles. By that time my father had dropped dead. He was a drinker so it wasn't much of a loss, and I started to keep my mother in a degree of comfort to which she had not been accustomed."

I wondered why he was telling me all this. He was an actor of a kind, for when he talked of people his voice and his expression would change. When he told me of the baked-potato seller, his face would be grizzled and he'd shout: "Come, me beauties, all hot and floury. Two a penny hot spuds. Fill your bellies and warm your hands."

"There, Miss Jessie," he would go on becoming himself. "I'm being a bit vulgar now, you'll be thinking, but that was the streets of London when I was a nipper. Life! I never saw such life . . . no, never. There it was all over the streets of London. It's something you don't take much notice of when you're there, but you never forget it. It gets in your blood. You get away from it, but you'll always love it and it'll always draw you back."

Then he would tell me of the orange woman and the sellers of pins and needles. "Five sheets a penny, pins," he sang out, "all neat and middlings"; then there were the vendors of what he called "green stuff," which was mainly water-cress gathered in the fields onto which, in those days, the city had not encroached. "Why there were fields just beyond Portland Place—meadows and woods; and there were market gardens too, so there was plenty of green stuff about. "Woorter creases," he shouted. "All fresh and green."

"Funny, when I talk of it, it all comes back fresh to me. Most clear in my memory is Eastertime. Good Friday was what I thought of as the Day of the Buns. It was the first thing I thought of when I got up on Good Friday morning. It was the day of the buns."

He began to sing:

"One a penny, two a penny, hot cross buns
If your daughters won't eat them, give them to your sons.
If you ain't got any of those pretty little elves
Then you can't do better than to eat them up yourselves."

"We used to go round singing that with our trays of buns on our heads."

I was fascinated. I had never met anyone like him. He talked all the time about himself. That didn't worry me, because I wanted to hear and I was getting a glimpse into a world hitherto unknown to me.

"I was born to make money," he said. "The Midas Touch, that's what I've got. Ever heard of that, Miss Jessie? Everything he touched turned to gold. That was how it was with old Ben Henniker. If *I* tossed with a pieman, I'd be the winner. You know what was done, don't you? There was the pieman with his tray of pies. You tossed your penny. 'Heads,' he'd say, for the pieman always called heads. And sure enough if it was old Ben's penny, it would come up tails. So I kept the penny *and* the pie. Other people—they'd lose every time. Never me. A proper gambler I was then and have been ever since. I found selling things was the answer. You find something people want and they can't do without and you bring it out much better and, if you can, cheaper than the next man. You get the idea? Even when I was only fourteen I knew how best to sell things. I knew where to get the cheapest and give the best value—sheep's trotters, pigs' trotters, whelks, sherbet, ginger beer, and lemonade. I had a coffee stall once, and when I got the idea of making gingerbread it seemed I was set fair to make my fortune. I hit on the idea of making it in fancy shapes—horses, dogs, harps, girls, boys . . . the Queen herself with her crown on her head. My mother made 'em and I sold 'em. It got so big we had a little shop right there on the Ratcliffe Highway, and a fine shop it was. The business grew and we were more comfortably off. Then one day my mother died. Right as rain one day and the next gone. She just dropped dead on the floor when she was making her gingerbread fancies."

"What did you do then?"

"I got me a lady friend. She hadn't got the touch though. Pretty as paint but a fiery temper, and she couldn't make the shapes and the cake wasn't right either. Business fell off and she left me. I was seventeen years old then, and I took a job in a gentleman's home looking after the horses. One day they went visiting friends in the country. It was my job to ride there at the back of the carriage, and when we stopped I'd jump out and open the door and see the ladies didn't muddy their skirts. Oh, I was very handsome in those days. You should have seen my livery. Dark blue with silver braid.

All the girls would look twice at me, I can tell you. Well, one day we went out visiting in the country, and where do you think we came to—the little village of Hartingmond. And the house we called on was named Oakland Hall."

"You were calling on the Claverings!"

"Quite right, but calling in a humble capacity, you might say. I'd never seen a house like that. I thought it was just about the most beautiful place I'd ever seen. I went round to the stables with the coachman, and we looked after the horses and then got ourselves refreshed while we talked to the stable men of Oakland Hall, and they were very superior, I can tell you."

"How interesting!" I cried. "That must have been years ago."

"Long before you were born, Miss Jessie. When I was seventeen or eighteen, and that's a good many years ago. How old do you think I am?"

"Older than Xavier . . . lots older, but somehow you seem younger."

The answer seemed to please him. "You're just as old as you feel. That's the answer. It's not how many years you've lived, it's how they've left you. Now I reckon I've lived mine pretty well. It was more than forty years ago that I first set eyes on this place, and do you know, I never forgot it. I remember standing there in those stables and feeling the age of it. That's what I liked—all those stone walls and the feeling that people had been living there hundreds of years, and I said to myself: One of these days I'm going to have a house like Oakland Hall and no one's going to stop me. In six months' time I was on my way to Australia."

"To look for opals," I cried.

"No. I hadn't thought of opals then. I was after what everyone else was after—gold. I said to myself: I'll find gold and I won't rest until I've made my little pile and when I've got it I'll come home and buy myself such a house. And that's why I went to Australia. What a journey! I worked my passage. I'll never forget that trip. I thought it would be the end of me. Such storms we had, and the ship—she nearly turned turtle, she did, and I thought it would be all hands to the pump and save the women and children first. I couldn't believe it when I stepped ashore. That sun! Those flies! Never seen neither like it before. But something told me it was the place for me, and I swore there and then that I wouldn't come home till I was ready to buy me a house like Oakland Hall."

"And you did, Mr. Henniker."

"Call me Ben," he said. "Mr. Henniker makes me sound like someone else."

"Ought I to? You're very old."

"Not when I'm with you, Miss Jessie. I feel young and gay. I feel seventeen again."

"Just as you did when you stepped ashore at Sydney."

"Just like that. Well, I was certain I was going to be rich. So I worked my way across New South Wales to Ballarat and there I panned for gold."

"And you found it and made your fortune."

He turned his hands over and stared down at them. "Look at them," he said. "A bit gnarled, eh? Not the hands of a gentleman of leisure, you'd say. Those hands don't fit Oakland Hall. Nor does anything else, as far as you can see. But something inside me fits." He tapped his chest. "There's something in here that loves the old place as it couldn't have been loved more by all the grand ladies and gentlemen who lived here. They took it for granted. I won it, and I love it because of that. Never take anything for granted, Miss Jessie. If you do you might lose it. If it's worth cherishing, cherish it. Think how I snapped up Oakland Hall."

"I am thinking," I said. "So you made your fortune."

"It wasn't done in a night. Years it took. Disappointments, frustrations . . . that was my lot. Shifting from place to place . . . living in the fields, staking my claim . . . I remember the trek out of Melbourne. There they were—a ragged army, you might say—a crowd of us all marching off to the promised land. We knew that some of us were going to strike it rich and others were going to die disappointed men, but which of us? Hope marched with us on that journey, and we all thought we'd be the chosen ones. Some of us had wheelbarrows carrying our load, some took what they had on their backs . . . across the Keilor Plains, through forests where the fires had blazed, making you shiver, for the first time realizing something of what these fires meant, never being sure whether some bushranger was going to spring out on us and murder us for our bit of tucker. We'd camp at night. Oh, it was something—singing round the campfires . . . all the old songs from Home we used to sing and I'm not going to say that there weren't some of us glad of the darkness so no one could see the tears in our eyes. And then on . . . to Bendigo then . . . living in a little calico tent. I sweltered there one summer and longed for the cool weather, but when it came with the driving rain and the mud I was longing for the sun again. Hard days—and there was no luck for me at Bendigo. It was Castlemaine where I had my first big find—not enough to make me rich but an encouragement. I banked it in Melbourne right away. I wasn't spending it on drink and women like so many did and then be surprised at the short time it lasted. I knew all about that. It wasn't bought women for me. It had to be love, not money. That's a wise way and you don't squander your hard-earned gold. But I'm talking out of turn. You can see why the Claverings didn't want to know me."

"This Clavering does," I assured him.

"Well, I'm beginning to discover she's a most unusual young lady. Now where was I?"

"Your women . . . for love not money."

"We'll skip them. It was Heathcote and after that to Ballarat. I wasn't a poor man any more—nor yet a rich one. I had time to look about and ask myself which way now. It's a funny thing—there's something about mining—finding something the earth has to offer. It gets in your blood. You've got to know what's under that hard crust of earth. It's not only for the money. When men talked of money out there they thought of gold. Gold! It's another name for money, you might say. But there's other things besides gold, as I was to find."

"Opals!" I said.

"Yes, opals. At first it was just a bit of fossicking. There I was with a nice little bit in the Melbourne bank and I thought I'd go on a trek into New South Wales . . . just to take a look at the country, you might say. I was in the Bush . . . camping at nights . . . when I fell in with a party who were looking for opal. Oh, not like proper gougers, oh no. Just a bit of fun. Weekend fossickers, you'd call them, just going out to see what beginner's luck would bring them. 'What you looking for, mates?' I asked and they answered 'Opal.' 'Opal,' I said, and I thought: Not for me! I was always a man to look for my market whether it was saveloys and pigs' trotters or gold and sapphires. Well, to cut a long story short, as they say, I went along with them for a bit of fossicking. All I had was a couple of picks—one was a driving pick, the other a sinking pick. Then I had my shovel and a rope and what we call a spider, which is a sort of candlestick

—for you may have to work in the dark. You want a snip too . . . that's a sort of pincers for snipping off the potch. Oh, I can see I'm getting a bit too technical for you, but with a name like yours you'll want to know."

"And you found opals?"

"Nothing to speak of . . . fossicking. That just gave me the taste for it. But I knew I had to go on, and within a month I was a proper gouger. Then I started to get my first real finds. I just knew as soon as I held it in my hands and it winked and twinkled at me that it was opals I was going after. Funny, you know. They say there's a story in each stone . . . Nature's pictures. I could show you something. . . ." He looked at me and laughed. "I'm going to show you. You're going to come and see my collection. We're not going to go on meeting out here, are we?"

"It seems the best way," I said, visualizing what would happen if I introduced him to my parents or Miriam and Xavier.

He winked. "We'll find a way. Leave it to me." He was laughing again. "I do talk, don't I? And all about myself. What do you think of me, eh?"

"I think you're the most exciting person I ever met."

"Here!" he cried. "It's time I went in. Next time you come to the house, eh? I'll show you some of my most precious opals. You'd like that, wouldn't you?"

"Yes, I would, but if they knew. . . ."

"Who's to know?"

"Servants talk."

"You can be sure they do. Well, let 'em, I say."

"I should be forbidden."

He winked again. "What do people like us care for a bit of forbidding eh? We're not going to let them stop us, are we?"

"They could forbid me to see you."

"Leave it to me," he said.

"When shall I see you again?"

"Tomorrow I have visitors, so it won't be then. Business, you see—and they'll be with me for a while. Say next Wednesday. You come and walk boldly up the drive to the front porch. They'll be expecting you, and they'll bring you straight to me and I'll entertain you in a fashion worthy of one of the Claverings."

I was so excited I could scarcely thank him.

Later I thought it would be the end, for we couldn't possibly keep my visits a secret. But I had a whole week to anticipate it.

2

Oakland Hall

That week seemed a long time in passing, for I was eager to hear more of Ben Henniker, who had shown me in our two meetings a different kind of world and made my own life seem colorless in comparison. I was not sure whether it was what he had to tell me or his manner of telling which made it so vivid to me, but I could picture myself in a calico tent fighting off the flies in the heat of the sun, wading through the mud and panning in the creeks. I could feel all the frustration of failure and the wonderful exhilaration of success. But that was gold. It was opal that I should look for. I could picture myself holding my candle, peering into crevices, gouging out the opal—the beautiful iridescent stone, the lucky stone which gave the gift of prophecy and which told a story, nature's story.

I never stopped congratulating myself on being at the stream that day when the chair came hurtling along and I had been able to save Ben Henniker from an accident which I had already convinced myself would have been certain death. I could have liked him for that alone and he would have liked me for saving his life, but there was more to it than that. There was something in our natures that matched each other. That was why it was so irksome to wait.

I would sit by the stream and hope he could come in his chair. "I know it was next Wednesday we were to meet," he would say, "but to tell the truth I thought it was too long to wait."

Then we would look at each other and laugh.

But it didn't happen like that. I just sat at the stream and nothing happened. I could see him so vividly, for his conversation had conjured up one image after another; I thought of the sun's beating down on him and what would have happened if the rock which had fallen on him had been a little heavier and had killed him.

Then I should never have known him.

That started me thinking of death, and I was remembering

the graves in the churchyard and they reminded me of the raised earth in the Waste Land where the archangel grew. Was it really a grave? And if so, whose?

It was no use sitting and staring across the stream. He wouldn't come. He had visitors who would perhaps be people who had come to buy or sell opals. I pictured them with a decanter of wine or whiskey between them, filling their glasses as soon as they were empty (for I was sure Ben Henniker drank heartily). He was the sort of man who would do everything with a special gusto. They would talk together and laugh a great deal and perhaps discuss the opals they had found or bought or sold. I wished I were with them. But I had to wait until next Wednesday and it was a long way off.

Sadly I stood up and wandered, aimless, along the stream and so I found myself in the Waste Land kneeling by the grave.

Oh yes, it was a grave. There was no doubt of that. I started to pull up the weeds which grew there and after I had worked for a while it was clearly revealed. It was not a dog's grave. It was too big for that. Then I made a startling discovery. A stake protruded slightly from the earth, and when I seized it and pulled it up, I saw that it was a small plaque and on it was a name. I knocked off the earth and what was revealed made me feel as though icy water were trickling down my spine, for on that plaque was my own name—Jessica—simply Jessica Clavering.

I sat back on my knees studying the plaque. I had seen such used before on the graves in the churchyard. They were put there by those who could not afford the crosses and angels holding books on which were engraved the virtues of those who lay beneath them.

In that grave lay a Jessica Clavering.

I turned the plaque over and there I could just make out some figures: "1880" and above it "Ju . . ." the other two letters were obliterated.

This was even more disturbing. I had been born on the third of June, 1880, and whoever lay in that grave not only bore my name but had died at the time of my birth.

Momentarily I had forgotten Ben Henniker. I could think of nothing but my discovery and wonder what it meant.

I found it impossible to keep this to myself and as Maddy was the obvious one to approach, I waylaid her as she was going into the kitchen garden to cut curly kale for dinner.

"Maddy," I said, deciding to come straight to the point, "who was Jessica Clavering?"

She smirked. "You haven't far to look for that one. She's her who asks too many questions and was never known to be content with the answer."

"That one," I said with dignity, "is *Opal* Jessica. Who is just Jessica?"

"What are you talking about?" I began to notice the signs of agitation.

"I mean the one who is buried in the Waste Land."

"Now look here, Miss, I've got work to do. Mrs. Cobb's waiting for her curly kale."

"You can talk while you're cutting it."

"And am I supposed to take orders from you?"

"You forget, Maddy, I'm seventeen years old. That's not an age to be treated like a child."

"Them that acts like children gets treated as such."

"It's not childish to take an interest in one's surroundings. I found a plaque on the grave. It says 'Jessica Clavering' and when she died."

"Well, now get from under my feet."

"I'm nowhere near them and I can only presume that since you behave like this you have something to hide."

It was no use talking to her. I went to my room and wondered who else would know about the mysterious Jessica, and I was still thinking of it when I went down to dinner.

Meals were dreary occasions at the Dower House. There was conversation, but it never sparkled. It usually centered around local affairs, what was happening at the church and to people of the village. We had very little social life and that was entirely our own fault, for when invitations came they were declined. "How could we possibly return such hospitality?" Mama would cry. "How different it used to be! The Hall was always full of guests." At times like that I would find myself watching my father, who would pick up *The Times* and cower behind it as though it were some sort of shield, and often he would find an excuse to get away. I once pointed out that if people invited guests they didn't necessarily ask for anything in return. "You are socially ignorant," said Mama; then with resignation: "How could we expect anything else after the manner in which we have had to bring you up." And I would be sorry I had given her the opportunity for reproaching my father.

On this occasion we were seated round the table in the really rather charming dining room. The Dower House had been built at a later period than Oakland Hall, for it had been added in 1696, and there was a plaque over the porch to confirm this. I had always thought it a beautiful house and it was only when compared with the Hall that it could be considered small. It was built of brick with stone dressings, and the roof sprang from a carved cornice which, with the mullioned windows, gave great charm. The dining room was lofty, although not large, and from its long windows we had a view of the lawn, which was Poor Jarman's pride.

We sat at the mahogany table with its cabriole legs, which had once been at Oakland Hall. "We were able to salvage some pieces," Mama had said, "but to bring all the furniture from the Hall to the Dower House was impossible, so we had to let some of it go." She spoke as though they had all been sacrificed, but I reckoned Mr. Henniker had paid a high price for them.

My father was at the head of the table saying scarcely anything; my mother at the other end kept a sharp eye on Maddy, who had to serve at mealtimes in addition to her duties—a fact which Mama found more distressing than Maddy ever did—and on my mother's right hand was Xavier and on one side of my father Miriam and the other myself.

Xavier was saying that the summer's drought had not been good for the crops and he was sure that when we did need the rain it wouldn't come.

This was said every year, and somehow the harvest was safely gathered in and there were great marrows and sheafs of wheat decorating the church to show that the miracle had happened again.

"When I think of the land we used to own. . . ." sighed Mama.

It was the sign for my father to clear his throat and talk brightly about how much less rain there had been this year compared with last.

"I remember what disaster there was last year," he said. "Most of Yarrowland crops were under water." This was a mistake because Yarrowland was a farm on the Donningham estate, and it had reminded Mama of Lady Clara. I looked at Xavier to watch his reactions. He gave no sign that he was wounded, but then Xavier never would because he was the sort of man who considered it ill bred to show his feelings. I wondered whether that was why he found it so difficult to show Lady Clara that he really did want to marry her.

"The Donninghams can take disaster in their stride," said Mama. "*They* retained their fortune throughout the generations."

"That's true enough," my father agreed in the resigned way which implied he wished he hadn't spoken. I was sorry for him, and to change the subject I blurted out: "Who was Jessica Clavering?"

There was immediate silence. I was aware of Maddy, standing by the sideboard, a dish of curly kale in her hands. Everyone at the table was looking at me and I saw the faint color begin to show under Mama's skin.

"What do you mean, Jessica?" she sad impatiently, but I knew her well enough to realize that this time the impatience was meant to hide embarrassment.

"Is it some joke?" said Miriam, her lips which seemed to grow thinner with the passing of the years, twitching slightly. "You know very well who you are."

"I'm *Opal* Jessica. And I often wonder why my first name is never used."

Mama looked relieved. "It is not very suitable," she said.

"Why did you give it to me then?" I demanded.

Xavier, who was the sort who always came to the rescue when he could, said: "Most of us have names we'd rather not own to, but I suppose when we were born they seemed suitable enough. In any case, people get used to names. I think Jessica is very nice, and as Mama says, it's suitable."

I was not going to be sidetracked. "But who is this Jessica who is buried in the Waste Land?" I insisted.

"Buried in the Waste Land?" said Mama tetchily. "What's that? Maddy, the kale will be getting cold. Do serve."

Maddy served, and I felt frustrated as I had so many times before.

Miriam was saying: "I hope Mrs. Cobb has given it an extra boiling. Did you think it was a little tough last time, Mama?"

"It was and I did speak to Mrs. Cobb about it."

"You *must* know," I said. "You couldn't have someone buried so near the house and not know. I found a stake with her name on it."

"And what were you doing in this—as you call it—Waste Land?" demanded Mama. I knew her tactics. If she was ever in a difficult situation she retaliated by going into the attack.

"I often go there," I told her.

"You should be better employed. There is a whole stock of dusters to be hemmed. Isn't that so, Miriam?"

"Indeed it is, Mama. There is much waiting to be done."

"It always seemed to me a wasted effort," I grumbled. "Hemming dusters? They collect the dust just as well without the stitching." I could never resist stating an obvious fact no matter how irrelevant.

This gave my mother the excuse she needed to go off on one of her sermons on industry and the need to give the poor as good as we took ourselves, for the dusters—made from old garments which had passed their usefulness and were cut up for the purpose—were distributed to the poor. If we could no longer afford to give them shirts and blankets we could at least cling to some of the privileges of the upper classes.

Xavier listened gravely—so did Miriam, and my father, as usual, was silent while the cheese was brought in and eaten. Then my mother rose from the table before I had time to pursue the matter of the grave and the plaque.

After the meal I made my way straight to my bedroom, and as I was mounting the stairs I heard my parents talking in the hall.

My father was saying: "She'll have to know. She'll have to be told sooner or later."

"Nonsense!" retorted Mama.

"I don't see how. . . ."

"If it hadn't been for you it would never have happened."

I listened, shamelessly straining my ears, for I knew they were talking about Jessica's grave.

They went into the drawing room and I was as bewildered as ever. It seemed that everything came back to the fact that my father had gambled away the family fortune.

As Wednesday approached I forgot my curiosity about the graves in the Waste Land in my excitement at the prospect of visiting Ben Henniker at Oakland Hall. In the early afternoon I set out and as I turned into the drive it struck me as strange that I should be a visitor to what so easily might have been my own home. Oh dear, I thought, I sound like Mama!

Oaks—solid, proud and beautiful—grew on either side of the drive which wound around—a fact which had caused me some irritation in the past because I had been unable to see the house from the road, but now I was glad of it. It added a sort of mystery, and as soon as I had rounded the bend I was out of sight, which was useful just in case anyone might be passing and see me.

When I saw the house I caught my breath in wonder. It was magnificent. It had always looked interesting seen through the trees from the stream, but to come face to face with it and have nothing impeding the view was thrilling. I could even understand and forgive my mother's years'-old rancor, for having once lived in such a place it would be hard to lose it. It was Tudor in essence, although it had been renovated since those days and added to so that there were hints of the eighteenth century here and there. But that lovely mellow brickwork was essentially Tudor, and it could not have been much different in those days when Henry VIII had visited Oakland Hall, as I had heard my mother say he did on one occasion. The tall dormer windows, the projecting bays and the oriels might have been added later, but how graciously they merged, defying criticism by their very elegance. The gate tower had been untouched. I stood awestruck looking up at the two flaking towers with the slightly lower one in the center. Over the gateway was a coat of arms. Ours, I supposed.

I went through the gateway and was in a courtyard, where I was facing a massive oak door. The ancient bell was fixed on the door. I pulled it and listened delightedly to the loud ringing.

It could only have been a second or so before the door was opened, and I had the feeling that someone had watched my approach and was ready and waiting. He was a very dignified gentleman and I placed him at once as the Wilmot of whom I had heard.

"You are Miss Clavering," he said before I could speak and somehow he made the name sound very grand. "Mr. Henniker is expecting you."

I seemed to grow in stature. I had caught a glimpse of the engraving by the carved fireplace, and as your own name will appear to leap at you from a number of others, I was aware of Clavering there, and I was thrilled by the implication that I was a member of that family which had once belonged to this house.

"If you will follow me, Miss Clavering. . . ."

I smiled. "Certainly."

As he led me across the hall I was aware of the big refectory table and the pewter dishes on it, the two suits of armor, one at each end of the hall, the weapons that hung there, the dais at the end towards which he was leading me and where there was also a staircase.

Did I imagine it or did I hear a faint murmur of voices, the slight hiss of whispering and the scuffle of feet? I saw Wilmot look up sharply and I guessed we were being observed.

Wilmot, realizing that I had been aware of something, no doubt thought it would be foolish to ignore it. A faint smile touched his lips. "You will understand, Miss Clavering, that this is the first time we have received a member of the Family, since. . . ."

"Since we were obliged to sell," I said bluntly.

Wilmot winced a little and bowed his head. I realized later that in anyone outside the Family this coming to the point and calling a spade a spade would have been considered bad taste. I wondered then how Ben Henniker and Wilmot got on together. There was little time for such thought for I was anxious to take in everything. I was led along a corridor and up another staircase.

"Mr. Henniker will receive you in the withdrawing room, Miss Clavering."

He opened a heavy oak door paneled with linen fold.

"Miss Clavering," he announced, and I followed him in.

Ben Henniker was seated in his chair, which he wheeled towards me. He was laughing. "Ha!" he cried. "So you're here! Well, welcome to the old ancestral home."

I heard the door shut discreetly behind me as I went forward to greet Ben.

He continued to laugh and I joined in. "Well, it is funny, don't you think?" he said at length. "You, the visitor. Miss Clavering—Miss..*Opal* Jessica Clavering."

"It's certainly extraordinary that I should be named Opal and it was opals that brought you all this."

"A little gold thrown in," he reminded me. "Don't forget I did very well with that. Come and sit down. I'll show you the place later." His shoulders shook with secret merriment.

"I shall begin to think you asked me just for the pleasure of showing a Clavering the family mansion."

"Not only that. I enjoyed our meetings and I thought it was time we had another. We'll have some tea . . . but later.

Now did you tell your family you'd made my acquaintance?"

"No."

He nodded. "Wise girl. Do you know what they'd have said? You're not to darken his doors nor is he to darken ours. Better for 'em not to know, eh?"

"Far better."

"It saves a lot of arguments."

"It also saves a lot of forbidding and disobeying."

"I can see you're a rebel. Well, I like that, and you've found out I'm a wicked old man . . . or if you haven't you soon will. So I may as well tell you in the early stages of our friendship."

I was laughing with that laughter born of pleasure. So this was the first stage of our relationship, and I was going to enjoy more and more of his stimulating company.

"So you would encourage me to come here even if my family forbade it?"

"I certainly would. It's good for you to learn something of the ways of the world, and you'll never learn much if you're going to cut out this one and that because they're not nice to know. You want to know those that are nice and those that are not so nice. That's why it's good for you to know me. I'm the wicked man who made his pile and bought the house that wasn't meant for his kind. Never mind. I won this with the sweat of my brow and the toil of my hands . . . with my driving pick and my sinking pick, with my shovel and my spider . . . I won this house and I reckon I've a right to it. This house represents to me the goal. It's like the finest opal ever gouged out of rock. It's the green flash of an opal."

"What's that?" I asked. "You mentioned it before."

He paused for a moment and his eyes were dreamy. "I said that did I? The Green Flash. Never mind. I won all this just as I meant to when I was a young shaver dressed up in livery at the back of a carriage . . . a flunkey you might say who's getting his first peep at the kind of life he's going to have one day. Now you . . . what are you? You're one of *them*, see? We're on different sides of the fence. But you're not one of them, are you . . . deep down inside? You're not just shut in with your cramped ideas that won't let you look outside your blinkers. You're free, Miss Jessie. You sent your blinkers flying long ago." He winked at me. "That's why we get along together . . . like a bush fire we get along.

I'm going to take you into my own special hideaway. I can tell you I don't let many see inside there since. . . . Well, I'm going to show you something so beautiful you'll be glad you're named after it."

"You're going to show me your opals?"

"That's one thing I wanted you to come for. Now you follow me."

He wheeled his chair across the room in the corner of which was a crutch; he reached for this and hoisted himself out of the chair. He opened a door and I saw that there were two steps leading down into a smaller room, which was beautiful with paneled walls and leaded windows. There was a cupboard, which he unlocked, and inside this was a steel safe. Twirling knobs, he opened the safe and took out several flat boxes.

"Come and sit down at the table," he said, "and I'll show you some of the finest opals that have ever been gouged out of rock."

He sat down at a round table and I drew a chair to sit beside him. He opened one of the boxes inside which, lying in little velvet hollows, were the opals. I had never seen such beautiful gems. The top row was of great, pale stones which flashed with blue and green fire; those on the next row, also of remarkable size, were darker—blue, almost purple—and in the last row the stones had a background which was almost black and the more startling because they flashed fire with red and green lights.

"There," he said, "your namesakes. What do you think of them? I see. Speechless. That's what I thought. That's what I hoped. Keep your diamonds. Keep your sapphires. There's nothing anywhere in the world to beat these gems. You agree with me, don't you?"

"I have never seen a great many diamonds or sapphires," I said, "so it wouldn't be fair for me to be so sure, but I can't imagine anything more lovely than these."

"Look at her!" he commanded as, with a gnarled finger, he gently touched one of the stones. It was deep blue and there was a touch of gold in it. "She's known as the Star of the East. They've got names, these opals. The Star of the East! Couldn't you see her, there in the sky just before the sun rises and shuts off her light. It must have been something like her that the wise men saw on that Christmas night years and years ago. I tell you this: she's unique. They're all unique, these opals. You'll find others that you think are just like them, then you'll see your mistake. They're like people, no two alike. That's one of the marvels of the universe . . . all those people . . . all those opals . . . and not two exactly alike. And sometimes you find something like the Star of the East and you think of all you've suffered . . . for believe me a gouger's life is no picnic . . . and you say it was all worth while. Now, for him who owns the Star of the East, it tells him the best is yet to come, for the Star is rising, you see, and wasn't it there to announce the birth of the Christ child?"

"So *your* best is yet to come, Mr. Henniker?"

"You're to call me Ben. Didn't I tell you?"

"Yes, but it's hard to get used to when you've been brought up not to call grown-up people by their Christian names."

"In here we don't care what was done because someone said it should be without rhyme or reason. Oh no. We do what's right for us, and I'm Ben to you as I am to all my friends and I trust you're one of them."

"I want to be . . . Ben."

"That's the ticket, and that's the idea. The best is yet to come for me while I've got the Star of the East."

I put out a finger and touched it.

"That's right," he said. "Touch it. Look at the light on the stone. And that's not the only one. Here's Pride of the Camp. A fine piece of opal there. Not quite up to the Star of the East, but a fine gem. She came from White Cliffs in New South Wales. A roaring camp, that was. Some prospector had been there and moved on; then some fossickers came by and started to tap round as fossickers do. And what happened? He finds opal . . . not potch . . . oh dear me no. Real, precious opal. What a find for a fossicker. Before the month's out there's a camp there and everyone's gouging like mad. I was caught up in it. It was my luck to hit on Pride of the Camp."

"Do you sell them?" I asked.

He was thoughtful for a moment. "Well, that would seem to be the object, but there sometimes comes a stone that no matter what it can bring you, you just can't sell. You get a sort of feeling for it. It belongs to you and you only. You'd rather have it than all the money in the world and that's plain straight."

"So all these you are showing me are stones which you felt like that about?"

"That's it. Some are there for their beauty and some for other reasons. Look at this one here. . . . See the green fire in it? That cost me my leg." He shook his fist at it. "You cost me dear, my beauty," he went on, "and for that reason I keep you. She's got fire, that one. Just look at her sitting there. She cares nothing for me. She says, 'Oh, if you want me, take me, but don't start counting the cost.' I call her Green Lady, for that was the name of a cat I once had. I'm rather fond of cats. They've got a sort of disdainful pride that I like. Have you ever noticed the grace of a cat? How it walks alone? It's proud. It never cringes. I like that. This cat I had was called Lady. It suited her, that name. She was a lady, and her eyes were as green as the green you see in her namesake there. So that's why I won't let her go, though she cost me my leg and you might think I wouldn't like to be reminded. There she was glinting at me in the candlelight . . . and I had to have her though the roof fell in and crippled me."

I took up the Green Lady in my hands and studied her. Then I laid her gently back in her soft velvet case.

"And look here, Miss Jessie. Look at this heart-shaped cabochon. See the violet in it. It's Royal Purple, this one. Look at the color. Fit for a royal crown she is."

I was fascinated, and he opened more boxes and I saw a variety of stones, from the milky kind flashing their reds and greens to the dark blue and black variety with their stronger colors.

He talked about them all, pointing out their qualities, and I was caught up in his enthusiasm.

One box he took out was empty. It was smaller than the others, for it was meant to cushion one single stone, and in the center of the black velvet was a hollow somehow almost accusing in its emptiness. He stared at it in a melancholy way for some moments.

"What was there?" I asked.

He turned to me. His eyes had narrowed, his mouth hardened, and he looked murderous. I stared at him, astonished by his change of mood.

"Once," he said, "the Green Flash at Sunset was there."

I waited but said nothing. His jaw protruded and his mouth was set and angry.

"It was a specially beautiful opal?" I ventured.

He turned to me, his eyes blazing. "There was never such

a beauty," he cried. "No, never such an opal in the whole world. It was worth a fortune, but I would never have parted with it. You'd have to see it to believe this, but you'd know it if you did. The green flash . . . it wasn't there all the time. You had to watch for it. It was the way the light caught it . . . and the way you held it . . . it was something about you as well as the stone."

"What happened to it?"

"It was stolen," he said.

"Who stole it?"

He was silent. Then he turned to look at me, his eyes narrowed. I could see how the loss of the stone upset him.

"When was it stolen?" I prompted.

"A long time ago."

"How long?"

"Before you were born."

"And all that time you never found it?"

He shook his head. Then he slapped the box shut. He put it back in the safe with the others, and when he had locked the safe he turned to me and laughed. But there was a slightly different note in his laughter than there had been before.

"Now," he said, "we're going to have some tea. I told them to bring it precisely at four. So let us go back there." He pointed to the drawing room. "You can pour out and entertain me, which is somehow right and fitting, as you're the Clavering."

The spirit lamp and silver teapot were already there, with plates of sandwiches, scones, and plum cake. Beside Wilmot stood a maid.

"Miss Clavering will pour out," said Ben.

"Very good, sir," replied Wilmot graciously; and I was glad when he and the maid had retired.

"All very ceremonious," said Ben. "I confess to you I've never quite got used to it. Sometimes I say: 'Enough of that!' You can imagine how a man feels when he's boiled his own billy can and cooked his own damper round a campfire. Today's special though. Today's the day when the first Clavering comes to be my guest."

"But not a very important one, I'm afraid," I said with a laugh.

"*The* most important. Never underestimate yourself, Miss Jessie. People are going to think you're not up to much if you think that way yourself. You've got to find a nice way between because it doesn't do to be too big for your boots nor for your hat. Then they won't fit."

I asked how he liked his tea, poured out, and when I carried it to him, he smiled at me appreciatively. I set his cup and plate on a table by his chair and felt very pleased with myself as I took my place behind the silver teapot.

"Tell me about this Green Flash at Sunset," I said.

He was silent for a second or so and then he asked: "Have you ever heard of the green flash, Miss Jessie?"

"Only this afternoon."

"I don't mean the opal . . . that other green flash. They say that there's a precise moment when the sun goes down— just before it disappears—that there is a green flash on the sea. You can only see it in tropical seas and then conditions have to be exactly right. It's a rare phenomenon. It's beautiful and exciting to see. People watch for it; some never catch it at all. If you as much as blink your eyes you could miss it. It's there and it's gone and you hardly know it's been. You've got to be in the right spot at the right moment, looking in the right direction, and you've got to be quick to see it. I saw it once. It was on the voyage back to England from Australia. There I was on deck, and it was at sunset time. I was watching that great ball of fire drop into the ocean. It's different in the tropics. There's little twilight like we have here. And there was this peaceful scene . . . no cloud and the great sun so low that I could just bear to look at it. Then it was gone and there was this green flash. 'I've seen it,' I cried out loud. "I've seen the green flash." Then I went and looked at my opal. It was very valuable, the finest opal of all. I remember on that journey home I carried it about with me. I'd look at it now and then just to assure myself that it was there. Now this opal reminds you of the green flash at sea. You'd look at it, you'd see its beauty, you'd see the red and blue flashes. There was a darkening of color right across it so that it looked like the meeting of land and sea, and there was such red fire in it that it was like the sun, and if you were looking at the right moment and you were holding it at a certain angle and the light was right, suddenly the red would seem to disappear and then you'd see the green flash. First I believe it was called the Sunset Opal and then when I had caught the green flash that was it. She couldn't be anything else but the Green Flash at Sunset."

"And you loved it best of all your stones?"

"There was never one like it. I'd never known that green

flash in a stone before. You had to watch for it. It was something that was rare, and you'd got to be ready for it. It was like no other green and if you missed it you might not get the opportunity again."

"Did you ever find out who took it?"

"I had my suspicions. In fact everything pointed to him, the young devil. By God, if I could lay my hands on him. . . ." He seemed to be lost for words, which was rare with him, and he was for the moment unaware of me. I guessed he was back in that time when he had opened the box and found the opal gone.

I went over to him, took his cup, and brought it over to refill it; and when I handed it back to him I said softly: "How did it happen, Ben?"

"It was here," he said, "in this house." He pointed over his shoulder to the room we had just left. "I hadn't had the place long then. I was anxious to show it off, for I had a great pride in it. It was more than just a house. That's how you'd feel about a place like this. I reckon your family felt it. Well, their loss was my gain. I used to have people stay here because I wanted to say: 'Look what I've got. This is what all these years of toil and disappointments have got for me. Success at last.' Some of them had never seen a place like this. It was pride, pride going before a fall, as they say. Look what I've got. Look at my mansion. Look at my opals. We went in there. . . ." He pointed to the study door. "There were four of us and on this occasion I brought out my opals just as I have for you and that was the last I saw of the Green Flash at Sunset. I put her back in her box and put that in the safe. The next time I went there, the box was in its place . . . all the opals were there except one—the Green Flash at Sunset."

"Who had stolen it?"

"Someone who knew the combination of the safe. It must have been."

"And didn't you know who it was?"

"There was one young man. He disappeared. I never saw him again, although I searched for him. He was clearly the one who had the Green Flash."

"What a wicked thing to do."

"There are wicked people in the world. Never forget it. Funny thing was I'd never have thought it of him. He had that dedication, that determination which almost always ends in success. But when he sets eyes on the Green Flash, that was his downfall. You see, there'll never be another like her. She's the Queen of Opals. The way you had to look for the flash and it never came for some, you see what I mean. And I'd lost her forever."

"Surely the police could find him."

"He was far away in next to no time. Sometimes I tell myself that one of these days I'm going to find him and the Flash."

"Do you think he sold it?"

"It wouldn't have been easy. She'd have been recognized. Every dealer knew her and would have reported the sale. He may have taken her with him . . . just to keep her to himself. She had a terrible fascination for everyone who saw her. In spite of all the tales of bad luck, everyone who laid eyes on her wanted her."

"What tales, Ben?"

"Well, you know how these things get round. She was unlucky, they said. There'd been one or two people who'd owned her and misfortune had come to them. The Green Flash meant death, they used to say."

"So *you* didn't find it in the first place then?"

"Oh, dear me no. It had passed through other hands before mine. You might say I won it."

"How did you do that?"

"I was always a bit of a gambler. Take a chance, that's me. I'd always keep a reserve though. I've never gambled to my last coin like some. I liked to be rich and then do my gambling from there, if you know what I mean. There was old Harry Wilkins who'd got this stone, and from the moment he showed it to me I wanted it. I'd fallen under its spell, you might say and I was bent on getting it. Ill luck dogged Harry. They said it was the stone. His son had never been much good and one night he went out and never came back. He was found with his neck broken. He'd always drunk too much. Old Harry went to pieces after that. He was a great gambler. He'd take a bet on anything. A couple of raindrops falling down a window pane. 'I'll bet you a hundred quid the right one gets to the bottom first,' he'd say. He just couldn't help it. Well, I wanted that stone and it was about all he'd got because this son of his had robbed him right and left before he died. To cut a long story short, he staked the Green Flash for a fortune. I took the gamble and won. He shot himself a few weeks later. Disaster follows the Green Flash, they used to say."

"And what about you?"

"I wouldn't believe in the curse."

"You lost the stone so perhaps you escaped it."

"One day she'll be back where she belongs."

"You talk about the Green Flash as though she were a woman."

"That's how she was to me. I loved her. I used to take her out and look at her when I was downcast. I'd watch for the flash and I used to say to myself: 'Times will change. You'll find happiness as well as stones, old Ben.' That's what she's telling you."

Suddenly it seemed as though he could no longer bear to talk of his loss and he started telling me of the days when he had been a young man and had done what he called "a bit of fossicking" and how he had first felt the lure of the opal. Then he said he reckoned I'd like to see the house, and as he was not able to get around as fast as he'd like, he'd tell one of the servants to take me.

Much as I disliked leaving him, I did want to see the house, and as I hesitated—which seemed to please him—he said: "You'll come again. We must make a point of these meetings, for there's one thing that's certain sure. You and I have quite taken a fancy to each other. I hope you agree with my findings."

"Oh I do, and if I can come again and hear more, I'd love to see the house now."

"Of course you would and so you shall. Then you can think what it would have been like if you'd lived your life here as you would have done if one of these get-rich-quick johnnies hadn't come along and grabbed the ancestral home."

"I shall always be glad of that now," I assured him, and he looked very pleased.

He pulled a bell rope and Wilmot appeared immediately.

"Miss Clavering would like to see the house," said Ben. "One of you must show her round."

"Very good, sir," murmured Wilmot.

"Just a minute," cried Ben. "Let Hannah do it. Yes, Hannah's the one."

"As you say, sir."

I went to Ben's chair and took his hand. "Thank you. I have enjoyed it so much. May I really come again?"

"Next Wednesday. Same time."

"Thank you."

His face looked strange for a second. If he had been anyone else I should have said he was about to cry. Then he said: "Off with you. Hannah will show you round."

I wondered why he had selected Hannah. She was the one who interested me most. She was a tall, spare woman with rather gaunt features and large dark eyes which seemed to bore right into me. She was clearly gratified that she was the one who had been chosen to show me round.

"I was with your family for five years," she told me. "I came here when I was twelve years old. Then I stayed on, and when they went they couldn't afford to keep me."

"That happened with so many, I'm afraid."

"Would you care to start at the top of the house, Miss Clavering, and work down?"

I said I thought that seemed an excellent idea, and together we climbed the newel staircase to the roof.

"You can see the turrets best from up here. And look what a fine view of the countryside." She looked at me intently. "There's a good view of the Dower House."

I followed the direction in which she was looking, and there it was, nestling among the trees and the greenery. The house looked like a doll's house from here. The clean lines of its architecture were very obvious and the smooth lawn looked like a neat square of green silk. I could see Poor Jarman working on the flower beds.

"You have a better view of us than we have of you," I commented. "In summer Oakland Hall is completely hidden."

"I often come up here and look around," said Hannah.

"You must have seen us in the garden now and then."

"Oh, often."

I felt a little uneasy at having been watched by Hannah.

"Do you prefer it now to the days when my family were here?"

She hesitated, then she said: "In some ways. Mr. Henniker goes away a lot and we have the place to ourselves. It seems funny that . . . at least it did at first, but you get used to most things. He's easy to work for." I could see that she was implying that my mother was not. "Miss Miriam was only a girl when she lived here," she went on.

"That was a long time ago. Before I was born."

"They won't be pleased to hear you've been here, Miss, I reckon."

"No, they won't," I agreed and added: "If they find out."

"Mr. Henniker is a very strange gentleman."

"Unlike anyone I've ever known," I agreed.

"Well, you just think of the way he came here. Who'd have thought a gentleman like that would take a place like this."

We were silent for a while contemplating the view. My eyes kept going back to the Dower House. Poor Jarman had straightened himself up as Maddy came out and started to talk to him. I was amused that unbeknown to them I could watch them.

"Shall we go in now, Miss Clavering?" suggested Hannah.

I nodded and we descended the circular stairs and entered a room. I admired the molded beams of the ceiling, the paneled walls and the carved fireplace.

"There are so many rooms like this that you lose count of them," said Hannah. "We don't use them all even when there's a house party."

"Is there often a house party?"

"Yes, gentlemen come to talk business with Mr. Henniker. At least that's how it was. I don't know if it will be the same since his accident."

"I suppose they come about opals."

"All sorts of business Mr. Henniker's engaged in. He's a very rich gentleman. That's what we say is so good about being here . . . in the servant's hall, I mean. There's never all this talk about economizing in, and wagers come prompt, not. . . ."

"Not like it was when my family was here."

"Most of the gentry have their money troubles it seems. I've talked to others in houses like this. But someone like Mr. Henniker . . . well, he's got to have a lot of money to buy the place, hasn't he, so it stands to reason he can afford to keep it up—not like someone inheriting it and finding it's a drain."

"I see that it must be a great comfort to work for Mr. Henniker after my family."

"It's all so different. Mr. Wilmot's always saying it's not what he's used to, and I reckon he sometimes hankers for a house with more dignity. But it's nice to know your wages are there . . . on the dot just when they're due, and there doesn't have to be all this pinching and scraping. He never locks up the tea or anything like that . . . never asks to see Mrs. Bucket's accounts, but I reckon he'd know fast enough if there was any fiddling."

We had come to a gallery. "Once," she went on, "there were pictures of the family all along here. They were taken away, and Mr. Henniker never put up pictures of his own. A gallery's not a gallery without pictures of the family, Mr. Wilmot says, but we don't know much about Mr. Henniker's."

The gallery was beautiful, with carved pillars and long narrow windows, the stained glass of which threw a lovely glow over the place. There were curtains of rich red velvet at intervals around the walls. They hid the part which wasn't paneled, Hannah explained.

"They say this is haunted," she told me. "There always has to be one haunted room in a house like this. Well, this is it. No one's seen or heard anything since Mr. Henniker's been here. He'd frighten any ghost away, I reckon. They used to say that they could hear music here . . . coming from the spinet that was once there. Mr. Henniker had it shipped out to Australia. It meant something special to him, I heard. Mrs. Bucket says it's a lot of fancy. Mr. Wilmot believes it though, but then he'd think that any family that didn't have a ghost wouldn't be fit for him to work for."

"But he works for Mr. Henniker now."

"It's something of a sore point."

We went on with our tour of exploration, and as Hannah had said, there were so many rooms of the same kind that it would be easy to lose oneself. I hoped that if I visited Mr. Henniker frequently I should be able to see it all again and enjoy exploring at my leisure. Hannah was not the most comfortable of guides because whenever I looked at her I would find her eyes fixed on me as though she were assessing me. I put this down to the fact that I was a member of the family she had once served. However I couldn't stop thinking of her looking down onto the Dower House and watching me.

I admired the carved fireplaces which had been put in during Elizabeth's reign; their theme was scenes from the Bible, and I picked out Adam and Eve and Lot's wife being turned into a pillar of salt and felt very ignorant when others had to be explained to me.

I thought the solarium delightful with its windows facing south and its walls covered in tapestry, which had no doubt been sold to Ben Henniker by my family, and I pictured my mother's pacing up and down here and in the gallery while they discussed how they could possibly go on living here.

Finally we came down to the hall and passed through a vestibule to what Hannah called the Parlor.

"In the very old days," she explained, "this was where guests were received." The walls were paneled, the windows leaded, and there was a suit of armor in a corner. "Right at the other end are the kitchens with the buttery and pantry and that sort of thing. That's the Screens end of the hall. You'll want to see them. Some of them go right back to the days when the house was built and that was long enough ago, goodness knows."

She led me back across the hall to what she called the Screens—a door which shut off the servants' quarters from the hall and I was in a vast kitchen. An enormous fireplace took up almost the whole of one side. In this were bread ovens, roasting spits, and great caldrons. There was a big table with two benches, one on either side; two arm chairs—wide and ornate—were placed at each end of the table, and I later learned that one of these was occupied by Mrs. Bucket and the other by the butler, Mr. Wilmot.

As I entered the kitchen I was aware of whispering voices. I knew that I was being watched from some vantage point. A large woman came sailing into the kitchen followed by three maids.

Hannah said: "This is Miss Clavering, Mrs. Bucket."

"How do you do, Mrs. Bucket," I replied. "I have heard of you."

"Is that so?" she asked, pleased.

"Maddy who is with us often mentions you."

"Ah, Maddy, yes. Well, Miss Clavering, this is a great day for us to have one of the Family here."

"It is wonderful for me to be here."

"Well," said Mrs. Bucket, "perhaps this is going to be a beginning."

I felt a little embarrassed because they were all assessing me. I wondered whether they were thinking that a Clavering who had been brought up in a Dower House was not quite a true one. After all, I had never known the grandeurs of a house like this.

"I'll never forget the day the Family told us they were going. Lined up in the hall we were . . . even the stable boys."

Hannah was signaling to Mrs. Bucket, but I blessed the plump cook, for I could see that she was one who could not stop herself talking and that the sight of me in the kitchen— a Clavering—had brought back such memories that she could not stop herself recalling them.

"Of course, we'd heard it before. Money, money, money. . . . It was affecting people all over the place. There was talk of this income tax and how it was ruining everybody. They'd already cut down in the stables. The horses they had when I first came here! *And* the gardeners! That's where the cuts always have to come first . . . the stables and the gardens. I said as much to Mr. Wilmot, which he will tell you is the truth if you will ask him. I said to him. . . ."

"It's a long time ago, Mrs. Bucket," interrupted Hannah.

"It seems like yesterday. Why, at that time you wasn't born, Miss Clavering. When we heard that a gentleman coming from Australia had bought the place, we couldn't believe it. You ask Mr. Wilmot. But it was so, and then it was all different and the Claverings went to the Dower House and we wasn't on speaking terms. And now. . . ."

"Miss Clavering has become acquainted with Mr. Henniker," said Hannah firmly, "so he asked her to tea with him."

Mrs. Buckett nodded. "And did you enjoy the scones, Miss Clavering? I always remember Miss Jessica. . . ."

Hannah was staring at Mrs. Bucket as though she were the Medusa herself. I could see that she was imploring her to be discreet.

But I was not going to allow that. I said: "Miss Jessica? Who was she?"

"Mrs. Bucket meant Miss Miriam. She loved the scones. Don't you remember, Mrs. Bucket, how she'd come down to the kitchen while you were baking them?"

"She said Miss Jessica," I insisted.

"She gets muddled sometimes over names, don't you, Mrs. Bucket? This is Miss Jessica. It was Miss Miriam and Mr. Xavier who used to love your scones. I reckon that Mrs. Cobb's are not a patch on yours."

"Nobody's was a patch on mine," said Mrs. Bucket emphatically.

"I thought they were delicious," I said, but I was asking myself why she had said Miss Jessica.

Hannah asked quickly if I would like to see the stables.

I said I thought I'd better not, for it had just occurred to me
that though my visits were supposed to be secret, some of
the servants would certainly talk, so the fewer I saw the
better. I could imagine my family's consternation if it was
discovered that I had become friends with Ben Henniker.
I was seventeen years old, still a minor, and I had to obey
orders to a certain extent, rebel that I was. It was therefore
better for the time being to keep my visits as secret as
possible, and the fewer people I saw the better.

I said it had been very interesting and I told Mrs. Bucket
that I was glad to have made her acquaintance, and when I
had thanked Hannah for showing me the house I left.

I felt they were watching me as I walked down the drive
and was glad when I reached the bend, although then I was
exposed to the road and wondered what would happen if
Miriam, Xavier, or my parents came along at that moment.
They did not, however, and I reached the Dower House
unobserved.

I kept thinking of what Mrs. Bucket had said about
Jessica and the scones, and I went straight to the Waste
Land and found the plaque which I had stuck back into
the ground with the name showing: Jessica Clavering Ju . . .
1880.

She must be the Jessica of whom Mrs. Bucket had spoken.

All through the hot month of August I went to Oakland
Hall. It was not only on Wednesdays because Ben said he
disliked regularities. He liked unexpected things to happen,
so he would say: "Come on Monday" . . . or "Come on
Saturday." And sometimes I would say: "Well, that's the
church fete day"—or some such engagement—"and they'd
miss me." Then we would make another date.

He seemed to be showing progress and could walk about
more easily with the aid of his crutch. He made jokes about
his false leg and called himself Ben Pegleg and said he
reckoned he'd do as well with wood as most people did with
flesh and blood. He used to hold my arm and we would
walk along the gallery together.

Once he said to me: "There ought to be family pictures
here. That's what a gallery's for, they say. My ugly face
wouldn't add much to it."

"It's the most interesting face I have ever seen," I told
him.

The face in question twitched at that. Underneath his tough exterior he was a very sentimental man.

He always talked a great deal, and I had vivid pictures of what his life had been. He made me see the streets of London clearly, and I could picture him with his bright eyes darting everywhere, discovering the best way of selling his wares and always being one step ahead of the rest. He spoke often of his mother and he was very tender then. Clearly he had loved her dearly. Once I said to him: "Ben, you should have had a wife."

"I wasn't the marrying sort," he replied. "Funny thing, there was never one who was there at the right moment. Timing plays a big part in life. The opportunity has to be there when you're in a position to seize it. I'm not going to tell you there weren't women. That would be a falsehood, and we want truth between us two, don't we? I'd be with Lucy for a year or so and then just when I'd be thinking it was time I made it legal, something would happen to change it all. Then there was Betty. A good woman, Betty, but I knew it wouldn't have worked with her either."

"You could have had some sons and daughters to fill the gallery."

"I've got the odd one or two," he said with a grin. "At least they claim me as father . . . or did when I began to grow rich."

"Who's to say?"

And so we talked.

I was friendly with the servants too. Mrs. Bucket had taken me to her heart. She liked to discover how Mrs. Cobb did certain things and questioned me closely. She would sit nodding in a superior way with a smirk on her lips as I talked, and I was sure she was unfair to Mrs. Cobb.

"Old Jarman would have done better to stay," she commented. "Look what he got. A cottage and enough children to fill it to overflowing, if you ask me. He would have been better to stay and wait for another five years. He'd have had five less to feed then."

Wilmot after a while accepted my visits to the servants' hall. I was sure he worked it out that although I was a Clavering, I was not really an Oakland Hall Clavering, for I had not been born in the great vaulted chamber where other Claverings had first viewed the world but in a foreign land. It had lowered my status in some way, and although he treated me with respect, it was tempered with a certain condescension.

I was amused, and Ben and I used to laugh a great deal over it, and I would wonder how I had endured the monotony of my life in pre-Ben days.

It was as we were approaching the end of August that Ben made me uneasy. We were taking our stroll along the gallery and he was now clearly able to walk quite easily with the aid of his crutch.

"If this goes on," he said, "I'll be off on my travels next year." He was aware of my consternation and hastened to reassure me. "It won't be this side of Christmas. I've got a lot more practice to do yet."

"It will be so dull here without you," I stammered.

He patted my arm. "It's a long way off. Who can say what will happen by Christmas."

"Where would you go?" I asked.

"I'd go up to my place north of Sydney . . . not far from the opal country where I'm sure there are more finds to be made."

"You mean you'd go mining again?"

"It's in the blood."

"But after your accident. . . ."

"Oh, I'm not sure that I'd go off with my pick. I didn't mean that. My partner and I have mines out there that we know are going to yield. We've got men working for us."

"What's happening to all that now?"

"Oh, the Peacock's looking after it."

"The Peacock?"

Ben began to laugh. "One day," he said, "you'll have to meet the Peacock. The name suits him."

"He must be vain."

"Oh, he's got a good conceit of himself. Mind you, I'm not saying it's not warranted. Ever seen a peacock's feather . . . that blue . . . unmistakable. He's got eyes that color. Rare, you know, deep, darkish blue, and my goodness can he flash them when he's in a rage. There's not a man in the Company who would dare cross the Peacock. That can be very useful. I know he'll take care of everything while I'm away. Why, if it wasn't for the Peacock I wouldn't be here now. Dursn't be. I'd have to be back there. You've no idea how wrong things can go."

"So you can trust this Peacock?"

"Seeing the closeness of our relationship, I reckon I can."

"Who is he then?"

"Josslyn Madden. Known as Joss or otherwise the Peacock. His mother was a very great friend of mine. Oh yes, a very great friend. She was a beautiful woman, Julia Madden was. There wasn't a man in the camp who didn't fancy her. Jock Madden was a poor fish who ought never to have been out there. Couldn't manage a job or hold a woman. Julia and I were very fond of each other. And when young Joss came along there wasn't a shadow of doubt. Old Jock was incapable of getting children anyway."

"You mean this Peacock is your son?"

"That's about it." Ben began to laugh. "I'll never forget the day. All of seven he was. I'd built Peacocks at that time . . . it might have been about five years before. I'd got the peacocks on the lawn and the house had its name. Julia used to come over to see me. She was thinking of leaving Jock and coming for good. Then one day on the way over, her horse fell. She was thrown, and the fall killed her. Jock married again. She was a tyrant, that one. No one would have her, even though there was a shortage of women, so she took Jock because he didn't know how to say no. Caught proper, he was. Our young Peacock didn't like the household at all, so he promptly packed a bag, and one day there he was walking across the lawn, frightening the peacocks, marching along like any swagman. They brought him to me, and he told me: 'I'm going to live here now forever.' Not, May I? but I am! That was Joss Madden aged seven and that's Joss Madden today. He makes up his mind what he wants and that's how it's going to be."

"You're fond of him, Ben. I can see you admire him."

"He's my son . . . and Julia's. I can see old Ben in him in lots of ways. There's nothing makes you admire people like seeing yourself in them."

"So he stayed at Peacock's and he became so vain that people called him the Peacock, and he's ruthless and he's your son."

"That's about the ticket."

"And is he one of those about whom you say he claimed you as his father when you grew rich?"

"At seven I don't know how knowledgeable he was about wealth. I think perhaps he just hated his home and liked the peacocks. He paid more attention to them than he did to me. He used to strut round the lawns with them. Then he became fascinated by opals—particularly those with the peacock colorings. He took an interest right from the start, and when Joss takes an interest it's a big one. I know the place is safe with him. He could soon manage it all without my help. But the urge comes over me to be out there. Sometimes I dream I'm there . . . going down the shaft . . . down down into the underground chambers . . . and there I am with my candle and the roof a mass of gems . . . lovely opal flashing red green and gold . . . and right at the heart of it another Green Flash."

"It's unlucky, Ben," I said. "I don't want any harm to come to you. You're rich. You've got Oakland. What does it matter about the Green Flash?"

"I'll tell you one of the nicest things I've found since I lost the Flash," he answered. "Well, that's you."

We didn't speak for some time. We just stumped along the gallery, but he had started misgivings in my mind and I knew the day would come when he would go away.

Sometimes I used to feel that there wasn't much time. If Ben went away I should no longer have an excuse for visiting the Hall, and there was so much I wanted to know before that happened.

I had learned a little about opals and how they were gouged from the earth. I had my own mental picture of the roaring camps he had talked of and the lives of the people who lived in them; I could picture the excitement when a brilliant gem was discovered; but I had learned more than that.

There was nothing Mrs. Bucket liked more than for me to go down to her kitchen, and I always made a point of doing this. I had discovered how little I knew of my own family and I often thought that Miriam, Xavier, and my parents were like shadow figures moving about in a dimly lighted room; the lights had been dimmed when my father's gambling lost them Oakland Hall.

Mrs. Bucket's main delight was to cook little delicacies for me so that I could compare them with the kind of fare Mrs. Cobb put on our table. I think she felt rather guilty because she had not gone with us to the Dower House. She liked to talk about the past, and from her I learned that Mr. Xavier had been a "bright little fellow."

"Mind you, at the time of the trouble he was getting his education. He liked my cooking. Used to call me Food Bucket." She purred and shook her head. "Nothing disrespectful, mind. 'Of course you're Food Bucket,' he used to say, 'because nobody can make food taste like you do.' Eat. He could eat. Miss Miriam could be a little tartar now and then. When she was a little thing I caught her more than once stealing the sugar. Fifteen years old she was when she came to me and she said: 'Mrs. Bucket, we've got to leave Oakland.' And she was near to crying she was—and I don't mind telling you I was too. Now, Miss Jessica. . . ."

What a deep silence there was before Hannah said: "Have you made those currant buns for tea, Mrs. Bucket?"

"Who was Jessica?" I asked.

Mrs. Bucket looked at Hannah and then she burst out: "What's the good of all this pretending. You can't keep that sort of thing dark forever."

"Tell me," I demanded rather imperiously, as though I were an Oakland-bred Clavering, "who was Jessica?"

"There was another daughter," said Mrs. Bucket almost defiantly. "She came between Miriam and Xavier."

"And she was called Jessica?" I went on.

Hannah bowed her head. It was tantamount to agreement. "Why is there this secrecy?"

They were silent again, and I burst out, "It's all rather foolish."

Hannah said sharply: "You'll know in time. It's not for us. . . ."

I looked at Mrs. Bucket appealingly. "*You* know," I said. "Why shouldn't I? What happened to this Jessica?"

"She died," said Mrs. Bucket.

"When she was very young?" I asked.

"It was after they left Oakland," Hannah told me, "so we wouldn't know much about it."

"She was older than Miriam, and Miriam was fifteen when they left," I prompted.

"About seventeen," said Hannah, "but it's not for us . . . Mrs. Bucket shouldn't have. . . ."

"I'll do what I like in my own kitchen," said Mrs. Bucket.

"This is no kitchen matter," protested Hannah.

"I'll thank you not to be impudent to me, Hannah Gooding."

I could see that they were making a quarrel of this to avoid telling me. But I was going to find out. I was determined on that.

I left the Hall and went to the churchyard and looked at all the graves. There was only one Jessica Clavering among them, and she had died about a hundred years before at the ripe age of seventy years.

Then I went to the Waste Land. There it was—the grave and the plaque engraved with her name and the date Ju . . . 1880.

"So this is where they buried you, Jessica," I murmured.

3

A Letter from the Dead

The next day, when I was sitting by the stream, Hannah appeared on the other side of it, carrying a package.

"I wanted to speak to you, Miss Clavering," she said.

"All right, Hannah. I'll come over." As I crossed the bridge I noticed how solemn she was looking.

"I've been thinking the time has come for me to give you this," she said.

"What is it?"

"It's something that was given to me to be given to you when the time came or on your twenty-first birthday—whichever came first, and I reckon, after all that's been said, that the time is now."

I took the packet which she thrust into my hands.

"What is it?" I repeated.

"It's writing. It was written to you and given to me."

"When? And who gave it to you?"

"It's all in there. I hope I've done what was right."

She hesitated for a moment, her brow puckered in consternation, then she turned and hurried across the bridge, leaving me standing there with the large envelope in my hands. I opened it and pulled out several sheets of paper on which someone had written in clear neat writing.

I glanced at the first page.

"My darling child, Opal," it began.

"It will be many years after I write this that you will read it, and I hope when you do you will not think too badly of me. Always remember that I loved you, and that what I am going to do, I do because it is the best way out for all of us. I want you to know that my last thoughts were of you. . . ."

I could not understand what this meant so I decided to take the papers to the Waste Land where few people ever came and there, close to the grave of Jessica, I started to read.

"I shall start right at the beginning. I want you to know

65

me, because if you do you will understand how everything happened. I think in every family there is one who is different, the one in the litter who doesn't bear much resemblance to the rest. They called it a winnick, I believe. Well, I was like that. There was Xavier who was so clever and good at lessons and ready to help everybody; and there was Miriam who could get up to mischief but mostly when I led her into it. Miriam was malleable; she could be molded any way and would at times be a model child. I was always a bit of a rebel. I used to pretend I was a ghost and play the spinet in the gallery and then go and hide when people came to look so that the rumor started that the gallery was haunted and the servants wouldn't go up there alone. I used to flatter Mrs. Bucket into making the special cakes which I liked and she would always bake an extra one for me. I was Papa's favorite, though not Mama's. Papa taught me how to play poker. I shall never forget Mama's face when she came to his study and found us there with the cards in our hands. I think it must have been then that I first realized the uneasy state of affairs in our household. She stood there, so dramatic that I wanted to burst out laughing. She said: 'Fiddling while Rome's burning!' I said: 'This isn't fiddling, Mama. It's poker.' She cried: 'I wonder you're not ashamed.' And she picked up the cards and threw them into the fire. 'Now it's cards that are burning, not Rome,' I said, for I could never guard my tongue and words always slipped out before I could stop them. Mama lifted her hand and slapped me across the face. I remember the shock it gave me because it showed how distraught she was. Usually she was calm and her reproaches were verbal. Papa was shocked too. He said sternly: 'Never lift your hand against the children again.' Then it came out: 'And who are you to tell me how to behave? You are teaching our daughter to be as dissolute as you are. Cards, gambling . . . and gambling means debts, which is why we are in the position we are in today. Do you realize that the roof needs immediate repair? There is water seeping into the gallery. There is dry rot under the floor boards in the library. The servants have not been paid for two months. And what is your answer: To teach your daughter to play poker!'

"I was standing there, holding my face where she had slapped it. Papa said pleadingly: 'Not in front of Jessica, please, Dorothy.' And she answered: 'Why not? She will know soon enough. How long before everyone knows that through your gambling your fortune away . . . and mine . . . we cannot afford to go on like this.'

"I saw the Queen of Hearts writhe in the flames and then Mama had gone and Papa and I were alone together.

"I don't know why I should tell you this. It's irrelevant really. But I do want you to know something of me, Opal, and what our lives were like. I don't want to be just a name to you. I want you to try to understand why things happened as they did, that's why I'm writing all this down. Perhaps I shall tear this up when I've finished. Perhaps I shall decide there is no need for you to know it. Perhaps it's just making excuses. However, just at first I will write whatever comes into my head, and that scene in Papa's study seems to me in a way a beginning because if it hadn't been for the fact that we had to sell Oakland Hall it would never have happened the way it did.

"It wasn't long after that that there were scenes quite often. It was always money. Money was wanted to pay for this and that, and it wasn't there. I knew Papa was wrong. It was some devil's streak in the family which had come down and was in him. He used to talk to me about it in the long gallery where he would show me pictures of his ancestors and explain what they were noted for. There was Geoffrey, born three hundred years before, who had nearly brought us to ruin. Then there was James, who had gone to sea and was a sort of buccaneer. He had filched treasure from Spanish galleons and we grew rich on them. Then there was Charles, who gambled again. This was at the time of Charles I and then came the war and we were naturally for the King yet managed to live somehow through the Commonwealth until the restoration when we acquired more land and riches because we had been loyal to the monarchy. For a hundred years we lived in comfort and then came Henry Clavering, the greatest gambler of them all—friend of George, Prince of Wales, a dandy and a spendthrift. We never recovered from him, although in the early part of this century we made an effort to. Papa's father, however, inherited the family failing and then it was passed on to Papa himself. Two generations running of gamblers was more than Oakland could take. That was how it came about that there was one course open to us. We had to sell Oakland.

"I was sixteen at the time. It was so depressing, Papa was so miserable that I feared he would take his life. Mama was bitter. She kept saying it need never happen. We had to sell not only the house but so much that was precious in it. The lovely tapestries, some of the silver and furniture. Then we went to the Dower House. It's a beautiful house, Xavier kept saying, but Mama wouldn't hear of it and grumbled continually. Nothing was right, and I used to hate the way she reproached Papa. She would bring it into everything that happened. As if it wasn't bad enough!

"We all seemed to change. Xavier was much quieter; he didn't reproach Papa, but he was withdrawn. We kept one farm and he managed that, but it was different from the large estate we had had. Miriam was fifteen and our governess was dismissed, so Mama taught her. I was considered old enough to dispense with lessons, and Mama said we must help in the kitchen, learning to bottle fruit and make preserves; we must try to be useful for the type of man who might be expected to marry us would be very different from those who would have come our way had the fecklessness of our father not driven us from our home. Miriam caught my mother's bitterness. I never did. I understood the irresistible urge, the compulsion which had beset Papa. I had that myself—not for cards, but for life. I was of a nature to follow my impulses, to act and consider the wisdom of that act afterwards. I hope you will not grow up to be of that nature, dear Opal, because it can bring you trouble.

"A Mr. Ben Henniker, who had made a fortune in Australia, had bought Oakland. He was a friendly sort of man and one day called on us at the Dower House. I shall never forget it. Maddy brought him into the drawing room where we were having tea.

"'Well, Ma'am,' he said to Mama, 'I thought that as we are neighbors we ought to be neighborly and as I'm having a little bit of a gathering next week, it struck me you might like to join us.' Mama could freeze people with a look—it was a habit she employed with the servants and it worked as well in the Dower House as it had at Oakland. None of the servants was ever allowed to forget that we were Claverings, however depleted our worldly goods.

"'A gathering, Mr. Henniker?' she said as though he were suggesting a Roman orgy. 'I'm afraid that is quite out of the question. My daughters have not yet come out and we shall most certainly be engaged on the date you mention.'

"I said: 'I could go, Mama.' Mama's look froze the words on my lips.

" 'You are not free to go, Jessica,' she said coldly.

"Mr. Ben Henniker's face was quite purple with rage. He said: 'I understand, Ma'am, you are engaged next week and will be any week if I were to have the impertinence to invite you. Have no fear. You are safe . . . you and your family. You'll never be asked to Oakland Hall while I'm there.' Then he walked out.

"I was so angry with Mama for her rudeness because after all he had tried to be friendly and it seemed absurd to me to resent him merely because he had bought Oakland. *We* had put it up for sale. *We* had sought a buyer. I slipped out and ran after him, but he was halfway up the Oakland Drive before I caught up with him. 'I wanted to say how sorry I am,' I panted. 'I'm so ashamed that my mother spoke to you like that. I do hope you won't think badly of us all.'

"He had such fierce blue eyes which were then blazing with fury, but as he looked at me, slowly he began to smile. 'Well, fancy that,' he said. 'And you're little Miss Clavering, I reckon.'

" 'I'm Jessica,' I told him.

" '*You* don't take after your mother,' he said. 'And that's the nicest compliment I can pay you.'

" 'She has some good points,' I defended her, 'but they are a little hard to recognize.'

"He started to laugh, and there was that about his laughter which made it impossible not to join in. Then he said: 'I like you for running after me like this. You're a good girl, Miss Jessica, you are indeed. You must come and see me in your old home. What about that?' He almost choked with laughter. 'After all she was only speaking for herself. You come and meet some of my friends. They're good people, some of them. It'll be an eye-opener for you, Miss Jessica. I reckon you've lived in a cage all your life. How old are you?' I told him I was seventeen. 'It's a beautiful age,' he said. 'It's an age when you ought to be setting out on your adventures. I reckon that's what you want, eh? You come over and see me sometime . . . that's if you think it's right and proper. Don't you find life pretty dull, living as you must have done?'

"I told him that I hadn't found it dull. There was a lot to interest me in the country. I liked to visit people and we had done a good deal of that at Oakland. As the squire's family we had had to see to the welfare of our tenants; our days had been divided into sections; lessons in the mornings, working on village affairs, sewing, talking, making some of our clothes, planning the dances we would have when we came out. Alas, we hadn't come out into society—only out of Oakland and our old life. But I had never found it dull, and it was only when Mr. Henniker opened a new vista for me that I discovered how uneventful the old life had been.

"What an escape those visits to Oakland Hall were. . . ."

I paused in my reading and stared at the grave before me, and I was beset by an uncanny notion that my life was repeating an old pattern. What had happened to Jessica was happening to me. I wanted to read on quickly, and yet to savor these events as I went. I felt it was important for me to know this Jessica, to see her life unfold before me; and that was what she wanted and was why she was telling me in such detail.

I went on reading:

"Of course I was deceiving the family, though I did confide a little in Miriam. I used to wish I could take her to Oakland with me. But I knew that if I were discovered there would be terrible trouble and I didn't want her involved because she was younger than I and I felt responsible for her. Miriam was so easily led. When she was with me she would be ready for a certain amount of mischief; in the old days we had had a governess, a rather forceful lady who was secretly a Buddhist; Miriam was for a while in danger of becoming one too. When she was with Mama she would become snobbish and scornful of Papa for bringing us down in the world. I used to call her the Chameleon, for she took her color from whatever rock she was resting on. Therefore I hesitated about taking Miriam with me. Instead I would satisfy myself by telling her of my adventures as we lay in bed at night. She would listen avidly and applaud what I did, but I knew that if Mama pointed out the wickedness of my actions she would immediately agree with her. She was not in the least devious—just incapable of having a view of her own. Malleable—that was the only way to describe her. When I watched Mrs. Cobb kneading the dough into cottage, wheatsheaf, and farmhouse loaves I would say to myself: That is just like Miriam; she will go into whatever shape she is put. It was different with Xavier, but who would confide in him? He felt very deeply about our change in fortune and saw it as a disgrace to the family. He had loved Oakland and had naturally been brought up to believe it would be his one day; therefore he necessarily felt a sense of outrage since it had been taken from him, though he never abused Papa as Mama did; he was just sad and withdrawn. I used to feel very sad about Xavier, but of course I didn't know him as I did Miriam.

"I'm digressing because I'm putting off what happened. I *do* want you to understand. Please don't blame me and don't blame Desmond. I met him at one of Mr. Henniker's gatherings. I was frequently going to the house and it soon seemed to me more like home than the Dower House ever could be. Life was so miserable there mainly because Mama could not stop baiting Papa. Sometimes I wondered whether he might do her an injury. He was so quiet and calm that I could imagine he was plotting against her, for there were times when I caught him looking at her oddly. There was a brooding tension in the house. I said to Miriam one night when we lay in bed: 'Something's going to happen. You can feel it in the air. It's as though Fate's waiting to strike.' Miriam used to get frightened and so did I. I little realized from what direction the blow would come.

"I was going more often to Oakland and getting really reckless. Mr. Henniker always welcomed me. Once when we were in the gallery I told him how I used to play the spinet and frighten the servants. He was very amused and thereafter asked me to play for him. He loved to sit there listening while I went through most of the Chopin waltzes. I used to think it would go on always, that Mr. Henniker would always be there and interesting people would come to the house. Then I learned that this was not so and Mr. Henniker's stays at the house were brief. He had what he called 'a property' in New South Wales. Oakland Hall was just a fancy, 'a bit of folly if you like,' he said. He'd seen it when he was a boy and had vowed to have it, and he was a man who believed in sticking to his vows. I wish I could tell you how he interested me. I had never known anyone like him."

She didn't have to try to make me understand that. I knew well enough, having experienced the same thing myself.

"As I was older than Miriam there had been a lot of talk about my coming out before we left Oakland. We had had little Minnie Jobbers making dresses for me and I had some lovely garments made. In particular there were two pretty ball dresses. I remember Mama's looking at them when we knew we were going to leave Oakland and saying: 'You'll never need them now.' One was more beautiful than the other; it was in cherry-colored silk trimmed with Honiton lace; it fell off the shoulders, and I had a pretty neck and shoulders. It had been cut in that style for the sole purpose of showing them. 'Poor neck, poor shoulders,' I used to say, 'you will never be shown off now.'

"One could talk to Mr. Henniker about anything so I told him about the dress. It was strange that he—a miner really and I suppose a rough one—could understand how I felt about almost anything I mentioned. He said: 'You shall wear the cherry dress. After all why should the world be deprived of a glimpse of your divine neck and shoulders just because your father was a gambler. We'll have a ball and you shall bring cherry red to it.' I said I would never dare and he answered: 'Nothing ventured, nothing gained. Never be afraid to dare.' Then he laughed and said he was a wicked man who was leading his neighbor's daughter from the straight and narrow path. He laughed a good deal over that. 'Straight and narrow paths are so restricting, Miss Jessica,' he said. 'The wide-open spaces are much more stimulating.'

"Well, I digress again. I didn't intend to. At first I meant this to be a brief letter, but as soon as I took up my pen I felt impelled to write like this. I had to make you see it all. I didn't want you to think I was just a wanton. It wasn't like that at all.

"There was a house party at Oakland. Ben Henniker often had them. His guests were mostly people who were in his business. They used to come bringing special stones to him. He bought them and sometimes sold them; there was a lot of talk about opals. I began to learn something of how they were mined and marketed and found it fascinating.

"He told me there was to be a ball and that I must come to it and be one of his guests. It was thrilling, but I knew I couldn't put on my cherry-red dress and walk out of the house in it, so Ben suggested that I smuggle cherry-red (as he called it) into Oakland and then on the night of the ball slip over and change into it there. He would get one of the maids to help me dress. So this was arranged.

"What a night that was, for during it I met Desmond for the first time. I must make you see Desmond. Everyone was wrong about what happened afterwards. That is what I want you to understand more than anything. It couldn't have been the way it seemed. It just wasn't possible.

"The gallery at Oakland looked beautiful with the musicians at one end and decorated with flowers from the greenhouses. It made a beautiful ballroom with the candles flickering in their sconces. It was like my coming-out ball and that was what Mr. Henniker intended it to be. He once said: 'I didn't mind taking Oakland from your father—he took a gamble and lost. I'm glad I took it from your mother because she deserves to lose it. I sometimes feel a twinge when I see your brother looking so mournful, but he's a young man and he should be seeing what he can do about getting it back, or some place like it. But for you, Miss Jessie, I'm right down sorry. So now we're going to have a ball.' It was an enchanted evening. There had never been such an evening in the whole of my life and never will be again, for it was at the ball that night that I met Desmond.

"He was young . . . not much older than I, but twenty-one seemed a responsible age to me. It was not a crowded ballroom because Mr. Henniker had asked none of the people from the neighborhood. He told me that he couldn't ask them because they would know me and that might cause trouble. This was to be my ball—the ball of the cherry-red gown and the divine neck and shoulders, he told me. So there were the house guests only and Oakland must have been rather full at that time, for there were so many rooms which could be used for guests. Right from the first Desmond found me. He asked me to dance and we did. I wish you could see the gallery as it was that night. It was so beautiful . . . so romantic. I expect over the centuries there have been many balls there, but I was sure there was never one like that one. He was tall and fair—though his hair was considerably bleached by the sun. He had what I call Australian eyes, which meant that they were half closed and had thick lashes. 'It's the sun,' he told me. 'It's brighter and hotter than here. You half shut your eyes against it and I expect nature provides the lashes as a protection.' He talked rather like Ben Henniker about opals. He was fanatical about them. He told me what he had found so far and what he intended to find.

" 'There never has been anything so fine as the Green Flash at Sunset,' he told me. 'Ben's got it. You ought to ask him to show it to you sometime.' I wasn't interested in the Green Flash at Sunset. I wasn't interested in anything that night but Desmond. Most of the other guests were older than we were. We danced together and talked and talked.

"He told me he intended to go back to Australia in about two or three weeks' time. He had been longing to get back because he had discovered land which he was sure was opal country, and he wanted to go out and prospect it. Ben and some others were interested in the project; it was going to need a good deal of money to develop it. He had a feeling about it. Some of the old miners laughed at him. They called it Desmond's Fancy. But he believed in it. He was going to make his fortune out of Desmond's Fancy.

" 'I can feel it, Jessie,' he said. (He always called me Jessie). 'It's Opal Country. Dry bushland . . . flat . . . lots of saltbush and not much timber—except the mulga—that's a sort of acacia—and mulga grass too. It's low-lying, scorched, eroded, with dry watercourses. I said to myself, That land speaks for itself. There's something there—gold or tin perhaps, wolfram or copper, but something tells me it's opal . . . precious opal.' He talked in an excited way . . . rather like Ben Henniker, and I couldn't help being excited too.

"We talked . . . how we talked, and I only realized how the time was flying when I heard the clock in the courtyard chime midnight. When the ball was over, Hannah helped me to change into my day dress. She was one of the servants who had stayed on at Oakland when we left. She hadn't been there very long and was about my age, which I suppose made her understanding. Maddy helped too. She crept down the Dower House stairs and let me in. Without those two it would have been very difficult for me. The next day Hannah was to bring my ball dress across the stream and I would be able to choose my moment to take it into the house unobserved. So there was only Miriam to placate. That was easy. All she wanted was to hear about the ball, so I told her. She was completely on my side then and thought with me that it was a wonderful adventure.

"When I brought the dress back next day there was a note from Desmond, delivered by Hannah at the stream. He must see me that afternoon. Of course I was there. We walked through Oakland Park and talked and talked, and that night I went once more to Oakland to dine. I knew the servants were very pleased to see me there. Hannah told me that I had always been a favorite with them and that they enjoyed working for Mr. Henniker, so the fact that I had become friendly with him—even though the rest of the family hadn't—pleased them. Hannah said they talked of little else in the servants' hall. 'They talked about you and Mr. Desmond Dereham,' she said. 'They think it's beautiful.'

"And beautiful it was. You guess, of course, that we were

in love. We were absolutely sure before the first week was out that there couldn't be anyone else for either of us. It was true. You must believe that, Opal, in spite of what happened. I know they were all wrong. I know how it appeared. But it couldn't be true. I never believed it for one moment . . . not even the very worst and most tragic moment. I knew it was untrue.

"He didn't go back at the end of two weeks. He kept putting it off. When he went, he said, he would take me with him. We would marry and go out together. 'How will you like being a miner's wife, Jessie?' he used to ask. 'It's not an easy life, but never mind, we'll make our fortunes just as Ben has, and then everything you wish for shall be yours.' Every night I would slip out across the bridge into the park and there he would be waiting for me. I cannot describe the bliss of those September nights. I couldn't have managed without Maddy and Hannah. They were wonderful. I must have been very deceitful, for Mama never guessed, and how I managed that I cannot imagine.

"We had planned it all carefully. We were going to be married in three weeks' time. Desmond would get a special license and afterwards we would go to Australia together. We had told no one . . . not even Ben. I was sure Ben would help us, but Desmond was not so sure. Ben seemed to think I was a fragile little doll who must not be subjected to the hardships of life, and life in a mining camp was very different from that lived in a gracious Dower House. I knew this and I was prepared. So we put off telling anyone . . . even Ben . . . and then we came to that terrible night.

"Desmond told me that several of Ben's associates were coming to Oakland and very soon Ben himself would be leaving for Australia. Such knowledge would have upset me some time ago, but now that I was to go to Australia too I was glad that Ben would be there. They would decide about this project of exploiting the land which Desmond was so sure of and discuss prospecting and setting up shafts. Desmond was very excited. 'There'll be Ben, myself, and one of the leading opal merchants there,' he told me. 'When we get the funds we shall start at once.' Because of this conference, which was to be held that night, he wouldn't be able to see me until the following afternoon, he told me. Then he would be waiting by the stream as usual.

"But he never came. I never saw him again. What happened on that night nobody really knew, but many thought they did. Desmond had gone. He had disappeared without saying good-bye to anyone, and the Green Flash at Sunset had disappeared at the same time.

"You can guess what people said, for they were both missing at once. They said there was only one answer—but it wasn't the right one. I *know* it wasn't. I will never believe it was. How could he have gone like that without telling me? We were going to be married in a few weeks. He was going to get the license and I was going to Australia with him, but he had gone without telling me, although we were to have met that afternoon. He had gone . . . and the Green Flash at Sunset was gone too.

"I waited for him the next afternoon. Hannah came to me there. She had been crying. 'He's gone, Miss Jessica,' she said. 'He went last night or early this morning. No one saw him go but he's gone.' 'Gone, Hannah,' I cried. 'Gone where?' Hannah shook her head, then she said angrily: 'As far as he can get from here. He'd better. He's taken the Green Flash opal with him.' I cried out: 'It's not true. It can't be true.' 'I'm afraid it is,' said Hannah mournfully and looking at me with such pity in her eyes that I wanted to weep. She went on: 'It wasn't until mid-morning that we discovered his bed hadn't been slept in. We couldn't make it out. He'd taken his things with him though, and his room was quite empty. Then just when everyone was wondering why he went off like that, Mr. Henniker went to his safe for something. He knew right away that someone had been there . . . things weren't just in their right places . . . and when he opened the case where he kept this Green Flash, it was empty. Mr. Henniker's raging mad. He's going to have that Desmond Dereham's blood, he reckons. He's calling him a thief, a scoundrel, and a lying hound. You should hear the names he calls him. Are you all right, Miss Jessica?'

" 'I don't believe it, Hannah. I just don't believe it.'

" 'You wouldn't, but everyone else does.'

"I felt sick with fear, but I kept telling myself how absurd it was. I couldn't forget how Desmond had glowed when he talked of the opals he would find. 'There'd never be one like the Green Flash,' he had said. Then he had added quickly: 'But why shouldn't there be?'

"The days started to pass while I felt that I was living through a nightmare. I kept telling myself that it was a silly mistake and that Ben would find he had put his opal in another case. I went to see Ben. He was like a raging bull.

'He's got it,' he shouted. 'He's gone off with the Green Flash. By God, I'll have his blood. I showed it to them that night. They were all three there when I took it out of the safe. He was sitting on my right . . . the young devil. I'll shoot him dead. He's got my Green Flash.'

" 'He didn't do it, Ben,' I cried. 'I know he didn't.'

"He stopped raging and stared at me. 'He's deceived you,' he said soberly. 'Such a good-looking boy . . . such a pleasant young man. But he wasn't all he appeared to be.'

"There was nothing to be done, nothing to say. I couldn't bear to talk to Ben. He was going away, he said. He was going to lose no time. He was going to follow Master Desmond Dereham to Desmond's Fancy because he reckoned that was where he had gone. He would not be able to stay away from that place. Ben had seen the opal lust in his eyes and he had thought it was for what awaited finding in the Fancy, but it was for the Green Flash. He hadn't realized this when he'd opened his safe and disclosed what lay in the box. He'd been blind, and he ought to have known what the young devil was after.

"I couldn't bear to hear Ben talk like that, so I stopped going to Oakland. I shut myself in with my grief, and they thought I was ill, for I grew pale and listless. For a time I simply didn't care what happened to me. Then Hannah told me that Ben was going back to Australia. 'He's going after the Green Flash,' she said.

"I saw him before he went, but our friendship had changed. Desmond was between us. Ben was so sure he was guilty; I was so certain that he was not.

"I cannot describe the desolation which had come into my life. Ben had gone and I had lost Desmond. I could not imagine greater tragedy. I still went to Oakland to see Mrs. Bucket and the rest, and they used to entertain me in the kitchen and talk about when Mr. Henniker would come back, for he would come back, they were sure. He had to keep coming back to Oakland; he had such a fancy for the place. They didn't mention Desmond to me, but I knew they talked about him when I was not there.

"Miriam knew what had happened because it hadn't been possible to keep her in the dark about my nocturnal adventures. In the past she had lain awake awaiting my return and then she would want to know all about it. Now she was aware that everything had gone wrong and was beginning to veer round to what Mama might say.

"It was towards the end of November when my suspicions became confirmed. When the fear first came to me I tried not to consider it. It couldn't possibly be, I told myself. Yet there had been those meetings in the park when we had talked and dreamed and loved so passionately. Desmond had said: 'We are married really. I shall never look at any-one else and at the earliest possible moment you are going to be my wife.' I thought of myself as his wife. I pictured our arriving in Australia and what a help I should be to him, and when I looked into the future I saw the children we would have. Before Christmas I knew I was going to have a child. I did not know what to do. I told Hannah because I could trust her. We talked and talked but could find no solution. If Mr. Henniker had been there I was sure he would have helped me, but he was far away and there was no one.

"I had to tell Miriam. It was on Christmas night, I remember. It had scarcely been a happy time. We went to the midnight service on Christmas Eve and in the morning of Christmas Day we went again to church. Such times as this brought back to my mother more vividly the old ways at Oakland Hall. During dinner—which took place at midday—she talked continuously of other Christmases, how they had brought in the yule log, and decorated the gallery with holly and mistletoe and how the house had been full of guests. I cried out suddenly: 'You should give Papa a Christmas present—silence about the glorious past.' I had been unable to restrain myself because I thought all this was so trivial set against what had happened to me, and the fact that Desmond had disappeared and was suspected of stealing the Green Flash.

"Everyone was horrified. No one—simply no one—ever spoke to Mama like that. Papa said rather sadly: 'You should show more respect to your mother, Jessica.' And I cried out: 'It's time she showed more consideration to us. We've lost Oakland. All right. This is a comfortable home. There are worse troubles in the world than having to live with your family in a Dower House.' Then I burst into tears and ran from the room. As I went I heard Mama say: 'Jessica is getting impossible.'

"I said I had a headache and spent the afternoon in the room I shared with Miriam, but I had to go down in the evening. It was a wretched day, and that night I told Miriam because I had to tell someone. She was horrified. She didn't understand much, but she did know that one of the servants had once 'got into trouble' as it was called and she had been dismissed and sent back to her family, disgraced forever. 'Disgraced forever,' she kept repeating until I wanted to scream. But what was I going to do? That was the question. I had no answer to that, and naturally, nor had Miriam. When I tried to explain to her she seemed to understand, but I knew that she would only have to listen to my mother and all her sympathy would vanish.

"I knew too that they would have to be told one day and I wanted to tell them before they discovered. I told Xavier first, for although he always seemed so remote I felt he would understand more than the others. I went to his room on a bleak January day when there were snow clouds in the sky, and when I told him he looked at me for some moments as though he thought I had gone mad. He was kind though. Xavier would always be kind. I told him everything—how I had become friendly with Ben Henniker and met Desmond, how we had intended to marry and how Desmond had disappeared. 'Are you sure you are to have a child?' he asked. I told him I was. 'We must make certain,' he said. 'You must see Dr. Clinton.' 'Not Dr. Clinton,' I cried out in horror. He had attended us for years and I knew he would be deeply shocked. Xavier understood and said he would take me to a doctor who did not know us, and he did. When it was confirmed that I was to have a child, there was nothing to do, said Xavier, but tell my parents. It could not be kept from them for long and we really should make plans as to what must be done without delay.

"It's strange but when a woman is going to have a child she seems to acquire some special strength. That was how it was with me. I was heartbroken because I had lost Desmond, but there was some new kind of hope in me. It was due to the baby. Even the scene with my parents did not distress me as much as might have been imagined. Xavier was calm and strong; he was a very good brother to me. He told Mama and Papa that there was something they must know and the four of us went into the drawing room. Xavier shut the door and said very quietly: 'Jessica is going to have a baby.' There was a moment's silence. I thought that that was how it must have been before the walls of Jericho came tumbling down. My father looked blank; my mother just stared at us. 'Yes,' said Xavier, 'I fear it is so. We have to decide what we must do.'

"My mother cried out: 'A baby! Jessica! I don't believe

it.' 'It's true,' I said. 'I am. I was going to be married, but there's been a terrible accident.' 'Accident!' cried my mother, having overcome her first surprise and taking charge. 'What do you mean? This is quite impossible.' 'It has happened, Mama,' said Xavier, 'so let us consider what action we can best take.' 'I want to know more about this,' said my mother. 'I can't believe that a daughter of mine. . . .' 'It's true, Mama,' I said. 'A doctor has confirmed it.' 'Dr. Clinton!' cried my mother aghast. 'No,' Xavier reassured her, 'a doctor who doesn't know us.'

"My mother turned on me like an enraged tigress. She said the most bitter things to me. I don't remember them; I deliberately shut my ears to them. I kept thinking of the baby. I wanted that baby, and I thought then, even in the thick of my trouble, that having it would make up for a great deal. My mother turned on my father. It was his fault, she said. If he had not been so feckless we should still have been at Oakland and no wicked miner would have come there bringing his evil friends to seduce silly, wicked girls. That was what came from having that sort of people living near one. Now I was going to produce a bastard. There had never been such disgrace in the Clavering family. 'Oh yes, Mama,' I said, 'there was. There was Richard Clavering, who shared a mistress with Charles II. . . .' 'As if this were the same sort of thing!' she said indignantly. 'That was Charles II and most of the aristocracy shared their mistresses with him.' 'But there was his bastard whose son married his legitimate cousin and came back into the family.' 'Be silent, you slut. The family has never been so disgraced and it is all due to the fact that your father. . . .' She raved for some time and I knew she would go on doing so as long as she lived. I told myself then: Desmond will come back. Something went wrong and we shall discover what and then it will all come right. So I shut my ears to her raving.

"It was Xavier who decided what should happen. It was unthinkable that anyone should know I had produced an illegitimate child. The fact that I was pregnant could be disguised for a few months. Perhaps as long as six. Skirts were voluminous and mine could be discreetly let out. The baby was due in June. In April my parents and I would go to Italy. My mother's health could be said to be giving my father some concern. We should have to sell the silver salver and punch bowl which had been given by George IV to one of our ancestors, because, being very valuable, they would provide the money for a two months' trip for the three of us and the expenses of the birth. My child should be born there, and when we returned we would say that my mother's ill health had been due to a pregnancy, which she had not suspected, and because of her time of life there had not been the usual symptoms. This would mean that we could return with a child and give no cause for scandal.

"How unhappy those months were! We took a villa in Florence for a while—Florence with its Medici Palace and its golden light! How I should have loved it in other circumstances. I used to escape from my misery by imagining myself strolling along the Arno with Desmond. When I saw opals in a shop window on the famous bridge I turned, shuddering, away and could not bear to look at them.

"A few weeks before my confinement we went to Rome and there my baby was born. That was June 1880 and I called her Opal. Mama said it was a foolish name and that she should be given another. So the baby had my name too; she was Opal Jessica.

"We came home, and such was my mother's indefatigable energy that although there might have been those who put a certain construction on our departure and return with a newly born baby, no one dared mention it. You, my dear Opal, as you have guessed, were that child. Never be ashamed of your birth. You were conceived in love. Always remember that, and no matter what people may tell you of your father do not believe them. I knew him well, and it could not be so. He was not capable of stealing that miserable opal. How I wish it had never been found. But he knew nothing of it. Someone else stole the Green Flash at Sunset. It was not your father. One day the truth will be known. I'm sure of it.

"Now, my dearest child, I come to the end of my story. After you were born I was beset by such despair that I did not know where to turn for comfort. We had never been happy in the Dower House; now Mama made our lives a misery—not only mine, but Papa's as well. I watched him as he grew more and more miserable every day. I would look up suddenly and see her eyes fixed on me with utter distaste. Constantly she blamed him. It was his weakness which had come out in me, she said. He was to blame for everything. Miriam took an interest in you, and I think she loved you in her way, though she was afraid to show it too much when Mama was around. You liked her too. You would always go to Miriam; and Xavier was fond of you, so was Papa.

"I was so unhappy. I used to go down to the stream which divides the Dower House from Oakland and I'd stare at the cool shallow water. I thought a lot about my life then, and the belief came to me that I should never see Desmond again, for since he would never have deserted me, he must be dead. The conviction was so strong that as I sat there by the stream it was as though the waters beckoned to me. It was as though Desmond himself was asking me to come and join him. The only solution could be that he was dead, for if he was not, why had he disappeared? Of one thing I was certain: he would never have gone away and left me. There was one answer only, someone had stolen the opal and laid the blame on him. They had killed him perhaps that he might appear to be the thief. I know no one else would believe this, but my conviction is strong. He would never come back. That was why he called me to the stream because he wanted me to be with him.

"My presence in the Dower House was bringing increasing unhappiness there. My mother was blaming my father more than she ever had before. I tried to think of what my life would be like because I was never going to see Desmond again on this Earth. The servants all loved the baby . . . everybody loved her . . . except Mama, and I don't think she ever loved anybody. So I used to sit by the stream and think of all the trouble I had brought the family and how much better they would be without me. Even the baby would be better off, because as she grew up the reproaches would go on. It would be better for her not to know that her mother had brought disgrace on the family, and while I was there Mama would always continue to regard me with contempt.

"I dreamed then of lying face downwards in that cool water, and when I dreamed thus, I experienced a perfect peace. I couldn't talk about it to anyone but Hannah. She knew the whole story, but she was very discreet. She told me that they talked about it in the servants' hall at Oakland. Although they had considered the possibility of the baby's being mine and not my mother's, they weren't sure about it. Even Mrs. Bucket was of the opinion that Mama would never have lent herself to such a thing and that it was a well-known fact that women getting on in years often 'got caught' when they least expected it, and her Aunt Polly had been just like that . . . feeling not up to the mark and the doctors not being sure what was wrong . . . and then all of a sudden she's pregnant and the baby almost ready to be born. 'I didn't tell them different,' said good, kind Hannah.

"A few weeks passed and I was still going to sit by the stream. When I talked to Hannah about what I felt she cried out: 'It's wrong. You mustn't think like that.' I said: 'It might be for the best. The baby would be all right. They'll care for her. It's better for me not to be there.' 'Perhaps you could go away for a while,' suggested Hannah. 'Time's not important,' I said. 'It's now that counts. Perhaps in twenty years I could look back at all this and find it tolerable, but it's not twenty years from now. It's *now*, and I've got to live through a lot before twenty years passes.' Hannah said: 'If you were to do away with yourself they couldn't bury you in consecrated ground.' 'Why not?' I asked, 'I tell you they won't if you were to . . . do that. It's a law, I think, a law of the Church. They bury people at the crossroads or some other place . . . never in consecrated ground in the churchyard.'

"I thought about that quite a lot, but I continued to go down to the stream, and one day I shall go down there and not come back. I think of you, my daughter, growing up, and I wonder what they will tell you about me . . . and your father . . . and that is why I have decided to write this so that you can know the truth as I saw it. And that is the real truth, Opal. So I sit by the stream and write and as I sit here the past comes vividly back to me. You see, you must know what happened and how it happened. I shall give this to Hannah, and she will give it to you when the time comes. It may be that the time will never come and that I shall tell you the story myself.

"Today I am giving this to Hannah so this will be the last I shall write to you.

"Good-by, little Opal. May God bless you, and one day you will discover the truth about your father. I promise you there will be nothing to discredit him. One last word, my dear little daughter, if I should not be here when you grow up—and if I am, you will not have read this—never let anyone say a word against him. Perhaps one day you will be the one to discover the truth."

I stared ahead of me. I was seeing it all so clearly.

Then I went and knelt by her grave and when I touched my cheeks I found that they were wet, although I had not known that I was weeping.

I did not appear at dinner that evening because I could

not face them. I was thinking of them as different people;
I was seeing them all so much more clearly than I ever had
before. I was angry with them. They drove her to it, I
thought. If they had been kinder to her, she would have
been alive today and I should have had a mother. How miserable she must have been! I wanted to storm at them—every
one of them; my poor ineffectual father—my grandfather
in fact; my proud unloving grandmother (how glad I was
that she was not after all my mother!); Miriam, who always
had to have her mind made up for her; and Xavier with his
negative kindness, so remote that he had not done anything
to save her.

I feigned a headache, and when Miriam came to see me
I closed my eyes and turned away.

The next day I saw Hannah who, I think, had been
watching for me.

"So you read it, Miss Jessica?" she said.

I nodded. "Tell me what happened afterwards."

"They found her in the stream. She was lying face downwards. The water was quite shallow. It just washed over
her."

"And they buried her there," I said, pointing to the Waste
Land.

"Reverend Gray was very strict about it. They don't bury
suicides in consecrated ground."

"How cruel!" I cried. "I'll make it consecrated ground!
She was good and meant no harm to anyone. I shall clear
her grave and grow plants on it and keep them watered."

"Best not, Miss."

"Why not? She was my mother."

"I knew you'd take it bad. She wouldn't have wanted that.
She wouldn't have wanted you to know if it was going to
make trouble."

"Tell me exactly what happened, Hannah."

"They found her there and buried her quietly. That's all.
People didn't speak of it . . . much. They said she'd always
been different from the rest of the family. It was put about
that she'd fallen in love and that he had gone away. Her
heart was broken and she, being young, had thought there
was nothing left to live for. I always put flowers on her
grave at Eastertime."

"Thank you, Hannah. Did anyone suspect I was her child?"

"If they did, it wasn't said. It was accepted that you were
an 'afterthought,' and Miss Jessica was drowned some time

after your birth. It was a hot July day I remember." She turned away, her lips quivering. "They'd only been home a few weeks so people said it was someone she'd met in Italy. It was the last day in July, and you were born on the first of June . . . so that tells how old you were . . . nothing but a baby, little knowing what your coming had cost."

"How she must have suffered! You must have known my father. Tell me about him."

"He seemed such a nice young gentleman. Tall with a pleasant face. He was quite a favorite with Mr. Henniker at one time. Then of course he couldn't say anything bad enough. I shall never forget the day. . . ."

"Tell me everything, Hannah, just everything."

"It began like an ordinary sort of day. We took the hot water up to the guests, and one of the maids came down and said, 'Mr. Dereham's not in his room. His bed's not been slept in and all his things have gone.' We said it couldn't be, but it was, of course. And then Mr. Henniker found his precious opal was missing, and it seemed only natural that he'd taken it with him."

"But it wasn't so, Hannah. You know it wasn't."

"That's how your mother used to talk, but he was gone and so was the opal."

"She knew he hadn't taken it."

"She was in love with him."

"She would never have fallen in love with a thief."

"Love don't take account of such things."

"I know it wasn't true."

"There again . . . you're talking just like your mother. I never thought she'd do it. I would have found some way of stopping her. She told me he'd come to her in a dream and said he loved her and he never would have left her in this life. 'Come to me,' he said in this dream. 'Come to me by the stream. Only death could keep me from you.' It was after that she made up her mind, I'm sure. She was certain he was dead. He had to be unless he had deserted her, and because she believed he would never do that, she was sure he was dead. They would be together now . . . forever."

"She should have lived to prove his innocence."

"But she had these strange fancies and she thought he was calling her to come to him."

"I wish I could find out the truth, Hannah, and discover what really happened to that opal."

"Bless you, Miss, there has been them that's tried to find

it these many years. I reckon Mr. Henniker has never given up the search. And you think *you're* going to be the one! You just don't know anything about these things. You've only just learned how you came into the world!"

"But he's my father. She's my mother. Don't you see that makes all the difference?"

Hannah shook her head sadly.

Although I could not talk to my family about the tragedy, I could do so to Ben, and at our next meeting I blurted out:

"I know about my mother and father and that you think he stole the Green Flash opal."

We were in the drawing room, he in his chair with his crutch propped up beside him. He did not speak for a few moments, and I saw that a great sadness had come to him.

"There's no one I can talk to about it but you," I went on.

"Who told you?" he asked.

I explained about the papers she had left for me.

He nodded.

"You knew?" I asked.

"I guessed. You're so like her with your dark eyes and those thick lashes and well-marked brows, with your turned-up nose and your mouth which somehow says you're going to laugh at life even at its worst. I could believe she was sitting there at this moment. You're about the same age now as she was then, but she was more innocent of the world than you are, less able to look after herself."

"Did you know about her and my father?"

"It was as clear as daylight."

"And you were pleased . . . at first? You didn't mind?"

It was the first time I had known him hesitate. "It wasn't for me to mind," he said at length. "I could see how it was with them from the moment they met. I thought he was a good, honest young fellow . . . then."

"He didn't do it, you know, Ben."

"What do you mean—he didn't do it? He broke her heart, didn't he? I'd kill him for that . . . yes, I would."

"You loved her, Ben," I said.

He was thoughtful. "I reckon you could say that. She was a pretty dainty creature . . . and look at me—a rough old gouger."

"You would have liked to marry her yourself, Ben."

"That wouldn't have been right."

"If you had," I reminded him, "I should have been your daughter."

"That's not a bad idea."

"I'd have been different though. I wouldn't have been a bit like myself."

"Then it's a mercy the tragedy was averted." He was becoming his old self again, and I was finding comfort in talking to him. "Yes," he went on, "I loved her. She was like this house . . . you know what I mean. A bit remote from me. Something I could covet and want to possess. But it's different with a woman . . . she's *not* a house. I blame myself for not being here. If I had been, it wouldn't have happened."

"What would you have done, Ben?"

"I would have married her. Perhaps she would have had me then."

I ran to him and putting my arms about him hugged him. "Oh, Ben, wouldn't that have been wonderful. We should all have lived here together and I should have escaped from the Dower House."

He stroked my hair and said: "You'd have liked that, eh?"

"It would have been wonderful."

"Well, it didn't work out that way, did it? No, here we are and it's no use looking back and saying 'if.' That's what fools do. Yesterday has to be forgotten. It's today that's important because of tomorrow. We got acquainted and we're good friends. I'd say friendship's a fine thing."

I went back to my chair and said: "Tell me your version of what happened."

"Your mother came to Oakland."

"Yes, I know, there was a party and she wore a cherry-red dress."

"That's right. She met your father, it was love at first sight, and they were going to be married and go out to opal country. I didn't think it was any place for such a dainty creature, but she was raring to go. As long as he'd be there, that was the place for her. She was fast catching opal fever; she swore she'd put up with anything as long as they could be together. And she would have too. I used to envy Desmond Dereham his happiness; he was a handsome boy, good family too. And honest . . . so I thought. He'd got adventure in his blood and that was what sent him out to Australia. He'd come for gold at first, like we all do, and when he found his first opal, he no longer cared for gold. He had a feeling he'd stumbled on one of the richest opal mines in New South Wales. He talked constantly about this place. He had a feeling for it and we joked about it, calling it Desmond's Fancy. Then we started to think there might be something in it. It was to discuss this that we all gathered together at Oakland. Then he met your mother and they fell in love and planned to marry. That was how it was up to that night."

"What actually happened on that night?"

Ben appeared to consider carefully. "There was Joss, Desmond, Croissant, and myself. Joss was fourteen then, going to school over here. My goodness, he was a sharp one. You'd never take him for so young. He already knew what he was going to do. He was going to be the biggest opal man in Australia . . . oh no, not just Australia . . . the whole world! That was his way of looking at everything. He was already telling me what I ought to do. That made me sit up, I can tell you. But the crunch was that he was sometimes right. He already towered above us all and he hadn't finished growing. Six feet five inches. That's Joss now and in his stockinged feet."

"Yes, yes," I said a little impatiently, being eager to hear about the fateful night and tired of the perfections of his son, Joss Madden.

"Well, Joss then and David Croissant. David had merchanted stones all over Australia, America, England, and the Continent of Europe. Where opals were concerned he was a man who knew what he was talking about. Then there was Desmond Dereham. Very enthusiastic he was. We sat here in this room and Desmond laid out his plans for the Fancy and we studied them. He'd examined the land, done a bit of prospecting, and although so far he'd found only the smallest traces of opal, he had the feeling that this could prove one of the richest fields in New South Wales. Of course we wanted proof, and so far there was little to go on. He'd found opal dirt there and he'd found round, hard lumps of silica—just fine grains of sand cemented together and in this are veins of opal. Anyway it's an indication that somewhere in land like this there could be big fine opals. We worked out where the best place to sink the shafts would be. We were going to keep it fairly small just at first, and then if Desmond's hunch proved correct we'd go all out in a big way. David Croissant was coming to examine the first finds and decide what would be the best way of marketing them. Then we'd need cutters and the latest equipment to get things in motion. There we were discussing all this, feeling our way, as it were. I remember Desmond's enthusiasm. He knew we were going to make a big strike, he said. Gougers are superstitious in a way. Some of them believe that there's a guiding hand that leads them to success, and that's how we all felt about Desmond's hunch that night. There was something in him . . . a sort of sheen of confidence. I know it sounds crazy, but I've seen it before. It nearly always means success, and I think that everyone of us sitting round the table that night believed that Desmond's Fancy was going to yield the finest opals yet come to light. We reckoned it would be black opal, and the market was growing for that kind. At one time it was all for the light, milky ones, as I've told you. Pretty enough, but black was coming into fashion. I said I reckoned we'd never find anything as good as the Green Flash at Sunset. Then we got talking of the Flash and they wanted to look at it.

"I brought them all in here and opened the safe to show them. There it lay in its velvet nest. What a sight! You haven't seen opal till you've seen the Green Flash. Desmond Dereham stretched out his hands to take the Flash. He let her lie in his palm for a moment, and then he called out: 'I saw it. I saw the Green Flash.' I snatched it from him and stared at the opal. I turned it round, but I couldn't catch the flash. You know, as I told you, I saw the real green flash once when I was coming home from Australia. Just as the sun dropped below the horizon I saw it as I had seen it once in the opal. 'You really saw it, Desmond?' I cried then. 'I'm sure of it,' answered Desmond. Joss swore he saw it too. He always had to be there right in the center of everything. No one must score over him. The next morning your father had gone. He had packed his bags and taken his belongings with him and quietly slipped away. And the Green Flash had disappeared."

"I can't believe that my father took it."

"Your loyalty does you credit, but it's never wise to blink facts when they're as plain as all the pikestaffs in the world. Desmond Dereham came here, lived here for a while in this house, seduced your mother, promised to marry her, and then the temptation of the Green Flash was too strong for him . . . so he took her and ran off with her instead."

"There must be another explanation."

Ben leaned forward and took my hand.

"I know what you're thinking. He was your father. Well,

I understand how you feel. But what happened to the Green Flash? David Croissant wouldn't have taken it. He'd never have had the guts. He was a salesman. He saw opals just as money. He knew their quality as few people did, but he didn't have the sentimental feeling for any one stone. He'd see its market value, and what market value would the Green Flash have had when it was offered? It would be recognized at once, and he'd be exposed as a thief. Joss?" Ben chuckled. "Granted Joss would be capable of anything. I knew how he felt about the Green Flash, but he could see it when he wanted to. Unless of course the urge came over him to own it. . . ."

"You said it was that sort of stone. It had a peculiar fascination."

"Now you're trying to put this onto Joss, are you . . . to exonerate your father? There were a lot of people who were afraid of the Green Flash. As I told you, it was sometimes known as the Unlucky One. There were legends attaching to it. It was said to bring misfortune. I never believed it. But look at me now."

"But you'd lost it. I just don't believe my father would have deserted my mother."

"He didn't know you were on the way then. Perhaps that would have made a difference . . . or perhaps not. You've never seen the Green Flash. If you had you might understand what effect it can have on people. There's a lot you've got to learn about men and the world and this thing called fascination, obsession . . . never mind what you call it, it's what it is that counts."

"What happened to my father's Fancy?"

"It's now one of the finest opal fields in Australia."

"So he was right about that."

"Oh yes, he was right."

"Do you think he would never have come back to look at it?"

"How could he when he had the Green Flash?"

"Do you believe he would have given up his dream . . . his Fancy . . . and my mother . . . for the sake of one opal which he would never be able—openly—to call his own?"

"I can only repeat, Miss Jessie, that you have never seen the Green Flash." He reached for his crutch. "You watch me walk across the room. I'm getting used to old pegleg. I'll soon be moving around as though I had two sound limbs. Then. . . ."

I looked at him searchingly, but he just shook his head. I knew what he meant and that he didn't want to tell me now. If he could get about more easily, he would be thinking of leaving Oakland Hall. I did not want to contemplate how wretched I should be without him.

When I left Ben that day and was coming down the Oakland drive, my grandmother, who had been taking some hemmed dusters to the "poor," saw me. She stood very still and stared at me as though she were dreaming. I felt defiant. There was not going to be any more pretense.

"Jessica," she cried incredulously, "where have you been?"

I answered almost flippantly: "Visiting Mr. Ben Henniker!" and waited for the storm to burst. It didn't immediately, of course. Her sense of decorum would always govern her anger, but as we went into the Dower House, Xavier and Miriam were just coming and she cried to them: "Come into the drawing room and, Miriam, ask your father if he can tear himself away from his cards and spare us a moment."

When we were all gathered together in the drawing room, my grandmother shut the door so that the servants couldn't hear.

"Now, Jessica, I should like an explanation," she said.

"It's simple," I retorted. "I was visiting my friend Mr. Ben Henniker."

"Your friend!"

"Yes, and a better friend than anyone in this house has ever been to me."

"Have you taken leave of your senses?"

"No. I am in full possession of them and that is why I seek friendship outside this house of pretense and sham."

"Pray, be silent. You had better explain at once how you came to be at Oakland Hall."

"First I should like you to explain why you have pretended to be my mother all these years and why you made her life so miserable that she drowned herself. . . ."

They were all staring at me. I was sure it was the first time in her life that my grandmother had ever felt at a disadvantage.

"Jessica!" cried Miriam, looking from her mother to Xavier, seeking a clue as to what she should think, I supposed, while my grandfather looked about him as though searching for *The Times* to cower behind; only Xavier was calm.

"I suspect someone has told you the story of your birth," he said.

"It's true, isn't it?" I answered.

"It depends on what you've heard."

"I know that my mother is dead and how she died and that she's buried in the Waste Land and you tried to forget her."

"It was a tragic time for us all," said Xavier.

"And mostly for her," I cried.

Then my grandmother spoke. "*We* had done nothing to deserve it."

"You deserved everything that came to you," I retorted scornfully.

"This," said my grandmother, "is what comes of friendship with miners."

"Please do not speak slightly of Mr. Henniker. He's a good man. If he had been here he would have helped her as none of you did."

"On the contrary," went on my grandmother, "we inconvenienced ourselves greatly to help her. We sold the silver salver and the George IV punch bowl to get her abroad, and I accepted you as my daughter."

"You didn't give her kindness, and that was what she wanted. You made her life miserable . . . you and your silly conventions. You didn't love her and help her. Don't you realize she had lost the one she loved?"

"The one she loved!" cried my grandmother. "A thief . . . a seducer . . . the stupid girl!"

"Oh, I can see how wretched you made her. You . . . who always do the right thing—or think you do. The right thing is to be cruel then, is it? Why didn't you comfort her? Why didn't you make life easier for her? You could have helped her. But you didn't. You let her die, you . . . my grandmother pretending to be my mother. I might have known you were not, for you were never a mother to me. And you"—I turned to my grandfather—"you haven't the guts" (I was talking like Ben Henniker and even at such a dramatic moment I saw my grandmother wince) "not you nor Miriam nor Xavier . . . not one of you helped her. You're despicable. Miriam can't face life with her curate because he's too poor. Xavier can't marry Lady Clara because she's too rich. It makes me laugh. What are you made of . . . all of you? Straw!" I turned on my grandmother. "Except you. You're made of the granite of unkindness and carelessness toward others put together with so much pride that there's little else but it . . ." And coming to the end of my tirade I turned to the door and ran up to my room.

I was shaking with emotion. I had told them what I thought of them, and for once they had no answer for me.

Miriam came up soon afterwards. She looked bewildered and what she said was: "We shall no longer have to hide the Family Bible." This struck me as so funny that I burst out laughing, which did something to relieve my feelings. Then she went on as though talking to herself: "I suppose it's better to be poor than let everything pass you by."

Later I saw the Family Bible, which had hitherto been locked away in the drawing room cabinet. There was my mother's name inscribed in beautiful copperplate and mine too. I turned the pages and looked at the names of long dead Claverings and wondered what trials and secrets they had had to suffer.

When I went down to dinner that night nothing was said about my outburst. It was as though it had never happened, and I couldn't help marveling at the conversation, which was all about the weather and village affairs as usual. No one would have believed that in the afternoon there had been such a storm. In a way I had to admire them.

But of one thing I was certain. No one was going to stop my friendship with Ben Henniker. Strangely enough, no one tried to, and after that I walked boldly up the drive to Oakland Hall and made no secret of my visits.

4

The Peacock

Change was in the air. Even my grandmother was slightly different. I often caught her watching me furtively; Miriam had grown a little bolder; Xavier was even more withdrawn; and I believed that the way in which I had stood up to my grandmother had impressed them all. It was clear that I had scored a victory, and they were less overawed by her than they had been before. Miriam grew mildly pretty. She was always going to church on some pretext or other, and I believed she was seeing more of the curate. The really alarming change, however, came from Oakland Hall.

Ben was gleefully hobbling round on his crutch. "This old wooden stump will soon be as good as a leg," he kept telling me.

"Then you won't be content to stay here," I suggested fearfully.

"Time never stands still," was his comment.

"Shall you go back to the opal fields?"

"I reckon I will at the end of the summer perhaps. That would be the best time to sail. The seas would be kinder and I'd be sailing from summer to summer."

There was a twinkle in his eye, which suggested he was making some plans, and I believed that I might be included in them.

There was certainly something unreal about that summer. The weather was hotter than it had been for many years and people were talking about records. There was not a cloud in the sky for days on end and the conversation at meals was concentrated on the weather and the possibilities of a drought, but I knew no one was thinking seriously about it. Even my grandfather had changed and was less subservient to my grandmother.

Ben was both elated and disturbed by my clear indication of what his departure would mean to me and encouraged me to come to Oakland more frequently. Not that I needed much encouragement.

I was there every day. The servants were now accustomed to seeing me and welcomed me. Hannah told me that Mr. Wilmot had said it was like the Family's coming back again.

One of my favorite places was the gallery. This was some hundred feet long and about twenty wide. The Family had used it as a ballroom and it was where my mother and Desmond Dereham had first met. There were window seats at either end, and sitting there I could imagine how grand it had looked when the Claverings danced through the ages while their family portraits lined the walls. The place where the spinet had stood was conspicuously empty, and the Persian rugs on the floor were those which Ben had purchased from the Claverings when he had bought the house.

I liked to sit in the window seat and picture my mother in her cherry-red dress and Desmond's setting eyes on her for the first time. Once she had thought her coming-out dance would be held here.

One day Ben said: "You'd miss me if I went away, Jessie."

"Please don't talk of it," I begged.

"But I want to talk about it. I've got something very important to say about it. You don't think I'd go away and leave you here, do you? If I went I'd want you to come with me."

"Ben!"

"Well, that's what I thought. We'd go off together. How's that?"

I immediately thought of myself going into the drawing room at the Dower House and announcing my departure. "They'd never let me go," I said.

"Oh yes they would . . . when I got at them."

"I don't think you know them very well."

"Don't I just. They hate me, don't they. I took their fine mansion away from them. For hundreds of years there had been Claverings at Oakland and then along comes Ben Henniker—an old gouger—and swipes the lot. Well, of course, they hate me. There's a bit more to it than that, though. I met your grandfather before I came here. I've got to tell you. I don't want any secrets between us . . . well, not more than we can help. Your family's got a special reason for hating me."

"Please tell me," I begged.

"I told you some of it. There's truth and there's half truth, and it's funny what a picture you can build up by telling just what you want to tell and holding back the rest. You

can make a fine picture of it and it all looks so natural . . .
but then out comes the truth and that puts a very different
complexion on it. I told you I came down here and saw
the house and made up my mind I was going to have it,
and I told you I made a fortune and put myself in a position
to buy it. All true. Well, there was I with my fortune, and
there was Grandfather Clavering finding it hard to make
ends meet but stumbling along somehow like his ancestors
had before him. I'm a wicked old man, Jessie. That's what
you've got to learn. I'm rich. I've got money to play with.
The world's my stage and I like to shift the players around
a bit to make them dance to my tune. I'm also a bit of a
gambler, as I've told you before. Not so much as the Claverings, though. I wonder if you're a gambler, Jessie. I reckon
you are. You're a Clavering, you know.

"Your grandfather belonged to one of those London clubs.
I knew it well . . . from the outside. I used to pass it with my
tray of gingerbreads when I was first starting out. Fine, im-
posing sort of place with stone lions guarding the door to
keep out poor gingerbread sellers like me. One of these days,
I promised myself, I'll strut up those steps with the best of
'em, and one day I did. I joined this club and there I met
your grandfather. We discovered a love of a game called
poker. It's one where you can lose a fortune in an afternoon
and I saw that he did. Well, it took two or three afternoons
actually. I made up my mind I was going to sit at that table
till the day came when he'd have to give up Oakland. It
was easier than I thought."

"You . . . deliberately did that!"

"Now don't look at me like that, Jessie. It was all fair
and above board. He had as much chance of winning as I
had. I wasn't staking all I'd got though. He was the more
reckless. Gamblers both—I was staking a fortune; he was
staking his house, and he lost. He had to sell, and I got
Oakland Hall. They never forgave me for that . . . particularly
your grandmother. It was no use trying to be neighborly
after that. Now I've told you."

"Ben," I said earnestly, "you didn't cheat? That's what I
want to know. I couldn't bear it if you had."

He looked straight at me. "Cross my heart . . . as we used
to say when I was a little 'un." He put his forefinger to his
lips and chanted:

"See my finger's wet
See my finger's dry *(he wiped it on his coat)*
Cross my heart *(waving his hand across his chest)*
And never tell a lie."

He grinned at me. "No. It was a gamble . . . nothing more. I just won."

"And my grandmother knew this?"

"Yes, she knew, and she's hated me ever since. Not that I care for that, but I shouldn't like it if you took against me because of it."

"No, I don't, Ben. It was a fair game and he lost."

"Goodo. Now we understand each other. I reckon I could arrange for you to come to Australia with me."

"It sounds so exciting I can't believe it."

"Well, we'll start hatching plots, shall we?"

"They'd be horrified, I know."

"That makes it all the more exciting, doesn't it?" he retorted mischievously.

He would sit there laughing to himself, and I wondered what was in his mind. He talked a great deal about the Company, the town which had grown up and was known by the name of the Fancy or Fancy Town. He often mentioned Joss; in fact he seemed to be obsessed by Joss, which I suppose was natural, since he was his son, but the more I heard of that arrogant gentleman the less I was able to share Ben's enthusiasm for him.

It was always: "When you're in Australia. . . ." But nothing was said about how I was going to escape from my family. I had only turned eighteen that June, so I was still not my own mistress.

I did enjoy our talks though. I loved hearing about his home out there and I felt I knew the ostentatious house already . . . for I was sure it was ostentatious with a name like Peacocks. I could never picture it without the peacocks on the lawn and the human Peacock strutting with them. There was a housekeeper, a Mrs. Laud, to whom Ben referred now and then and who seemed to be a most efficient woman for whom he felt some affection. She had a son and daughter —Jimson, working with the Company, and Lilias, who helped her mother in the house; there were also a number of other servants, and among them were several what he called "A bos," the term for aborigines.

I would listen avidly and again and again I asked: "Yes,

Ben, but how am *I* going to get there?"

Then he would give his sly laugh. "You leave that to me," he would say.

I saw Hannah now and then and was still on good terms with the servants at the Hall, for I always found time to visit them.

"Mr. Henniker's told me he'll be leaving soon," said Mrs. Bucket. "He's told Mr. Wilmot too. So then we'll arrange to shut up again and it'll be as it was before he came back without his leg. I don't think it's right for a house like this. The servants don't like it. That's what comes of people who don't belong. You'll miss him, I reckon."

I almost blurted out that he had plans, but I realized then how wild those plans were, and it occurred to me then that he talked of them to placate me and that he knew as well as I did that I should never be able to leave.

There was a knock on the door of my room and Miriam came in. She looked quite pretty.

"I want to talk to you, Jessica," she said. "What do you think? Ernest and I are going to get married."

I put my arms round her and kissed her, because I was so pleased that she had at last come to her senses. I didn't remember when I had last done that, but I knew it pleased her because she went pink to the tips of her ears and nose.

"I'm very happy," she went on. "We decided that no matter what Mama said we would wait no longer."

"I'm so glad, Miriam," I cried. "You should have done it years ago. Never mind. You have at last. So when shall you be married?"

"Ernest says there is no sense in waiting. We have waited long enough. We were waiting, you know, for him to get St. Clissolds, because the vicar there is very very old, but he just goes on living and could live for another ten years."

"No use waiting for dead men's shoes or dead vicars' vestments. I think it's wonderful, and I'm glad you've come to your senses. It's lovely and I hope you'll be very happy."

"We shall be very poor. Papa can give me nothing, and I still have to tell Mama."

"Don't let her stop you."

"Nothing could stop me now. It's rather a blessing that we have been so poor lately—though not as poor as Ernest and I shall be. It means that I have learned how to make everything go a long way. . . ."

"I'm sure you're right, Miriam. When is the wedding to be?"

Miriam looked really frightened. "At the end of August. Ernest says we'd better put up the banns right away and then no one can stop us. There's the little curate's cottage in the vicarage grounds where Ernest lives alone. But there'll be room for two of us."

"You'll manage very well, Miriam."

I was glad she had made the decision, and the change in her was miraculous. My grandmother was naturally angry and skeptical. She referred slightingly to "our lovesick girl" and how some people seemed to think they could live like church mice on the crumbs which fell from the rich man's table. I bubbled over with mirth at that and pointed out that she did not know her Bible, as it certainly was not the mice who had devoured those very special crumbs.

"You have become impossible, Jessica," she told me. "I don't know what this household is coming to. How different things might have been if some people had taken their responsibilities more seriously. Perhaps then we shouldn't have foolish old maids making laughingstocks of themselves in the mad rush to marry *any*body—just *anybody*—before it is too late."

Miriam was wounded and wavered, but only slightly. She was Ernest's future wife now, not merely my grandmother's daughter, and she quoted him whenever possible. I was delighted. I talked to her often and we grew more friendly than we ever had been. I told her she was doing the right thing in escaping from my grandmother's tyranny, that she was fortunate to be able to and that she was going to be very happy.

"I wonder what will happen here when I have left," she said on one occasion. "Jessica, what of *you?*"

"What do you mean?"

"You're going a great deal to Oakland Hall. Sometimes that frightens me. It's what your mother did."

"I enjoy going there. Why shouldn't I go? You must admit life is not exactly hilarious at the Dower House."

"Her trouble began there."

"It's going to be quite different with me. Stop worrying, Miriam. Think of the future. I know you're going to be happy."

"I'm determined to be," she said defiantly, as though she was thinking of her mother.

Miriam was married, as she had said she would be, at the end of August. My grandmother went to the wedding because it would look unsuitable if she did not, and this seemed to be her sole reason for going. My grandfather performed the giving-away ceremony, and I was a bridesmaid. It was a quiet wedding—necessarily so, my grandmother pointed out about a hundred times after the banns had been called, in our reduced circumstances.

There was no wedding feast. "What is there to celebrate?" demanded my grandmother. "Just an old maid's folly."

She was cruel, but Miriam seemed impervious to her insults; she was so happy to be married at last and to have made the decision which had hung over her for so many years. There was a permanent sneer about my grandmother's lips when she referred to the married pair, and she took to calling them "the church mice," gloating over their future poverty and making it out to be so much worse than it was.

There was no honeymoon. "Honeymoon," sneered my grandmother. "You know what their honeymoon will be—a piece of bread and cheese eaten from that *cottage* wooden table which my daughter will have to learn to scrub. Then she will discover her folly. A honeymoon in that miserable little hut . . . for it is no more! I wish them joy of it."

My grandfather spoke up: "Sometimes there can be more joy in a humble cottage than in a mansion. It says something like that in the Bible, and it seems to me that Miriam can only congratulate herself that she has escaped from this place."

My grandmother stared at him, and he picked up *The Times* and walked out of the room.

Change indeed when my grandfather stood his ground with his wife.

It was a week after Miriam's wedding when the accident happened. Ben was walking in the grounds one morning when his crutch apparently slid on some damp leaves and he fell. He was in the grounds for an hour before he was discovered. He was carried in by Banker and Wilmot, who called the doctor. It seemed that his injuries were by no means slight. The wound on his leg had burst open and he would have to remain in bed until it was healed.

He was looking not only disgruntled but ill when I called. "Look what the old fool's done, Jessie," he grumbled. "There was I sprinting along you might say one minute and the next my crutch has gone flying and I'm rolling on the grass and there's the old leg letting me know it was once there and mad because they'd lopped it off and it's there no longer. Why weren't you there to save me this time?"

"How I wish I had been."

"Well, you'll have to come and see me now and then."

"As often as you like, Ben."

"You'll get tired of this sick old man. But I'll be up and about soon, you see."

"Of course."

"It means postponing our going to Australia. Why, that doesn't seem to upset you."

"I couldn't bear to think of your going."

"Not when you were coming with me."

"I don't think I ever really believed I would."

"That's not like you, Jess. You wanted to come, didn't you? You didn't want to stay in that house. You'd be stifled there. What's going to happen to you if you stay there? It's no place for a bold spirit like yours. You want to live, see the world, spread your wings. . . . You're a gambler, Jessie. Oh yes you are. It's in your blood, the same as it's in mine. Look at it like this. It's a postponement. One day you're going off to Australia. I promise you."

"Are you going to gamble with them for *me* this time?" I laughed.

"That's not a bad idea, I'd take your grandfather on any day." He grimaced. "But suppose I lost, eh Jessie? What then?"

"You're a gambler. You'd take a risk."

"There are some things too important to take a chance on." He gripped my hand firmly. "You're going to Australia. That's something I've made up my mind about."

"Well, Ben, all you have to do is get well."

"Leave it to me. Next week I'll be on the hobble again."

But he wasn't.

September passed and October was with us, and still the wound did not heal. Until it had, the doctor insisted, he must stay in bed.

He raged a good deal, cursed doctors, declared they didn't know what they were talking about, but he was uneasy. Why wouldn't the miserable wound heal? He was not going to stay in bed. He had plans. He tried to get up, but the effort of attempting to walk was too much for him and he had to admit defeat.

I went in every day to see him and I knew that he watched the door at half-past two every afternoon, so I made a point of never being late, and it made me happy when I left him more cheerful than I found him.

Then one day—it must have been towards the end of October—the doctor arrived with another member of his profession whom he had called in, and there were grave faces at Oakland Hall. There was something wrong—something more than a wound which obstinately refused to heal. This was indeed a symptom of something else.

Ben at first insisted that it was all a lot of nonsense and wanted to get up to prove it; that was where *he* was proved wrong. He simply could not get up and in time he had to admit that the doctors were right.

Being Ben he insisted on knowing the truth and when I called he told me what he had got out of them.

"I'm going to talk to you very seriously, Jessie," he said. "I made them tell me the truth. They didn't want to but they soon saw the sort of man I was. 'Its *my* body,' I told them. 'Now don't you go treating me as though I'm a child or a weak old woman. If it's the end of Ben Henniker then that's Ben Henniker's business. I want to leave everything in order!' Well, they told me I've got some blood disease. That's why the old leg won't heal. If I hadn't had the fall it would have shown itself sooner or later. That just gave them the clue they wanted. They reckon I've got a year at the most and that I'm not going to get up from this bed. You might think that there goes all Ben Henniker's fine plans . . . but if you think that you don't know Ben Henniker. It means an adjustment, and I made them tell me the truth because I wanted time to make this adjustment. You follow me, Jess?"

"Of course," I said.

"All right then. I've not got long. I've got to be prepared. So I'll make preparations. Don't look so sad. I'm an old man. I've had my day and a pretty good day it's been. The point is, I don't want to be snuffed out like a candle. You know, there was a light there and then suddenly there's no light . . . and that was Ben Henniker that was. No. It's not going to be like that. It's always been a dream of mine to see my grandchildren peacocking on my lawn."

"You mean Joss's children."

"That's right. I used to picture them . . . sturdy little 'uns . . . looking just like him. Not just one of them . . . I wanted lots of 'em. Little boys and little girls. He'd have pretty girls if they inherited his eyes. I'm glad he's shown no signs of marrying yet and there's a reason for it."

"What reason? He's not so very young is he?"

"He's the other side of thirty. To think it's all that time since he came strutting across that lawn with his suitcase. 'I've come here. I like it here. I like peacocks. . . .' What a boy! I reckon he's liked it there ever since. I want him to marry the right woman. That's important. So I'm glad he hasn't married yet."

"You were going to tell me the reason."

"Oh, he's been involved here and there. He's a man who likes women and they like him." Ben chuckled in that fond way which I always found irritating in this connection. "Everything Joss does is done with more energy than ordinary people use. So it's like that with women. He's got the roving eye all right, but he never seemed anxious to settle."

"He gets more attractive than ever," I said sarcastically. "He's now added promiscuity to his arrogance."

"Joss is a man, remember. He's strong, proud, sure of himself. He's all that a man should be. He's myself made tall and handsome and got the right education too, which was what I missed. I sent him to school over here when he was eleven years old and he stayed here until he was sixteen. I was a bit worried about that. Afraid it might change him too much. Not a bit of it. An English education just gave him something more. When he was sixteen he refused to stay at school any longer. He was raring to get to work. He was mad about opals and mining and all that went with it. When I showed him the Flash that night I remember the look in his eyes. . . . But that's past. What I want to talk about is now. A year at the most, they say. Well, perhaps old Ben can make it a bit longer. But before I go everything will have to be in order. Now you can do all sorts of things for me. You can write letters and such like."

"I'll do everything I can. You know that, Ben."

"Well, the first letter I want you to write is to my solicitors. Now they're in London and in Sydney. I want you to write to the London address right away and tell them their Mr. Vennor is to come and see me down here without delay. Will you do that?"

"Of course. Immediately. You must give me all particulars."

"It's Mr. Vennor of Vennor and Caves, and they're in Hanover Square and you'll find the complete address in a book in that drawer over there. That's the first thing."

I wrote the letter and said I would post it.

I sat by his bed, and he said: "I'm glad there's some time left to us, Jessie."

"The doctors could be wrong," I insisted. "They have been known to be."

"That's so. I wonder if it is the curse of the Green Flash after all. I told you that misfortune dogged those who owned it, didn't I?"

"But you don't own it. You—lost it . . . nearly twenty years ago."

"Yes. Yes, of course. But there was my accident in the mine . . . and there's the suggestion that I might have caught this infection of the blood, or whatever it is, in those mines. Perhaps that's the price you have to pay for gouging those beauties out of the rock, taking them from where they belong—a sort of revenge they have."

"Surely something beautiful shouldn't be hidden in rock. It should be brought out for people to enjoy."

"Who knows? But it could be the curse of the Green Flash getting me."

"You don't believe that, Ben. How can you? You were well enough to see me out when you owned it."

He didn't answer. He merely took my hand and held it. "Later on," he said, "I shall send for Joss."

"You mean bring him here?"

His shrewd eyes were on me. "I can feel your pulse quicken. He excites you, doesn't he . . . I mean the thought of seeing him does."

"Why should it?" I asked. "I know you think a great deal of him, Ben, but what I have heard doesn't make me admire him very much."

He started to laugh so hard that I thought it might be bad for him. "Stop it, Ben," I said severely. "It's not a bit funny."

"It is, because I know you're going to change your opinion when you meet him."

"So you really are going to ask him to come here?"

"Not yet. I've got some time left to me. When he comes it will be to see me out. He's got work to do out there. He can't dilly-dally shilly-shally for a year. But when the end is near—and I'll know it—there's no doubt of that, I'll send for Joss. I'll have to tell him what I want him to do before I go."

I was unhappy, for I could see the change in him every day. Being Ben, he would cling to life tenaciously, but in the end he would have to give way.

This time next year . . . I thought; and I was filled with melancholy.

The weeks passed, and I continued to visit Ben every day.

My grandmother could not be kept in ignorance of my visits, and while she expressed disapproval she did not attempt to stop them. I was sure she knew that if she did I should blatantly disobey her.

"Your friend, the miner, seems to be getting his just desserts," she commented sourly. "People of his station clambering about in mines so that they can ape their betters are bound to come to grief."

I couldn't respond with my usual flippancy. I felt too deeply about Ben.

He used to talk incessantly about the days in Australia, and I would encourage him to do so because it comforted him. He often mentioned the Green Flash opal and once or twice he seemed to be wandering in his mind because he talked as though he still had it.

"People get fancies about opals," he said, "and the Green Flash was no ordinary gem. Diamonds can be of greater value, but they don't seem to have the same effect on people. I've seen men going for gold . . . it's a sort of fever, but the lust is not for the gold in itself. It's what gold can bring them. Perhaps it's because opals are different. One nugget looks very like another, but opals are varying. There are such legends about that stone. People read messages in the colors. In the past they were omens of good fortune. People say they can bring bad luck though. I always used to say this was because some of them could be so easily chipped, and a stone a man has regarded as his fortune can thus lose much of its value. I've known men desperately in need of money and yet refusing to part with a stone that could save them. That's how it was with the Green Flash."

"Yet you say it was called the Unlucky Stone."

"There's bound to be legends about a stone like that. It was one of the first black opals to be found. It's odd that there should never have been anything like it since. There never will be in my opinion."

"Who found it?"

"It was an old miner . . . fifty years ago. He'd had bad luck all along . . . the sort of fellow who'd give up just as he was almost on a find . . . and then someone else would come along and reap the reward of his labor. He was called Unlucky Jim. Then . . . he found her. It was rather like what happened to me with Green Lady. The rock collapsed on him, and he was found dead clutching the Green Flash in his hand. Perhaps that's what started it all. I think bad luck's sometimes wished on to you . . . if you follow. Unlucky Jim finds the Flash and, taking her, loses his life. His son found him and the stone and he knew right away that she was a winner. One look at her was enough . . . though she was in the raw state then. He wanted to get her into Sydney right away, but he'd showed her round a bit. He couldn't help it, he was proud of her. He was warned by an old gypsy woman that it wouldn't be wise for him to carry that stone through the Bush because already people were talking of it . . . how it was the finest opal in the world and worth a fortune. So he had a plan. He gave it to his younger brother to take . . . and none knew he had it. A bushranger shot him on the way, determined to get the opal, but of course he couldn't find it because the brother had it. So that was two deaths already."

"And what happened to it then?"

"It was cut and polished and, by heavens, what emerged dazzled just everyone who saw it. The size . . . the color . . . it had never been suspected that such a stone existed. This younger brother had it then. I only half remember what happened to him. His daughter eloped and he tried to stop her and in the scuffle with the would-be husband, the owner of the Green Flash was thrown downstairs. He spent two years in acute pain before he died but he wouldn't give up the Green Flash. I heard he used to carry it with him so that he could look at it every day and he thought it was worth while . . . everything that had happened . . . just to possess it. His daughter though was afraid of it, and she put it in the hands of a dealer and from him it passed to some Eastern ruler. That'll give you an idea. It was worthy to fit into some jewel-studded crown. He was assassinated a year or so after, and it passed to his eldest son who was sold into slavery but not before the Flash was taken from him by his captors. One of them stole it and ran off with it, and when misfortune started to hit him he blamed the stone.

He died of a fever but not before he'd told his son to take it back where it belonged. That was how it was brought back to Australia. Old Harry I told you about gambled for it. It was one of those occasions when Harry won."

"Did he believe the legend?"

"All I know is that when people get that stone they want to keep it at all cost."

"And you weren't afraid when you had it?"

"No. But look what happened to me. Look at me now."

"You can't blame that on the ill luck the stone has brought you because you no longer have it. I wonder what happened to whoever took it?"

He held my hand firmly and began: "Jessie. . . ." I waited for I thought he was going to tell me something, but he seemed to change his mind.

He looked very tired, and I said: "I'm going to leave you to sleep now, Ben."

Oddly enough, he made no protest, so I quietly left him and went back to the Dower House.

The next year was with us. Every now and then Ben rallied so that I thought he was going to defy the doctors and get well, but there would be days when he would appear to be exhausted in spite of his efforts to hide it.

It was in the middle of February, a cold day with a north wind blowing and flurries of snow in the air, that I went to see him.

There was a fire in the grate and Hannah looked sad.

She whispered: "He's failing, I think. Lord help us. What's going to become of us all?"

"I daresay he will have made some provision," I assured her.

"That Banker is really cut up, and Mr. Wilmot hasn't mentioned Mr. Henniker's not the right sort of master of Oakland for the last six weeks. I reckon he'd give a good deal to have things go on as they were."

"We all would, Hannah," I said.

So I was prepared when I went into his room. It may have been the cold white light of the snowy weather which gave his face that bluish tinge, but I didn't think so.

He smiled when he saw me and tried to appear jaunty.

"What I call roast chestnut and hot spud weather," he said. "I once did very well with them . . . chestnuts and roast potatoes cooked on a little brazier at the corner of the street. Lovely to warm your hands on. It's a cold day today, Jessie."

I went to the bed and took his hands. They were indeed very cold.

"I can't seem to keep myself warm these days," he said.

We talked of Australia and the mines and men he had known; and I made tea on the spirit lamp, which he liked to see me do.

"I picture you boiling the billy can out in the Bush. That's what I used to think we'd be doing one day. They say Man proposes and God disposes. He's disposing a bit today, I'm afraid, Jess."

I gave him the tea and watched him drink it.

"Good strong stuff," he said. "But, you know, tea never tastes as good as it does out in the Bush. I'd like to have been out there with you, Jessie. I'd have liked to see you— a damper in one hand and a cup of good brew in the other, and I'd like to have heard you say you'd never tasted anything so good. Never mind, you'll know it all one day." I must have looked very sad because he went on: "Cheer up, my girl. Oh yes, you're going out there. I'm certain of that. I won't have it otherwise."

I didn't answer. I let him go on with his fancies, and I wondered what I was going to do when he was gone and I should no longer come to Oakland Hall.

"I've been thinking of something," he said. "I reckon the time has come. Joss should be told. He ought to start thinking about coming over now. It'll take him time. You can't expect him to catch the first ship. He'll have things to arrange. Without Joss the Company will be in need of a bit of organizing."

"You want to write to him?" I said. I took paper and pen and sat down by the bed. "What do you want me to say?"

"I'd like you to write it in your own way. I want it to be a letter from you to him."

"But. . . ."

"Go on. It's what I want."

So I wrote:

> "Dear Mr. Madden,
>   Mr. Ben Henniker has asked me to write to you
> to tell you he is very ill. He wants you to come

to England. It is very important that you should leave as soon as possible.

> Yours truly,
> Jessica Clavering"

"Read it to me," said Ben, and I did.

"It does sound a bit unfriendly," he commented.

"How could it be friendly when I haven't met him?"

"I've told you something about him."

"I suppose it doesn't make me feel particularly friendly."

"Then I haven't told you the right things and I'm to blame. When you meet him, you'll feel like all women do . . . you'll see."

"I'm not a silly little peahen to goggle at the magnificent peacock you know, Ben."

That set him laughing so much that once again I was afraid it might be bad for him.

When he was quiet he lay back smiling happily as though, I thought, he had discovered a rich vein of opal.

"Anyone would think you'd found the Green Flash," I told him, and a strange expression crossed his face. I could not guess what he was thinking.

He rallied a little after that, and in due course I received a reply from Josslyn Madden. It was addressed to Miss Jessica Clavering at Oakland Hall, and Wilmot handed it to me on a silver salver when I arrived.

I saw the Australian postmark and the bold handwriting, and I guessed from whom it came so I took it up to Ben and told him that Joss Madden had answered my letter.

I opened it and read aloud:

> "Dear Miss Clavering,
>   Thank you for your letter. By the time you receive this I shall be on my way. I shall come immediately to Oakland Hall when I arrive in England.
>
> Yours truly,
> J. Madden"

"Is that all he says?" cried Ben querulously.

"It's enough," I replied. "All he has to tell us is that he is on his way."

April had come. I should be nineteen in June.

"You're growing up," said my grandmother. "How different

it *might* have been. We should have done our duty by you and you would have come out with dignity. Here . . . in this place . . . what can we hope for? There isn't even a curate for you. Mind you, your fondness for low company might exclude you from such as Miriam has turned to."

"Miriam is very happy, I think."

"I'm sure she is . . . wondering where her next meal is coming from."

"It's not as bad as that. They have enough to eat. She enjoys managing and I know she is much happier than she was here."

"Oh, she was glad enough to get someone to marry her . . . anyone . . . it didn't matter who. I hope you're not going to get into that desperate state."

"You need have no anxieties on that score," I retorted.

I was feeling very sad because I knew that Ben's health had taken a turn for the worse; he was visibly deteriorating and I wondered what would happen when he died. The future stretched out drearily before me. I was still doing what my grandmother called those duties expected of people in our position even though we were in such reduced circumstances. That meant taking to the poor dusters and the preserves which had not turned out as well as my grandmother had expected them to, taking charge of a stall at the church fête, attending the sewing class held at the vicarage, putting flowers on the graves, helping decorate the church, and such activities. I could see myself growing old and sour as Miriam had been before she married her curate—but even she had had him in the background. I was no longer very young. I was now a woman and the older I grew the more quickly would the years slip by.

The day began ordinarily enough with prayers in the drawing room, where the family assembled with the servants while my grandmother, as I once irreverently observed to Miriam, gave the Almighty His instructions for the day. "Do this. . . ." and "Don't do that. . . ." By force of habit I counted up the injunctions.

That April Mrs. Jarman had been delivered of another child and Jarman was more melancholy than ever. Nature, he told me, showed no signs of curbing her generosity. My grandmother sharply retorted that he was not so simple that he did not know that a little restraint might ease the situation. He was indeed Poor Jarman; he looked at my grandmother with such reproach that he made me want to laugh.

"Talk of Poor Jarman," she said to me sharply. "*I* think it's a case of Poor *Mrs.* Jarman."

In an outburst of generosity she packed a basket for the fertile lady and even put in a pot of raspberry jam which had not started to go moldy, a small chicken, and a flask of broth.

"You can take this over to Mrs. Jarman, Jessica," she said. "After all her husband does work for us. Take it while he is working, for I am sure he seizes the best of everything for himself and she needs nourishment, poor woman."

That was how on a breezy afternoon in late April I came to be walking over to the cottage where the Jarmans lived, a basket on my arm, thinking as I went of Ben and wondering how soon the day would come when I would go over to Oakland Hall and find that he had left it.

Outside the Jarman cottage was a muddy pond and a scrap of garden overgrown with weeds. It was strange that Poor Jarman, who spent his days making other people's gardens beautiful, should so neglect his own. I contemplated that they could have grown some flowers there, or perhaps some vegetables, but instead of daffodils and flowering shrubs there were little Jarmans playing games which seemed to involve the maximum of noise, confusion, and an abundance of litter.

One of the young ones who must have been about three years old had a small flowerpot into which he was shoveling dirt and turning it out into neat little mounds which he patted with hands understandably grimy, after which operation he rubbed them over his face and down his pinafore. Two others were tugging at a rope, and another was throwing a ball into the pond so that when it bounced a spray of dirty water rose, splashing him and anyone near to the immense delight of those who were thus anointed.

There was a brief silence as I approached, all eyes on the basket, but as I went into the cottage the noise broke out again.

I called out: "Good afternoon, Mrs. Jarman."

One stepped straight into the living room, and I knocked on a door which I knew from previous visits to be that of the connubial bedchamber. There was a spiral staircase leading from the room to two rooms upstairs which were occupied as sleeping quarters by the ever-increasing tribe.

Mrs. Jarman was in bed, the new baby in a cradle beside her. She was very large. Like a queen bee, I had once re-

marked to Miriam, and indeed nature had clearly furnished
her for a similar destiny.

"Another little girl, Mrs. Jarman," I said.

"Yes, Miss Jessica," said Mrs. Jarman, rolling her eyes
reproachfully up to the ceiling as though Providence had
whisked this one into the cradle when she wasn't looking,
for she shared Poor Jarman's complaint that it was Nature
at her tricks again.

The little girl was going to be called Daisy, she told me,
and she hoped God would see fit to bless her.

"Well, Mrs. Jarman," I said, "you have your quiverful
and that's supposed to be a blessed state."

"It'll mean getting another bed in time," she said. "I only
hope the Lord sees fit to stop with Daisy."

I talked for a while and then came out of the house to
where the noise seemed to have increased. The maker of
dirt mounds had had enough of them and was cheerfully
kicking them down to the pond. The ball went straight into
the pond, and the Jarman who had thrown it shrugged his
shoulders and walked away.

I was about to cross the road when the mound-maker,
having seen the ball go into the pond, decided to retrieve it.
He walked in, reached for the ball and fell flat on his face.

The other children were all watching with interest, but
none of them thought of getting the child out. There was
only one thing for me to do because he was in imminent
danger. I waded into the pond, picked up the little Jarman,
and angrily strode with him onto dry land.

As I stood there with the child in my arms I was aware
of a man on horseback watching the scene. The horse looked
enormous, so did the man; it was like a centaur or some
legendary creature.

An imperious voice said: "Can you tell me the way to
Oakland Hall?"

The eldest Jarman present, who must have been about
six, shouted: "Up the road there. . . ."

The man on horseback was looking straight at me expecting the only adult to give the answer.

I said: "You go straight up the road, turn to the right
and you will see the gates a little way along the road."

"Thank you."

He put his hand into his pocket and brought out some
coins which he threw at us.

I was furious. I hastily put down the little Jarman and

stopped to pick up the coins with the intention of throwing them back at him, but before I could reach them two Jarmans had swooped on them and had run off as fast as they could with their prize.

I looked angrily at the back of the horseman and turned on the small Jarman whose mud-spattered face was lifted to mine, one finger in his mouth while he regarded me with curiosity.

"You dirty little creature," I stammered. Then I was sorry because it wasn't his fault.

"All right," I said. "Go in and get one of your brothers and sisters to dry you. And don't dare walk into the pond again."

I strode off to the Dower House. As soon as I reached my room I looked at myself in a mirror.

There was a smudge of dirt on my cheek; my blouse was muddy, my skirt wet at the hem and my shoes saturated.

What a sight I looked! And the man on horseback had taken me for a cottage girl! I guessed who he was. Hadn't he asked for Oakland Hall? Hadn't he behaved in a perfectly arrogant manner? Hadn't he the conceited looks of a peacock!

To think that my first meeting with him should have been like that!

"I knew I'd hate him," I said aloud.

I could not bring myself to go to Oakland Hall the following afternoon. I thought: He'll be there, and I don't want to see him. Ben will be all right, I thought jealously. He's got his precious Peacock. He won't want me.

I was wrong.

Maddy came knocking at my door. "Hannah gave me a message for you. It's from Mr. Henniker. He's asking you to go over there. He wants you particular."

I had to go then, so I dressed with care. I wore my blue alpaca, which if it was not my most becoming gown gave me an air of dignity.

As soon as I arrived at the Hall I was aware of the change. There was tense excitement in the atmosphere. Wilmot greeted me in the hall, urbane and dignified.

"Mr. Henniker wishes you to go straight up to his room, Miss Clavering."

"Thank you, Wilmot," I said.

I knew it was no use asking the questions which came into my mind. Wilmot would be too correct to discuss one

visitor with another. But I did see Hannah at the top of
the staircase where she was lurking, obviously hoping to
catch me.

"Oh, Miss Jessica," she said in an awestruck voice, "he's
come . . . the gentleman from Australia."

"Oh?" I said, waiting.

"My word!" The expression on her face irritated me.
Usually sensible Hannah looked quite foolish.

"He seems to have had an extraordinary effect on you," I
said sharply.

"Mr. Henniker's that pleased. I reckon it's given him a
new lease of life. Joss came into the hall, yesterday it was.
. . . You'd have thought he owned the place. Wilmot says
it looks like the place could belong to him. I don't know when
I've seen such a *big* gentleman, and he's got a way of talking
too. You can hear him all over the place . . . one of them
carrying voices. My word! I reckon he knows what he's
about. Wilmot seems to think he's some sort of relation. A
son, Wilmot's heard. Though we didn't know Mr. Henniker
had been married, and he's a Mr. Madden."

"I suppose I'm to meet him," I said, cutting her short, "so
I must go and see this"—I was going to say "peacock" but
I changed it to "paragon"—"of yours whose huge body and
booming voice seems to have bewitched you."

I went past her, knowing she was thinking I was very
touchy today.

I knocked at Ben's bedroom door and heard him say: "This
will be Jessica." Then loudly: "Come in my dear."

I went in. Ben was sitting in the chair by the bed in a
dressing gown and with a rug about his knees. A tall figure
rose and came towards me. I was annoyed because I had to
look up so far.

Of course it was the man I had met on horseback outside
the Jarman cottage.

He took my hand and kept it too long for me.

"So," he said, "we meet again."

"Hey? What's this?" cried Ben. "Come over here, the two
of you. I want to make a proper introduction. This is a very
important occasion. I want you two to know each other,
and when you do, you're going to like each other a good
deal. I've never had any doubt of that. You're two of a
kind."

I couldn't help showing the resentment which flared up
within me at the thought of being compared with this man.

I noticed his eyes then—those deep blue eyes the color of a peacock's feather; I noticed the rather large nose, slightly aquiline, which suggested the arrogance I was convinced I would find, and the long, rather thin lips, which could have been cynical or sensuous or both. It was not so much a handsome face as distinguished—one that would never be passed in a crowd. Once seen, it would be remembered. The brown velvet jacket and the very white cravat suggested fastidiousness, but the brown riding boots and corded breeches were essentially masculine.

What I disliked most was the mocking expression in his face, which told me that he was remembering the sight of me emerging from a muddy pond with a grubby Jarman in my arms. That was his first impression and it was something he was not going to forget.

"We have met before, Ben," he said.

"Come and tell me all about it."

I said quickly: "I went to the Jarmans. Mrs. Jarman has produced again and my grandmother sent me over with some things. As I was coming out of the house one of the children fell into the pond. I got him out and Mr. . . . . er. . . ." I nodded towards him.

"You must call him Joss, my dear," said Ben. "We don't want any formality. We're all too friendly for that."

"But I don't know him," I protested.

"We have met before," said Joss Madden, and I sensed the mockery.

I said firmly: "Mr. Madden came by, asked the way—and paid for the information." I turned to him. "I can assure you the fee was unnecessary and would have been returned to you had not the children seized whatever it was and run off with it."

Ben laughed. "Well, fancy that. And you didn't know each other."

"Having heard that Mr. Madden was due, I guessed it was he. His actions fitted what I had heard of him."

Joss Madden laughed. It was a quick bellow of a laugh. It exploded and was over. "I trust that was meant as a compliment," he said, "because I'm going to take it as such."

"I will leave you to judge," I replied.

Ben was smiling as though—I found I was using this simile often in connection with him—he had found the Green Flash.

"It does me good to see you here getting along so well

with Jessica," said Ben. "It's the best thing that's happened since my fall. Now, let's all sit down and get comfortable, shall we? We've got a lot to talk about, and I don't know how much time there is left to us."

"Don't say that, Ben," I cried. "You're going to be so much better now that, er . . . Mr. Madden has come."

"Let's look the truth straight between the eyes," said Ben. "It's always the best way. That's so, eh, Joss?"

"I believe it to be," Joss Madden answered.

"Now come on . . . bring the chairs up . . . one of you on either side of me. There. That's what I've been wanting for a long time. Now I'm going to be sentimental. It's allowed for a poor old man who hasn't got much time left to him. There's two people who mean more to me than anything else in the world, and I've set my heart on one thing and that is that I want them to be together . . . work together. . . ."

I could feel Joss Madden's eyes on me, assessing me in a way I felt offensive. No man had ever looked at me like that before. It made me strangely aware of myself. I had expected him to be arrogant and offensive, but I had not guessed he would arouse such hitherto unexperienced feelings in me. I found myself remembering that there was a strongish breeze which had made my hair untidy and that my alpaca was not very becoming. I must have looked quite terrible yesterday when I had emerged from the pond.

I heard myself say shrilly: "Work together . . . ! Whatever do you mean, Ben?"

"Well, that's something I'm coming to. I can see Joss here thinking it's a bit soon. I reckon he's thinking you and he ought to get better acquainted first. Is that it, Joss?"

"It may be that Miss Clavering would find the shock too great. Give her a day or two to get used to me."

"This is all rather mysterious."

"It's really straightforward and practical," said Joss Madden. "Are you practical, Miss Clavering?"

"Now what did I say," interrupted Ben. "No formality."

"Are you practical, Jessica?" asked Joss Madden.

"I think I am," I answered.

"Yes. You have that air. I would say you take a pride in being a sensible young woman."

"It seems a sensible thing to take pride in," I retorted.

"Brisk," he said. "No nonsense. That's going to be very helpful, I can see."

"Look here," said Ben. "I'm rushing things. I begin to see

that. I'll tell you what we'll do. Tomorrow we'll have a good talk. The three of us together, eh?"

"That seems a good idea," said Joss Madden.

"All right then," said Ben. "That's settled. We'll just chat now, eh? Tell me how things are back home."

"I've told you the essentials already," said Joss with a laugh. "Things are running as smoothly as they can be expected to. There are no dire problems. We struck a rich vein out near Derry Creek."

"Good black opal, eh? And not too much potch. That's what I like to hear. Jimson Laud coming along all right?"

"He's all right."

"You sound lukewarm."

"Jimson's the one who's lukewarm."

"Can't expect everyone to blow hot like you, Joss. Jimson's a figure man. They don't get excited—but accounts are important to the business. And Lilias?"

"The same as ever."

"And Emmeline?"

"The entire family has changed little since you last saw them."

Ben looked into space, murmuring: "Oh, I'd like to see Peacocks once more before I went. Mind you, I've got a pretty clear picture in my mind's eye. I've loved every brick of that place . . . every blade of grass on those lawns. Not the same as here . . . of course . . . that sun, that burning sun . . . all those months of drought. What was it like when you left?"

"Dry as a bone. There were some forest fires a few miles away."

"It's a perpetual danger, Jessica," said Ben to me. "You'll find it very different from here. Won't she, Joss?"

"If she decides to accept your terms."

"Terms?" I demanded. "What terms?"

"I thought you said it was too soon to talk," said Ben.

"So it is," replied Joss Madden. "If we did, I reckon we'd get a blank refusal. You've got to give Miss Clavering time . . . er, I mean Jessica. You're not the puppet master, Ben, simply because neither Jessica nor I are of the stuff which puppets are made of. Don't you agree . . . Jessica? You wouldn't want to be jerked round on the stage. Go this way . . . go that way . . . because that's the way the master's twitching the strings."

"I can assure you that I would not and that you are talking of something of which I know nothing. I think you ought to let me into the secret without delay."

Ben looked at Joss who shook his head. Then Ben said: "There's something I have to tell you first, Jessica. Joss knows it already. I'll tell you when we're alone, and then you'll understand."

I looked at Joss meaningly because their mysterious talk was giving me a burning desire to discover what it was all about.

"I see," said Joss, "that's a sort of hint. I'm going to have another look at your stables, Ben. I want to see if there's anything good enough to ride there."

"Impertinence," laughed Ben. "We breed horses here, I might tell you. You'll find several there as good as that one you hired to arrive on."

"I hope so. I had to take him because he was all they had. Then shall I leave you? You can have your talk. You and I will meet again soon . . . Jessica."

He went out, and Ben turned to me at once. "What do you think of him?" he asked eagerly.

"He's exactly what I expected."

"So I gave you a good description of him, did I?"

"I based my judgment on the little anecdotes you told me."

"And you like him, Jess?"

I hesitated. I didn't want to hurt Ben by telling him that the more I saw of Joss Madden the less I liked him.

I said cautiously, "I don't feel I know him."

Ben shook his head. "You'll soon get to know him. I wish I'd asked him to come earlier."

"Ben," I said, "you were going to tell me what you and he have been hinting at. What is it?"

He hesitated. "I hardly know where to begin. I've been very wrong, and I'm sorry for it. But it's a good thing really. You'll see that and understand I'm sure. It's to do with the Green Flash at Sunset."

"That seems to be at the center of our lives," I commented wryly.

"That was all true . . . what I told you about how I won it. I'd got the stone and it made a difference to my life. Funny how the possession of that opal changed everything. It was true that those who had owned it had been dogged by bad luck. I knew that everyone was watching me . . . waiting for the ill luck to hit me. There were those who wished me well. There were others who had seen it, felt its fascination, and wanted it. Men are strange creatures, Jess. A girl like you . . . a sensible girl, Joss called you . . . wouldn't know about this. And you've never seen the Green Flash either. Perhaps if you had seen it you'd understand more. That flashing blue and the red of the sun . . . it just bewitches you. So where was I? There were those who watched me and others who sought to steal it. I reckon my life wasn't worth what it was before I had that stone. There were some who would have cut my throat or put a bullet through my heart for the sake of it. I'd got a red hot property on my hands and I was going to burn myself pretty badly one way or another.

"Then there came the day when they were all here and I showed them the stone. This is going to hurt a bit, Jessie. I didn't want to tell you. I know you have a beautiful picture of your father and his love for your mother, and it's right for young ladies to have these feelings for their parents. But it wasn't quite like that. Your mother was a sweet, pretty creature. She was like you . . . oh very much . . . but different. You've got your feet more on the ground, that sensible quality eh? She could be gay, a bit willful; she was a bit of a gambler too. It's in the family. You can't escape it. I bet you'll be ready to take a gamble when the time comes. I hope you will be, and I'll tell you you're going to come out a winner. I was more than a bit in love with your mother."

"Yes," I said. "I know that."

"I thought it would be nice rounding off if I married her and brought her back to her old home. I thought we'd have children and my name would be on that family tree in the hall. I couldn't see her in Australia though . . . not like I can you. She was more delicate, fragile-like. Well then Desmond came along. A handsome young fellow he was, with what I call the gift of gab. A bit of a rogue too. Oh yes, I've got to tell you the truth. He'd roamed the world a bit and learned a few tricks. He was dead serious about his Fancy though, and he'd got opal fever as bad as the rest of us. He was always one for the ladies, and when he came down here to stay for a while to persuade me to invest in the Fancy and we waited for David Croissant to join us, he took up with your mother and in his way he was in love with her. She was innocent and believed all he told her. He might have married her. I reckon he would have, but he couldn't, the way it turned out.

"I was mad with him . . . mad for his being young and

handsome and having his way with the women. Joss was here as I said before . . . home from school, agitating about not going back, and he was learning a lot about opals. That brings me to the night when I showed them the Green Flash. I saw the way it had got Desmond. He couldn't take his eyes from it. He picked it up, and I remember how his fingers curled round it. Desire! There's no other word for it. Mad, demanding desire . . . like thirst in the desert, like food to the starving. You look skeptical, Jessie. That's because you haven't experienced it. But I saw it and I knew what the result would be, so I was ready. When I went to bed that night I left my door open and I sat fully dressed listening. Then I heard the sound of creeping footsteps so I came down to the study.

"He was there at the safe. He had the Flash in his hands. I said: 'What are you doing, Desmond Dereham?' He just stared at me . . . white as these sheets. I said: 'You've seduced little Jessica Clavering and now you're trying to steal the Green Flash. And when you've got it what would you do? There's only one thing you could do. Get out of here . . . sharp . . . and leave her, eh. You'd desert her, wouldn't you, for the sake of the Green Flash? Do you know, I reckon you're not fit to live.' "

"Oh, Ben," I cried, "you killed my father!"

He shook his head. "No . . . no . . . not that. Though I had a gun in my hand and would have done it too. But I thought, No. I don't want this man's life on my hands. It's not worth it. So I said: 'I've caught you red-handed. You'll put that opal back in the safe where it belongs and you're going to get out of here fast. You'll never show your face here or at the Fancy, for if you do I'll expose you for the thief you are. Get out. Leave my house . . . now. I'll swear you've got your bags packed and are ready to leave.' Oh, I was mad with him. I can tell you what restraint I had to put on myself to prevent my pulling the trigger. That would have been silly . . . messy . . . and wouldn't have done me any good. So he put the opal back in the safe and I marched him back to his room. Sure enough, there were his bags . . . already packed. He planned to get the opal and clear out . . . like a thief in the night . . . which was what he was."

"So you sent him away . . . away from my mother."

"He would have been no good to her. He knew he'd have to keep out of the way if he'd got the Flash. He'd planned it all. He was going to take the opal and get out."

"My poor mother!"

"There'd been women in his life. Nothing had lasted. I knew this. I wanted him out of the way . . . for her sake. I didn't know you were on the way then. That could have been different."

"You said he had stolen the Green Flash."

"That's what I want to tell you. It was a pretense on my part. He'd gone . . . disappeared in the night. He wasn't coming back. He wouldn't dare face me, for I'd let it be known that he was a would-be thief. We're very rigid in Australia. We have to be. There's a rough-and-ready justice. We don't tolerate thieves and we don't tolerate murderers. We can't. There's too much to take care of. He was finished for the Fancy when I found him at the safe. He knew that and he had been ready to risk everything for the Green Flash. I thought then: I'll make people believe he's got the Green Flash, then no one would seek to rob *me* of it. No one would ill wish me with that certainty that misfortune was going to overtake me. I left soon after for Australia . . . taking the Green Flash with me."

"Does Joss know this?"

"He does now, because I've told him as I've told you. Believe me, Jessie, I'd have acted different if I'd known you were on the way. . . . You don't speak."

"I feel so shocked.'

"It's in the past. Your life is about to open out. You're going to be happy. You're going to have all your mother didn't have. I promise you you're going to find life a great adventure."

"I can't think of the future. I can't stop thinking of my mother."

"You've got to forget all that."

"I wonder where my father is."

"He'd fall on his feet . . . he always did."

"All those years you have allowed him to be suspected, and my poor mother. . . ."

"She should never have done what she did."

"She was driven to it."

"No, Jess, we're none of us driven. We act of our own free will, and if we find life too much to be borne, then clearly there's no one to blame but ourselves."

I turned my face away. I was going over it all, my father caught at the safe, Ben forcing him to get out. His belongings already packed, so he had meant to go with the Green

Flash . . . and leaving my poor little mother to bear me and then destroy herself.

Ben was caressing my hand.

"Don't think badly of me, Jessie," he said. "I'll not be here much longer you know. I couldn't bear there to be bitterness at the end. I'm a violent man. I've lived dangerously. I don't belong in a historic manor like this. I've had to fight throughout my life and it's made me hard and strong and ruthless. Perhaps I don't set so much store on morals as I should. In the Outback there were men who were ready to kill me for the Green Flash. Do you understand? Tell me you do understand."

"Yes, I do understand, Ben."

"And we've loved each other, haven't we? Didn't your life change when we met, and wasn't it for the better?"

"It did, and I love you, Ben."

"Then you'll have learned something. When you love it's not for rhyme nor reason. And whatever the loved one's done makes no difference . . . not to true love. I don't love you any less because I'm a wicked man on some days. I'm still the same old Ben, sentimental and loving where he gives his love, and when he gives it he gives it for good."

"It's true, Ben. I could never do anything but love you. I can't bear to think of your not being here. . . ."

"Never mind, never mind, because I'm not leaving your life empty. There's better coming into it than was ever there before. That's what I'm going to promise you if you'll listen to me, if you'll take my advice. There's a lot I know about human nature and that means I know you perhaps even better than you know yourself. I'm going to talk to you tomorrow. You've had enough for one day. You're a gambler, as I am, and you're going to have to gamble a bit with life. I always have. You wouldn't want to turn your face away from life. You wouldn't want to live out your days in that dismal old Dower House, would you?"

"Oh, Ben," I said, "I wish it hadn't been like that . . . about my father, I mean. And the Green Flash is still in your possession . . . with its ill luck. Is that why you had your accident? Is that why this is happening to you now?"

"That's what people would say, but I've never regretted having it. It's meant a lot to me. I used to go down in the dead of night and take it out and look at it . . . and I felt it was telling me 'Go on . . . enjoy your life. Never mind if you live dangerously. I'm yours and if you have to pay for having me, pay cheerfully.' "

"Does Joss know all this . . . about my father and mother?"

"He knows it all."

"And the Green Flash will be his when . . ."

"When I die. Oh, I've plans, and that's something the three of us are going to talk about tomorrow."

"Tell me now, Ben."

"Oh no. You've had enough to digest for one day, I reckon. You've got to be in the picture to see it all clearly. Don't fret, Jessie. I want my last weeks to be cheerful. There aren't many left to me."

"Please, Ben, *don't*."

"All right, I won't. Go home now and come back tomorrow afternoon. Then I'll tell you my plans, and don't worry, my dearest girl."

I left him then and went to the Dower House. I was very disturbed ; the revelations coming immediately after my meeting with Joss Madden had completely bewildered me.

As I went into the house my grandmother was in the hall arranging a bowl of flowers.

"Oh dear," she said, "it's so difficult here. How I miss the flower room we had at Oakland! By the way, I see your friend has a visitor staying there. He looked slightly superior to the mining type . . . almost a gentleman. He sits his horse like one."

I did not answer. I was too full of emotion to think of one of my retorts so I merely went quietly to my room.

I spent a sleepless night and fancied I looked a little haggard next day. Why this unaccustomed attention to my appearance? I asked myself; but I knew of course that it was due to that man. He had a way of assessing me, and there was something in his expression which I felt was shaming. I began to wonder about him, and remembered Ben's saying something about his being fond of women. I thought: I know the type—wondering whether every woman he meets is going to find him irresistible. He really is an odious character. But I was still too upset by Ben's confession to think very much about Joss Madden. I wished that he would not keep intruding into my thoughts when my desire was to keep him out.

When I arrived that afternoon, it was to find them awaiting me and I sensed an impatience in them both.

"Oh here you are at last," said Ben. "Now come and sit down."

He was in bed. I supposed the excitement of yesterday had exhausted him. He certainly looked less well, and I noticed the bluish tinge about his mouth.

"One on either side of me," he commanded, and as we sat there I saw those peacock-blue eyes on me and again I sensed that uncomfortable feeling Joss Madden's too close scrutiny aroused in me.

"Now, I'll start," said Ben. "I'm going to die very soon and I don't want to. There's so much I wanted to see before I went. One of my dearest dreams was to watch my grandchildren playing here on these lawns or those of Peacocks. You see, I never had any little ones around me. I was always too busy making a fortune, and then because it was not orthodox my children were never with me. Not until Joss came marching across the lawn with his suitcase . . . and he was never a little 'un. You were a giant for your age even then, Joss, and you talked like a man and acted like a man. So I was cheated out of babies. Joss, you never married and I used to fret about that . . . until I came here and met Miss Jessica Clavering. I've always had a feeling for the Claverings. I can't tell you how much I've wished I was one when I look at that family tree in the hall. It's grand to belong to a family like that. So what I want more than anything is to bring the families together. I want our blood mingled . . . that of the boy who sold gingerbread fancies in the Ratcliffe Highway and those who served kings in their historic battles . . . those who have been born to riches and those who had to fight their way to the top. I reckon there couldn't be a better combination for future generations."

I lifted my eyes and met that dark blue stare. What is he suggesting? I asked myself. Oh no, Ben, even you could not be so audacious as that. I tried to read what was in Joss Madden's eyes. He must be as horrified as I was.

"So that's why I want you two to be friends . . . more than friends. The plain fact is that more than anything I want to see you two marry. Don't fly into a rage, Jess. I know it's a shock. But you haven't heard it all. Joss will be a good husband . . . if you go along with his ways. And Jessica will be a good wife, Joss, if you're careful how you handle her."

I said hotly: "Please, Ben, let us have an end of this. I'm sure I could never go along with Mr. Madden's ways, nor would I agree to place myself in his careful handling."

"You see, Joss, our Jessie can fly into a temper pretty quick," said Ben. "But you won't mind that. You wouldn't want a mild and meek gentle little dove, would you?"

Joss did not reply. I imagined he was regarding me with the same horror I felt for him.

"Now I should have had time to condition you," went on Ben, "but time is running out for me. Who knows when the powers that be will come for me? Could be tomorrow. Could be the next day . . . or six months hence. All we can be sure of is that they're coming. Now I'd like the wedding to take place soon because I want to know it's done. Then I'll rest happy."

"You don't know what you're suggesting, Ben," I cried.

"Oh yes I do, my dear. I've been thinking of it for a very long time. As soon as I got to know you I said to myself: That's the one for Joss. That's the girl I want to bear my grandsons. I've thought of nothing else for weeks."

"Now, Ben," said Joss, "you see from Miss Clavering's horror that your little scheme will have to be abandoned."

For the first time I gave him a look of approval.

"Marriage is a bit of a gamble," said Ben. "Well, you've both got gamblers' blood in you. When you've considered everything involved, Jess, you'll fall in with my schemes. Joss is already halfway there."

"Not now," he replied, "not now that I see Miss Clavering's repugnance."

"Oh, proud . . . proud as a peacock! You always wanted others to do the running. You thought it was your right." He turned to me. "That's Joss for you. Now why are you both being so stubborn. Jessica's an attractive girl. Don't you think so, Joss? Now, Jessie, you've got to admit Joss is a fine figure of a man. You could search through England and Australia and where would you find a better mate? Be sensible, both of you. I tell you this is my dying request. You can't refuse me that, can you?"

"We can," said Joss. "Ben, you're outrageous."

"I know," he replied with a hoarse chuckle. "But I never wanted anything in my life so much as I want this. I can only die happy if I see you two married first. I just know it's right. I can see into the future."

I thought: He's mad. Surely the old Ben would never have talked like this.

"Now listen to me," he went on. "I've made all the arrangements. I'm leaving everything to you . . . except for a few minor legacies . . . that's if you're married."

"And if we aren't?" said Joss.

"My dear Joss, you get nothing . . . nothing."

"Now look here. . . ."

"You can't argue about a man's estate when he's on his deathbed," said Ben, and there were lights of mischief in his eyes. "You don't get a thing . . . either of you . . . unless you marry. That's plain fact. Joss, do you want to see the Company pass out of your hands?"

"You couldn't do that."

"You'll see. Jessica, do you want to spend your days in the Dower House with that virago of a grandmother . . . looking after her when she gets more fractious . . . or do you want a life of excitement and adventure? It's for you to choose. You're right, both of you, when you say I can't force you. I can't. But I can make it very uncomfortable for you if you don't do what I want."

We looked at each other across the bed.

"This is absurd," I began, but Joss Madden did not answer. I was aware that he was contemplating the loss of the Company. Ben had conjured up a picture for me too. I saw myself ten . . . twenty years hence, growing pinched about the lips just as Miriam had begun to look . . . decorating the church, taking baskets to the poor, growing old, growing sour because life had passed me by.

Ben knew what I was thinking. "It's a gamble," he said. "Don't forget that. What are you going to do?"

He lay back on his pillows and closed his eyes. I stood up and said I thought he was tired.

He nodded. "I've given you something to think about, haven't I?" He seemed full of secret amusement.

Joss Madden came with me to the door.

I said: "I'll go by the back way across the bridge and the stream."

"I'm afraid this has been a shock to you," he said.

"You are right," I answered. "How could it be otherwise?"

"I should have thought young ladies in your position often had husbands chosen for them."

"That does not make the position any more acceptable."

"I'm sorry I'm so repulsive to you. You have made that very clear."

"I don't think *you* showed any enthusiasm for the proposed marriage."

"I suppose we are both the sort of people who would want to choose for themselves."

"I think Ben must be losing his senses."

"He believes he's in full possession of them. You Claverings have cast a spell on him. It's those grand antecedents of yours with your ancestral home and so on. He wants your blue blood to be brought into his family."

"He will have to think of another way."

"I hardly think he can if you refuse to comply."

"You surely don't mean that *you* would?"

I had stopped short in my amazement and looked at him searchingly. His lips twisted into a wry smile. "There's a great deal at stake for me," he said.

I said shortly: "I'll leave you here. Good-by."

"*Au revoir*," he called after me as I sped across the grass.

I went back to the Dower House in a kind of daze. As I came into the hall the familiar smell of lemon wax struck me forcibly, although I should have become accustomed to it after all these years because it was always there. My grandmother used to say that even though we had come down in the world we must show people that we had not given up our standards and there was no excuse for even the most humble dwelling not to be spotlessly clean. There was a bowl of flowers in the hall—lilacs and tulips arranged by my grandmother neatly and without artistry. I could hear voices in the drawing room—those of my grandmother and Xavier, and I wondered whether my grandfather was there in his usual role of penitent. I paused for a moment and contemplated the confusion which would result if I opened the door and announced that I had had a proposal of marriage and would in due course be leaving for Australia. That would scarcely be true, for I could hardly call it a proposal since the intended bridegroom was more reluctant than prospective. It then occurred to me how deeply I should have enjoyed confronting them with such news.

I went to my room—a pleasant little one with a picture of one of our ancestors on the wall. She had once graced the gallery at Oakland. My grandmother had been hard put to it to find suitable spots in which to accommodate all the pictures in the Dower House. With a characteristic desire to improve us all, she had distributed ancestors with considerable judgment. I had Margaret Clavering, circa 1669, a handsome young woman with a hint of mischief in her eyes. I had never heard exactly what she did, but I knew that it was something shocking, something to make even my grandmother's lips twitch with amusement. Her misdemeanor must therefore have been committed in high places—I suspected the King himself was involved as indeed he was with so many. Even so, poor Margaret did come to an untimely end when she was thrown from her horse while escaping with a lover from one of her husbands—she had apparently had many of the former and three of the latter.

In my grandfather's room gamblers looked down from the walls. I always thought they were a jolly-looking crowd, all those wastrel Claverings, and might prove an inducement rather than a deterrent; and they certainly looked nicer to know than the virtuous savior of our fortune from the eighteenth century who looked down primly, and I am sure approvingly, on my grandmother.

The four-poster bed was a little overpowering for my small room; and there was one chair with the tapestry seat and back worked by another ancestress, and its fellows were distributed around the house. There was also a beautiful Bokara rug—another relic of Oakland. I saw all these articles with greater clarity it seemed than ever before. I suppose because Ben had suggested that if I were wise I should soon be leaving them and if I were not I might be with them for the rest of my life.

I couldn't stay long in my room. There was one to whom I could talk, though the idea of doing so a few months ago would have been out of the question. Miriam!

I ran out of the house and went along to Church Cottage— the name of the tiny house at one end of the vicarage grounds. It looked quite pretty, I thought, with the shrubs on either side of the crazy paving path which led to the front door.

Miriam was at home. How she had changed! She looked several years younger, and there was a new dignity about her. I did not need to ask if she was happy.

I stepped straight into the living room; there was only a kitchen and this room on the lower floor and from this living room a staircase twisted up into two bedrooms above. Everything was highly polished and a bowl of azaleas and green leaves stood on the red tablecloth; there were chintz curtains at the window and another bowl of flowers on the hearth on either side of which were two chimney seats. One or two of Miriam's possessions—brass candlesticks and silver ornaments —looked rather incongruous, but charming, in this humble room.

Miriam's hair was dressed in a less severe style than she had worn it before, and she looked very domesticated in her starched print gown as she carried a duster in her hand.

"Oh Miriam," I cried, "I had to see you. I wanted to talk."

That she was pleased, there was no doubt. "I'll make some tea," she said. "Ernest is out. The vicar works him too hard."

I put my head on one side and studied her. "You're a joy to behold," I said. "You make a splendid case for the married state." It was true. How she had changed! She was indulgent, in love with her curate and with life; and the fact that she had turned her back on this blissful state for so long only made her appreciate it more now that she had achieved it.

"I've had a proposal," I blurted out. "Well, a sort of proposal."

Little lights of fear showed in her eyes. "Not . . . someone at Oakland?"

"Yes."

"Oh, Jessica!" Now she looked like the old Miriam, for my words had transported her back in time to that other occasion when another Jessica had had a proposal from a visitor to Oakland. "Are you sure. . . ."

"No," I said. "I'm not."

She looked relieved. "I should be very careful."

"I intend to be. Miriam, suppose you hadn't married Ernest . . . suppose you had gone on as you were. . . ."

I saw the look of horror in her face. "I couldn't bear to think of that," she said firmly.

"Yet you hesitated so long."

"I think it was a matter of plucking up courage."

"And even if it hadn't worked out so well with Ernest would you still be glad you left?"

"How could it possibly *not* have turned out well with Ernest?"

"You didn't always think that, did you, or you would have done it before."

"I was afraid. . . ."

"Afraid of your mother's sneers and prophecies. They don't worry you now."

"I don't care how poor we are . . . and we can manage. I've discovered I'm a good manager. Ernest says so. And even if things hadn't turned out so well, to tell the truth, Jessica, I should have been glad to get away from the Dower House."

"Who wouldn't?" I thought of living there for years and years without the compensation of going to Oakland to see Ben, and I knew I couldn't face it. Rather . . . oh no . . . not marriage with that man . . . and yet I wanted to contemplate it. What would it be like? It would be a marriage of convenience if ever there was one. Perhaps we could come to terms. Perhaps we could do it for Ben's sake and lead our own lives.

I began to tingle with excitement. I knew I could not face dreary years at the Dower House.

"But let's talk about you," said Miriam. "What about this man?"

"He's Ben Henniker's son and he's come over from Australia."

"You can't have known him very long."

"One does not have to know people all one's life . . . just because you and Ernest did."

"But then you can be so much more sure."

"Perhaps it's more exciting not to be."

"Whatever do you mean? Oh, Jessica, you are headstrong. You're like your mother, but she had a more gentle nature."

"Miriam, I can't stay forever in that miserable Dower House listening to Grandmother's saying the litany ten times a day: 'We've seen better days, O Lord, don't You forget it. Look down on this miserable husband of mine who brought us to this and never let him forget it because I'm not going to.' "

"You can be very irreverent, Jessica."

"Perhaps, but what I say is true. I don't want to be a prisoner all my life as you were for so much of yours. This proposal is a secret as yet so don't mention it."

"I shall have to tell Ernest. We never have any secrets. He might consider it his duty. . . ."

"Let him remember how Grandmother kept you apart all those years. This is my secret and I expect it to be kept.

I've only told you because I wanted to talk about marriage, and I've not made up my mind yet. I thought you'd understand."

"Oh, I do, and I think that if you really love each other you shouldn't hesitate. I do wonder what Mother will say."

"She is my least concern. You were scared of her all those years. I wouldn't be. But you took the plunge eventually. You snapped your fingers at your mother who had been keeping you and Ernest apart all those years and now you're glad."

"Yes, I'm glad," said Miriam fervently.

She was thoughtful for a while, swaying in her opinions. The same old Miriam! Much would depend on what Ernest thought, for he was the rock on which she rested now, and she would change her color—chameleon that she was— according to his views.

She went to a cupboard and brought out a bottle of wine— her own make, which she had brought from the Dower House. She had always been proud of the wines which she had made in the still room. My grandmother had said: "You'd better learn to be useful about the house, for soon we shall have no servants." Miriam had busied herself, and how glad she was of that now!

"We'll drink to your future," she said. "This is more suitable than tea."

So as we sat at the table and drank to my future and hers, I was wondering why I had talked to Miriam as though I were actually contemplating marriage.

I scarcely slept that night. Next morning at prayers I did not listen to my grandmother's voice but said my own personal prayer, which was a call for help, and I thought ironically that I had never prayed so fervently before and that it was only when I wanted something that I really prayed at all.

After breakfast I performed the tasks my grandmother had set for me, since she insisted that I too learn to manage a house. So I helped Maddy bring in the early lettuces from the kitchen garden and clean the preserving jars for the fruit which would, in due course, be bottled or made into preserves later in the season.

Her sharp eyes had detected that something had happened.

"You're up to something," she said. "You're not here . . . no, you're not. You're miles away. What's brewing, Miss?"

"I'm no longer a child," I retorted. "I think you sometimes forget that. I have a perfect right to be preoccupied with matters outside the trivial preparation of bottles to receive the fruits of autumn."

"Hoity toity," she replied. "You've not been the same since you've been on visiting terms at Oakland. And I'm sure I wonder why it's allowed."

"As long as you keep your opinions to yourself, Maddy, it is of no consequence."

"Talk about giving yourself airs. . . ."

"That will be all for this morning," I said with dignity.

Immediately after luncheon I went to the stream. The world seemed to have turned upside down. Ben, whom I so dearly loved, had lied about my father. How could I reconcile myself to that . . . and yet how could I stop myself loving Ben and feeling miserable because I feared he would not be with us much longer? And now he had come along with a proposition which he knew was repugnant to me and to Joss, whom he so clearly loved—adored might be a more apt word. I just could not understand him. The alarming fact was that I did not understand myself, because, somewhere at the back of my mind, I was assessing the situation. I was actually considering the possibility of making this marriage.

As I sat there, I saw Joss Madden emerge from the copse and come towards me.

"I saw you from the turret," he said. "I thought it would be a good idea to have a talk. Come over."

It seemed to me that it would be more convenient to be on the Oakland side of the stream than on that of the Dower House, where I could be seen by someone from the house, so I obeyed.

As we walked across the grass and into the copse he said: "Have you decided?"

"It's an impossible situation," I cried.

"It exists and therefore can't be impossible. On the other hand it's a straightforward proposition."

"Have *you* made up your mind?" I asked.

"Yes, I'm ready to go ahead."

"You mean . . . you would marry me?"

"That was the proposition I thought. Oh come, don't look so mournful. You won't be going to your execution, you know."

"It feels rather like that."

He gave that loud, explosive laugh. Then he was serious. "I'm afraid Ben won't live much longer. He was very weak this morning. And he wants the ceremony to take place before he dies."

"That could be . . . soon."

"Once you've agreed there'll be no reason for delay."

We came to a tree trunk, and he took my hand and pulled me down to sit beside him. He dropped my hand immediately but I was very much aware of him. I felt an excitement which I could not suppress.

"I gather," he said, "that you had no one else in mind?"

"In mind?"

"Let's talk plain English. You haven't a lover . . . you weren't contemplating marriage with someone else?"

"No."

"Then it's fairly straightforward. I could get a special license, I think . . . in view of Ben's illness. We could be married very shortly."

I replied: "What of you? Were you contemplating marrying someone else?"

"I was not," he said.

"You seem to take all this in your stride."

"How else could I take it? I see what Ben feels. He had a fixation on your mother. It was not only herself . . . it was all this . . . the stately mansion, the family tracing itself back to the Conqueror . . . and he wants the families linked. He has the house, but he hasn't got the blood. If you and I married, our offspring would have a modicum of the blue-blooded variety through you, and with the generations to come the family could be rather proud of itself." He laughed cynically.

I was scarcely listening because I had been caught up in what he had said about offspring. That was too much.

I said sharply: "I'm afraid I never could."

He looked straight at me, and it was as though he were probing my innermost thoughts. I felt very uncomfortable, because I knew that he understood what had alarmed me.

"There's a great deal at stake," he said. "Ben means what he says. I know him well. He's set on this and he knows that the only way he could get us married at such short notice is to threaten what will happen to us if we don't. He can be ruthless, our Ben."

"I know that."

"He's told me a great deal about you. That family of yours . . . your life here . . . how stultifying it is. He's sentencing you for life to the Dower House unless you marry me. The devil or the deep blue sea. That's your choice. And for me: The loss of command of the Company which I have helped to build up as surely as Ben has. I have some shares in it, but Ben has the major holding, and he's threatening to pass them to someone else. It would mean if I stayed with the Company I'd be there in a minor capacity. He knows very well I never would. So he has netted me. He knows I'd accept anything rather. . . ."

"Even me?"

"Even marriage. Which for thirty-two years I have successfully eluded."

"So there have been those who have angled for you?"

"Countless numbers."

"Perhaps they came in time to regard their lack of success as good fortune."

"They wouldn't realize that. The lost prize is always more desirable than that which is won. Did you know that?"

"I don't believe it's true—but that's beside the point."

"You're quite right. We don't want to be sidetracked into frivolous discussion when there is something so much more important to occupy us. We are both faced with a dilemma. If we marry we benefit considerably. We both have a great deal to lose if we don't. I know what it will mean to me. You must have realized that too."

I was contemplating going back to the old life before I had known Ben—older now, knowing a little more of how exciting life could be, and I knew I should hate it.

"So," he went on, "I've made up my mind. I'll marry you immediately, so all you have to do is say you'll marry me."

He put an arm about my shoulders, and I drew back in dismay. Again he gave that brief laugh.

"All right," he said. "I'll make it easy for you. We'll marry and it'll be, as they say, a Marriage in Name Only. That's until both parties want it otherwise. What about that?"

I was silent, and he went on: "I sense your relief."

I said: "Ben may not agree to those terms."

"They would be a matter for us to decide surely."

"I'm not sure. It's grandchildren he wants."

"He can't have it all his own way. Listen to me. We'll

marry and go our own ways. You will escape from the Dower House, and I shall have the full command of the Company. Now you must admit that does seem a way out."

I stood up suddenly. He did the same, towering above me. There was an amused twitch to his lips as he laid his hands on my shoulders.

"Negotiations seem to be progressing favorably," he said. "Shall we go and tell Ben?"

"Not yet. I'm undecided."

"All right. But don't delay too long. At least it's just a matter of indecision and not a blank refusal."

I turned and left him, going back over the stream to the Dower House.

I went to see Ben. I was glad that he was alone. He looked a little better and I commented on this.

"Yes, I'm determined to live until I see you two married. Tell me, Jess, have you thought any more about it?"

"I have thought a great deal."

"Of course you have. You're going to wake up and live now. You'll have to keep your eyes on Joss. He's a favorite with the women."

"It's too much to ask, Ben."

"Now then, are you going back to the Dower House life? I'd rather go to the penitentiary, that I would. That grandmother of yours . . . she's like vinegar now. What'll she be like in ten years' time . . . gall, bitter aloes. . . . She's not like a wine that'll improve with age. You'll love the excitement of it. The Company . . . Fancy Town. . . . It's in your blood. You'll come back here to Oakland now and then. . . . It'll be a wonderful life."

I was silent, and he went on: "Look, Jess, you've got to grow up . . . if you're going out there. Life's lived in the raw there. But it's life. That's the great thing. I can see you at Peacocks. Has Joss talked to you of Peacocks?" I shook my head. "He will. He loves the place. This will be yours, too. Just think of that. When you come to England you'll be the lady of the manor. I wonder what the old lady of the Dower House is going to say to that! I'd like to see her face . . . that I would. Just think of your little 'uns . . . playing on these lawns, in the copse, just as you would have done if you'd had your right."

"There's one thing I have to tell you, Ben. If I did marry him, I couldn't. . . . I couldn't live with him as his wife, and that means that your idea of the little ones on the lawn would simply not be possible. I'm sure that in these circumstances the whole thing falls through."

I had expected dismay, but there was nothing of the sort. Ben laughed so much that I feared he would exhaust himself.

"You know, Jessie," he said when he had recovered from his laughter, "you're enlivening my last days, you are. You never fail to please me. So you've made up your mind to marry him, have you?"

"I didn't say that. I've just told you why it's impossible."

"Listen. I want you two married. I knew Joss would agree. There was too much to lose. I could rely on the pride of my peacock. As to the other little matter, well, I'm ready to leave that to Joss."

"What do you mean by that?"

"Ah, danger signals! I'll leave it like this. I'll see you married, and I'll die hoping that one day you two are going to see what's staring you in the face and that is that you were meant for each other. It's the looker-on that sees the best of the game, and I'm a very observant looker-on. I've lived every minute of the days God gave me. I'm like a cat that's had nine lives. I'm coming to the end of my ninth now, but I've picked up a lot in those lives and I know what I am talking about. So it's settled, is it? I accept your terms and you'll accept mine. I want a nice wedding in the church . . . so that everyone knows."

"That will take a little time."

"I reckon I've got that little time left to me. I just won't go until I've seen you and my boy Joss joined together in holy matrimony."

"Ben," I said, "if you love us, how can you ask so much of us?"

"It's just because I do love you both that I'm making this bargain. Years ahead when you and the family are visiting England and you're sitting on those lawns, the like of which you don't see outside this green land, there'll be the shade of old Ben looking on with contentment because it's all come about as he meant it to. I'll be here . . . and I'll be at Peacocks . . . a happy ghost who saw what should be and did his little bit to make it come about."

"You're tired, Ben," I said.

"Happy tired. A good sort of tired to be. And don't forget, in years to come, remember me."

"I'm never going to forget you."

"And you'll be grateful to old Ben, I promise you."

I kissed him gently and slipped away.

I knew as I went out of Oakland Hall that I was about to burn my boats. I had accepted this incongruous situation. I was going to marry Joss Madden.

I don't know what Joss said to my grandmother. He was in the drawing room with her, my grandfather, and Xavier for an hour. From my bedroom window I saw him stride across the lawn to the bridge. He walked as though the place already belonged to him.

Maddy was knocking at my door. They wanted to see me in the drawing room, she said.

As I entered I was aware of the change in their attitude towards me. I had become important, but my grandmother was not going to show me her gratification too readily.

"So," she began, "you have clandestinely been meeting this man from the wilds."

"If you mean Mr. Josslyn Madden, it is true I have been meeting him."

"And become engaged to him! He did not ask our consent before asking you, which would have been the proper thing to do. But I suppose we cannot expect good manners from people brought up as he must have been."

"He has been educated in England."

She grudgingly admitted that she realized this saving grace.

"Of course after all we have done for you we might have expected a little gratitude. When our terrible tragedy was brought upon us"—she sent a venomous look towards my grandfather, who nodded in a rather jaunty way, I fancied—"we had to prepare ourselves for our great sacrifice. Our daughter disgraced us, and now Miriam has committed herself to a life of penury."

"I always thought she endured that here."

"Compared with what she was accustomed to before our fortune was wantonly thrown away, Miriam once lived in grace and dignity with her family." She laughed. "Now this cottage. I believe she scrubs the floors." She shivered. "No matter. Don't let us distress ourselves by even mentioning Miriam's folly. The fact is that you should have kept me informed. After all we did for you, giving you a home. . . ."

"And selling the silver salver and the George IV punch bowl."

She smiled—very rare with her and this was an indication of her true feelings. "At least you have spared us the humiliation of seeing you scrub floors and living in abject poverty. I only hope this offer is genuine. You will not, I hope, inconvenience us as your mother did. If it is genuine, all may not turn out too badly. But I must let you know that I am displeased that you should associate with people who have been no friends to your grandfather. However, I can see the hand of fate in this. We have suffered great misfortune. We lost Oakland . . . and if this man is telling the truth, he will in due course inherit the Hall in which case you as his wife will live there."

I thought she was like an eagle about to pounce on its prey. Oakland Hall coming back to the family . . . and through me!

I couldn't help being thrilled that I was doing this. I knew then that if a way out was offered me, if Ben said he had been joking after all, I wouldn't want to take it. The extraordinary fact was borne home that I wanted the excitement of marrying Joss Madden—providing of course that we kept to that all-important clause which he had laughingly acknowledged he would respect and which Ben had thrust aside as though he did not believe it was important.

Xavier spoke then. "Mr. Madden has told us that he has asked you to marry him and that you have accepted. We understand he is Mr. Henniker's heir and that Oakland as well as property in Australia will pass to him. They ask for no dowry for you, but Mr. Henniker will make a settlement on you of Blueberry Farm, which as you know went to him with the Oakland estate. The management of this will be left to me, so it is in a measure as though the land has been returned to us. It seems to be a very satisfactory arrangement."

My grandfather's eyes looked watery. "It's almost like Oakland coming back to us through you, Jessica," he said.

My grandmother would not be left out of the conversation.

"In spite of your deception, this seems to have turned out better than we could have expected," she said. "I hope your children will be born here. Perhaps we could get Mr. Madden to change his name to Clavering. That has been done before in the family."

"I know that would be quite impossible."

My grandmother waved the matter aside as though that was something she would deal with later.

"We must be practical," she went on. "It must be a wedding worthy of the old days before we were reduced to this. I think we should sell the silver candlesticks so that we can do everything as it should be done. As you know the candlesticks were given by William IV to Jeremy Clavering in 1832, and they are worth a great deal."

"Then please don't sell them on my account."

"It is not on your account but for the good name of the family. Oh dear, how I wish you could be married from Oakland itself."

"Never mind, Mother," said Xavier, "perhaps Jessica's daughter will be."

"Pray let us get her married first before we mention such things," said my grandmother, forgetting that a moment before she had done so. I had never seen her look so pleased, and the knowledge that it was due to me seemed very ironical.

The next Sunday, Ernest, officiating for Rev. Jasper Crey, read out the banns.

Ben seemed to recover quite a bit. It was obvious that he was delighted, and his pleasure seemed to give him a new energy.

"So they read the banns," he cried. "So there was no opposition from the family. I should think not! See what this means to them."

My grandmother had engaged a dressmaker and I was to have a white satin wedding gown—the best possible satin from Liberty. My grandmother made a journey up to London to buy that and other materials on the proceeds from the silver candlesticks.

"I hope William IV won't haunt you in his displeasure," I commented.

"You are much too flippant," was her retort. "You always were. You will have to be more sober when you marry."

"I can't change my nature, Grandmother," I said.

She sighed, but even she could not criticize me too much, considering the change I had brought about in the family fortunes.

I stood for hours while the seamstress, her mouth full of pins, fitted my dresses, for I had to have a trousseau besides the wedding dress. "We don't want people in Australia to think we're savages," said my grandmother. She was determined that I should go not only adequately but elegantly clothed.

The banns had been called twice and the excitement at the prospect was beginning to be replaced by apprehension. Joss Madden had to spend a week in London negotiating some business, and I felt easier in my mind when he was not there.

When he returned, however, he seemed determined to spend a good deal of time with me. "Doing his courting," as Ben described it to my chagrin.

Joss said: "We'd better get to know each other, as this wedding is imminent. How good are you on a horse? You'll have to ride a good deal in Australia."

I said that I had been taught to ride but had little opportunity of doing so. There had been a pony, but when that died it had not been replaced. We only had one horse now, which Xavier used.

"There's a small stable at Oakland," he said, "I'll take you riding. I want to see what you can do."

I immediately felt resentful, objecting to his patronizing manner.

He chose my mount, a brown horse with a frisky look in his eyes which made me somewhat apprehensive. Our pony had been of about thirteen hands, and I had never ridden a better steed.

I was about to protest when I caught his eyes on me—amused, a little triumphant, so superior and arrogant—every inch the peacock.

I mounted uneasily. He said: "These horses need exercise. They're too fat. Riding here is different from riding in Australia. You'll have to get used to the difference because you're lost without a horse in the Bush."

"Is this house Peacocks in the Bush then?"

"It's in its own grounds and Fancy Town is about two miles away. Surrounding all this is some pretty wild country. You'll need to feel as much at home in the saddle as you do on your own two feet."

My equestrian knowledge was not great, but it was obvious even to me that he chose the finest horse in the stable for himself. As we walked our horses side by side I could feel his eyes on me appraisingly—my posture, my hands, my heels, everything . . . and that smile which I hated played about his lips.

"In other words," he was saying, "you could loosely say that we`live in the saddle."

"Have you a good stable at Peacocks?"

"It would be hard to find a better in Australia."

"Naturally," I commented.

"Oh yes, naturally."

"So you ride everywhere?"

"Yes, everywhere. There are Cobb's coaches which ply between the big cities. I rarely use them. You'll find the country different out there, I can tell you."

"I expected to."

"This . . . why, it's like a garden. You don't go far without some sort of habitation. And these little fields and roads . . . oh, it's very different."

"So you have said more than once."

"Then I must apologize for repeating myself."

"A common fault," I said lightly, to remind him that he was not without them, which I was sure he imagined himself to be.

He broke into a canter, and I tried to follow him, but my horse refused. Instead he lowered his head suddenly and gripped a bush by the roadside.

"Come on," I whispered urgently. "He'll laugh at us."

But the horse seemed determined to mock me too.

Joss Madden turned and I heard that quick gust of laughter. "Come on, Joker," he said, and the response was immediate. The sly Joker immediately relinquished the bush and went on with an injured air as though to say: What can you expect me to do with this amateur on my back?

"You have to *control* your horse, you know," said Joss, smiling, well pleased with Joker's co-operation.

"I'm very well aware of that," I retorted.

"He knows who's the master. You see, I only had to call his name and he obeyed."

"I've never *seen* this horse before," I protested.

"He's a little mischievous when he thinks he can get away with it. It's understandable. Now, Joker, no more nonsense. You'll do what the lady tells you. Come on."

I hated that morning because I sensed that he was trying to show me how inferior I was. He proved that to me more than once. There was one occasion when he galloped across a meadow and called Joker to follow. I thought he was hoping I'd fall and break my neck. It was maddening that he should be commanding my horse, and when it sped after him I knew that I couldn't control it and the thought came into my mind: He's trying to kill me so that he won't have to marry me. If I'm dead Ben won't cut him out. He'll get the precious Company without having to pay the price—marriage—for it. Oh, he is so arrogant. He's nothing more than a peacock . . . flaunting his superiority as a peacock flaunts its tail.

He was beside me suddenly. He had seized my bridle and for a few moments we galloped side by side. When we stopped he was laughing at me.

"I'll have to teach you to ride," he said, "and I'll do so before we leave. You can't go out to Australia like this."

"Don't you think it would be a good idea if we abandoned the whole thing?" I asked.

"What! With the dress being made, the banns being called. . . ." He was serious suddenly. "Besides, what of Ben?"

"I hate it all," I said vehemently.

"You mean you hate me?"

"You can look at it that way if you like."

"A firm basis on which to build a marriage," he mocked. "Feelings often change, they say, afterwards, so at least yours can't change for the worse since they are as bad as they can possibly be before."

"Isn't the whole thing rather farcical?"

"Life often is rather farcical."

"Rarely as much as this ridiculous wedding."

"Don't you think it makes it rather piquant? You and I will go to church and take our vows and everything we vow to do we shall be promising ourselves not to do. Marriage is for the procreation of children. That comes in the service. But for us . . . marriage in name only."

"Your expression," I said.

"It's a good one. It conveys the meaning as well as anything could. To love and to cherish, we shall say, and here are you telling me you hate me."

"You're giving very adequate reasons why the whole thing should be called off."

"But we're not going to, are we? We're two sensible people—don't you agree? There's too much to gain and too much to lose. We're better off making the best of it. Who knows, I might succeed in making a tolerable horsewoman of you and you might succeed in keeping me at a distance." His eyes glittered suddenly, and I saw the pride there which I was beginning to think was his main characteristic. He was put out because I was not attracted by his virility . . . or masculinity . . . whatever it was. "Let me say," he said with a hint of anger in his voice, "I think the latter will be easier to achieve than the former."

We walked our horses back to Oakland—a pace, he commented dryly, more suited to my accomplishments.

I certainly hated him, and he appeared to despise me. Well, there was no need to fret about that, for I should not have to worry about his forcing his attentions on me; and because he had made this so obvious I began, perversely, to hope that he might—solely that I could have the pleasure of rebuffing him.

The servants were excited about the wedding. Miriam was making the wedding cake; my grandmother continued to be slightly benign towards me and my grandfather regarded me as the savior of the family fortunes. Ben would lie in his bed or sit in his chair chuckling to himself. It was certainly a popular wedding—with everyone except the bride and groom!

Twice a day Joss insisted that I ride with him.

"It's a necessity," he said. "You must know how to master a horse before you get to Australia."

I saw the wisdom of this and decided to put up with his patronizing attitude. I worked hard, and I was sure that I was an apt pupil. Not that he would admit when I showed improvement. He seemed to enjoy humiliating me.

Once skilled, I promised myself, I should be independent of him, and I was really beginning to enjoy riding as I never had before. He never complimented me; and I inwardly accused him of showing off. To myself I always referred to him as Peacock.

At last my wedding day arrived. It was like a dream, standing there at the altar while the Rev. Jasper Crey married us. I felt a shiver of emotion as Joss slipped the ring on my finger and I couldn't quite define it. Apprehension was certainly there, but if I was honest with myself I would have to admit that if I could have canceled it, I shouldn't have wanted to.

Ben was in the church. Banker had wheeled him there. I could imagine his contentment. His will had been done.

Miriam at the organ played the Wedding March, and as I came up the aisle later on the arm of Joss Madden, aware of those watching us—Xavier, my grandfather and grandmother—gleams of contentment in their eyes, I remembered my grandmother's saying that God had brought Oakland Hall back to the family because of all they had done for me. It was His reward for their virtue.

We went to the Dower House, where the reception was held, and when it was over Joss and I walked across the bridge to Oakland Hall.

Ben was in his bedroom, but he had left word that he wanted to see us as soon as we came in. He was sitting up in bed and his eyes were shining.

"You two have made Ben Henniker a very happy man today," he said. "Come and sit on either side of me. There, that's good. Give me your hands. You're going to bless me for this day. Before it's over there's something I want to say to you and I've been saving it up till now."

"You're exhausted, Ben," I said. "You should rest."

"Not till I've told you this. You know the story of the Green Flash. You know how I took it to Australia with me all the time, pretending it was lost. I had to have a hiding place for it. You're the only two who'll know where that hiding place is. It belongs to you both now. Now this hiding place . . . I made it myself . . . so that no one else should be in the picture. Ha, that's a joke. You know 'The Pride of the Peacock' in the drawing room, Joss. It was always a favorite of yours. It's a picture, Jessie, of our lawn, and there's a magnificent peacock on it, looking as a peacock does. Look-at-me attitude. Don't you think I'm the most wonderful creature in the world? This picture is set in a beautiful frame . . . carved wood and gilt. It's a thick frame . . . a very thick frame. At the right-hand corner of the frame, there's a spring catch. No one would know it was there. It's so cunningly placed. You touch the spring and the back opens like a door. There's a cavity there and wrapped up in cotton wool is the Green Flash. I've locked myself in that room many a time and I've taken it out and gloated over it. Well, that stone is yours when I die . . . yours jointly. It'll be up to you to do what you like with it."

He was getting too excited. I felt alarmed for him, so I

said soothingly: "Thank you, Ben. Now you must please rest. Everything is settled now."

He nodded. Joss pressed his hand and for a moment or two they looked steadily at each other. Then I bent over and kissed him.

"Bless you both," he said; and we went out.

The bridal suite had been prepared for us. Apparently Oakland brides had used it through the ages.

I was apprehensive when I entered it. Joss shut the door behind him. He stood leaning against it looking at me mockingly.

"They tell me that all the future mistresses of Oakland Hall spend their first night of marriage in this room," he said.

I glanced quickly at the four-poster bed. He followed my gaze and I knew he was amused.

"This is a rather different case," I said.

"One's own case always is," he replied. He walked across the room. "Here's the dressing room. Shall I occupy it or will you?"

"Since you say it is a tradition of Oakland brides to occupy this bed I will do so. The dressing room can be yours. It will be quite comfortable, I dare say."

"A nice wifely concern for her husband's comfort is always to be admired," he said.

"So . . . good night."

He took my hand and kissed it, and when he did not immediately relinquish it I felt afraid.

"I trust you are a man of your word," I said.

He shook his head slightly. "It would be unwise to trust me too far."

I snatched my hand away.

"But," he went on, "have no fear. I would never force myself where I am so clearly not wanted."

"Then I will repeat Good night."

"Good night," he said.

He walked to the communicating door.

When it shut behind him I ran to it and to my dismay saw that there was no key. As I stood there the door opened. He was there with the key in his hand. He gave it to me with a bow.

"You will want to feel safe," he said.

I took the key and locked the door. I *was* safe.

Two weeks after the wedding Ben took a decided turn for the worse. It was as though he had made up his mind that as his mission was accomplished he was ready to go.

We were with him constantly. He talked a good deal about Peacocks and how he would be there with us in spirit.

"Remember me, Jessie," he said, "and particularly remember that everything I wanted was for your happiness . . . yours and Joss's. You're going to see that one day. I always knew it. You don't like plans being made for you. Sometimes though you can't see the woods for the trees and that's how it is with you two just now. It'll change. I'd like to see you together; I'd like to hear you sparring. You were meant for each other. And now you're man and wife. God bless you both."

Joss and I rode together each day. I both dreaded and enjoyed the lessons. I knew I had improved and Joker would not now dare refuse to come when I ordered him to.

They were long days of waiting, and with the passing of each one it became clear that Ben could not be long with us.

He died in his sleep. Hannah called me, and I went to his bed and was struck by the utter peace of his face. It was almost as though he were smiling at me. I kissed his cold brow and went away.

We buried him in the churchyard not far from the Clavering section. It was what he would have wanted. Joss and I stood side by side at the graveside, and as I listened to the clods of earth falling on his coffin I knew that was the end of a phase.

My new life was about to begin.

There were solicitors to be seen. I had begun to wonder whether Ben had played a trick on us and had not changed his will at all with the new conditions. I was wrong. It was precisely what he had done.

Joss and I were joint owners of Oakland and the house in Australia known as Peacocks. I was given a good share of Ben's holding in the Opal Mining Company, and Joss was given another to match mine. There were other legacies to people including the Laud family, his housekeeper and her children, and the opal known as the Green Flash at Sunset was left to Joss and me jointly.

It seemed as though Ben was determined that we should be together. This bequest depended on our marriage, and if it had not taken place at the time of his death it must do so immediately afterwards, and on its taking place the properties would be ours. We were to be given a year, and if we had not married at the end of that time the shares and the houses and the Green Flash opal would be in trust for the Laud family.

"There is no need for us to consider this," said Mr. Venning, "for the marriage has already taken place before his death, so I may congratulate you both."

During the next weeks preparations were made for our departure. Miriam was frankly delighted that it had all gone so smoothly. Ernest thought I was doing the right thing and therefore she did. She was an expert at tatting and gave me some exquisite mats for a wedding present.

Xavier wished me happiness. "Weddings are infectious," he said; and I wondered whether that meant he and Lady Clara might at last come to an understanding.

My grandmother tried to hide her gratification by faintly amused skepticism right until the wedding was over; now and then she would shoot the occasional barb and refer to life in the wilds and comment that some people had strange tastes and like fools rushed in where angels feared to tread. When people had perfectly good homes in civilized surroundings she could not understand why they must go dashing off to the other side of the globe. How much more satisfactory it would have been if I had stayed at Oakland and entertained in a manner to which the old house was accustomed. I knew that she sometimes mentioned me at prayers, commanding God to look after me and not to punish me too severely for my thoughtlessness in leaving Oakland, when it would have been so much more pleasant for the family if I stayed, in a manner which in fact admonished Him not to be too slow in bringing me to my senses.

I could laugh more than ever. I was free of her.

Joss went to London on business and I was alone for some time. It was strange sleeping in the big four-poster bed in Oakland Hall, the mistress of it all.

Wilmot was delighted. So were the other servants.

It was right and proper, Wilmot told her, according to Hannah. "Now Claverings would be back at Oakland Hall."

I rode every day, determined to improve; and when Joss returned he said we would be leaving England very soon.

Banker went back soon after the funeral. He was going to settle in Melbourne, he said. It was October before Joss and I sailed for Sydney.

5

Outward Bound

It was a golden autumn day when we embarked on the *Hermes*, which was to take us to the other side of the world. I quickly realized that Joss was a person of some importance and was known, as Ben had been, to the captain and a number of the crew. He told me that when the ship docked in Sydney they were often entertained there by some members of the Company and this meant that innumerable little concessions were granted to us.

"One of these," said Joss, "is being provided with single cabins which they think is rather unorthodox in a newly married pair, but I am sure you will feel exceedingly grateful for that."

"I do."

It was quite adequate, that cabin; and Joss's was next to it. I was thankful for the partition which divided us.

The weather was rough at first, but I was delighted to find that I was a good sailor. He was, of course! I should have hated to have given him an advantage over me in that respect.

There was little to do on board except sleep, eat, talk, and study our fellow passengers. Naturally Joss and I must spend a good deal of time together. He talked then about the Company and life in Australia and I had to admit that I found it enthralling.

We breakfasted at nine and dined at twelve. On one particular occasion the ship was rolling and pitching badly and as the atmosphere below was stuffy I decided it would be more pleasant on deck in spite of the high seas. I staggered up there to find it was almost impossible to stand upright. The waves were pounding the side of the ship, which was so much at the mercy of the sea that as the prow rose up towards the sky it seemed as though it would never come down again; then after a while it would plunge down so deep that I feared we were going to turn over. The wind tore at my cape and threw back my hood, and my hair streamed all over my face so that I could scarcely see. I found it exhilarating.

I tried to walk the deck, but I had reckoned without the wind. It tore at me and lifted me off my feet. I was caught suddenly and held. It was Joss and he was laughing at me. There was spray on his eyebrows and his hair stuck up round his head. His ears looked more pointed than usual.

"What are you trying to do?" he demanded. "Commit suicide? Don't you know it's dangerous to walk the decks in weather like this?"

"What of you?"

"I saw you come up and followed you, guessing you'd be foolhardy enough to defy the wind."

He was still holding me and I made an effort to free myself.

"I'll be all right now," I said.

"I beg to contradict." The ship rolled and we fell against the rail.

"You see?" he taunted, his face close to mine.

"Yet another occasion when I have to admit you're right, I suppose."

"There'll be so many. I wouldn't bother to count."

"Perhaps I might turn the tables one day."

"Who knows. Miracles have happened. Look. There's a bench over there set against the bulkhead in the shelter of those hanging lifeboats. We'd get the freshness without the buffeting there."

He put his arm through mine and held it close against him. He gave the impression that he enjoyed such contacts not because they pleased him physically but because he knew they disturbed me.

We sat down and he put an arm about me. "Safer," he said with a grimace. "The only reason, I assure you."

"Had I in my folly been washed overboard everything you now share with me would have been yours, wouldn't it?"

"That's true."

"A consummation devoutly to be wished surely?"

"Perhaps there are other consummations which would be more devoutly so." I drew away from him. "Be prepared, Jessica," he went on. "One of these days you're going to grow up."

"It seems that you never speak to me without attempting to denigrate me in some way. So of what interest will it be to you when I reach this adult stage?"

"That's what I can't wait to discover."

"You seem to think you should instruct me in this art of growing up?"

"A husbandly duty perhaps."

"And when I do. . . ."

"Ah, then we shall see. I am impatient to discover."

"Tell me about the Company and the life I'm going out to."

"It's something you'll have to experience for yourself. Ben has told you a great deal. You'll be right in the midst of opal company. We're all opal men in Fancy Town. You know the town got its name because Desmond Dereham had a hunch about it. Tell me how you felt about Ben. You were fond of him, I know. He fascinated you, didn't he? He was a great man. But he sent your father away, branded him a thief and deceived us all about the Green Flash. You don't brood on that, do you? One of the things you'll have to learn is to accept our code of behavior out there. It's something you'll have to adjust to. Ben felt no compunction for having behaved as he did towards your father. He was going to steal the Green Flash and desert your mother. Ben was fond of your mother and when he got fond of people, he was really devoted to them. He was a gambler at heart. We all are. We wouldn't be there if we weren't. That's how it is with men who go after gold . . . sapphires, diamonds, opals, whatever it is. Nature plays tricks and you compare it with playing a card game. You don't know what card is given to you till you turn it up. It might be the ace of spades; it might be the ace of hearts; that's death and love, they say. But it might be the deuce of clubs and that won't mean much either way. There's a lot of luck in life, and I've always thought you've got to believe in luck to get it."

He told me about some finds which had come to light in the Fancy. He explained to me how there were pieces attached to fossilized wood which itself was impregnated with opal, but only fragments of it—nothing that could be used.

"Sometimes," he said, "it's like a sandwich. What a sandwich! There's the precious bit in the middle and on top you get the sandstone and underneath the opal dirt. It's in between that there's the meat. But these are not the lumps I've been telling you about. They consist of a lot of fine grains of sand stuck together . . . and in the cracks there'll be this hint of opal. There are times when you can gouge out enough to make a small stone, but the effort is hardly worth it. But I tell you this—when you find these, you can wager that not far off you're going to come across the precious stuff. It might be opal matrix, opal dirt, or just plain potch, but where it is there's always hope that somewhere, nearby, if you can only find the spot, is the precious stuff, and every miner believes that what he is going to find is going to be better than anything that ever came to light before."

It was fascinating listening to his talk. He seemed then as though he forgot the need to score over me which I believed had its roots in my repugnance to him and the terms I had insisted on before marrying him. When I saw him as the director of the Company, the man who understood opals and loved them—for this came out whenever he talked of them—I saw a different side to his nature from that of the conceited male whose dignity had been affronted because the woman he had been forced to marry for the sake of a fortune had insisted on the marriage's being, as he called it mockingly, "in name only."

So we sat there while the storm raged around us, and as I listened to his talk of the life to which I was going, my feelings towards him changed a little. I had realized that there were many sides to his nature and I must not allow my dislike of one to blind me to the existence of the rest.

Our first port of call was Teneriffe, and when we called there Joss took me on a tour around the island. We went to Santa Cruz in a gay little carriage drawn by two donkeys, and Joss, who was very knowledgeable about the place, enlightened me a good deal. The weather was gently warm, and I felt so exhilarated that I did not want the day to end. I admired the wonderfully colored flowering shrubs and the lushness of everything. Joss showed me banana plantations, and we lunched in a small restaurant overlooking the sea on *potage de berros*—a sort of water-cress soup—and fish which we had been told had been caught that morning and was served with a delicious sauce with the name of *mo-jo picon*. It was very exotic and exciting. As we sat overlooking the sea, Joss told me that when the Romans had come there they had found this group of islands to have a larger population of dogs than any other country they knew, so they called them Canaria, the Islands of Dogs. The natives were the Guanches—a savage people—who were in due course subdued by the Spaniards.

As we ate, young men and women came to dance the local dances, and there were singers too. We enjoyed the *isa* and the *folia* which, said Joss, were characteristically Spanish. He was clearly gratified by my wonder and delight in everything and even his pleasure in his superior knowledge failed to dampen my pleasure.

I was sorry when we had to go back to the ship, and as we sailed off he and I leaned over the rail and watched the dominating peak of Pico de Tiede fade out of sight.

When we reached Cape Town, Joss had some business to do, and he suggested that I go with him to the house of a man whom he had to see. It would be good for me, he said, now that I was a shareholder in the Company, to learn everything I could about it.

Cape Town must surely be one of the most beautifully situated cities in the world. I was overwhelmed by the magnificence of Table Bay, with the flat-topped Table Mountain clear in the sunshine and the Twelve Apostles Mountains looming up beside it.

We had a horse-drawn carriage to take us up the slope to Joss's business associate. The house was delightful in the Dutch Colonial style, and to step inside those beautifully cool rooms was like walking into a Dutch painting. There were stone steps leading to a terrace, and on this was a table with chairs ranged round it.

As we went up the steps, Kurt van der Stel and his wife came to greet us. They were clearly very pleased to see Joss, who introduced me as the wife he had recently married in England.

Grete van der Stel was a rosy, plump woman, rather severely dressed, and she bustled around, serving us with wine, which she explained came from a nearby vineyard, and with cakes which she had made herself.

When Joss told them of Ben's death, they were deeply distressed.

"It's sad to think we shall never see him again," said Grete.

"He had never been completely well since his accident," replied Joss.

"That is one of the hazards of mining," Kurt reminded him.

"And one of the reasons why people like you must pay

high prices for that which the miners have risked their lives for," answered Joss.

The Van der Stels talked for a long time about Ben, his exuberance, his unpredictability. They agreed that the opal world would not be the same without him.

Then Grete asked me if I would like to see the house and I told her that I should.

How beautiful that house was with that ambience of peace and order which I had experienced before through the intriguing interiors of the Dutch school of painting. Everything was highly polished and treated with loving care.

Grete told me that her family had been in Cape Town for 250 years.

"It is beautiful and it is home," she said. "Life is full of chance. Nearly two hundred and fifty years ago, two Dutchmen were shipwrecked here. They were enchanted by the place, as all must be—the climate, the fruit, the flowers— and the possibility of making a great colony occurred to them. They went back to the Dutch East India Company and reported what they had found. As a result they sent out three ships under the command of Jan van Riebech. Here they settled and then more Dutch came out to join them and so we built a city, and it has been home to us through the generations."

I stood at the window and looked out at the sparkling sea with the mountain—indeed resembling a table—rising proudly out of the waters. Grete took me into the garden, where exquisite shrubs flowered in abundance about the one-story dwelling where her servants were housed, and then we went back to the terrace on which the two men were sitting, before them the roll-up cases which I had so often seen in Ben's possession. They were discussing the opals which lay in the cases.

Grete said that luncheon would be served in a few moments, so Joss rolled up the cases. As he did so we heard the sound of horses' hoofs on the road below.

"He's here," said Kurt van der Stel.

"I'll be interested to see him," said Joss. "Perhaps he'll be able to give me some news about what's going on at the Fancy."

A man mounted the steps to the terrace, and Joss rose and shook hands with him. "It's good to see you, David," he said.

"You too, Joss." The newcomer shook hands with Kurt,

and as he did so Joss drew me forward.

"I want you to meet my wife," he said.

The man found it difficult to hide his astonishment.

"Jessica, this is David Croissant," said Joss.

I had heard that name before. David Croissant, the merchant who knew more about the quality of opals than any other. He was not tall, and his dark hair grew low on his forehead, forming in the center what we called a "widow's peak." He had light eyes, which because of his general darkness gave him an unusual appearance, and those eyes, I noticed, were too closely set together.

"You've not heard about Ben," said Joss. David Croissant looked startled, and Joss told him.

"Good God!" said David Croissant. "I had no idea. Ben . . . old Ben!"

"We shall all miss him sadly," said Kurt.

"What bad luck," murmured David Croissant. "If he'd still got the Flash, you'd think it was that did him in. I wonder whatever happened to Desmond Dereham? He disappeared off the face of the earth. Went to some outlandish place, I don't doubt. Perhaps he'll escape the bad luck."

"Why should he?" asked Grete.

"Some say there's evil in that stone, and if that were so it might favor someone who stole it."

"What a crazy idea," said Joss. "I'm surprised at you, David, an opal man, talking such nonsense. Ill luck! For heaven's sake let's put a stop to all that talk. It's not good for business."

He flashed me a warning look, which told me that he did not want me to mention the fact that the Green Flash had not been stolen. I wondered why and felt resentful that my father should go on being accused of stealing something which at the very most he had only attempted to. However, I was unsure of myself and remained silent.

"It's true," said Kurt. "Who's going to buy opals if they're considered unlucky?"

"Lucky! Unlucky!" said Joss vehemently. "It's a lot of nonsense. Long ago opals were the good-luck stones, and then it was discovered that they could sometimes be brittle and this talk of bad luck started."

"What have you brought to show us, David?" asked Kurt.

"Ah," replied David, "some stones that will make you dance with joy. There's one in particular."

"Let's see it," said Joss.

"Mind you," answered David, "it's not cheap."

"If it's what you're implying, who'd expect it to be?" retorted Joss.

When I saw the Harlequin Opal, I had my first real understanding of the fascination a stone could convey. It was aptly named. There seemed so many colors which changed as one watched. There was a gaiety about that stone. It definitely had a quality which even I could recognize.

"You're right," said Joss. "It's a beauty."

"I only know of one stone I'd compare it with."

"Now we're back to the Green Flash," retorted Joss. "You can't expect anything to compare with that."

"Of course not. But this is superb."

"I wonder you're not afraid to travel around with it."

"I only show it to people I know. I keep it apart from the rest. I'm not going to tell you my secret hiding places. How do I know you might not turn bushranger?"

"That's wise of you," said Joss. He held out the stone to me. "Take a look at that, Jessica."

I held it in the palm of my hand and felt a reluctance to let it go.

"You see the beauty of it?" said Joss eagerly. "Not a flaw in it. Look at those colors and the size. . . ."

"Don't praise it too much, Joss," begged Kurt. "You're putting the price up. Not that I'm going to bid for it. I know I can't afford it."

"I've others you'll like, Kurt," said David Croissant. "I'll put Harlequin away or she'll outshine everything else."

I was still staring at the stone I held.

"You see," said David, "your wife doesn't want to lose it."

"She's beginning to understand something about opals. That's true, eh, Jessica?"

"I'm very ignorant," I said, handing the stone back to David, "but at least I'm aware that I know nothing about them."

"Which is the first lesson," answered Joss. "So you've mastered that."

We looked at the other opals as David Croissant unrolled case after case and Joss explained the properties of each to me.

Then suddenly he looked at his watch. "We must go, unless we are going to miss the ship. I'll see you in Australia, David. I dare say you'll be coming back soon."

"As soon as I can. One or two calls to make and then it's the next ship back."

So we said good-by, and our horse-drawn carriage, which had been waiting for us, took us back to the ship.

There were long days in calm waters when the ship seemed to move hardly at all. I would sit on deck with Joss and we would talk desultorily while we sipped cool drinks. There was a quality about these days which suggested erroneously that they would go on like this forever. Now and then we would see a school of porpoises or dolphins sporting in the water and the flying fishes rising from the deep blue depths to flutter on its surface. Once an albatross followed the ship for three days, and we would lie back in our chairs watching the infinite grace and calculate the immense strength of that twelve-foot span of wing as it circled above us.

Even my desire to discover the truth of my father's disappearance receded. This was peace, and I wondered whether Joss felt it too.

We would sit on deck until sunset, which was about seven o'clock, and it was fascinating to experience the quick descent of twilight. How different from home, where the subdued light lingers for a long time after the sun has set. Here it was bright day with that great ball of fire shedding its heat upon us until it sank into the sea, followed by almost immediate darkness.

The sunsets were superb, and one night Joss said: "In waters such as this we could see the green flash."

So each night we sat there and we were all hoping for a glimpse of it. Anxiously we would scan the sky for the signs. "Everything has to be perfect for it," Joss explained. "No clouds, the sea calm, every little detail has to be just right."

Each evening when we sat there I would say: "Will it be tonight?"

"Who shall say?" answered Joss. "One sits and waits as for an important visitor. If it comes and you are not watching for it with your complete attention, you'll miss it. Don't forget it's there in a flash and gone again. If you blink an eye you'd miss it."

It had become a fetish with us. Joss had seen it of course but, he admitted, only once. "And I've been where it could be many a time," he told us. "And only once was I honored."

So each evening at sunset we watched—but we waited in vain. The natural phenomenon was as elusive as its namesake.

We were on deck as we sailed into Bombay, and before us lay a wonderful panorama of mountainous islands and away to the east the gently swaying palm trees and high peaks of the Western Ghat Mountains. Here was the gateway to India.

Joss and I spent an exhilarating morning in exotic surroundings the like of which I had never seen before. How beautiful the women were in their brilliantly colored saris, and the contrast between them and the multitudes of beggars who surrounded us appalled us, touching our pleasure with a depression created by such horror. We gave to the beggars, but the more we gave the more seemed to gather around us, and we had in the end to turn away from those big pleading eyes and little upstretched brown hands.

We had stopped to watch a group of women washing their clothes in the river, but because of the beggars we returned to our gaily colored mule-drawn carriage and left the river. Yet I could not get them out of my mind.

We were taken to a market where there were stalls of the most exciting merchandise and voluble salesmen, eager to sell their wares. There were beautiful carpets, all kinds of objects in carved wood, ivory, and brass; and we were fascinated.

The bright black eyes of one of the salesmen were on us.

"You give a little present, eh?" he suggested. "To show love . . . to bring good luck."

I hesitated, and Joss whispered: "He's going to be very disappointed if we don't."

"This lady, very lucky," said the salesman. "It was ivory charm. The goddess of good fortune . . . talisman against evil."

"I'm going to buy that for you," I said. "The Green Flash is yours now . . . you may need it."

"It's partly yours, too, and to show that I don't believe in bad luck I'm going to buy you that cherry-colored silk to make a gown."

So we made our purchases with the minimum of bargaining, for, said Joss, the salesman would be disappointed if we did not haggle a little.

I felt as we walked away that that incident seemed to imply that our relationship was changing.

We had a light luncheon and during it I asked Joss why he had allowed David Croissant to believe that the Green

Flash was still missing and that it had been stolen by my father.

"There's always a great deal of speculation about that stone," said Joss. "And David's a talker. I don't want people talking about it until I have it secure. I think that's the wise thing to do."

And I did not feel I could argue with him on that score.

After luncheon we drove in the carriage to the impressive Rajabai Tower built in the fourteenth century and went up Malabar Hill to Malabar Point. We paused by the Tower of Silence where, so our driver told us, the Parsees disposed of their dead according to their religious tradition, which was to leave the bodies to the sun, the weather, and the birds.

"No woman is allowed in," we were told.

"Why not?" I asked. "Why should they be excluded?"

The driver could not understand us, for his English was limited, but Joss replied: "The inferior sex, you know."

"That's quite absurd," I retorted hotly.

I could see he was pleased to have aroused my indignation, and the change in our relationship which I had fancied I detected had evaporated. We were back to where we had started.

As we were approaching the end of our journey, a restraint had grown up between us. Joss was often thoughtful, and once or twice I caught him regarding me intently.

We continued to sit on deck together in the evenings at sunset. We would sit in silence watching the great ball of fire slipping down to the horizon.

When we did talk, we often mentioned Ben. Joss quoted him frequently. It was clear that he had been greatly influenced by him throughout his life.

"Do you think we'll see the real green flash one day?" I asked.

"Perhaps. Though there's not much time left. You have to wait for it. I believe some people imagine they've seen it."

"Are you one of those?"

"Not I. I'm much too practical. I don't have daydreams."

"Perhaps it might be better if you did."

"Why should one want to indulge in fancy when there's reality all around one?"

"It shows imagination."

He laughed at me. I knew he enjoyed laughing at me, proving to me that I was young, inexperienced of life, and somewhat foolish.

Once he said: "Ben used to say love comes quickly in a flash sometimes, but you have to recognize it for the real thing. Lots of people think they've found it because they want to. That's how it is with the green flash. They want to have seen it so they delude themselves into thinking they have."

"I can assure you that I never delude myself."

He went on: "Look at the sun. There are opal lights in the sky today. Look at the touch of yellow over there . . . with the blue. I found an opal just like that once. We called it The Primrose because someone fancied he saw the shape of the flower there. In half an hour the sun will be going down. Who knows? Tonight we could see it. It's a night for the green flash."

We sat there watching.

"Any minute now," said Joss. "How bright it is! It's as though it wants to blind you so that you'll miss it. Be careful. Be sure you don't blink."

The great red ball low on the horizon was dipping into the water—now only half of it was visible, now less and then just that red rim.

"Now!" whispered Joss; and there was a quick intake of breath to indicate disappointment, for the sun had completely disappeared below the horizon, and neither of us had seen the green flash.

6

The Burned-out Inn

There was great excitement on board when we approached the land, and I don't think there was one passenger who was not on deck looking out with eager, fascinated eyes. And it was a sight worth looking at, for I suppose there is no harbor in the world to compare with Sydney's. The captain had given me a book in which I had read of the arrival of the first fleet there. I wondered what the convicts had felt when they stepped ashore after months of confinement in the noisome hold of a ship to find themselves surrounded by so much that was beautiful. In those days the scene would have been made more colorful by the brilliantly plumaged birds—parakeets, lovebirds, and those delicately colored galahs with the exquisite mingling gray and pink of their feathers, all of which I was to see later. It was different now. Buildings had sprung up where beautiful wild flowers had grown and the birds had retreated inland. They had named the place after Lord Sydney, the Secretary of State for the Home Department. Captain Arthur Philip, the first governor of the new colony, who had had a port named after him, had declared that here was "the finest harbour in the world in which a thousand sail of the line might ride in the most perfect security."

Perhaps because what I had read had given me such a sense of the past or perhaps merely because this was one of the most beautiful places I had ever seen, I was filled with exhilaration which completely eliminated the mild depression I had begun to feel at the prospect of leaving the ship which had been my home for so long.

I stood leaning on the rail as we went through the Heads —past numerous covelike indentations and sandy beaches fringed with lush foliage. Then the buildings began to appear and it was obvious that we were coming to a considerable city.

"What a beautiful place!" I cried.

Joss looked pleased. "We shan't be so far away up at

Fancy Town," he said. "You'll be able to take the odd trip into Sydney and do your shopping. There are some fine shops there—and hotels too. Of course you'll have to camp out for a night or two very likely on the way. Though there are homesteads where you might stay."

"It sounds exciting."

"It will be. You'll see. I wonder if anyone's come to meet us. We're staying at the Metropole. It will take us a couple of days to get out to Peacocks."

"How shall we go?"

"There's Cobb's coach, but it doesn't go our way, so it would be best to ride. You'll be glad of those riding lessons I gave you."

Everyone seemed to know Joss, which made disembarkation easy. Our baggage would in due course be unloaded and sent to the hotel.

"We'll spend a week at the Metropole," Joss told me. "I have business to do in Sydney, and I reckon you'd like to see a bit of it before we go to Fancy Town. Get into the buggy and it'll take us to the hotel. We'll just take a few personal things with us."

The hotel was situated in the heart of the town and the reception area was crowded with people who talked loudly to each other, but Joss forced his way through to the desk and emerged with two keys.

I saw the ironical grin on his face as he handed one to me.

"All according to contract," he said.

I flushed with irritation. He had completely lost that tenderness which I had fancied I glimpsed during the voyage.

Our rooms adjoined and there was a communicating door between them. Maliciously he watched my anxious glance towards it, and he went to it at once, took the key from the lock, and handed it to me as he had on the first night of our marriage.

The room was pleasant with French windows leading onto a small balcony. I went out into it and looked down on the streets teeming with people and horse-drawn vehicles. We had indeed come to town.

I washed and when I was ready sat down on my bed to wait. It was not long before there was a knock on my door, and Joss came to conduct me to dinner. We went down the wide staircase to the lounge which was full of men talking earnestly.

"Graziers from all over New South Wales," Joss told

me. "Some from the other side of the Blue Mountains. There are some gold men here too. There's something about a gold man. It's the look in his eyes. It's as though he's searching for something. Hope deferred, I suppose. And that makes the heart sick. That's how so many of them are . . . sick at heart because their dreams have been grander than reality. Then you pick out those who have struck their bit of gold. They're not often happy men because they've found that there are things gold can't buy and they're the things they want most. Then there are those who have made their little pile and are going to spend it. They're all here. Now the grazier . . . he's a different species . . . though God knows he has his troubles . . . droughts, floods, swarms of pests that can destroy his land and animals. I can tell you there are more plagues here than there ever were in the land of Egypt."

We went into the dining room, and he said: "We'll have a steak. It'll be a treat to eat fresh meat."

And although I felt vaguely resentful of his taking command and telling me what I should eat, I nodded agreement.

The steak was certainly good, and after we had eaten it we took coffee in the lounge, but it was so noisy that we could scarcely hear ourselves speak.

Joss said it had been a tiring day for me and I should retire. I didn't know whether to be pleased by his concern for me or to resent his giving orders.

It was true I was tired, so I said good night and went to my room, assured myself that the communicating door was locked, and enjoyed a good night's sleep.

We met at breakfast—a hearty one for Joss consisting of lamb chops and kidneys.

"We're good trenchermen here," he said. "It's the outdoor life. I'm going to spend the day taking you round, and then I shall have business to attend to. I want you to meet some of the people who buy and sell opals, and though it will be just social here, you'll pick up quite a bit. Then you'll probably find it a good idea to shop. First though I'll show you something and you'll get your bearings."

I said it was an excellent idea, and after breakfast we set off.

He drove the buggy himself and first he wanted to show me the harbor. I had seen it from the ship of course, but this was different. We could drive in and out of the coves, and from the heights we could look down on those wonderful bays. The sea was the color of sapphires.

"It looks beautiful," he said, "but I can tell you that there are sharks lurking beneath that innocent blue. If you ventured in you might easily end up by providing a shark with his dinner."

"What a horrible thought."

"Things are not always what they seem," he said with a grin.

"It's certainly true of the water and it looks so calm and peaceful."

"That's the time to be wary. If sharks frighten you. How are you going to like it out at Fancy Town?"

"That's something I shan't know till I've experienced it."

"You'll find it very different from England." He had brought the buggy to a standstill and was looking intently at me. "Some people come out here and get so homesick they can't endure it. They just pack up and go home."

"It's hard to leave your native land."

"My ancestors came out here seventy years ago."

"Were they homesick?"

"It wouldn't have mattered if they were. They had to stay. My mother's father came out on a convict ship. He was no criminal, but he was a man of certain opinions that didn't fit in with what was thought right and proper. He offended some people and a charge was trumped up against him and out he came. Fourteen years was his sentence. Her husband's mother was a lady's maid accused of stealing her employer's valuable brooch. She was innocent, says the family, but all convicts were innocent according to their families. Most people have a yearning to go back to England."

"And do you?"

"Sometimes. It's a second home to me and I get torn between the two. When I'm here I want to be in England and when I'm in England I'm longing for Australia. Perverse of me, but then I'm a perverse sort of person."

I did not disagree, which amused him. He made me uncomfortable often because he liked to read my thoughts.

"Like Ben," he went on, "I was taken with Oakland. Part of me would like to stay there and become a sort of squire. Now I'm married to a Clavering perhaps I qualify. On the other hand, opals are here and opals are my life. You see the dilemma I'm in."

"An *embarras des richesses*, I believe."

"Yes, but I shall not allow it to embarrass me. I'm the sort who's determined to get the best out of both worlds."

"So you will return to Oakland for visits?"

"Yes. It's a pity it's on the other side of the world, but what are a few thousand miles?"

"Nothing to you," I replied blithely.

"I am sure," he said, "that you would like to visit the old place now and then."

"Indeed I would."

"Now we have one matter on which we agree. I think we are progressing."

"It's natural for me to want to visit so it hardly seems like progress."

He just laughed at me.

We rode back through the city, where he showed me how the streets wound around in an inconsequential manner because in the beginning, when the settlement was founded, the tracks around the hills were made by carts and riders and in time became streets.

"Sydney grew rather than was planned," he said.

"Which is what a city should do," I replied. "How much more interesting that something should be in a certain place for a reason other than because someone drew it on a plan."

"I can see you're romantic."

"It's not a bad thing to be."

"That's too profound for me to consider when I'm driving a buggy through the streets of Sydney."

"I should have thought nothing was beyond your powers."

"So that's your opinion of me. I must say I'm happy to have made such a good impression."

"Ben used to say that people are taken at their own valuation."

"And that's what you are doing in my case?"

"I have yet to discover what other people's opinions of you are."

Joss was at least an informative companion. He talked quite lyrically of Captain Cook who had arrived in 1770 and taken possession of New South Wales for the British Crown, and how it had been named New South Wales because those who first saw it thought it bore a resemblance to that coast at home; and then seventeen years later, when it had been decided to use this beautiful land as a convict settlement, the first shipboard had come out in 1787.

"They were little better than slaves," said Joss, "and

flogged for the slightest offense. Those were cruel times, and although some of those who came out were hardened criminals, many were political prisoners and men of intellect."

"Like your grandfather."

"Exactly. Then later others came out to make a new life for themselves. Land could be bought for the sum of ten pounds a block and a block was five miles square, so it wasn't necessary to have a great deal of capital to start with. Convict labor was available and all that was needed was hard work. And how they worked! You've seen the graziers in the Metropole. Rugged men most of them—hard-headed, shrewd men who knew the meaning of disaster. You've heard about the plagues, the floods, and the droughts. There's another evil, the forest fire. It can do terrible things in our Bush. You see, there's plenty to contend with out here. You have to forget the easy, cozy life."

"You're warning me again."

"If you feel in need of warning, take it."

"I believe you have a poor opinion of me. I'm surprised because I have quite a fair opinion of myself and if Ben was right. . . ."

He laughed, and for a time I felt he was no longer laughing at me but with me.

As we drove back to the hotel he said: "Everyone who comes out here is in a sense a gambler. The miners, of course, are all lavishly endowed with the gambling mentality. Every day they start out to work they say to themselves: "This will be the day." At sundown they know it is not, but there's always hope. Those who go after gold are the same . . . and after opal. They always think they'll find another Green Flash at Sunset."

"You've seen the real thing, of course."

"Yes, as I told you, I saw it once as the sun was setting."

"You would succeed where others failed."

I enjoyed those days in Sydney. In the evenings I met some of Joss's business associates and one of them had his wife with him, so she and I did some shopping excursions together.

In bustling George Street I bought material to be made into practical garments for my new life, and we roamed through Pitt and Elizabeth Streets, marveling at the merchandise. I acquired two large straw hats that my companion advised me to buy, for I should need them against the fierce Australian sun, which was far more brilliant than that which we experienced in England. I was pleased with them because they were quite becoming and served two purposes—use and decoration. In King Street I bought ribbons and hairpins.

In due course the time came for us to leave. Joss spent a long time choosing the horses we should hire. Most of our baggage would come by coach to Fancy Town, where we should pick it up. We took one pack horse with a few belongings and provisions. Our journey from England had taken a little over six weeks, and we were at the end of November, which was the equivalent of our May. The wild flowers were so colorful that I kept exclaiming at their beauty, which I saw was very gratifying to Joss; but most impressive of all were the tall eucalypts—aloof, indifferent, towering over the tree ferns and native beech and ash as they reached for the sky. Joss was as knowledgeable about the countryside as he had been about Sydney, and I found a new excitement in having such a good mentor beside me.

"Look at these eucalypts," he said. "We call them stringy barks. That's because of their tough, fibrous barks. The term is Bush slang for bad whiskey too. You'll find the language colorful and you'll have to learn some of it."

"I shall be interested to," I told him.

"Glad to hear it. It'll help you along a bit. Look over there. That's what we call a spotted gum. See the markings on the bark?"

The country was flat, and the dryness of the land was particularly noticeable after the green fields at home. Having no other as contrast, I had never before realized how green they were. The roads were rough and full of holes, and our horses raised a cloud of dust.

We climbed small hills and crossed more flat country; we went over dried-up creeks and at length came to a homestead—a one-storied building surrounded by grazing land. Joss said he thought we should stay the night there for the pull from where we were to Fancy Town would be too long to do in one day. The next night he planned to stay at Trant's Homestead and reach the Fancy the day after that.

He rode into the yard and dismounted, by which time a woman in a voluminous black dress and a white apron had come out.

Joss talked to her and then he came back to me.

"They've only one room," he said. "This is not a London hotel, you know. What about it? Shall we take it or spend the night out of doors?"

The woman had come forward.

"You're welcome, my dear," she said. "It's a nice room. Are you man and wife?"

"Yes we are," answered Joss.

"Then I'll bustle too and get the bed-made up. It's a very good bed . . . lovely, soft feathers brought out from England. Jack here will see to the horses. Jack. Set to, lad. And Mary. Where's Mary?"

Joss helped me to alight. I could see that he was enjoying the situation.

"Cheer up," he whispered. "The unnatural embargo is bound to put us into some awkward situations, but I'm very resourceful."

The room was pleasant—very clean—and dominated by the big double bed. Joss regarded it ruefully. "That's a comfortable chair," he said. "It would serve me well or I might lie at the foot of the bed like a knight of old." He placed his hands on my shoulders and looked at me earnestly. "There is one thing you must never forget," he said. "I have never yet forced my attentions on a woman who didn't want me, and I feel no temptation to do so now. I'm proud you know. . . ."

"I do know it. I believe the Peacock is a nickname of yours."

"I believe it is, but no one dare call me by it to my face. Remember what I said. It might save you considerable uneasiness."

We washed the grime of the road from ourselves in tepid water and went downstairs. Steaks were cooking on a gridiron on a fire out of doors, and close by was a long table with benches. We were told to sit down and were given kangaroo soup in thick earthenware mugs while the steaks sizzled over the grid. Our hostess made dampers, which were ready at the same time as the steaks. Afterwards cheese was served with johnnycakes—dampers the size of scones—and there was a beverage which tasted like ale to accompany the food.

It was not dark when we had finished, and we strolled about and watched the sheep being rounded up by kelpie dogs who answered the farmer's whistle and got the bewildered animals into their pens, keeping them close together by running nimbly right over their backs.

For all Joss's protestations, I was disturbed at the thought of sharing a room with him. He said he would take the chair, which seemed to offer greater comfort than the floor. I removed only my skirt and bodice. I slept fitfully, which perhaps was to be expected in the circumstances; and I suppose the same applied to Joss.

We set off on our journey in the pure morning air. It was about eleven o'clock when we came to a river which Joss thought would be a good place to stop. The horses were in need of a rest and they could drink. He told me to gather some sticks of bracken, which I did, and with an expert touch, which I could not but admire, he quickly made a fire and brewed what he called quart-pot tea. We found a tree under which we could sit comfortably. Our landlady of the previous night supplied us with sandwiches, and we had some cheese. Strangely enough I felt I had never drunk tea or tasted sandwiches so good.

The sun grew hotter and both of us were feeling drowsy. I quickly dozed and dreamed that I was on the ship. There was a storm and I was walking on deck, being buffeted from one side to the other. I was caught suddenly in a vise-like grip, and there was Joss. "Are you trying to commit suicide?" he asked, and I was stung into replying: "That would be a good way out for you, wouldn't it? Everything would be yours then. You wouldn't have the encumbrance of a wife who doesn't want you any more than you want her. Everything would be yours . . . the houses, the shares, the Green Flash at Sunset. . . ." As I mentioned the opal, his expression changed and his grip on me tightened and there were murderous lights in his eyes. "You're right. I'd be better off without you. Suicide . . . well, it could look like that, couldn't it?" I cried out: "No . . . no! You're going to murder me."

I awoke with a start, and my heart leaped in terror, for there he was, his face close to mine, watching me intently. For a moment I thought the dream was real.

"What was that about?" he asked.

"I was dreaming."

"It seemed like a nightmare."

"It must have been."

"A nightmare in broad daylight! You must have something on your mind . . . something that frightens you."

"I think I'm able to take care of myself, so I'm not afraid."

"What was the dream?"

"Oh, nothing. It was all confused as dreams are."

"It's a big undertaking to leave your native land and come out to a strange one. Are you disturbed about that?"

"I sometimes wonder how I shall fit in."

"And marriage . . . with a stranger . . . a meaningless sort of marriage. Let's hope that in due course we shall come to some compromise about that."

I wondered what he meant by compromise.

"There are lawless elements out here," he went on.

"There are in all countries."

"Have you ever heard of bushrangers?"

"Of course."

"But you do not know what they are really like. Desperate men . . . perhaps they've failed in the gold fields or the opal and sapphire mines. They're desperadoes who live by robbery. This is the ideal background for them. They can hide in the Bush and ply their trade with comparative ease. They're determined not to be caught, which would mean hanging from a tree as a warning to their kind. They don't hesitate to kill if the occasion arises."

"I believe you'd like me to go straight home."

He laughed. "I'd like to see if you're the sort of person who would go straight home because of a few discomforts."

"I'll tell you one thing. I'm the sort of person who would put up with a great deal to prove you wrong."

That made him laugh, and I stared straight ahead because I did not care to meet his eyes, which I thought overbold.

"Looking for bushrangers?" he asked. "Don't fret. You've got a protector."

"You?"

"And this." He took out a small pistol from a belt at his hip. "A beauty," he said. "I never travel without her. Neat, insignificant in appearance, and deadly in action. They wouldn't stand much chance, I can tell you, with us around."

We rode side by side through the Bush.

"The Trant Homestead is about fifteen miles on," he said. "The horses will be in need of a rest when we get there and so will we."

I looked about me at the scenery which was wild and interesting. "What are those pale-looking trees over there?" I asked.

"Ghost gums. Some people believe that when people die violently in the Bush they take up their habitation inside the trees and that where there is a ghost gum there will in time be others to join it. You should see them in moonlight; then you would believe the legend. There are some who won't pass a clump of ghost gums after dusk. They think the branches will turn into arms and that in the morning there will be another ghost gum to stand beside those who were there the day before."

"Every country has its legends."

"And we're a down-to-earth people here."

There was a sudden cackle of laughter above us, which startled me so violently that I moved sideways in the saddle. Joss noticed and laughed.

"It's only a kookaburra," he said, "the laughing jackass of a kingfisher. Ah, there's his mate. They are often in pairs. They seem to find life very amusing. You'll hear them often round Peacock House."

We rode on over dried-up creeks and gullies.

"The wild flowers would have been a picture," said Joss, "if it hadn't been for the drought."

It must have been about seven in the evening when Joss pulled up on a slight hillock and looked about him at the Bush spread out around us.

"We should be able to see Trant's from here," he said. "It's built in a hollow."

"It'll be dark soon."

"Yes, I want to get there before sundown. The Bush can be treacherous. I know it well, of course, but even old stagers have been known to be lost. You have to be careful, and not wander out alone. You see how the same kind of landscape goes on and on. I've known people to be lost in the Bush; they walk miles and often end up literally going around in circles. They can't make a landmark because the scenery repeats itself again and again. So take care. I think I can see Trant's. Look. Over there in that hollow."

We rode on. The sun had sunk below the horizon. The first stars had started to appear and there was a thin crescent of moon.

He galloped on and I followed. Suddenly he pulled up short and I came up beside him.

"Good God!" he cried. "Just look at that!"

It was an eerie sight in the pale light of the moon and

stars—a shell of a house. Joss rode on and I followed him, picking my way carefully over the sparse, scorched grass. Fire had ravaged one side of the two-story building; the rest had been severely licked by the flames.

"We'll look round," said Joss, "and see what there is."

We dismounted, and he tethered the horses to a piece of iron fence.

"Careful how you go," he called over his shoulder. Then he turned and took my hand and together we stepped over the blackened threshold.

"They must have lost everything," he said. "I wonder where they went."

"I hope their lives were saved."

"Who can say?"

"How far are we from Fancy Town?"

"Thirty miles or so. Trant's! People used to stay here. It was like an oasis in the desert . . . there's nothing else for miles around." He turned and looked at me. "We'll have to stay here for the night. The horses can't go on. There's a river close by. Let's hope it's not dried up. The horses could drink and there might be some grass that's not been scorched by the fire. Wait here. I'll go and look."

As I stood in that burned-out shell, I felt a sudden horror of the place. There was an atmosphere of doom about it. Tragedy had happened here, and death and disaster seemed to have clung to the air. I shivered and a sudden coldness came over me. I felt that I was alone with the dead. I touched the blackened walls. This had once been a parlor, I imagined, where people had sat and talked and laughed together; within these four walls they had lived their lives. I imagined their coming from England, settlers who had sought a new life and had hit on the idea of making an inn where travelers through the Bush could stay for a night or so. They would farm the land as well, for not enough people would pass this way to give them a living as innkeepers; they would go for walks without seeing anyone . . . nothing but wild bush. I wondered if they had lived in fear of bushrangers. Those blackened walls filled me with foreboding and I don't think I fully realized the loneliness of the Bush until that moment.

I noticed that there were some remains of habitation—a half-burned table, pieces of metal which could have been part of some fitting, two battered candlesticks which had once been shining brass, and a tin box such as the one Maddy had at home. She always referred to it as "my box" and it carried her possessions in it. It had come to Oakland Hall when she had and it would be with her all her life.

A figure loomed up beside me, and I gasped in horror.

"Sorry I scared you," said Joss. "Why, what's the matter?"

"It's this place. There's something haunted about it."

"Why, there's little left but the walls. I found the stream and mercifully there's grass there. We'll take the horses down."

"Are we going to stay *here?*" I asked.

"It's shelter, and we're not equipped for camping."

"Couldn't we go on?"

"For thirty miles? The horses need rest. We'll stay here till dawn and then we'll get going. Let's see if there's anything we can use. We'll explore. But be careful."

I said: "There's a tin box over there. There might be something in that."

As we moved across the floor, my foot struck something. I stooped and picked up a half-burned candle. Joss took it from me and said: "Someone's been here recently and must have had the same idea as we have of using it for the night." He examined the stump and then took matches from his pocket and lighted it. He held the candle high, and the place looked more forbidding than ever in the dim light. His face looked different too. His eyes were darker and the bronze of his skin less obvious. There was something half amused and enigmatic in his expression as he regarded me; I noticed again that his ears were large and faintly pointed at the tips, which gave him the appearance of a satyr. I caught a glint in his eyes which suggested to me that he was not altogether displeased with our situation. This gave me more than a twinge of uneasiness.

"It was lucky to find the candle," I said.

"I wonder who left it. Some bushranger perhaps."

"Why shouldn't it be travelers like ourselves?"

"It might be, of course." He patted his belt. "Now you see why it's well to be prepared. Don't be alarmed. You're not alone, you know."

He kept his eyes on my face, and I had an idea that he was trying to frighten me.

"There could be something in the tin box," I said.

He went over to it and touched it with his foot. "It seems

to have stood up to the fire pretty well." He stooped down and opened it and holding the candle high, peered in.

"Why look. A blanket. It must have escaped the fire. The tin box has protected it. What a find! We can spread it on the floor." He took it out and sniffed at it. "You can smell the smoke."

I came over to him and took the blanket. "Do you think whoever used the candle used it too?"

"Who knows? We can't afford to be fastidious. We'll have need of it."

As I lifted it out, I saw a book. It was a kind of ledger. I picked it up and opened it. Inside was written "Trant Homestead, 1875. This book is the property of James and Ethel Trant who left England in the year 1873 and settled here in this house which they called Trant's Homestead."

I pictured James and Ethel leaving home full of hope and settling in this isolated spot. As I turned over the pages of the book I saw that it had been used as a kind of register. There was one column for the date, a center one for names, and another for comments. There were remarks like "Thanks, James and Ethel. It was good." And another "Just like Home." Another said "My third visit. Speaks for itself."

The discovery of the book had made real people of Ethel and James, and I deeply hoped they had survived the destruction of their property.

Joss was looking over my shoulder. "Oh, I see, a hotel register. Look and see when the last guest was here. That should give us some idea of the date of the fire." I looked. A Tom Best and Harry Wakers had stayed three months before.

"As recent as that," commented Joss.

"I wonder what happened to James and Ethel Trant."

"Who can say? Now we've got to rest. Don't forget we must be up at the crack of dawn."

"Somehow I don't like the idea of staying here."

He laughed aloud. "It's a shelter. Not much but a bit. There's water close by for the horses and a bit of grass too. We're in luck. Oh, I know you were thinking of a comfortable bed, but things don't always work out that way in the Bush. Here, hold the candle."

I did so while he spread the blanket on the rough, charred floor. He took the candle from me and, tilting it, let some of its grease drip onto the floor and in this he stuck the candle so that it was held upright.

"How long do you think that will last?" I asked.

"A few hours with luck. It's amazing good fortune to have found it. You appreciate your luck out here."

"I should think one should anywhere."

I sat down on the spread-out blanket, still holding the register in my hand. I turned the pages, glancing idly at the names and comments. Then one name leaped out at me. "Desmond Dereham, June 1879" and his comment: "I shall surely come again."

"What's the matter?" asked Joss.

"My father stayed here. His name's in the book. I think people ought to know the truth, that he did not succeed in stealing the Green Flash and that Ben had it all the time. It'll have to be known that we have it."

"We'll see. It's not a thing I want to decide quickly about. There's so much depending on it."

Perhaps he was right, I thought, and it was better that no one should know that we had the famous stone.

I glanced down at the book and saw David Croissant's name.

"There's someone else we know," I said.

Joss looked. "I dare say I could find many people I know in that book. This place was used by everyone. We might try and make a fire and boil some tea. I thought you and I would be sitting at mine host's table and perhaps sharing a room as we did last night. Rooms are scarce in these homesteads you know. They don't cater for people with fastidious notions. That chair was damned uncomfortable. I was telling myself I didn't fancy repeating the experience, and here am I doomed to spend the night on a smoke-ridden blanket in a burned-out homestead."

He had stretched himself out full length and was staring upwards at what was left of the roof, which in candlelight looked like some prehistoric insect. I could see stars through the gaps in the roof.

He said: "This is a good introduction to your life here. At least after this you'll be prepared for anything. Are you sleepy? It wasn't a very good night last night, was it? A pity . . . and they said it was such a comfortable feather bed."

. He put out a hand and pulled me down beside him.

"Such a small blanket," he said quietly.

I shrank to the edge of it.

"You disappoint me, Jessica," he said. "I didn't think you'd be so easily frightened. Why don't you be bold. Why don't you prepare yourself for new experiences?"

"What experiences?"

"I didn't want to marry you any more than you wanted to marry me. We were two sensible people with eyes open to the main chance. This marriage suited us both. We stood to lose a lot if we didn't go along with Ben. Well, now it's done, why don't we try to make something of it?"

"I intend to learn all I can about the Company. I want to play a part in that."

"That's not what I meant. You're frightened. What a dilemma! Here you are alone in the burned-out inn with your husband. Don't be such a child, Jessica. You're a woman now."

"You promised," I cried. "You said you were too proud. . . ."

"You are the most maddening woman I ever knew."

"Because I'm not panting for you?"

"Yes," he cried. "I wish to God. . . ."

"That you had refused Ben. You wouldn't have done that though, would you? You wanted Oakland, Peacocks, and the Green Flash. It was unfortunate that you had to take me too, but that was part of the bargain. If you could be rid of me you'd be contented. You've shown me that. I'm not such a child that I can't see it. I expect there's someone else you'd like to marry. That would be just like you . . . to take the main chance. Do you think I don't understand you? I'm doing that more and more every day, and I don't like what I discover. I wish. . . ."

I seemed to see Ben's face rising before me, admonishing me: "Now tell the truth, Jessie. Did you want to stay behind in the Dower House for the rest of your days?"

Joss had risen. "I'm going to see that the horses are safe," he said, and he strode out, leaving me alone.

As I looked about that burned-out inn, a feeling of foreboding came to me. He didn't want me. He resented me. It must have occurred to him how much more convenient it would be if I were not here. He wanted to be free and lose nothing by his freedom.

I could hear his voice echoing through my mind: "This is a country where life is cheap." Bushrangers roamed the land. How easy it would be for him to kill me. He could find a hundred excuses for it.

"I went down to the horses. . . ." I could hear his explanations. "When I came back she was lying there dead . . . strangled . . . or shot. There were bushrangers in the neighborhood. . . . Some jewels she was wearing were missing . . . so was some money she had. . . ." Or: "She was not accustomed to riding in rough country. I'd given her lessons in England but this was different. She took a toss. I saw that her neck was broken . . . so I buried her close to the burned-out inn. . . ."

Had he wanted to make love to me? Perhaps. Ben had implied that he was something of a rake. To make love and then to kill. There were people like that.

O God, help me, I whispered and I thought: again I am asking Him when I'm in trouble. It's the only time I pray, so what help can I expect?

There was something about this place. Was it the dark, the pungent smell, was it the eeriness? My father had stayed here. Where was he now? Perhaps he was dead and his spirit haunted the place and he was warning me now. After all I was his daughter.

Had Joss really gone to see the horses or would he come creeping up behind me. . . .

Nonsense, I told myself, this man is your husband.

My husband who was forced to marry me because he would gain a good deal if he did and lose it if he didn't. He stood to keep everything and my share too if he disposed of me.

I started. Footsteps, slow, stealthy, creeping up to the inn—and not from the direction of the river.

I was on my feet. I was at the door, crouching there. What was left of the door creaked as it was pushed open.

A man stepped into the inn. I heard his quick intake of breath, then he said: "Good God."

I cried out and he spun round. I thought I was dreaming, for it was David Croissant.

"Mr. Croissant. . . ." I stammered.

He stared at me. "What . . . in God's name. . . ."

I said: "The inn was burned out. Joss and I had planned to stay here."

"Why, it's Mrs. Madden. It gets stranger than ever. So you're here. Where's Joss?"

"He's looking after the horses."

We heard Joss coming then and David Croissant called out to him.

There were explanations. He had caught a ship in Cape Town about a week after he had seen us. He was on his way to the Fancy and had planned to stay at Trant's.

"I was hoping for a plate of Ethel's stew," he said. "My horses have had just about enough for today."

"Strange you should turn up," said Joss. "We saw your name in an old register we found here."

"Not surprising. I often stayed here. The most comfortable homestead for miles round. I wonder what became of poor James and Ethel."

"I'll show you where I've put our horses," said Joss. "It's a good spot. What have you got in your saddlebags?"

"We'll see," said David Croissant, and he went down to the water with Joss leading the way.

My feeling was one of immense relief because I was no longer alone with my husband.

It was not long before the two men were back from the horses and Joss made a fire and boiled a billycan of tea. David produced cold chicken and johnnycakes, and we all ate ravenously.

David talked as we ate about the many times he had stayed at the Trant Homestead. "Used to make a regular thing of it. I stayed here once with Desmond Dereham. I wonder what happened to him and where he went with the Green Flash. His name will never be forgotten."

"Not while people remember that Fancy Town was really named for him."

"Ah, Desmond's Fancy. That was what it was called, Mrs. Madden, before they got to work on it. That was before he'd stolen the Flash and disgraced himself. I'd like to know what happened to him and the stone. An opal like that shouldn't be allowed to fall into oblivion in my opinion. I wonder if we shall ever see it again."

"I wonder," said Joss, and it was all I could do to keep quiet and not cry out that my father had not stolen the stone. It was only the fact that, according to Ben, he had intended to, which kept me quiet.

David Croissant had several blankets with him, so we were able to sleep more comfortably in the shelter of the burned-out inn.

We set out at dawn and I rode between the two men into

the sunrise; and later that day we arrived at the town which was so named because of my father's certainty that he had found a prosperous opal field. And that day, for the first time, I saw my new home: Peacocks.

7

Peacocks

Fancy Town had sprung up on the banks of a creek which nature, by great good fortune, had set near the opal field. Some of the workers lived in calico tents, but there were a few huts made of logs or mud bricks with rough chimneys of clay or bark; and the shops were like sheds open on one side that their goods might be displayed. After the wide open spaces it was rather a depressing sight.

It was late afternoon when we arrived and the excitement our coming aroused indicated that visits were rare occurrences. Children came running out to stare at us—rather unkempt, most of them, which wasn't surprising, since the only homes they had were those huts and tents.

A man called to Joss: "Glad to see you back, sir."

"Thanks, Mac," answered Joss.

"Sorry about Mr. Henniker, sir."

Peacocks was about a mile from the town, and what a contrast it made to that poor place. We turned into a gate, and before us lay a drive of about a quarter of a mile to the house, which was built in the old Colonial style—gracious and shining white in the clean air. The porch and terrace were supported by rather ornate pillars which had a Grecian touch, but the house itself was periodless—it had something Gothic, Queen Anne, and Tudor about it—and the intermingling was not without charm.

A peacock appropriately appeared on the lawn followed by his meek little peahen; he strutted along beside the terrace as though asking for our admiration. The lawns were so immaculately kept that one would have thought they had been there for hundreds of years. In fact the immediate impression was that the house was posing as an ancient mansion, which it obviously could not have been, but was not quite sure which age it was meant to represent.

"Take the horses, Tom," said Joss. "Who's at home?"

"Mrs. Laud, sir, Mr. Jimson, and Miss Lilias."

"Well, let someone tell them we've arrived."

We dismounted and Joss took my arm as we went up the steps to the porch, David Croissant following. The door was open so we stepped into the hall. It was cool inside the house, for the thin wooden venetian blinds were slatted to shut out the fierce sunlight. The hall was large and lofty with a floor of mosaic paving all in peacock blue. In the center was one large flagstone in which was depicted a magnificent peacock.

"The motif of the house," said Joss, following my gaze. "Ben decided to call the house Peacocks and to have plenty of the aforementioned strutting around. I'd like to tell you that Peacocks will always belong to this family as long as there are peacocks here, but it wouldn't be any use, for we don't have those legends and old traditions here. We're too young a country. One thing Ben was determined on and that was that everyone who set foot in the house would know it was Peacocks. There's something to remind you everywhere."

There was a wide staircase winding up from the hall, and I saw a woman standing there watching us. She must have been standing there for some seconds listening to Joss's explanation.

He saw her as soon as I did. "Ah, Mrs. Laud," he said.

She came down the stairs—a tall, slender woman with fine, graying hair which she wore parted in the center and brought down to a knob in the nape of her neck. Her gown was of gray—high-necked with a very clean white collar and cuffs. The utmost simplicity of her dress gave her the appearance of a Quaker.

"Mrs. Laud!" cried Joss. "I've got a surprise for you. This is my wife."

She turned a shade paler and clutched at the banister as though to support herself. She looked bewildered, and then a faint smile touched her lips. "It's one of your jokes, Mr. Madden," she said.

Joss slipped his arm through mine and drew me forward. "No joke at all, is it, Jessica? We were married in England. Ben came to our wedding."

She came down the stairs rather slowly. Her face had puckered a little, and for a moment I thought she was going to burst into tears.

She said shakily: "The sad news of Mr. Henniker's death reached us only a week ago. You didn't mention . . . your marriage."

"No. That was to be a surprise."

She came forward and I held out my hand, which she took gently in her own.

"What will you think of me? I had no idea. . . . We have all been so sad. We have lost a good friend and master."

"I share your sadness," I told her. "I felt he was my very good friend."

"Mr. Croissant is with us, as you see," said Joss. "We picked him up on the journey from Sydney. Are Jimson and Lilias at home?"

"They're somewhere in the house. I've sent one of the servants to look for them. I am sure they will be here shortly."

"Mrs. Laud will be able to tell you all you want to know about the house, Jessica," said Joss.

"I shall be very interested to learn," I answered.

Mrs. Laud smiled at me almost ingratiatingly. I remembered what Ben had told me about her and was expecting someone of a more dominating nature. She appeared gentle, and her voice was soft and soothing.

"I think we'd better have some refreshment," said Joss.

"What am I thinking of," said Mrs. Laud, fluttering her hands helplessly. "I'm so shaken . . . by all this. First Mr. Henniker's death. . . ."

"And then this marriage," said Joss. "I know. But you'll get used to it. We'll all get used to it."

"I'll get them to make some tea," said Mrs. Laud. "Dinner will be served in an hour or so, unless you would like me to put it forward."

"We had chicken and johnnycakes on the road," said Joss, "so tea will do and then we'll wait for dinner."

Mrs. Laud opened a door and we were in a drawing room. It had long windows which reached from floor to a ceiling which was beautifully molded; the room was lofty and the curtains were of the same tinge as a peacock's feathers, but the daylight was shut out as the blinds were drawn. Mrs. Laud went to them at once and opened the slats so that the room was brighter.

My eyes immediately went to the picture of the peacock hanging on the wall. Joss's did the same; our eyes met, and a tremendous wave of excitement passed between us. The Green Flash at Sunset was hidden in that picture and we were going to take the first opportunity of seeing it.

There was a cabinet in this room in which were black-velvet-covered shelves and on the shelves were not polished stones but different types of rock with streaks of opal in them.

Joss saw me looking at them and said: "That was Ben's idea. Everything in there meant something to him. They have all come from different mines which were important to him. Ah, here's Jimson."

Jimson Laud was a man who I reckoned to be about Joss's age; he had the same gentle manner as his mother.

"Jimson, this is my wife," said Joss.

Jimson was startled, as well he might be, I thought. Joss grinned at me, obviously enjoying his surprise. "We seem to have delivered a bombshell," he said. "Jessica and I were married before we left England."

"Con . . . congratulations."

"Thank you," I said.

"I am so pleased to meet you," he said, recovering a little from his surprise. He then said he had been deeply shocked by Ben's death.

"We have all been shocked," answered Joss. "I'm afraid there was no hope of saving him. That was why he wanted me to go to England."

"And there you met your bride," said Mrs. Laud softly.

"Jimson works for the Company," Joss explained to me. "He and his sister Lilias live here in their mother's apartments."

"It's a large house," I commented.

"Mr. Henniker was always determined that there should be plenty of room for guests," said Mrs. Laud. "We often had a houseful. Well, here is my daughter, Lilias."

How alike the family were! Lilas was a younger edition of her mother—meek, unassuming.

"Lilias, this is Mrs. Madden . . . our future mistress," said Mrs. Laud.

Lilias's surprise was as evident as that of her mother and brother. I caught her expression as her eyes rested on Joss and I was not quite sure what it meant. She was certainly overwhelmed by the fact that we were married. The expression was fleeting; it had gone scarcely before it was there and she was the meek girl of a few moments before.

"You'll be staying for a while, Mr. Croissant, I dare say?" said Mrs. Laud.

"For a couple of nights, I hope. Then I have to get on to Melbourne."

"Has everything been going well while I've been away, Mrs. Laud?" asked Joss.

"Everything has been well in the house, Mr. Madden, which is all I can speak for."

Joss was looking at Jimson Laud, who said: "There have been one or two spots of trouble in the Company but nothing serious. I expect you will be down there tomorrow."

"You can be sure of that," replied Joss. "Tomorrow you must show my wife the house, Mrs. Laud."

Mrs. Laud bowed her head.

"I shall be most interested to see it," I told her.

Then the tea arrived.

"Shall I pour?" asked Mrs. Laud.

"I believe my wife would like to do that," said Joss, which was dismissing her, I realized.

"Lilias will see that they prepare the rooms," said Mrs. Laud.

"I'll talk with you later, Jimson," said Joss, "and then you can give me an idea of what's been happening."

We were alone with David Crossiant. I could feel that Joss was a little impatient by the manner in which his eyes kept straying to that picture.

I felt as impatient as he did. Very soon I was going to see the wonderful Green Flash.

David Croissant talked about some of the stones he had brought with him, a few of which he had shown us in Cape Town. He was most eager, he said, to see what the Fancy had thrown up lately.

"Not more eager than I," Joss reminded him.

In due course we had finished tea and Joss said he would take me up. As we mounted the stairs he said: "I noticed how your eyes kept straying to the picture. Were you thinking what I was?"

"I expect so."

"At the first opportunity we'll look. I shall lock the door because I don't want us to be disturbed. I hardly like to do it while David Croissant's in the house. He's got a nose for opals. I felt he was going to sense it in that room. We'll choose our moment. Well, what do you think of your home?"

"I have seen very little of it yet."

"It can't compare with that of your ancestors, of course, but it comes pretty near it. I believe Ben had Oakland in mind when he planned this. You'll discover several similar features. Imitation is the greatest form of flattery, it's said.

Well, this place is a piece of flattery to Oakland Hall. So you should like it."

"I like very much what I have seen."

"You must reserve your judgment until after your tour of inspection. By rights, you know, I should have carried you over the threshold."

I ignored that.

"What do you think of the Lauds?" he asked.

"I thought that they were very unassuming . . . eager to please."

"They're a sort of institution. Mrs. Laud came to work here . . . oh, it must have been quite twenty-seven years ago. She was a widow with two children. Her husband had come out after gold. He'd had some bad luck; he died and left them penniless. Ben took them in. Lilias was only a year or so old and Jimson was about five. She's been more than a housekeeper."

"I gathered that."

"She and Ben were *very* friendly at one time."

"You mean . . .?"

He looked at me maliciously. "You wouldn't understand," he said.

"I think I understand . . . perfectly," I contradicted.

"It gives them a certain standing in the household. Jimson was taken into the Company. He's good at figures . . . quite a good worker but uninspired."

"And Lilias?"

"A pleasant girl . . . more talented than you'd think."

"How do you know what I think?"

"My dear wife, I read you like a book. I saw your eyes on her contemplatively."

"She seemed eager to please *you*. Is that why you consider her talented?"

"Of course. It shows her wisdom. Ah, they have prepared the bridal suite for us."

He opened the door and turning to me swiftly, swept me off my feet and carried me into the room. I did not protest because that was what I realized he was hoping I would do. I remained passive until he set me down.

"Oh dear, oh dear," he said cluckling his tongue. "They've made the same mistake." He was regarding the big four-poster bed with feigned dismay. "There is a dressing room." He slipped his arm through mine and took me to it. "Designed for those occasions when all is not harmony between the married lovers. The bed looks uncomfortable. Moreover its proximity would be distasteful to you." He went to a bell-rope and pulled it.

It was Lilias who came, and I suspected that she had not been far off.

"Lilias," said Joss, "will you have my old room made ready for me. I shall need it."

She looked startled, but I saw the speculative gleam in her eyes. I was again wondering what the relationship had been between her and Joss.

"I will see to it immediately," she said. As she went out Joss turned to me. "You see what consternation you arouse in us all."

I did not answer. My cheeks were burning.

A maid came in with hot water.

"I'll leave you," said Joss, "and I'll come for you in just under an hour's time for dinner."

He went out and I looked round the room. The curtains were a light shade of yellow, the carpet a darker one; and there was a primrose-colored counterpane on the bed and touches of varying shades of yellow, all blending beautifully with each other throughout the room.

It was indeed pleasant. I washed, changed into a green silk dress and wondered when the rest of my baggage would arrive.

Then I went to the window and pulled up the blind. The sun immediately blazed in. Looking out I could just see beyond the grounds to the calico tents of Fancy Town. I imagined Ben in this house reveling in the similarities of Oakland and looking out on the town which had begun with my father's dream. "Ben, are you satisfied now?" I whispered, and I thought of the sudden fear which had come to me in the burned-out inn. I knew those fears were still there in the back of my mind waiting to emerge.

I longed for Ben then. I wanted to explain to him that when he had arranged our lives he had not been aware of what danger he was putting me in.

I seemed to hear his laughter. "It was a free choice, wasn't it? You didn't have to, did you? You wanted everything the marriage brought you . . . both of you. You took what you wanted; well, now you must pay for it."

Oh Ben, I thought, you were a ruthless man and your son is the same. You lived hard; you brushed aside those who stood in your way. Did you ever think, Ben, that *I* might be in Joss's way?

What was this idea which had been creeping into my mind since I had had my nightmare in the Bush? It was almost as though it had been a warning.

When Joss came to take me down to dinner I was ready and waiting for him.

He said: "The Lauds dine with us. They always have. You'll have to get to like them. They'll go out of their way to please you. Mrs. Laud is a wonderful manager. You can leave everything to her. We often have people in and out . . . for meals I mean. She manages that sort of thing very well."

The dining room was paneled like the one at Oakland and had long windows reaching from floor to ceiling at which there were blue draperies bordered with silver. A candelabrum stood in the center of the table and at either end was a decoration of variegated leaves that was very effective. Mrs. Laud had arranged everything very tastefully.

I saw her sharp eyes take in the details as though doubly to assure herself that they were as they should be. Soup was followed by roast chicken, and these were excellently served.

I felt ill at ease because I was aware of a certain tension at the table. I had a feeling that there was a great deal I had to discover about my new home. I believed that beneath the surface was something which would change the entire atmosphere if it came to light. It was an odd feeling. When I looked in her direction I would find Lilias's eyes on me; she smiled or looked hastily away and I asked myself whether I had been right in assuming she had some deep feeling for Joss and that our marriage was a great blow to her.

Mrs. Laud gave a kind of silent direction to the servants and I had the idea that she missed nothing.

I was mostly a listener at the dinner table that night, for the conversation was all about the Company and of this, of course, I had everything to learn.

Mrs. Laud said: "Tom Paling was badly hurt when the wheel came off a buggy he was driving. He'd been up to the house to see Jimson and on the way back to the town the wheel came off and he was nearly killed."

"Paling!" cried Joss. "Good God! He's all right now, I hope."

"He'll never walk again. Jimson took over his work . . . and I believe the department is running better than it ever did before. But you tell Mr. Madden, Jimson."

"Well you see," said Jimson, "this happened, and we thought it was the end of poor Tom. He injured his back and he's partly paralyzed. I took over his work at once."

Joss was clearly disturbed. "Paling was one of our best men. What about his family?"

"They've been looked after," said Jimson. "You'll see tomorrow that nothing has suffered in the department."

"Jimson was working day and night," said Mrs. Laud.

"That's a shock," murmured Joss. "What else happened?"

"Trant's Homestead was burned to the ground," said Lilias.

"We know that," replied David Croissant. "We called there on the way here."

"What happened to the Trants?" asked Joss. "They escaped, I hope."

"By great good fortune, yes. And they've set up a sort of cookhouse in the town. It's quite useful."

"It must have been a terrible blow to them."

"It was. James was quite broken, but Ethel rallied him, and they got this idea and now they're doing fairly well. It's useful for those who are working in the offices. They can slip out and get a meal—and a lot of people buy cooked food to take away."

"Some good has come out of it then," said Joss.

"I think you will find that some good has come of Tom Paling's accident," said Mrs. Laud. "I've heard that the department has never been run so well as it has since Jimson took over."

"We'll see," replied Joss.

"I thought," went on Mrs. Laud, "that you would want the Bannocks to come up to dine. You'll see Ezra tomorrow in the town, of course, but perhaps you would like me to ask them for dinner tomorrow."

"Isa will want to see what I've brought with me," said David.

"Yes, I think it's a good idea," Joss said. "There'll be a lot of detail to discuss." He turned to me: "Ezra Bannock is our manager-in-chief. He lives not far from here—about five miles actually, but that's close out here. They have a homestead . . . he and his wife Isabel—Isa."

"So it will be for tomorrow then," said Mrs. Laud.

"That will do very well," Joss told her.

"Oh," cried Lilias, "we haven't told Mr. Madden about Desmond Dereham."

"What?"

Everyone seemed to be leaning forward in their seats . . . I with the rest.

"It came from the Trants," said Mrs. Laud.

"Yes," went on Jimson, "someone came to stay there just before the place was burned down. He had recently arrived from America and he said he had been with Desmond Dereham out there and that Desmond had died. They'd become friends and gone into business together, which was buying and selling precious stones, mainly opals. Desmond was ill for some time, he was dying of some disease of the lungs and he told this man an extraordinary story about the Green Flash."

"What story?" demanded Joss.

"He swore he'd never stolen it. He said he had been tempted to and had been caught in the act of trying to take it by Ben himself. Ben had forced him either to face exposure or leave immediately, leaving no trace of his whereabouts. If he didn't, Ben had said, he'd have him arrested for theft because he'd caught him red-handed. Ben told him that there'd be no future for him in Australia, he'd see to that. So he went to America."

"And of course," said Joss, "this story is being repeated all over the town."

"People are talking of nothing else," agreed Jimson. "Apparently Desmond Dereham had said he had had nothing but bad luck since the night he had tried to steal the opal. He said that for a few minutes he had actually owned it because he held it in his hand, and if Ben hadn't come in and caught him, the stone would have been his . . . and that was why he had been unlucky ever since."

"In that case," said David, "where is the Green Flash?"

"According to Desmond Dereham it never left Ben's possession," said Jimson, "so it's either in England or here. . . ." He was looking at Joss. "Unless you know . . ."

"I haven't seen the Green Flash since the night it was supposed to have been stolen," said Joss. "I hope people are not making too much of this story about opals being unlucky. It's bad for business. Stop it when you can."

"The Green Flash has had rather a history," said David Croissant.

"Well, don't let's dwell on it," retorted Joss.

"I wonder if that fellow was telling the truth," went on

David. "If so it'll be a matter of finding where Ben has hidden the Green Flash."

"Would you like a little more of this apple pie, Mr. Madden?" asked Mrs. Laud. "I made it especially, knowing it was one of your favorites."

Joss began to talk about our journey out from England. It was clear that he was dismissing the subject of the Green Flash.

Coffee was served in a small parlor close to the dining room.

"Tomorrow," said Joss to me, "Mrs. Laud will show you round Peacocks while I go into the town to see what's been happening during my absence. Later on I'll take you in and explain a few things to you."

"That will be very interesting," I said.

The bedroom looked very different by candlelight. He had called it the bridal chamber and the four-poster bed was overpowering. Of course it had never been a bridal chamber. The house had been built by Ben, and he had never married.

I sat down at the dressing table and took the pins out of my hair, letting it fall about my shoulders. Images passed in and out of my mind—scraps of conversation came back to me. The Lauds, so meek and unassuming, interested me. There was something I didn't understand about them . . . secretive, was it? I thought of Lilias, who seemed to watch me so intently. Was she emotionally involved with Joss? Jimson was mild enough, but when they had talked about how he was conducting the department since Tom Paling's accident, had I detected something . . . I wasn't sure what.

It was clear that I myself was a little overwrought emotionally. It had been such a strange day. Too much had happened and my imagination was running amok.

I took off my dress and put on a dressing gown—part of the trousseau which my grandmother had insisted that I have. It was made of red velvet and was, I thought, becoming.

I sat down at the mirror and started to brush my hair. My reflection looked back at me—wide-eyed, a little apprehensive, watchful, waiting. I could see the room reflected behind me . . . the posts of the bed, the curtained window, the shadowy furniture, and I thought of my room at the Dower House where my naughty ancestress Margaret

Clavering looking down at me was supposed to provide a lesson. I thought how safe it was. Safe! That was the word which occurred to me.

Then suddenly I was so startled that I caught my breath and listened. It was a footstep in the corridor. Someone was out there stealthily coming towards my room. Whoever it was had paused outside my door.

I half rose, and as I did so there was a quiet knock.

"Who's there?" I cried.

The door was opened, and Joss stood there holding a candle in a silver candlestick.

"What do you want?" I cried in alarm.

"To talk to you about the Flash. I think we ought to find it."

"Now?"

"The household is asleep. I was going to wait until Croissant had gone, but I've changed my mind. I can't wait to see it. Can you?"

"No," I answered.

"Then there's no time like the present. We'll go down now and see it."

"And when we've found it?"

"We'll leave it where Ben put it until we decide what to do about it. Come on."

I wrapped my dressing gown more closely round me and he led the way to the drawing room. He locked the door and lighted more candles. Then he went to "The Pride of the Peacock," took it down, and laid it face down on a table.

"The spring Ben talked of would be somewhere here," he said. "Not easy to find, of course. That would have defeated the object if it had been. Hold the candle higher."

I obeyed. Some minutes passed before he cried: "I have it. The back comes right off."

He took it off and there in the right hand corner of the picture was the cavity large enough to hold a big opal. Eagerly he explored the cavity.

"Jessica," he whispered with a note of excitement in his voice, "you're going to see the most magnificent thing you ever saw in your life. . . ." He stopped and stared at me. "It can't be. . . . There's nothing here. Look. Feel it."

I put my fingers into the cavity. It was empty.

"Someone has been here before us," he said briefly.

It was then, as we stood there looking at each other that

I was sure I saw a shadow pass the window. I turned sharply but there was no one there.

"What's wrong?" asked Joss quickly.

"I thought there was someone at the window."

He took the candle from me and looked out. Then he said: "Wait a minute." He unlocked the door and hurried through the hall and out of the house. I saw him pass the window. I looked furtively over my shoulder, expecting, I did not know what.

In a short time he was back.

"There's no one about. You must have imagined it."

"I suppose that's possible," I admitted. "But I was almost sure. . . ."

"Who could have known . . . ?" he murmured. Then he became brisk. "The point is what are we going to do? It looks as if someone discovered the hiding place before we did. We've got to find out who, and where the opal is. There's nothing to be done now but put the picture back and go to bed. I'll decide tomorrow how we'll tackle this."

"It must have been someone who's in the house or who came to it . . . someone who knows the house. . . ."

"Ben was full of tricks. I wonder if he didn't leave it in the picture after all."

"But why should he tell us that he had?"

"I don't know. It's a mystery to me. The most likely solution is that it's been stolen. But there's nothing to be done tonight."

He put the back of the picture in place and hung it on the wall. The proud peacock again faced the room as before looking as though he had nothing in his thoughts but his own glory.

"I'll conduct you to your room," said Joss.

I followed him up the stairs and he left me at my door. Understandably I passed a restless night.

When I arose next morning, Joss had already gone into Fancy Town accompanied by Jimson Laud and David Croissant. I felt bewildered by all that had happened on the previous day culminating with the scene in the drawing room where we had made the discovery that the opal was missing.

Mrs. Laud was waiting for me when I went down.

"Mr. Henniker liked things done as they are in England," she said, "so we serve an English breakfast. There are bacon, eggs, and kidneys. Would you like to help yourself from the sideboard?"

I did so.

"I trust you slept well."

"Oh yes, thanks, as well as one can in a strange place."

"Mr. Madden was very anxious that I should show you everything, and if there is anything you want to change please say so. I have been running this household for twenty-seven years. Mr. Henniker was very kind to us. My daughter Lilias helps me in the house. It's a large place to run, and so many people come here. Merchants and such people when they come on business invariably stay here, though they are sometimes at the Bannock homestead. Managers from the Company dine here often when there is special business to discuss. Then there are certain gatherings . . . parties you'd call them. Mr. Henniker was all for getting people together. The Bannocks are here a great deal."

"I believe I am meeting them tonight."

"Oh yes." Her lips tightened almost imperceptibly. I wondered whether there was something about the Bannocks she did not like.

"I understand Mr. Bannock is the manager-in-chief."

"Yes. He's said to be very knowledgeable about opals. They all are, of course, but some are supposed to have this special gift. His wife is quite a collector."

"I shall look forward to meeting them. Of what age are they?"

"He would be about forty-five. She's much younger . . . ten years I'd say . . . though not admitting to it." Again that slight tightening of the lips. I guessed she was not as calm as she would like to imply, but she was a woman, I guessed, who was determined to keep her feelings to herself.

When I had eaten, we started on a tour of the house. I could not help feeling half amused, half sad, because it brought Ben so vividly to mind. He had tried to make an Oakland Hall of this house and had of course failed to do so. The rooms were lofty; there was the drawing room— and I couldn't help glancing at the peacock on the wall as I went in—with the study leading from it as at Oakland, but that was really where the similarity ended. At all the windows were the essential blinds to shut out the fierce sunlight so different from that benign and often elusive English version.

Through the different rooms she took me and it was true that there were a great many of them, and finally we came to the gallery which was a replica of that at Oakland.

"Mr. Henniker was very fond of this," Mrs. Laud told me. "He was anxious that it should be exactly like the one in his English home."

"It is," I said. "Oh . . . there's a spinet."

"He had that brought out from England. Someone he was fond of used to play it. She died. So he brought it here."

I felt emotional. That was the very spinet my mother had mentioned, the one she used to play and then hide when anyone came in, so that the servants thought the gallery was haunted.

Ben had been very sentimental.

She took me to the kitchens and introduced me to some of the servants. Several of them were aborigines.

"They are quite good workers," she told me as we came out into the gardens, "but every now and then the urge comes over them to 'go walk about' as they call it. Then they drop everything and go off. It makes them very unreliable. Mr. Henniker swore he wouldn't have them back when they returned . . . but he often relented."

She took me to the English garden, which was walled in the Tudor manner such as Ben had had at Oakland.

"He used to say this is like a bit of England," said Mrs. Laud. "It was difficult, he always said, with the droughts over here, but he always liked it to look as much as possible like home. Over that trellis we grow passion vines, but he put the convolvulus there to mingle with them and make it homey, he said. You must see the orchard."

There grew oranges, lemons, figs, and guavas with vine bananas.

"Mr. Henniker grew a lot of apple trees too, but he always said they weren't as good as those grown at home."

"It seems as though he had an obsession for home."

"Oh, he was a man who could be drawn many ways at once. He wanted to live several lives all at one time and enjoy them all."

"I think he succeeded," I said.

"He was a wonderful man," she replied. "It was a pity he ever saw the Green Flash."

I looked at her sharply, and she lowered her eyes. "It brings bad luck," she went on passionately. "Everyone knows it brings bad luck. Why do they want it? Why don't they let it alone?"

"It seems to fascinate everyone."

"When I heard it had been stolen by Desmond Dereham I was glad . . . yes, glad. I said it's taken its bad luck with it. Then there was Mr. Henniker's accident. He was never right after that. Then he died. I thought that was because he had had the Green Flash and had to pay for having it . . . but if Mr. Henniker had it all the time that would account for it. And where is it now?"

She looked at me steadily and I shook my head.

"It could be in the house. Oh, I don't like that. I'm afraid of it. It will bring bad luck to the house. It already has, and we don't want any more."

I was surprised, for though she endeavored to keep her emotions under control, she was agitated. Before this she had seemed so serene.

"You can't believe all these stories about bad luck, Mrs. Laud," I said. "There's no real foundation for them. They just grow out of gossip and rumor."

She laid a hand on my arm. "I'm afraid of that stone, Mrs. Madden. I hope to God it's never found."

I could see that she was distracted, and so was I when I thought of our discovery last night, so I suggested that I should go to my room and unpack some of my things which had arrived, and this I did.

8

Harlequin

I did not see Joss until dinnertime, but Lilias came to my room in the afternoon to ask if she could help me unpack.

I thanked her and said I could manage very well, but she sat down and watched me, admiring my clothes as I took them out. She thought them very elegant, she said, and they would surely make Isa Bannock jealous.

"She thinks she is a *femme fatale*," Lilias added.

"Is she?"

"She's reckoned to be so. There's no one like her in Fancy Town or hereabouts."

"It will be interesting to meet her."

"I hope you'll find it so. My mother has shown you the house, hasn't she?"

"Yes, it's fascinating."

"So like the one in England?"

"It's not really like it."

"It just tried to be, I suppose."

I smiled. "Mr. Henniker set out with the idea in the first place, I expect, and then found it didn't work."

"We're very anxious that you should put us right about anything you don't like. I hope you don't think we're too presumptuous."

"Certainly not."

"You see, when my mother came here Mr. Henniker was so good to us and I was only two . . . slightly less than that. . . so it's always been my home."

"And must continue so . . . until you marry."

She cast down her eyes again. It was a habit which she shared with her mother.

"We were rather anxious. We had no idea Mr. Madden would marry . . . over there."

"I know it was a shock to you all. You should have been warned."

"It's not for us to say what should and should not be done."

"Well, I'm sorry you weren't told before. I am sure we shall all get along well together."

"My brother, Jimson, is doing well at the works, especially now that he has Tom Paling's job. We're sure Mr. Madden will be pleased."

"It was a good thing that he was able to take over after Mr. Paling's accident."

"Oh yes, they would have been in difficulties without Jimson. We're proud of him. You may think it's a strange name . . . Jimson. Our father was Jim, so they called him Jimson."

"Very neat," I commented.

"Oh, we're a very close family. Jimson and I never forget what we owe to our mother. But I'm boring you, Mrs. Madden. I only wanted you to know that I'll be ready to help. Have you got plenty of room for your things? Mr. Madden's seems to be all in the other room."

She had lowered her eyes again. Was it a certain triumph she was hiding?

"I have plenty of room," I said coolly.

"Dinner will be at half-past seven," she said. "The Bannocks will be here by then. Will you come down when you're ready?"

I said I would, and she left me.

I had a suspicion that she might be pleased that Joss and I did not share a room. Her remarks about Isa Bannock had seemed rather pointed too.

I was becoming imaginative. Was I looking for mysteries and secret tensions? Too much had happened to me in too short a time, and the discovery last night had really startled me and made me wonder what was going on in this house. Then there was the niggling thought that someone had watched us from the window, and if I had been right about that, it must have been someone in the house.

I dressed with care and I thought it appropriate to choose a dress of peacock blue silk. "This," my grandmother had said, "will serve for a *dignified* occasion." And so I went down to meet the Bannocks.

They were in the parlor drinking apéritifs when I arrived. Joss came forward and took my arm.

"Come along, Jessica," he said, "and meet Isa and Ezra."

I did not see her immediately, for Ezra, a powerfully built man, had taken my hand and was nearly crushing it in an oversincere handshake.

"Well, this is a surprise," he cried in a booming voice. "Congratulations, Joss. You've got yourself a beaut."

I was not quite sure how to respond to this fulsome greeting so I smiled and said how pleasant it was to meet him, for I had heard a good deal about him.

"Nothing bad, I hope," he cried.

"On the contrary," I answered.

"And here's Isa," said Joss.

She was obviously several years younger than her husband, I thought, as she turned her lovely topaz-colored eyes upon me and scrutinized me with probing interest. She reminded me of a tigress. There were tawny lights in her hair to match her eyes; and there was something about her that reminded me of the jungle, for she moved like a cat with immense grace.

"So you're Joss's wife," she said. "We never thought he'd marry. What a sly thing to do . . . to spring it on us like this. I hope you'll like it here. It's good to have women around. There's a shortage of them here, you'll soon discover. It makes us all so much more precious than we should otherwise be. Don't you agree, David?" She was smiling at David Croissant, who seemed overwhelmed by her charms.

"I think it would depend on the woman," said David.

"What nonsense!" retorted Isa. "When there's a shortage the value automatically rises. You as a merchant should know that."

David grinned at her. It seemed as though his shrewd common sense deserted him in the presence of this siren.

"Let me get you something to drink, Mrs. Madden," said Mrs. Laud.

When it was brought to me, Isa was saying: "What have you brought in your peddler's pack, David? I can't wait to see."

Joss said: "After dinner, he'll show us, I dare say."

"The market's pretty good for black opals now," said Ezra. "I only hope they're not going to flood it."

"You've had some good finds hereabouts, I gather," put in David.

"You can be sure of that," added Ezra.

Isa smiled at me. "Aren't you longing to see them?" she asked.

"Yes, I am. I did see some in Cape Town when Mr.

Croissant was there. Joss and I were at the home of the Van der Stels."

Isa's eyes were dreamy. "That must have been a wonderful experience for you! A honeymoon at sea. And coming to a new home. How romantic! And then David arrived and showed you some of his precious opals."

"Yes. There was one I remember specially. The Harlequin Opal. I don't think I ever saw anything so beautiful."

"The Harlequin!" cried Isa. "What a marvelous name! I long to see it. Have you got it with you, David?"

"You shall see it after dinner," he promised her.

"And it's a real beauty?"

"It'll fetch a big price," said David.

"Opals mean business to David," Isa told me. "He doesn't see the beauty of the stones, only their market value. I'm not like that. I *love* beautiful stones . . . particularly opals. That flash of fire excites me. What was the finest opal you experts ever saw? I know what you're going to say: The Green Flash at Sunset."

Mrs. Laud said: "I think we should go in to dinner now."

Joss sat at one end of the table and I at the other. Isa was on his right hand, Ezra on mine. It was soon clear to me that the attention of the men was focused on Isa, and that this was what she expected as a right. I felt at a disadvantage and irritated by her manner, particularly as I guessed she was aware of this and was reveling in it, perhaps more than she usually did, and this was on account of me.

Thick, juicy steaks were served with fresh vegetables followed by passion-fruit jelly, but I scarcely noticed what I ate. My attention—like that of the men—was on Isa, and in particular on Isa and Joss. I noticed how once or twice she placed her hand over his and the manner in which he smiled at her. And it seemed to me that Mrs. Laud and Lilias were watching me in order to gauge my reactions.

Ezra seemed to be pleased by the effect his wife had, and it was clear that he was one of her greatest admirers. I tried to tell myself that she was an empty-headed and frivolous woman, but I knew there was more to her than that. She was secret, subtle, and cunning, and while she scolded Joss for marrying so hastily without letting them know and pretended it was all something of a joke, I was sure she was exceedingly piqued by it.

She returned to the subject of the Green Flash and repeated the story of Desmond Dereham's death in America and his confession.

"It seems that Ben had the opal all the time," she said. "In that case what on earth happened to it?"

There was a brief silence, and then Joss lifted his eyes and looking straight at me said: "Before Ben died he told my wife and me where he had hidden the Green Flash. He left it to us jointly."

Isa clapped her hands. "I want to see it. I can't wait."

"I'm afraid I can't show it to you," said Joss, "because when we looked in the place where Ben said he had hidden it, it was no longer there."

Mrs. Laud had turned very pale. "Do you mean, Mr. Madden, that it was in this house . . .?"

"When Ben put it there. Since then it seems someone has stolen it."

"It's no longer in this house then," said Mrs. Laud quietly. "Thank God for that."

"You've been listening to those tales, Mrs. Laud," said Ezra. "There always are tales about a fine stone. It's a sop to people's vanity. They don't want anyone to enjoy what they can't so they say it's unlucky and these tales get around. But, I say, what a thing to happen! What'll you do, Joss?"

"I'm going to find it, but where to start looking?"

"Who could have known where Ben had hidden it?" said Ezra. "Would he have told anyone?"

"I am sure he didn't. He didn't tell me until he was dying. Then he told us both . . . Jessica and me."

"Where was it?" demanded Isa.

"He had had a cavity made in a picture frame."

"How exciting and mysterious!" cried Isa. "I do wonder who has stolen it."

"I don't envy them," murmured Mrs. Laud.

"Oh, Mother, you take the rumors too seriously," said Jimson.

"There's one thing I want to say," said Joss. "I've said it before. I don't doubt I'll have to say it again. I don't want a lot of talk about unlucky stones. People could stop buying opals because of such talk."

"Joss," whispered Isa, "how can you start looking for the Green Flash?"

"It's no use putting up a bill saying 'Will the thief return priceless opal he stole from Peacocks sometime during the last two years,' is it?"

"Hardly. So how will you begin?"

"I shall have to work that out, but I'm determined to find it."

"And what Joss determines he always does, doesn't he, Mrs. Madden?" The tawny eyes mocked me. "You will know that as well as any of us."

"I'm sure he's very determined."

"I don't want talk in the town about this," said Joss.

"They're already talking about Desmond Dereham's not having stolen it and Ben's having it all the time," said Ezra.

"I know, but let that die down." He addressed Ezra, and I noticed afresh how when he wanted a subject changed, he made it clear. "Have you added any good horses to your stables lately?"

"One or two. You'll be interested, Joss. I've got a little beauty . . . a gray mare. She's called Wattle. I've never known any horse with such feeling. She's really fond of mè."

"All horses are fond of you," put in Jimson. "You have a way with them."

"Horses and women," said Isa, looking at her husband.

"Horses anyway," replied Ezra. "Have you got a good horse for Mrs. Madden?" he asked Joss.

"I've been thinking what there is in the stables. I'll probably have a look round."

"I'd like to give her my Wattle. She's just the ticket. She's strong, will of her own, but she's malleable, too. If I drop a word in her ear she'll be just the mount for the lady."

I said: "This is too generous."

Ezra waved his hand. "Oh, it's all in the Company. You're one of us now, you know."

"I'm most grateful. . . ."

"You'll love her. She's a real beaut . . . and such a good girl too. Treat her right and she'll treat you right and if I just give her the word . . . all will be well."

"It's true," Jimson told me. "I've never known anyone talk to horses as Ezra does."

"It's very kind of you," I said. "Thank you."

"Well, that's settled," said Isa. "David, I can't wait to see your treasures."

"Perhaps after coffee," suggested Mrs. Laud.

Isa was obviously impatient for coffee to be over and

this was soon taken in the parlor. Then we went into the drawing room, and before the eyes of the haughty peacock on the wall, who, could he have spoken, might have told us who had stolen the Green Flash, David sat at a table and opened the rolled-up cases. The blinds had been raised to let the light in with sundown, and as there was no gaslight at Peacocks several candles were lighted to shed their soft glow over the room.

We were all seated at a round table—Joss and Isa on either side of David Croissant, myself next to Joss, and Ezra on the other side of his wife. The three Lauds sat together. I was beginning to think their position embarrassed them; they were of the family and yet not quite of it, something which they themselves by their very manner called attention to, and which existed for that reason.

In the center of the table was a candelabrum, and as David unrolled the cases the gems glowed in their wonderful colors and I was fascinated by the flashes of fire.

"You've got some fine specimens there, David," said Ezra.

"Mostly from South Australia, this lot," replied David. "They're hard come by. You're lucky here. Conditions are not so good in the gibber country. It's dry as a bone and gougers there suffer great hardship—hardly any firewood, and water scarce as gold in a worked-out mine."

"He's trying to put the prices up," said Ezra with a wink.

Joss turned to me. "Gibber country is flat plains strewn with stones. Hard to live with, you can imagine." And I was irrationally pleased because he had remembered me.

"But David," said Isa imperiously, "where is this Harlequin we've heard so much about?"

"All in good time," replied David. "If you saw it first, you wouldn't want to look at the others."

"What a tease you are!"

He unrolled another case, and the men examined the opals, commenting on their size, color, cut, and other technicalities.

"Please David," wailed Isa, "*I* want to see the Harlequin."

So he opened a case, and there it was in all its glory—even more beautiful than it had seemed on the previous occasion—but perhaps I was a little more knowledgeable and able to recognize its superior qualities.

David lifted the stone and let the light fall on it. He touched it caressingly. I wondered whether he was thinking of its beauty or its worth.

Isa reached for it impatiently. She cupped it in her hands. "It's magnificent," she crooned. "I love it. Look at those colors. Harlequin, yes. No wonder Columbine loved him. Light, fantastic colors. . . ." She lifted her glowing face. "I think it's one of the loveliest stones I ever saw."

"I reckon it's worth a tidy sum," said Ezra.

"You're reckoning right," said David.

"I'd give a good deal to add that one to my collection," sighed Isa.

"I can see I'll have to start saving up," commented Ezra.

Joss turned to me again. "Isa has one of the finest collections of opals. She doesn't necessarily want to deck herself out in them. She takes them out and gloats over them."

Isa laughed, her tigress face animated by an expression I could not fathom. There was triumph in it and a certain greed.

"They're my inheritance," she told me. "If Ezra ever decides to discard me, I might have to realize my fortune."

"You think there is a possibility of his doing so?" I couldn't stop myself asking coolly. I was a little tired of her thrusting her superior attractions under my nose.

"As if I ever would!" said Ezra fondly. "Isa's a jackdaw," he went on, again to me as though since I had come here to learn about opals and the country I must also learn about the delectable Isa. "When she hears of the best stone of the year she wants it for her collection."

"Oh, how I should love to add this beautiful stone to it," said Isa. "If I had it I would stop these commercially minded men treating this beautiful object as though it represents nothing but a certain amount of money. You do understand that, don't you, Mrs. Madden?"

"Of course," I answered.

"A stone like that will eventually go into a private collection, I imagine," said Joss.

"And you want to add it to yours, I suppose?" Isa asked Joss pertly.

A look I did not understand passed between them, and he said quietly: "I'm considering."

Isa turned to me. "It's true that over the years I have got together some really fine stones. I should so much enjoy showing them to you sometime."

"I should very much like to see them."

"Please come over to us. We're only five miles from here. Wattle will bring you over. *She'll* be delighted to come and visit Ezra while you come and see me and my collection."

"Thank you."

Isa reluctantly laid the Harlequin on its velvet background, and David rolled up the case.

After that everything else seemed an anticlimax.

The Bannocks left soon afterwards and Joss went out to see them off.

I went up to my room and brooded on the evening. I kept thinking of Isa leaning forward, holding the Harlequin Opal in her hands. I felt there was something significant about the scene . . . all those people sitting around a table, their attention concentrated on that stone, the intentness of their gaze, the manner in which they handled the opals and the way in which they spoke of them; it was as though they admitted to a certain supernatural power which flashed in those colors. It was like a Greek play, I thought, with the Lauds as the Chorus, and I could not rid myself of the conviction that everything was not as it outwardly seemed. There was something uncanny hanging about the atmosphere of my new home.

Dominating my thoughts was the memory of Isa's attitude towards Joss and his towards her. She was flirtatious by nature, but she betrayed something deeper in her manner towards him. There had not been one of the men present who had not been attracted by her . . . even Jimson Laud, in a retiring sort of way.

"A *femme fatale*," Lilias had said.

I felt angry. How dared she behave in that way towards my husband in my very presence!

It was the first time that I had referred to him to myself as "my husband."

I shrugged that aside. Women like Isa irritated me, and whatever her relationship with Joss might be, I did not care.

I was ready for bed when I heard a sound in the corridor which startled me. I went to the door and listened. The footsteps were slow and stealthy. At my door they paused. I found myself trembling. Someone was standing close to my door, listening. Cautiously I lowered my hand and found the key; I turned it quickly in the lock. The sound it made would be heard from outside.

For some seconds there was silence, then I heard the sound of retreating footsteps.

The incident had shaken me considerably.

When I went down to breakfast next morning, Ezra Bannock was there. I was surprised to see him so soon after last night. He and Joss were at the breakfast table, and Ezra laughed heartily when he saw me.

"Ah, you're surprised," he said. "Well, I thought you and Wattle ought to get together right away. I've told her all about it and she's agreeable. A bit put out at first about leaving me, but she knows it's what I want so she'll play. As soon as you've had a bite to eat, we'll go to the stables and I'll make a formal hand-over. I'd like to be there just to see how you two get along."

"Then we'll go into the town together," said Joss, "and I'll show Jessica round."

I took to Wattle immediately, as she did to me. I was rather amused by the way Ezra patted her and talked to her.

"Now, old girl, we'll see each other often. I'll be over there and you'll be over here. I want you to look after this young lady. It's a bit rough going out here for her, so you'll look after her, now won't you?"

Wattle nuzzled against him.

"That's the idea. She's just come out here, you see, and we want to give her a good impression. There! That's my girl." From his pocket he took a lump of sugar and gave it to Wattle. She took it and crunched gratefully.

When I mounted her she seemed docile enough, but I sensed the fire in her. I leaned forward and chatted to her, trying to give a good account of myself for she seemed to be assessing me.

As we rode out, Ezra on one side of me, Joss on the other, I felt confident and grateful to the big, rather clumsy man, and I wondered why Isa had married him and what he thought of her behavior.

Very soon the town came into sight. It was not beautiful by any stretch of imagination. There in the heart of the arid land was a crudely constructed town bordered by a fringe of calico tents. Outside these were trestle tables and benches and on the tables were rather primitive cooking utensils.

"You'll have a few surprises," said Joss. "Remember this is a town which sprang up overnight. The people living in the tents haven't been here long enough to acquire a more solid dwelling, so they temporarily pitch their tents. Some have wives and families, which is easier for them in a way. The wives cook and mend and there are jobs the children can do."

Some of the children came out of the tents to stare at us as we passed into the center of the town, and the dwellings on either side were like little cottages. There was a store where all kinds of goods were sold. I noticed how respectful everyone was to Joss and what curiosity was directed towards me.

We passed a blacksmith busy at his anvil shoeing a chestnut horse. Joss called out: "Good morning, Joe."

"Good morning, master."

"This is Mrs. Madden, my wife. You'll be seeing a good deal of her in the future, Joe."

The blacksmith came forward rubbing his hands together. "Welcome to the Fancy, Ma'am," he said.

"Thank you, Joe."

"And happy congratulations if you'll accept 'em."

"I will and thanks again."

" 'Tis good to see the master wed at last," commented Joe.

Joss gave his sudden burst of laughter. "So that's your opinion, is it?"

" 'Tis well for gentlemen to settle down, master, when they'm no longer boys."

"Yes. You see Joe doesn't mince his words. He's a wizard with horses, though. In fact he believes they're more important than anyone else. That's so, eh, Joe?"

"Well, master, we'd be hard put to it to do without 'em."

"True. Tether the horses here, Joe," said Joss.

Ezra alighted and I noticed how he spoke to his horse and didn't forget Wattle, asking her how she was and if she didn't think me light as a fairy on her back. "A bit different from old Ezra, eh?"

I noticed Wattle nuzzling against him lovingly and being rewarded by yet another piece of sugar. He left us and said he would go on to the offices and see us later, and Joss took my arm and we sauntered along what he called The Street. He stopped and introduced me to several people. It was hot and the flies were beginning to pester. Joss grinned as I tried to brush them aside.

"It's nothing to what it will be later on in the day," he said with a certain satisfaction. "You'll have to be careful of the sandflies. They can give you sandy blight which, believe me, is not very pleasant. And they're particularly partial to fresh English blood—especially when it's of the blue variety. You see, they're used to coarser stuff. So watch out."

"I think you're trying to make me dislike the place."

"I just want you to see it in its true colors. I think you had rather a romantic idea in the first instance. You thought we walked around in beautiful sunshine all the time and now and then stooped to pick up a valuable opal."

"What nonsense! I did nothing of the sort. Ben had told me so much. I know what hazards miners face. Ben's accident was enough to tell me that."

"Don't look so angry. People will think we're quarreling."

"Aren't we?"

"Just a little friendly banter. But we have to create a good impression. It wouldn't look good for the newlyweds to be quarreling already."

"Good for what?"

"Business," he replied promptly. "Friction is not good for the Company."

"Do you think of nothing but the Company?"

"Now and then I think of other things."

"I believe it would be better if you allowed me to form my own impressions."

"Very well. Form them."

Men wearing cabbage tree hats to keep off the sun and others in straws on the brims of which were attached corks which danced as they walked—again a precaution against the flies—were going to and from the field which lay stretched out beyond the township. I looked at the dried-up land and the shafts and piles of mullock which had been dug up that the land might be explored.

"There are two thousand people here," Joss said rather proudly, "so there have to be traders to supply them. The Trants' Cookshop has been a great success already, I've gathered."

"I'd like to meet the Trants," I said.

"I'll have a word with them now. They'll expect it."

We went on and there in one of the wooden dwellings I met James and Ethel Trant. James was seated on a stool at the door peeling potatoes, and he scrambled to his feet when he saw Joss.

They shook hands.

"I was sorry to hear what happened," said Joss.

James Trant nodded. "We're getting on all right now though. We're making quite a success of this."

"And it's a good thing for the town, they tell me."

"We like to think so, sir. We were lucky to find a place. Mr. Bannock suggested it and it works."

"Good. This is my wife. I'm taking her round to have a look at the place."

James Trant shook hands with me and said: "Welcome to Fancy Town." He added that he would go and tell Ethel.

Ethel, wrapped in a large apron, came out wiping floury hands on a cloth. I was introduced to her and Joss and I repeated how sorry we were to hear of their misfortune and how we had discovered it when we had spent a night at the burned-out inn.

"Don't do to look on the black side," said Ethel. "There's not much hope of saving a wooden house when you're in the Bush, and it had been so dry . . . the grass was ready to flare up if you so much as looked at it. When I saw that the fire was getting a hold, I knew we hadn't a hope. Well, we've been lucky. As soon as Mr. Bannock said why shouldn't we have the corner place and turn it into a cookshop, we got going. It's the very thing they wanted at the Fancy. Things are not so bad now, are they, James? I used to take such pride in feeding them. They could eat like horses, those cattlemen and miners. They'd come to me tired out with a day's riding and longing for a taste of the sort of food they'd had at home. Stews they loved and there was always roast beef. A lovely bit of sirloin . . . that was the favorite . . . red and juicy; and they loved my potatoes done in their jackets. Done in the coals they couldn't be beaten. And a good beef stew swimming with onions and dumplings, and damper to go with it . . . and of course tea with everything."

James interrupted by saying that as long as the field continued to yield good opal they were sure of a living.

"May it be for a good many years to come," said Ethel fervently.

"It will," Joss assured her.

"The funny thing was," said Ethel, "that it was only a few days before the fire that this man came along."

"What man?" said Joss sharply.

"Him who'd been with Desmond Dereham in America. He said Desmond had never stolen the Green Flash and

that all the time it had been here in Australia. I wondered
if that had brought us bad luck."

"What utter nonsense," said Joss sharply.

"That's what I tell Ethel," agreed James.

"Well, it seemed funny to me. Whenever that Flash is
about there's bad luck. Look at Mr. Henniker. Who'd have
thought that accident would have happened to him."

"Accidents happen to anyone at any time," retorted Joss
tersely.

"But you see, he had the Flash all the time if this man
was right . . . and then he had the accident and now he's
dead."

Joss said angrily: "If that sort of talk goes on you'll have
no cookshop. All this nonsense about ill luck has got to be
stopped, and I'll put an end to it."

James and Ethel looked crestfallen, and I felt sorry for
them and angry with Joss.

I said gently: "I'm sure nobody takes that sort of thing
seriously."

"But they do," snapped Joss, "and it's got to stop."

I smiled apologetically at James and Ethel and Joss said:
"We must be going."

When we were out of earshot I said: "Need you have
been so curt?"

"There is every need."

"Those poor people have suffered a dreadful tragedy and
you can't even be civil to them."

"I'm being kind to them. Talk like that could make the
price of opals slump and cookshops with them. It's something we have to fight against."

"I see. Being cruel to be kind."

"Exactly, and you object to it?"

"It's a mode of self-righteousness which I particularly
dislike."

"I've discovered something."

"What?"

"That there's a great deal about me that you particularly
dislike."

I was silent and he went on maliciously: "You've burned
your boats, I'm afraid. You've accepted the conditions of
Ben's will. Just think . . . all this . . . and me too. . . .
You've accepted us. You've made your bed and now you
must lie on it. . . ." Again that mocking laugh. "Though

I have to admit that's a rather unfortunate analogy in the circumstances."

I said angrily: "I came out this morning determined to like everything. It's you who are spoiling things."

"Isn't that how it's always been? Now had Ben produced a pleasant gentleman for you instead of me, all might have been as merry as a marriage bell—as you see I'm in a quoting mood today."

I said: "I think we should at least try to behave in a gracious manner, whatever resentments we feel for having been pressed into a situation distasteful to us both."

"I believe that's a good old English custom."

"It's not a bad one."

"You set me an example. Pretend that all is well. It's a great help. Who knows in time you may enjoy being here among the shafts and the gougers. And one day this is going to be a real town with a town hall, a church and a steeple. We'll get rid of the shacks and build proper houses, and the calico tents will be gone. It'll be more to your taste then."

"Perhaps," I said.

"Here are the Company's offices," he told me as we came to quite the most impressive building in the township. "You'll want to know what goes on in here, as you are now part of it. It's no use despising what you have a share in, is there? You'll gradually find out what goes on, but this morning I'll content myself with introductions."

"I hope they won't feel resentful towards me."

"Resentful towards my wife! They wouldn't dare!"

We entered the building. It was good to get out of the sun and enjoy a little respite from the flies.

There were several rooms in which people were working. Again I was aware immediately of the effect Joss had. There was no doubt that they were all in great awe of him. Ezra had gathered some of the heads of departments into the boardroom, and there they were introduced to me.

"Mrs. Madden is one of our new directors," Joss explained.

There were six men present, including Ezra and Jimson Laud. Of the others I felt particularly drawn to Jeremy Dickson, blond, fresh-faced, and not long out from England. Perhaps it was for that reason that we seemed to have something in common.

Joss explained to me that mining was only the beginning

of the industry: there was expert sorting into categories and snipping and putting the stones on facing wheels; all these tasks had to be performed by experts. One mistake could mean the loss of a great deal of money.

"These gentlemen," he explained, "are all experts in their various fields."

As we sat around the table, he told them the terms of Ben's will and that Ben's shares in the Company had been divided equally between himself and me, which made me of course an important figure.

He turned to me. "You will no doubt want to acquaint yourself with all that goes on here . . . that's if you decide to take an active part. It's a decision you won't want to make in a hurry. You can of course always allow me to take care of everything for you."

"I feel I want to be able to take my place here with the rest of you," I said.

My decision was applauded.

"In that case," Joss went on, "we'll have a run through of what has been happening during my absence. That should teach you something."

I sat there while they talked. Secretly I found a great deal of it beyond my comprehension, but I was determined not to allow Joss to score over me. I had already made up my mind that I was going to take my place in the Company and show these men, who I was sure had made up their minds that I would soon tire of it, that I could grapple with problems as well as they could.

When they had talked for about an hour and I was very little wiser at the end of it, Joss asked if I would like to see some of the departments or would prefer to return to Peacocks. If the latter was my choice he would send someone back with me.

I said I would see the departments. Jeremy Dickson was told to take me around. Afterwards he could ride back with me to Peacocks, for Joss would be engaged at the township for the rest of the day.

With Jeremy Dickson I saw how opals were sorted in one room and in another put under the facing wheels. I watched the men at work, and Jeremy pointed out how quality was recognized. I learned to distinguish pieces likely to contain first-, second-, or third-class opal from what was merely what they called "potch." This was Jeremy's particular forte.

I was fascinated by the snippers, who were able to cut away worthless stone and, by means of whirring wheels which had to be used with the utmost care while the worthless layers were removed, reveal the beautiful colors beneath. One false move, it was explained to me, and a precious opal could be lost.

Later I was to see opal revealed in all its flashing beauty when the worthless stuff was whittled away; and men almost weep with frustration when a stone on which they had been working proved to be sand-pitted through and through, making worthless the beautiful stone which otherwise could have brought a handsome price on the markets.

It was a most interesting day, but one thing I knew Joss was right about: it would have been a mistake for me to try to absorb too much at once. After the heat and my experiences I was ready to go back to Peacocks.

Wattle was submissive as I mounted her, and although I had the impression that she was trying me out, I didn't think I had offended her so far.

I enjoyed talking to Jeremy Dickson, who told me about his home in Northamptonshire. He was the son of a curate, which immediately made me sympathetic—I suppose reminding me of Miriam and her Ernest. He had come out to Australia eight years previously and had thought he might make a fortune out of gold as so many people had before him. However, he had not done very well at this and suffered many disappointments. Then he had discovered opal and these stones had begun to exert their perennial fascination over him. He met Ben Henniker in Sydney and in characteristic manner Ben had taken a liking to him and offered him a place in the Company. He had worked hard and soon found he had special skills which impressed Ben. Three years ago he had been put in charge of the department.

"And you enjoy the life out here?" I asked.

"I love opals," he replied. "They do something to me. I can't express how I feel when I see the colors emerging. I could never find anything to do which would give me the same pleasure."

"Don't you miss Northamptonshire?"

"One always dreams of home. There is, of course, a lot one misses, when the day's work is over mostly. But Ben was always aware of that and he did his best to keep us happy. We often had invitations to Peacocks. Ben used to ask us to dinner to discuss business and there were occasions when we'd all gather together there and have parties. We missed him very much when he went to England, but your husband carried on in the old tradition and when he went Home I was invited to call by the Lauds, which I found very enjoyable."

We had reached Peacocks and I said: "You'll come in now, won't you?"

"For half an hour, please. Then I must get back to work. But I shouldn't like to call and not say hello to Mrs. and Miss Laud."

I took him into the drawing room and sent one of the servants to tell Lilias and her mother that we had a visitor.

It was Lilias who came. I was amazed at the change in her. She smiled and went forward, holding out both her hands which Jeremy Dickson took. "I brought Mrs. Madden back," he explained.

"You must be hot and tired," said Lilias. "Shall I send for something refreshing?"

"Please do," I told her.

She pulled the bellrope and asked for lemonade.

She had made it herself early that morning, she told us, and had stood it in ice so that it would be delightfully cooling.

We sipped and talked, and I thought how pleasant it was. Jeremy Dickson was so English that I felt completely at home with him. As for Lilias, she seemed like a different person. I wondered whether she was fond of the young man, since he seemed to have such an effect on her.

We talked of the township and what I had seen that morning, and he told us about a piece of opal that had just come in and could be wonderful if there was no flaw in it, and how breathtakingly exciting it was to watch the layers of useless stuff being removed to reveal the gem beneath.

Then Mrs. Laud came in.

She stood at the door looking at us, her expression enigmatical and her eyes not on me but on Lilias.

"So Mr. Dickson has called," she said.

"Yes, Mother. He brought Mrs. Madden back. The lemonade I made this morning has come in useful."

"How nice," said Mrs. Laud, her eyes downcast as though she did not want to look at any of us. She seemed nervous.

"I found it most refreshing," I said, feeling the need to

say something while I asked myself: Why are we talking about lemonade when something dramatic seems to be happening?

My eyes went to the proud peacock looking down on us with his disdainful stare, and he reminded me of Joss. Again I had the impression that I had stepped into a drama with a plot which was a puzzle to me—but in this scene it was not I who was playing the principal part.

Each morning for the next three days I rode into the town with Joss. The first event on arrival was the meeting with the heads of department when the business of the day was discussed, with Joss presiding. If any finds of special interest had been brought in by the gougers on the previous day they were closely examined. Joss would always hand the rock to me with what I thought of as a superior smile, and, as I examined it, I determined to learn quickly just to confound him. But that was not really my only reason. Each day I became more and more genuinely fascinated.

I made a point of getting to know, as soon as possible, many of the people who worked in the building . . . the few clerks and those who did their job at the benches. I talked to the miners when they came in, and although at first I was aware that they thought my presence something of a joke, when they discovered that I wasn't quite as ignorant as they expected me to be, they began to have a little respect. I was finding it all a tremendous challenge—not only to confute Joss but to show these people that a woman was not only fit to manage a house and bear children, which I knew was what they were thinking.

I was most interested in the sorting and snipping and the work that went on at the facing wheels. As this was Jeremy Dickson's concern, I was seeing more of him than other members of the Company. There was little that was practical about his approach to opals; he was a romantic.

On my fourth morning he boiled water on a spirit lamp in his tiny office and made tea in a billycan. As we sat drinking it, he talked of opals and told me marvelous stories about them.

"The ancient Turks," he said, "had a theory that a great fire stone was thrown out of Paradise in a flash of lightning. It was shattered and fell in a great shower which was scattered over certain areas of the world. That is now opal country." His eyes glowed. "Do you know, it used to be called the Fire Stone. You can understand it, can't you? That glow! Does it thrill you, Mrs. Madden, in a rather unaccountable way? Do you have to keep gazing and feel you could lose yourself in it?"

"I'm beginning to."

"You'll get more so. I've often thought these stones have some odd power because of the hold they get on people. It seems to be universally felt that they have some uncanny influence."

As we talked, the door opened and Joss looked in.

"Am I interrupting a tea party?" he asked.

"It's a working tea party," I replied. "Mr. Dickson is teaching me a great deal."

"I hope you are finding my wife an apt pupil." He stressed the words "my wife" as though he were reminding Jeremy Dickson who I was. Quite unnecessary, I thought, and as he shut the door and went off I felt annoyed because he had spoiled our tête-à-tête. I could see that Jeremy Dickson was thinking he should be back at work.

The day after that, when I went down to breakfast, Joss said: "It's time I showed you something of the countryside. I thought we'd take a ride this morning. You'd better get some idea of the layout of the land. It wouldn't be wise for you to go riding alone until you had."

"I dare say I could find someone to go with me for a while."

"That's what I'm offering to do now. You'd surely find others too. I dare say young Dickson would be ready to oblige."

"He's very knowledgeable about opals."

"He wouldn't hold the job he does if he weren't," replied Joss curtly.

We walked our horses away from Peacocks in the opposite direction of Fancy Town.

I said: "Are you doing nothing about the theft of the Green Flash?"

"Can you suggest what should be done?"

"Surely when something so valuable has been stolen some effort should be made to retrieve it."

"This is rather an unusual theft. In the first place, no one knows when it took place."

"It must have been some time after Ben left for England. I wonder why he didn't bring the stone with him."

"It would have been risky traveling with such a valuable

piece and he thought it was safe where he had put it."

"But someone found the hiding place. Surely we should make some effort. . . ."

"I am," he said.

"Don't forget it's partly my stone."

"I don't."

A thought entered my head then that he had been in Peacocks after Ben had left. Suppose he had been the one who had found the stone in the picture!

Surely he would not have stolen the opal from Ben! Yet that stone had a strange effect on people. My own father had been so bewitched by it that he had contemplated leaving my mother for it. Who could say . . . ? And it would explain why he was doing nothing about finding it.

"Leave this to me," Joss said. "I'll think of something. We're going to find the stone, but in due course. You want everything done so dramatically. Life's not a melodrama, you know. Things can't be tied up into neat little parcels and labeled. The thing I'm most anxious about at the moment is to stop all this talk about the Green Flash because with it comes the idea that opals are unlucky. I can't tell you how hard Ben and I used to fight to quash that. We want to keep the old legends going when they were said to be talismans against evil. So remember, not too much talk about the Green Flash."

"You make it sound like an order."

"That's not a bad way of looking at it. For everyone's comfort, forget it."

He turned from me and made his way towards a range of low hills. The ground was dry and sandy so that a cloud of dust was displaced by his horse's hoofs, and as he galloped straight through a gap in the hills, I lost sight of him for a few moments. How I should have liked to turn back, but already I was aware of the fact that one part of the Bush looked very like another and there were so few distinguishing landmarks. I knew I should not be able to find my way back to Peacocks without his guidance.

I came through the gap and there he was waiting for me.

"This is known as Grover's Gully," he told me. "There was a very flourishing mine here at one time. Now it's duffered out, as we say out here, which means it's no longer productive. Yet it was once one of the biggest-yielding opal mines in New South Wales. It's full of underground chambers. There's a rumor that it's haunted."

"I thought you were too down to earth to believe in such things out here."

He grinned at me. "Not all of us. In fact some of us are very superstitious. Men who work in dangerous operations are. Fishermen, miners . . . they are some of the most superstitious people on earth. There are so many occasions in their lives when they tempt fate. The story is that a man named Grover made his fortune here and then went to Sydney to settle down. He found a woman, married her, and together they gambled his fortune away. Then he found out she was only interested in his money when she left him, and he was bitter. He turned into a bushranger, and some said he used to hide in the underground chambers of his old mine which had made him rich. He was always masked, and he was actually known as the Masked Ranger of Grover's Gully. Of course when he was operating nobody knew he was Grover. It was only when he was shot dead by the driver of a small carriage he was holding up that they took off his mask and discovered who he was. After that people said he haunted the place, and they don't like passing it at night. Some have sworn they've seen a masked man. I reckon it was mulga bush and imagination did the rest. Well, that's the legend of Grover's Gully so make sure you don't pass this way after sundown. If you do you might see the masked ghost or hear Grover crying for his woman and his fortune."

"There's certainly something desolate about the place."

We walked our horses until we were close to the old mine. A deep shaft had been sunk, and I saw an old iron ladder, which had been used for the descent, still in position. In spite of the fact that I knew he was watching me closely, I could not repress a shudder.

He came closer to me. "You will sense it," he said. "The eerie atmosphere, the presence of the dead." He spoke in a low, mocking voice.

"I'm just wondering what I should have thought if you hadn't told me the story. I should have said it was just another . . . what did you say . . . duffered-out mine?"

"Good. You're learning. Come on. That's enough of Grover's Gully."

He moved off and I followed. He was a little way ahead of me when he pulled up once more and pointed away to the horizon.

"Can you see a building there?"

"I can just make it out. Is it a house?"

"A homestead."

"Whose?"

"You'll see," he called over his shoulder, and rode on.

A white house lay ahead of us gleaming in the brilliant sunshine.

"This is the Bannock homestead," said Joss, and my spirits fell. The last person I wished to see was Isa Bannock.

As we approached the dogs started to bark and Ezra Bannock came out. He cried out in his hearty way when he saw us: "Well, look who's here." He opened the gate and took us into a grass enclosure. Wattle gave a whinny of delight as he stroked and patted her and asked how she was getting along and told her how glad he was to see her.

"Come along in," he said. "Isa will be pleased. Come to the stables first, and I'll show you the new little filly I've got. I reckon that's what you came out to see, eh, Joss?"

Joss answered: "I knew Jessica would like to come." And he looked at me quizzically as though he was amused and knew it was the last place to which I wanted to come because of the antagonism between me and Isa.

We went into the stables, which were as big as those at Peacocks. Wattle was clearly in good spirits to be where she considered was home. She had been an easy mount for me and I wondered whether this really was because Ezra had told her to be. That seemed rather fanciful, but to see Ezra with horses made one feel that he had a special magic for transforming them into human beings while he talked to them.

We went into the house. An artistically arranged bowl of flowers stood on an ornately carved oak chest. The hall was tiled, which gave a gratifying coolness to the place.

"Isa," shouted Ezra. "Visitors."

Then I saw her. She was wearing a kind of morning gown in a soft, voilelike material with a frilly skirt and flowing sleeves. She looked fresh and, I had to admit, beautiful; the dress of a light-brown color brought out the tawny lights in her hair and eyes.

"But this is fun," she said, coming towards us. "Mrs. Madden *and* her husband."

Joss took her hand and kissed it. I was shocked and surprised that he should do that for it seemed out of character. But apparently he could be different with Isa than with anyone else.

"My *dear* Joss," she murmured tenderly, "it *is* good of you to come to our little homestead."

"I hope we haven't come at an inconvenient time," I said to draw her attention to the fact that I was also present.

"My dear Mrs. Madden . . . but don't you think we should call each other by our Christian names? After all we are going to see each other frequently, and Joss has always been Joss to me, so it seems only right and proper that I should call his wife by her Christian name. Jessica then . . . it suits you. . . ." The manner in which she said my name suggested a rather prim woman, tight-lipped, stern-faced, inclined to take life very seriously. She laughed. "Jessica, there can never be a wrong moment for calling. We get so few visitors out here that they are always welcome."

"It's a short time ago that we met."

"Too long," she cooed. "You will stay for luncheon," she went on eagerly. "Ezra was working at home this morning so it will be good to have you join us. You can talk business to your hearts' contentment, but over my table instead of in that gruesome boardroom of yours."

"That does sound an excellent idea," said Joss warmly. "In fact I was hoping to be asked. Then we can go back in the cool of the afternoon."

I was deeply conscious of the change in his voice when he addressed her, and it filled me with resentment.

"First cool drinks in my parlor," said Isa. "Now Ezra, my darling, please summon Emily."

The parlor was essentially hers. Indeed I wondered what part Ezra played in this ménage. I had thought of her as a jungle cat; now I saw her as a female spider who devours her mate—but only of course when he has ceased to be useful to her. It was a frilly, feminine room with muslin curtains and the inevitable sun-blinds. Pots of brightly colored plants gave the room an air of gaiety and the chintz-covered chairs and the curtains augmented that impression. Tall cool drinks were brought in and we were very grateful for these.

"We're very neighborly out here, Jessica," said Isa. "You must never think that we shouldn't be pleased to see you. We like all visitors . . . especially those who are friends." She threw a coquettish glance at Joss, who was smiling at her in a way which was beginning to madden me. At least, I thought, he might not show his besotted admiration so blatantly in front of his wife . . . for even though our relationship is not the usual one, there are conventions to be observed.

They chatted about people of whom I had never heard. Isa made sure of that because I guessed she was determined to shut me out until they mentioned the yearly treasure hunt which was held at Peacocks.

"Oh, haven't you heard about it, Jessica? Oh, Joss, you are very slack. Fancy not telling Jessica about the treasure hunt."

Joss turned to me. "It's a little entertainment we do once a year. It's due in a few weeks' time. I must tell you all about it."

"It's the greatest fun," said Isa. "We all go . . . how many Joss . . . about fifty, sixty, seventy of us . . . to Peacocks and there we're given clues and we search and search. It's one of the events of the year. Ben thought of it to keep the people happy. He was always trying to keep his workers from being bored. He used to say trouble starts with boredom."

"It sounds interesting," I said. I looked at Joss coldly. "I should like to hear about it."

"There's been such a lot to show you," he said. "I forgot to explain about it. It's a little childish perhaps. . . ."

"But it's fun," cried Isa.

"And people seem to enjoy it," added Joss.

Isa changed the subject as abruptly as she had introduced it.

"I did promise to show you my collection, Jessica, didn't I? Perhaps I will. What do you think, Joss?"

She and Joss exchanged a glance, which I was aware of without—then—fully understanding.

He said: "By all means show her, Isa. Jessica's getting really interested in opals. It'll be part of the education she's rapidly acquiring."

"Then after lunch," promised Isa. "And we'll have that now."

We went into the dining room for luncheon which consisted of cold chicken and salad and there was fruit which she told me her servants bottled and preserved when there was a glut.

"*You* will probably do your own bottling and preserving, Jessica. I am sure you do it beautifully. I'm afraid my talents stop short of housekeeping. Still, I have other uses I believe."

Ezra laughed loudly and Joss smiled as though she had said something very witty.

My irritation was growing and my great desire was to get

away from this woman for among those talents she mentioned there was certainly one for making me feel unattractive. It was all the more galling because I felt that Joss was aiding and abetting her in this.

After lunch we settled down to see her collection. We went back into the shady parlor with its frills and femininity—Isa's room. We sat at a table and from a safe she took out the now familiar rolled-up cases. She had some magnificent stones and she was clearly knowledgeable about them. They were of all varieties and all exquisite.

"I only want the very best," she told me.

"That's what you have," replied Joss.

"Coming from such a connoisseur that's gratifying," she said, smiling at him.

"Yes," said Ezra, "Isa always wanted her collection to be the best in Australia."

"In the world," she corrected him. "Now. . . ." She had taken a small case and opened it. She laid it on the table, and there on the black velvet in all its glory was the Harlequin Opal.

I stared at it. It couldn't be. It must be something similar and I was not experienced enough to see the difference. It couldn't possibly be the Harlequin, for how could it have come so soon into her possession?

Isa chuckled. "She recognizes it," she said.

I looked up and caught Joss's eyes on me. He was watching me intently.

I stammered: "I thought it had a look of the Harlequin."

"It *is* the Harlequin."

"Oh. . . . It's certainly very beautiful."

"Pick it up," commanded Isa. "Hold it in the palm of your hand. I know you love it. I saw by the way you looked at it before. It's a beauty. I reckon it's one of the finest I have."

"You are very fortunate to have such a stone," I said.

"I have to thank my very good friend. . . ." She was smiling at Joss, and I felt such cold anger in my heart that I was astonished at myself.

"Your . . . very good friend?" I said.

"Dear Joss! He knew how I coveted it. He gave it to me, didn't he, Ezra?"

"It was a generous gift," said Ezra complacently.

"How . . . interesting," I said.

I put it back on the black velvet and hoped my fingers were not trembling with the rage which consumed me. I was shocked and angrier than I have ever been.

I glanced at Ezra. He did not seem in the least perturbed. How should a man feel when his wife accepted expensive gifts from another man? The same as a woman would feel when her husband bestowed those gifts on another woman?

I heard myself say coolly: "So you acquired it after all. I know you wanted it badly."

"I always get what I want, don't I, Ezra?"

"It seems so, my dear."

"You certainly have a most interesting collection. Has it taken you many years to amass it?"

"Not really. Only since I came out here and married Ezra. Fifteen years or thereabouts, isn't it, Ezra?"

"Such a short time?" I said, pointedly implying that I thought it might have been longer, which was a feeble barb compared with the blow she had just delivered. I could see that Joss was amused by the asperity in my voice. I hated him.

The collection was put away and I thought: The object of the visit is over. We sat awhile and as I listened to their talk and now and then managed to join in, I kept seeing Isa's tiger eyes and the smoldering response I fancied I detected in those of Joss.

It was a great relief to go down to the stables where Ezra took a fond farewell of Wattle, and then we rode back to Peacocks.

I was deep in thought and tried to keep aloof from Joss, but he rode beside me and insisted on walking our horses.

"You're silent," he said.

"You should have warned me that we were going there."

"I thought it would be a pleasant surprise. Isa made us very welcome, didn't she?"

"Especially you."

"Well, she has known me for a long time."

"And very well, I imagine."

"Oh, we're very old friends."

"And she must be grateful to you. You give her such wonderful presents."

"It's rather a beauty, isn't it?"

"I can agree with that."

"Something has occurred to me. Is that rather pleasant little retroussé nose somewhat out of joint?"

"What do you mean?"

"You show such stern disapproval."

"I thought it was an odd thing to do."

"Did *you* want it? You did rather fancy it, I know, and now you are beginning to learn something through the good offices of Jeremy Dickson, you can recognize opal when you see it. You should have asked me for it. Who knows, I might have been persuaded to give it to *you*."

"Unlike that woman, I have no wish to take expensive gifts from you."

"Yet you seem rather angry because I gave it to her."

"And what of that . . . so-called husband of hers?"

"He doesn't really mind any more than my so-called wife does . . . or so I thought. I may be wrong."

"I think it was a very foolish thing to do."

"Why? She wanted it. She appreciated it. What's wrong with giving people things they want?"

"It seems to me very . . . unusual . . . to give someone's wife such a present and then ask your own wife . . . who knew nothing about it . . . to applaud your action."

"I didn't ask you to applaud my action. What action of mine have you ever applauded?"

"It's most unconventional."

"We can't always observe the conventions out here."

"You are that woman's lover."

He was silent. "Are you?" I demanded.

"We have to be conventional, don't we? Now it is considered right not to divulge the secrets of others. That's the only reason why I don't answer your question."

"You have answered my question."

"And you have shown me clearly that you disapprove of my actions. But have you any right? You don't want me. You have rejected me. Can you take me to task if I look for affection elsewhere?"

I turned to look at him. His eyes were lowered in an expression of resignation. He was mocking me. When had he ever ceased to mock me?

I could endure no more. I started to gallop.

"Steady," he called. "Where do you think you're going? You'll be lost in the Bush if you go that way. Just follow me."

So I followed him back to Peacocks.

I went straight to my room. I felt wretched and angry at the same time, and I tried to feed my anger because it was the only way to soothe my wretchedness.

He's in love with Isa Bannock, I thought. Of course he would be. She's feminine and attractive. She's everything that I am not and she's his mistress.

I lay on my bed and stared up at the ceiling.

I dislike him, I told myself. He's arrogant and conceited, heartless and ruthless. He's everything that I hate.

"Peacock," I muttered. "Nothing but a peacock flaunting your glory."

But the flashing light of the Harlequin Opal had revealed something to me. I wouldn't face it. At least I was trying not to, but how stupid that was. Why should I be so angry? Why should I care so much? Because . . . I must face it because I knew it was true. I was either in love with him or fast getting into that terrifying state. It had taken his devotion to another woman to make me face up to what had been slowly revealed to me. I had so far refused to see the signs when I had felt that certain exhilaration in his company which I could not find elsewhere. Why hadn't I been wise enough to understand the true nature of this excessive hatred?

At least now I faced the truth. I was in love with Joss Madden, my own husband, and it made no difference to me what fresh revelations I discovered. He was everything that I should have thought I would most dislike in a man, and yet I had to fall in love with him!

"You must be mad," I said to myself angrily.

I was. Perhaps one sometimes is in love.

I had been in my room for more than an hour considering this extraordinary situation which had burst upon me when there was a knock on my door. I called: "Come in," and Mrs. Laud entered.

"Oh," she said, "you are resting."

"No. I had not changed. It was so hot out today and we had ridden quite a distance."

"Mr. Madden mentioned that you had taken luncheon with the Bannocks."

"Yes."

"I believe their cook is very good."

"I'm sure she is. The food was delicious."

"I had come to speak to you about the Treasure Hunt."

"I heard of it for the first time today."

"I had thought Mr. Madden must have mentioned it. It's an event which takes place every year. Mr. Henniker started it because he felt the men and their wives were getting restive without any diversion. He used to talk to me a great deal about such matters, you know."

"Do tell me more about the Treasure Hunt, Mrs. Laud."

"Well, clues are made up and we make believe that the house is a desert island. The treasure is two opals of some value which have been found during the year. The servants make up the clues and plant them. They're very simple. Mr. Henniker used to think that it was good for the servants to have a part in it. They think about it for the whole year. It keeps their minds busy."

"It sounds most diverting."

"I help them, of course, because I don't take an active part, though Mr. Henniker used to insist that I did sometimes." She smiled reminiscently. "So that part of it will be taken care of, but I wanted to discuss the other arrangements with you. There's always been a buffet supper and the guests have to be asked, formal invitations sent out. We like to do it some time in advance because it gives people the pleasure of anticipating."

"Who comes to the Treasure Hunt?"

"All the heads of departments and people in the higher positions. There would be about sixty or seventy of them. Then a few days later there's another, different sort of celebration for the rest of the workers, with contests and prizes. Mr. Henniker used to say: 'Bread and circuses are necessary to keep the people happy.' He was full of sayings."

"I dare say you could arrange all this perfectly well without any help from me, Mrs. Laud."

"Oh, I thought it only right and proper that you should know how we had conducted it in the past in case you wished to make new arrangements."

"I'm sure I shan't want to do that. I'm such a newcomer. I'd like to see how this one works, and then for the next one if I have any suggestions to make that would be different."

"I usually send to Sydney for what we need for the buffet. Then we do a good deal of the cooking here in the kitchens of course."

"You must please carry on as before."

"I thought you would know how these things should be conducted . . . coming from such a good family. . . ."

I looked at her in surprise and she lowered her eyes in the way to which I had become accustomed.

"Mr. Henniker confided in me a good deal. I heard Mr. Madden refer to Oakland Hall and your being one of the

Claverings. I knew Mr. Henniker bought the house from them."

"It's true I was a Miss Clavering, but I never lived in Oakland Hall. My family became impoverished. That was why they sold Oakland."

"Oh, I know, but being one of that family I felt you would know how things should be done."

"I'm not at all sure of that," I replied. "I think it would be better to leave this Treasure Hunt in your capable hands."

"I'm glad you have no objections to us, Mrs. Madden."

"Objections! How could I have? You're so efficient."

"I mean the whole family of us . . . living here and enjoying so many privileges."

"I believe it is what Mr. Henniker would have wished."

"Oh yes, he remembered us in his will. He was always fond of Jimson and Lilias. They were only children when we came here. . . . Lilias nothing more than a baby. I will always be grateful to him. Heavens knows, I was at my wit's end. Jim—that was my husband—had been so close to me. I had thought it was a mistake to come out to Australia but Jim wanted to. Then he died and there was I . . . homeless, penniless when Mr. Henniker came along."

"It worked out very well then."

"Yes it did for all those years. Then he died and I thought there'd be changes, and when Mr. Madden came back with a wife. . . ."

"You were all amazed, I know. But don't worry. I'm very happy that you should stay. In fact I don't know what we should do without you."

She seemed overcome with emotion and said in a practical voice: "Perhaps I could show you the draft of the invitations I'm sending to Sydney to have engraved. They're the same every year."

"Don't bother to show me. Just go ahead as you always have. I'm sure that's best."

She looked at me so anxiously that I went on: "I'm really more interested in learning the affairs of the Company than running a house, Mrs. Laud."

"You're a very unusual lady. I realize that. I think you're the kind who will master what you set out to do."

"I hope so, Mrs. Laud," I said.

I could not sleep that night. I kept thinking about that moment when Isa had unrolled the case and revealed the

Harlequin Opal. Joss had known that she was going to show it to me. He had given her permission to do so. It occurred to me that he had taken me there for that purpose. It was tantamount to an act of defiance.

It meant: I don't care for you any more than you care for me. And yet I fancied he did not like my growing friendship with Jeremy Dickson. How dared he resent something so innocent when his relations with Isa were far from innocent?

And what did Ezra think? Was he prepared to stand aside for Joss because of the power Joss held with the Company? What sort of husband was he? He seemed equally besotted— ready to grant her every wish. What was the power she had over them? Hers was an evil sort of beauty. She was what was known as a siren, the sort who would lure men to destruction when all the time they knew that would be their end. They couldn't resist it.

I was more upset than I would have believed possible, but the revelation was clear. In spite of everything, I had allowed myself to be caught up in some sort of fascination. While I hated him, I wanted Joss to be near me, to take my hands, to laugh at me, to thrust aside my resistance.

What had happened to me?

If it had not been for Isa. . . . But what was the use of saying that? Isa was there. She existed. It had taken my jealousy to reveal the true state of my feelings.

I dozed fitfully and dreamed we were all sitting round the table and Isa unrolled the case and showed us the Harlequin Opal.

"Look at it," she said, and I looked into the fire that extended all across the table and in it I could see pictures. I saw myself and Joss, and Joss was saying: "Of what use are you to me? You are no wife. I don't want you. I want Isa. You are in the way. If you weren't here, the Green Flash would be mine. You're in the way . . . in the way . . ." I felt his hands about my throat and I awoke calling out.

I lay in the darkness trembling.

It was only a dream, I assured myself. But as I lay there the thought came to me that the dream was a warning. There was something strange about Peacocks. If Ben had been here it would have been different. He would have blown drafts of fresh air through the place, blowing away . . . I knew not what.

How I longed for Ben. I could have explained to him how

I felt. The Lauds with their meek unobtrusiveness were pale shadows of people, and it seemed to me that all of them were living two lives—the real one which I didn't see and the shadow one which I did. Both Jimson and Lilias seemed afraid of their mother . . . not exactly afraid . . . protective, was it? I suppose that was natural and yet. . . .

And then as I lay there I heard the sound of footsteps outside my door as I had heard them before. Someone was prowling out there . . . right outside my door now. I got out of bed and sat on it, watching the door. I had locked it as I always did.

In the faint moonlight I saw the handle slowly turning.

There was a brief silence and then the sound of retreating footsteps.

I lay still, trembling, wondering what would have happened if the door had not been locked.

9

Treasure Hunt

For several days the bustle of preparation went on at Peacocks. The servants were absent-minded, giggling together.

"It's always like this when Treasure Hunt approaches," Lilias told me.

She asked how I was getting on with the Company and I told her that I was growing more fascinated every day. I was tremendously interested in the processes and was thrilled when I saw colors emerging.

"I dare say you see a great deal of Jeremy Dickson," she said.

"He happens to be in charge of the side which interests me most."

She looked a little mournful and like her mother, as though she were afraid of betraying something. I wondered whether their attitude had something to do with their living with the family and yet not quite being of it. Rather like poor relations, I thought; but in this case there was never any attempt to treat them as such. Joss was the same in his manner towards them as he was to me. In fact, I thought ruefully, perhaps a little more considerate.

I was trying not to think of him, but I couldn't help it. Every time I heard his voice I felt excited, eager to hear what he had to say. When he rode out, I wondered whether he was going to Isa, how they were together. I wondered about Ezra and whether he was afraid of Joss in some way. Everyone was afraid of Joss. Once when I had remarked that everyone seemed to hold him in great respect he had retorted: "They'd better, hadn't they? They depend on me for the jobs."

"On me too perhaps," I suggested.

"You're going to be someone to reckon with," he replied. "Don't mock."

"Mock," he cried. "I'm in deadly earnest."

I remembered the things he said so vividly.

Ezra was a skilled man, but he was not a big shareholder in the enterprise. If he displeased Joss he could be asked to go. Did pleasing Joss extend as far as turning a blind eye on his affair with his wife?

I couldn't believe that. I thought of his affection for Wattle and hers for him. Surely a man who was so beloved by his horse—and dogs too, I had discovered—could not so degrade himself. But who could say? There were so many facets to all our characters.

And there was something overpowering about Joss. Perhaps people behaved differently with him. I wished I could stop thinking of him.

I had learned that he did not like my being in the company of Jeremy Dickson. He did not say so, and I longed for him to, but he somehow implied it.

On some mornings I rode into the town with Jimson Laud as my companion, for I would arrive downstairs to find that Joss had already left. I would pretend to be quite pleased at the prospect, although I found Jimson like his mother and sister—strangely indeterminate.

He would talk to me about bookkeeping which he had taken over from Tom Paling who had apparently run everything in a most primitive way.

I supposed I should have to learn something about bookkeeping sometime, but I was too fascinated by the active side to feel any great interest.

Sometimes I would be overcome with amazement to think that Ben had given me a major share in this thriving Company, and I used to fancy that he was beside me, urging me on. I could hear his voice coming back to me often; his racy conversation was something I would never forget. He had loved opals and he had wanted me to do the same. He had loved my mother and thought of me as his daughter, I believed, so he had loved me too. He had admired Joss . . . the son who had been all he wanted his son to be. That was adventurous, hard, ruthless, not too scrupulous—a man of this land and his times. And he had forced us into this marriage. Why? He was a wise man and he had loved me dearly. He had wanted to rescue me from the Dower House. Had he known me so well that he had had a premonition that before the year was out I should be in love with Joss?

Had he known of Joss's infatuation for Isa? I did not think Ben would have liked Isa very much. Perhaps he had wanted to break that connection by giving Joss a young wife.

Ben had loved me and perhaps he thought that because he did others must too. How wrong he had been! No one had ever really loved me except Ben. My mind went back to the days in church when I had asked Miriam about the she-bear. How could my mother's love cease when it had never existed? I had asked. A tragic question on the lips of a child. But then the woman whom I had thought was my mother was not after all. My real mother had loved me, but not enough to live for me.

I longed to be loved as Isa was loved; and I knew then how happy I should have been if my marriage had turned out differently, if we had grown to know each other and Joss had in due course fallen in love with me as I had with him.

It was the night of the Treasure Hunt. Thousands of candles blazed throughout the house, for the party started at sundown. I thought how romantic it looked and how excited I should have been to have shared such a house with a husband who loved me.

Lilias came to my room while I was dressing to see, she said, if I needed any help.

"Why, your dress is beautiful," she cried.

It was another of the shade of peacock blue, which strangely enough I had always loved. I had been allowed to choose my own materials which I had thought a great concession at the time, but now when I considered all I had brought my family, I understood why I had been shown this clemency. I had not adhered closely to fashion because the mode of the day was not, I considered, very becoming. I had been wise in this, for fashions meant little out here. So I had gone back to an earlier and more charming age, and my skirt resembled, though not quite, a crinoline. It billowed out in tiers of chiffon and my bodice was close-fitting, falling off the shoulders in an elegant austerity which made a contrast to the skirt.

Lilias herself looked pretty in a modest gown of pale gray silk embroidered with pink moss roses, which she admitted she had worked herself.

"I wondered if you needed any help with your hair," she said.

I had piled my thick, dark hair high on my head—again defying fashion and going back to an even earlier age than the style of the dress.

"I've always done it myself."

"I'm sure you'll be much admired. I've never seen such beautiful clothes as yours except Isa Bannock's."

"Of course," I answered.

"She has her materials sent out from England. I wonder what she'll look like tonight. You know we choose our partners for the Treasure Hunt. It's a tradition. Mr. Henniker used to say: 'This is the night the ladies choose.'"

The prospect excited me. I would choose Joss, I promised myself. Perhaps it would be a start. To be fair I had to admit that the unsatisfactory state of our relationship was to a large extent due to me, so perhaps it was for me to set the pace. I remembered the first days of our marriage. It was not he who had then suggested separate rooms. But I was glad that I had, for I did not want a makeshift marriage. I wanted to explore these new and fierce emotions, but I wanted him to feel the same. I would never be the sort of wife who would compromise. I wanted to be the one in his life. He would have to abandon Isa and his philanderings.

Lilias was saying timidly: "I thought I'd ask Mr. Dickson, unless, of course. . . ."

I looked surprised and she went on quickly: "Unless you wanted to ask him."

"I hadn't thought of it," I replied, and she looked relieved.

The door opened and Joss came in. He looked magnificent. He, too, wore the shade of peacock blue almost identical with mine. It was a velvet dinner jacket and he wore white ruffles at his neck and the edge of his cuffs. He looked even taller than usual and the blue jacket brought out vividly the blue of his eyes.

Lilias said: "Excuse me," and scuttled out.

"She's like a frightened rabbit," he said.

"You look rather formidable."

He regarded himself in the mirror, approvingly, I thought. His eyes met mine and he smiled. "I know what you're thinking," he said. "Peacock!"

"It's the right color. Do you know, I've never heard any but Ben call you by that name."

"They do it behind my back. They wouldn't think of using it before my loving wife. They would think she might find it offensive. I collected the name when I was a boy. I used to strut round with the peacocks and I was rather fond of myself."

"An endearing quality which you haven't lost." Why did I have to continue in this strain, I asked myself. I suppose the fact was that I was afraid of betraying my true feelings.

He smiled at me ironically. "So you admire my pride, my

arrogance, my conceit. It makes me so happy to please you in some way."

It was hard to meet his eyes, for I feared to reveal the true state of my feelings. The time was not ripe. His complacence would be intolerable. I had a horror of his going to Isa and telling her that I had at last succumbed to his attractions and that I was going to be a good and docile wife in future.

He had caught me by the shoulders and turned me around so that we were standing side by side looking at our reflection in the mirror. "We're a good match, you must agree. A handsome pair. You're not exactly displeased with your appearance, are you? Is there a bit of the peacock in you?"

"I hope that people will share my good opinion," I retorted. "The difference is that you don't care whether they like yours or not. That's the peacock element."

"How clever of you to discover that. I believe you're beginning to learn something about me at last."

"I think I know a little."

"A little knowledge, they say, can be a dangerous thing."

"I'll keep out of danger."

"Don't be too sure of that."

"This is a very cryptic conversation."

"Ours is a very cryptic relationship."

"Perhaps it won't remain so," I said, and I wondered if he noticed the little catch in my voice.

"Nothing remains static, I've heard."

A great impulse came to me then to tell him that I wanted to change everything. I wanted us to see more of each other. I wanted him to tell me everything about his true relationship with Isa and how deep it went. I wanted to say: "Let us give ourselves a chance to make something of our lives." One little sign from him and I should have done so.

I said on impulse: "I understand it's the lady's privilege to choose her partner for the Treasure Hunt. I suppose I should choose you."

It sounded ungracious—as though I didn't want to, as though I regarded it as a duty when all the time I wanted to say: I want to be with you. I want us to walk through this house hand in hand, searching for the treasure which will be symbolic in a way . . . searching for that happiness which we can only find together.

A few seconds passed when everything seemed to be silent . . . watching—an important moment. I had taken the first step and this could be a beginning. I saw a fierce light in those dark blue eyes as they came to rest on my bare shoulders fleetingly, almost caressingly, and my heart beat fast.

Then he said: "My dear, there is no need to choose me. In fact it would hardly be right. Suppose we found the treasure. They would think it was collusion."

I felt deflated. I knew of course that he had already allowed Isa to choose him.

"It's time we went down to greet the guests," he said.

We stood side by side in the hall and received them as they arrived. People whom I had not met before shook my hand warmly, congratulated me on my marriage, and welcomed me to Fancy Town. They were noisy, friendly people all out for an evening's enjoyment—the high spot of the year, the greatest of Ben Henniker's circuses.

The prize, as usual, was two opals which had been found in the Fancy field, cut, polished, and recognized to be of fair value.

"It's not the opals themselves which are so important," one of the wives told me. "It's the fact of winning. Everyone wants the honor of having solved the clues first."

There was one fair-haired young woman who came to talk to me and told me that she was glad her baby had arrived in time to let her come to the Treasure Hunt. The baby, with his young brother, was in the charge of her elder sister who herself was too heavily pregnant to come.

"It's the luck," she told me. "Treasure Hunt opals are always lucky. That's what people say. They must be to the ones who find them, because that's luck isn't it? That's one reason why people want them. They really are lucky."

The buffet was attacked with gusto, and after people had eaten their fill the hunt began.

"All ladies must take their partners," announced Joss.

I felt sick with misery, for I saw Isa with her arm through that of Joss. She looked beautiful, of course, in one of her tawny brown and yellow gowns touched with green—a mass of silk, ribbons, and lace. She wore a band of topaz like a tiara in her hair, and it brought out the strange color of her eyes. Predatory, prowling, very much the jungle cat that night.

"I've taken your husband," she cried with a hint of malice in her voice. "I hope you won't mind."

"I'm sure he doesn't," I answered.

Joss was watching me closely, an unfathomable expression

in his eyes. Ezra stood by sheepishly.

"He made no objection," retorted Isa.

"Then perhaps I'd better retaliate by taking yours."

Ezra beamed on me. "Why, that's wonderful," he said. "There was I wondering who would ever choose me and the beautiful hostess herself comes along."

"I'm sure you'll be very good at solving the clues," I said.

"I'm going to do my best to win with you, Jessica."

"We'll work together," I told him.

I heard Isa's laughter and saw her white hands with their long clawlike fingers on Joss's arm as I turned away with Ezra.

Mrs. Laud handed out the first clue. Like her daughter, she was dressed in gray, but instead of moss roses she wore touches of white. Jimson was at her side. I think he had been hoping I would ask him to partner me. I noticed Lilias looking almost gay with Jeremy Dickson.

The game was the old English one which most people had played before. I was one of those who had not. We did not indulge in such frivolities in the Dower House, but I imagined the rest of the family must have had similar occasions in the Oakland days. Players were given a clue to start with which led them to the next; they kept their clues which were written on small pieces of paper and the first to collect the entire set was the winner.

The first was traditionally easy, to give everyone a start and interest in the game.

It was something like:

> "You have come to pay a call
> Take a drink beside the wall."

This meant, of course, that it was the hall where callers would come on their arrival and there was a large pewter punch bowl on a table close to the wall. The second clues were in this.

Then the real hunt began.

We found the second in the drawing room and the next led us upstairs, and it occurred to me on occasions like this when there were so many people in the house, it could have been possible for one of them to have come upon the hidden Green Flash. How ironical if it had been lost through a Treasure Hunt. I thought of the remark that any opal found in this hunt must be lucky for the one who found it because he or she had been led to it by luck.

"How are you getting on with Wattle?" asked Ezra.

"Very well."

"She's happy, I think. There's something very special about that little filly, Jessica."

"I know it."

"Bright as a button. All there, as they say. That's our Wattle."

"She still remembers you."

"She'll remember me till the day she dies. Faithful creatures, horses. That's more than you can say for some human beings, eh?"

I looked at him sharply, wondering whether he was referring to Isa.

"You have a way with animals. That's perfectly clear. Even the peacocks on the lawn seem to be aware of you. In a mild way of course, because they can't think very much about anything but themselves."

He laughed. "I always have had this. Was born with it. Funny. I was never much to look at. I could never make out why Isa fancied me in the first place. Mind you, when I came out here I had big dreams . . . everyone has. I was going to find the crock of gold."

"Well, you've done very well haven't you?"

"I know my job, and there's nothing I'd rather work with than opals."

"Then you're fortunate. It's not everyone who finds satisfaction in his work. Where are we going?"

"Into the gallery. There's bound to be something in the gallery."

"I suppose so, but I expect others will think the same."

We opened the door. There was no one there. Six candles flickered in their sconces. It looked eerie and remarkably like the gallery at Oakland Hall. My eyes went to the spinet at one end.

"It looks as if it ought to be haunted," said Ezra. "But I don't suppose it's old enough for that. Why are those drapes placed at intervals around the room?"

"That's how they are at Oakland. There the walls are partially paneled and the drapes hang where there is no paneling. It's quite effective."

"Can you play the spinet, Jessica?"

"A little. I had lessons when I was a child. My Aunt Miriam taught me. I was not very good."

"Play something now."

I sat down and played a Chopin waltz as well as I could remember it.

"Hello! This place is haunted then." It was Joss's voice. I swung around sharply, for he and Isa had come into the gallery.

"Why," he went on, "the ghost is Jessica."

"Why did you think I was a ghost?" I demanded.

"I didn't. I don't believe in them. But Ben used to say in his sentimental moments that he used to fancy he could hear the spinet being played and he'd like someone who used to play it at Oakland to come back and play for him here. He had strange fancies sometimes for such a practical man."

"He always said he had an open mind about everything," said Ezra.

"Yes," went on Joss, "Ben was prepared to believe anything if it could be proved to him, so he believed that if he built a gallery just like the one at Oakland and put a spinet in it, his ghost might come."

"How are you getting on with my husband?" asked Isa, with a hint of mischief in her voice.

"Tolerably well," I replied. "We've solved three so far. How are you getting on with mine?"

"More than tolerably well," she replied. "Come along, Joss. I want that opal."

"It won't be worthy of your collection," he told her.

"Then I shall ask you to swop it for one that is."

I said to Ezra: "We should be going. I don't think there's anything here."

We went out. Joss and Isa had disappeared, and shortly afterwards we found ourselves at the top of the house in a section which was unfamiliar to me. The rooms here were smaller and there was one which was furnished as a sitting room. A lighted oil lamp stood on the table which held a pot of dried leaves and a wooden workbox with the lid open. A piece of needlework lay on the table with a needle case, cottons, and scissors. A door leading from this room was half open and I looked out onto a narrow terrace bounded by a low wall. We were at the very top of the house.

"I believe these are the Lauds' quarters," I said.

"Sounds rather holy," answered Ezra with a chuckle.

"L.A.U.D.," I spelled out. "I don't know whether we're supposed to be here."

"Isn't where you're not supposed to be the very spot where

you're most likely to find the vital clue?"

"I shouldn't think so. The Lauds are so unobtrusive. I doubt whether Mrs. Laud would have allowed any clues to be placed in their apartments."

"Nevertheless, we'll look around."

"I'm interested in this little terrace," I said. "I had no idea it existed."

I stepped out on it and looked up at the sky where the Southern Cross shone down, reminding me that I was far from home, where no one would be missing me very much— and I thought, with a trace of bitterness, no one here cared either.

I looked over the side of the terrace wall to the sheer drop below. We were indeed very high.

Then I heard voices. Mrs. Laud was speaking and I stepped back into the room. Ezra was standing at the table and Mrs. Laud was at the door.

She was saying: "I had no idea anyone was here. There's nothing up here, you know. I wouldn't have dreamed of letting them put clues here. Oh, there's Mrs. Madden."

"I'm sorry we intruded," I said.

"Oh no, it's not that. But there simply isn't anything here."

"Then we'd better get on," I said. "We've wasted our time, it seems."

Mrs. Laud laughed apologetically. "It's of no importance. I was just startled when I opened my door and saw a man in the room."

Ezra apologized in his hearty way, and we went downstairs.

"You've got a treasure in that woman," he said. "I remember old Ben's saying what a manager she was. Mind you, he's done a lot for her children . . . brought them up, you might say. She's very grateful, is Mrs. Laud. I've heard her say it again and again."

"I don't know what we'd do without her."

"And Jimson's good. The way he can juggle with figures just takes your breath away. It's rare to find people out here who can do that. Most of them want to do the exciting things . . . but to find someone who really likes figures . . . that's a godsend. We thought we were lucky to get Paling, but Jimson beats him . . . as we discovered after the buggy accident."

"Do you know the daughter?"

"Lilias. Why, yes. Sweet on Jeremy Dickson if you ask me.

I reckon they might well make a match of it. I don't know. Lilias seems to blow hot and cold."

"Does she? I thought she liked him."

"Well, I reckon it's just a bit of coyness or something. It would be nice to see them wed. Married men are much better in the town. They get more settled and stable."

"I can hear the sounds from below," I put in. "I believe they've got a winner."

I was right and delighted that it was the little fair-haired woman and her partner—the one who had left her new baby in the charge of her pregnant sister.

Joss made me stand with him to present the prizes. "Don't forget," he whispered to me. "You own half of this now and everyone must be made to realize it."

The fair-haired woman came up with her partner, the opals were presented and everyone crowded round to examine them.

Joss said to me: "Tactful of you not to win."

"You too," I answered. "But did this please your acquisitive friend?"

"My acquisitive friend was forced to accept the inevitable."

"I wonder if she will demand another Harlequin as compensation."

His eyes met mine—a little stormy, a little mocking and veiled.

"I wonder," he murmured.

10

Saturday Night

The next morning when I went down to breakfast, Joss was alone in the dining room. He asked how I had slept after last night's revelries. I told him very well and trusted he had done the same.

"It gives you an insight into one of our traditions here. It's Ben's idea to keep the workers happy. They're far away from the bright lights of a big city so we have to make their entertainment."

"When is the next occasion?"

"My dear Jessica, there are occasions once a week. Saturday nights are regular. It's time you attended a Saturday night. I must introduce you to them."

The prospect of being with him delighted me, and I must have looked eager.

"There's no time like the present. We'll go next Saturday."

That day in the office an incident took place, and I did not realize until later how very disturbing it was. I overheard raised voices coming from Joss's office, and as I passed, Joss and Ezra came out. I had never seen Ezra look angry before, but then his large face had completely lost its benignity. It made him look quite different. Joss looked fierce and stern. They both acknowledged me rather curtly as though they were not in the mood to talk to me at that moment.

Later when Joss and I were riding back to Peacocks I said to him: "You and Ezra seemed at cross purposes this morning."

"It happens now and then," said Joss lightly. "We don't always see eye to eye. Ezra's a good man, but he's not always practical. There's always trouble about the houses in the town. Those who have been living in the calico tents are naturally anxious to get them when they fall vacant. Ezra had promised one to a man he liked, but I've given it to someone who is a much better worker and who has been with us longer. Ezra had the unpleasant task of telling his man he'd have to wait a bit."

"So that was it."

Joss looked at me quickly, but he said nothing. I was thinking: Ezra can stand up for himself then. Was it really about the dwelling house, or had he perhaps told Joss that he was getting tired of seeing him with his wife?

The next time I saw Ezra he was his beaming, hearty self so I thought no more of the matter until later.

Saturday had come, and it was dusk as Joss and I rode into the township.

"Saturday night at the camp," said Joss. "There'll be revelry. Oh, not what *you'd* call revelry. No masked balls and powdered footmen, I do assure you."

"You've no need to reassure me. I am not expecting them, nor am I accustomed to them. Didn't I tell you that I was brought up in a Dower House and though the family had seen Better Days, I was only with them in the worse ones."

"What a mercy!" He surveyed me ironically. "Now perhaps we shan't disappoint you so much. Saturday night has to be seen. The week's work is over. Sunday is a day of rest, but not for the gougers who have to do their washing and clean their homes then, but there has to be revelry before the work begins again."

"What sort of revelry?"

"You'll see."

As we approached the township I saw that outside it a bonfire was burning.

"We'd rather have it in the center of the town," Joss explained, "but it's too dangerous with so many wooden buildings. A wind in the wrong direction and the whole town would be ablaze. We'll take the horses in and leave them at Joe's and then we'll wander out to the bonfire. They're starting to cook, and it's a communal feast. No stranger is turned away. You'll find a few sundowners coming in on Saturday nights."

I sensed the atmosphere of excitement as we rode through the town to the blacksmith's forge and came away on foot.

Joss took my arm, and we went past the wooden shacks and tents. Outside the children were dancing and calling to each other and the elderly were seated watching them.

"Supper will be in that large tent over there," Joss told me. "It's kept for Saturday nights. Roast pig, I believe, and there'll be beef and mutton."

"Who provides the food?"

"The Company. It's part of their wages. They look forward to Saturday nights all the week. Ben always believed that incentives make people work harder, and so do I."

"So it's not for charity."

"Not a bit of it. That's Madden policy, as you'll discover."

"You're a little calculating, aren't you?"

"We're in business and it's got to be successful. If it wasn't what do you think would happen to these people? They might find places elsewhere, some of them. Many would starve and some would die of despair."

"And you like seeing them enjoy themselves?"

"Of course I do. It means they're contented. We'll get a better day's work out of them than if they have grievances."

"Why do you always present yourself as the hard-headed businessman?"

He turned me around to face him, and his face glowed in the firelight. "Because that's what I am," he said.

"You look like a demon in this light."

"I've often thought they might be more exciting to know than the angels. I'm sure you'll agree, because you're not exactly angelic yourself."

"Indeed."

"Oh, most certainly. There's a flash of fire in you. They named you Opal rightly. . . . Opal Jessica. There's no one who knows more about opals than I do."

"Naturally," I mocked.

"Of all varieties," he pointed out.

"I think perhaps you overestimate your powers in some directions."

"Don't you believe it. All opals come within my province. Particularly those which are in my collection."

"What about Isa Bannock?"

"What about her?"

"Do you see her as an opal?"

"That's an interesting idea."

"Of course I couldn't hope to compare with her brilliance."

He pressed my arm against his. "You mustn't underestimate yourself . . . or pretend to, must you?"

"What a foolish conversation!"

"Yes, isn't it . . . and on a Saturday night!"

Just ahead of us lay the calico tents, looking weird in the firelight. Someone was playing on a fiddle the old tune "Ash Grove" and it made me think of Home suddenly—the fields and lanes and the Dower House with Poor Jarman working on the flower beds, and Miriam and her curate, and I wondered whether Xavier had married Lady Clara yet.

Two children in gingham frocks were turning somersaults and they stood upright and bobbed curtsies as we passed by. Someone had joined the fiddler with a mouth organ, and now I could smell the roasting pork.

Joss and I sat down on one side of a hillock on which grew clumps of mulga, and from this slight eminence we had a good view of the scene. From the tent came the smell of food and excited voices.

"They're cooking in there," said Joss. "It's safer inside. We don't want to start a fire. God knows where that would end here. When they've eaten the fun will start. After the pork, there'll be plum pudding. You should take some just to show you're not too proud to join in." He grinned at me. "Don't forget you're one of the family. You'll have to follow our customs."

"You find this a pleasant one?"

"One of the bosses is expected to join in most Saturdays. We take turns. Ben used to go often. Then I'd go, or Ezra would. We have to show we are one of them. That's very important. Here Jack's as good as his master. Don't forget it."

"Yet it seems to me that there are some masters who think themselves highly superior."

"Only because they are. A man commands respect for what he is out here."

"Doesn't he everywhere?"

"I mean he's not superior just because he has had a better education or has money. He's got to show himself as a man and then he'll be accepted as such."

"And if men rely on others to provide them with the means of earning a living they might think it advisable to show them some respect?"

"They'd be fools not to."

"Your philosophy of life is worked out to give you all the advantages."

"Now isn't that the wise way?"

"You bring everything to your personal view."

"It's you who do that. You brought me into this analysis."

I shrugged my shoulders.

"That's right," he went on, "a woman should always admit when she's beaten."

"Beaten! I!"

"Only in argument of course. There's a saying at Home:

A woman, a dog and a walnut tree
The more you beat them the better they'll be."

"Some arrogant man no doubt made that up. I've never
heard of beating walnut trees and the thought of beating
dogs nauseates me. As for women, men who use physical
violence against them usually do so because they know they
will be beaten in verbal battles."

"You do very well. I hope it doesn't become a test between
us. My strength, your brains. Oh dear, what a contest!"

"We do seem to get involved in the most absurd bickering."

"It's really due to your verbal agility."

"Now you're mocking me."

"And once again we're forgetting we're here to enjoy
Saturday night."

I turned my attention to the scene before us. People were
crowding into the tent and some were coming out with slices
of roast meat and bread which they were eating with great
enjoyment. They sat about and talked together, shouting from
group to group and taking little notice of us seated on the
hillock. Children came out with trays on which were slabs of
pudding with which they were drinking what Joss told me
was home-brewed ale.

I was given a piece of the pudding which was like hot
cake. Both Joss and I took it in our fingers and ate it. It
was good.

When the eating was over the revelry began. The two
children who had been turning somersaults darted about
turning cartwheels. One man did some conjuring tricks. There
were two violins and several mouth organs in the camp and
they played the songs the people knew and everyone sang
them. It was a moving scene there in the light of the campfire which glowed on the faces of men, women, and children
as they sang the old songs we knew so well. Always they
were songs from Home which many of them must have
learned before they left and others had picked up from those
who had brought them across the sea.

There was one song which they sang with more feeling
than any other and that was "The Miner's Dream of Home."
This told the story of how the miner fell asleep and dreamed.
Everyone joined in. I remember some of the words and I
think I shall never forget them:

I saw the old homestead, the faces I loved
I saw England's valleys and hills.
I listened with joy
As I did when a boy
To the sound of the old village bells.
The moon was shining brightly
It was a night that would banish all sin
For the bells were ringing the Old Year out
And the New Year in.

As the song finished there was a deep silence in the company. They were in no mood to sing more for a while. They wanted to think of the people they had left at home; perhaps some of them longed to return and knew they never would.

The silence was broken by the sound of horse's hoofs and a man came riding up. The tension was relaxed.

He cried: "Is Mr. Madden here? I must see Mr. Madden."

Joss rose and went over to the rider who was surrounded by a group of people.

"Oh, Mr. Madden sir," I heard him say, "Mrs. Bannock has sent me to find you. She says to tell you, sir, that Mr. Bannock has not been home all last night and not through the day and now his horse has come back without him. She's worried and says would you go over to the homestead."

I heard Joss say: "Go back at once, Tim. Tell her I'm coming over right away. Like as not I'll be there before you."

He walked off and left me standing there. I felt sick with rage and anger. She only had to send for him and he forgot my existence. Then I thought of Ezra and was ashamed. What could have happened to him? I made my way to the blacksmith where Wattle was patiently waiting for me. Someone was already there. It was Jimson.

"I'm to take you back to Peacocks, Mr. Madden says," he told me.

"Thank you, Jimson," I answered. "Let's go."

So I rode back to Peacocks with Jimson, all my pleasure in the evening departed and a terrible anxiety about Ezra beginning to disturb me.

I went to my room and took off my riding habit, put on my trousseau dressing gown, and loosened my hair.

I sat up waiting. It was midnight when Joss returned. He came straight to my room as I had hoped he would.

"Jimson brought you home all right?" he said.

"Yes. What of Ezra?"

He frowned and looked very anxious. "I can't think what's happened. He's missing. I don't like it. There must have been some accident. His horse coming back without him. I'll send out search parties tomorrow. Isa will let me know if he turns up."

"You've said so often that people can get lost in the Bush," I said.

"Not a man like Ezra. He could only have been going between the Homestead and the town. He knows his way around blindfolded."

"You don't think he's gone. . . ."

"Gone?"

"He might have been tired of being Isa's husband."

Joss looked at me incredulously. "What about his horse's coming back like that?"

"He might have wanted to make it look like an accident. . . ."

Joss shook his head and then his eyes dwelt on me almost tenderly. "It was a bad ending to your first Saturday night."

"I do hope Ezra's all right. I like him so much. He was very nice to me."

He laid his hand on my shoulder lightly and pressed it.

"I didn't want to disturb you, but I thought you might be awake and wanting to know."

"Thank you," I said.

He smiled, hesitated and I thought he was going to say something, but he seemed to change his mind.

"Good night," he said, and left me.

11

Discovery at Grover's Gully

Rumors regarding Ezra's disappearance grew as the days passed. Some of the stories were quite horrific. He had tempted fate in some way. He had always been a man who had laughed at legend. He had never minded going past Grover's Gully after sundown. He had been heard to say that Grover was an old fool and should have taken better care of his money.

The favorite story was that he was the one who had stolen the Green Flash, because in spite of Joss's desire to keep the theft secret the news of it had spread like news of a lucky strike. It was clear, said rumor, that Ezra had found it and stolen it and the bad luck of the stone was pursuing him. Anything could, therefore, have happened to him.

Joss did not express his usual anger at the revival of the stories about the ill luck of the opal. He seemed very subdued. I supposed he could only think of what this meant to Isa.

Search parties had gone out in all directions, but there was no sign of Ezra. Some people said he had made off with the Green Flash because that wife of his was not all she should be. . . .

Three days passed while there was talk of nothing but Ezra's disappearance.

I rode out on my own one late afternoon, and as usual Wattle turned her face towards the gap in the hills leading to Grover's Gully and the road to the Bannock Homestead.

It was a hot day and the wind was blowing from the north. It grew stronger and started stirring up dust. It would be very uncomfortable later, but at the moment it was not unpleasant—hot, dry, and smelling of the desert.

I rode through the gap and looked about me uneasily. The place looked desolate. Little eddies of dust swirled just above the ground, and I thought: The wind is certainly rising. I'd better get back soon.

"Let's go home, Wattle," I said.

Then Wattle behaved in a most extraordinary manner. I

247

urged her to turn so that we could go back through the gap in the hills but she had grown suddenly stubborn and refused to do what I wanted.

"What's wrong, Wattle?" I asked. She started to move then towards the mine. "No, Wattle, not that way."

What had happened to her? She was not going my way but hers.

I pulled on her reins and then Wattle did something which she had never done before. She showed me that I rode her so easily because it was her wish that I should do so. When she changed her mind and decided not to go along with me, I must give way to her. It was a startling discovery.

She began to move forward.

"Wattle!" I cried in a dismayed tone. She ignored me and at that moment I heard two kookaburras laughing. They always seemed to be at hand to witness my discomfiture, but perhaps at other times I heard them without noticing them.

I felt a tingling horror in my spine that I was in the presence of something uncanny which was quite beyond my powers of understanding.

Very resolutely Wattle was making her way forward.

"Wattle, Wattle," I coaxed in vain, for I could sense her indifference to me. She seemed, indeed, to have forgotten that she carried me on her back. I tried coaxing again and then a little anger; it was no use. *She* was in control.

What was she going to do? I asked myself. Never before had I been so conscious of the fact that I was a novice with horses. I could ride well enough when all was well, but when it was not, I was incapable—as Joss had hinted. At that moment I was at the mercy of Wattle, and I knew that she was aware of something of which I was ignorant. Wasn't it said that horses and dogs had an extra sense, higher powers of perception in matters which were beyond our comprehension?

I don't know exactly what I expected, but I should not have been surprised to see the spectre of old Grover rise up from the mine to beckon to Wattle.

I had never been so frightened.

Wattle stopped suddenly; she pawed the ground and started to whinny. Then she turned from the mine and made her way to the right, where the ground was very sandy and a ragged mulga bush was growing.

She pricked up her ears and began wildly pawing at the

sand. Then she gave a sudden snort. It was obviously one of distress.

"What's wrong, Wattle?" I asked.

Then I saw that she had uncovered something. I leaned forward.

"Oh God!" I whispered in horror, for I saw that what she had uncovered was what was left of Ezra Bannock.

He had been shot through the head and someone had thought it safe to bury him there under the mulga bush not far from the mine, where, but for Wattle who had loved him, he might never have been discovered.

There was consternation throughout the community when they brought him in. He was taken to the Homestead and the blacksmith made a coffin for him. Then he was laid to rest in the graveyard on the edge of the town and there was a full day's holiday so that all might go to the funeral and pay their last respects to Ezra.

Joss held a meeting in the Company's offices which I attended. It was to discuss what had happened and what was to be done about it.

Ezra Bannock had been murdered and his murderer must be discovered. Crimes of violence must not go unpunished. In a community such as this, certain laws of conduct had to be rigorously observed so every effort must be made to bring the murderer to justice.

Notices would be printed offering a reward of fifty pounds to anyone who could give information about the murderer. Everyone who had seen Ezra on the day he disappeared was questioned.

It was discovered that he had ridden over to Peacocks during the morning of that day and he and Joss had been together for an hour or so. Then he had ridden off presumably to go home. Joss had gone into the town some time later.

A terrible suspicion had come into my mind, for it occurred to me that when Ezra had come over to Peacocks he and Joss might have been quarreling about Isa. I asked myself whether the true cause of that disagreement they had had some days before in the Company's offices was indeed about housing one of the gougers and his family. Was it really about Isa and was Ezra putting his foot down at last and saying he would have no more of it? And if so. . . .

No, I would not continue with such thoughts. I wished I

could stop thinking of Joss and Isa together. I had no doubt that they were lovers. Hadn't he given her the Harlequin Opal? If she had not been married to Ezra she would have married Joss, and then there would have been no question of his marrying me. They must both have regretted that. Had they decided to do something about it? Isa was free now . . . but Joss was not. Where were my thoughts leading me?

At the funeral Isa was swathed in black, which became her well. Indeed her widowhood seemed to have added an extra dimension to her charms. She was mysterious and, I thought, not entirely desolate. Her eyes gleamed like topaz through a fine veil and her tawny hair seemed brighter than ever.

Several of us rode back to the Homestead afterwards, where ham sandwiches and ale had been prepared by her servants.

I found her beside me. She said she hoped I would come and see her sometime. It was comforting to have a woman in the neighborhood not so far distant.

I said I would call.

"Poor Ezra. Who would have thought this could happen to him? Who *could* have done it?"

I shook my head. "I know so little of what goes on," I said. "I'm such a newcomer."

"He didn't have any enemies. Everyone liked Ezra."

"You don't think he quarreled with someone?"

I saw the speculative light in her eyes. "It . . . could have been," she admitted.

"The most likely theory is that a bushranger took his purse and shot him."

"His purse was missing," said Isa. "And it was full of sovereigns. He liked to carry a good deal of money around with him. He said it made him feel rich, and he used to fill his purse every morning. It was one of those leather ones with a ring over the top. You know the kind . . . red leather."

"And that's missing? It clearly must have been a thief."

"So he died for a few pounds. Poor Ezra! But perhaps that's too easy a solution and it was someone who wanted him out of the way."

"Who could?" I asked.

"There might have been someone. . . ." I could not fathom the expression in her eyes. "Perhaps," she went on, "you'll come soon. I want to show you my collection."

"You have shown me, remember?"

"I didn't show you everything. Some day I will."

Joss came up, and she immediately turned from me to him. I heard him tell her that if she needed any help she was to call on him.

No, Isa had not become less attractive because she was a widow.

Joss and I rode back to Peacocks together. Absent-mindedly we made our way past the peacocks on the lawn. Later we sat on the terrace to take advantage of the cooler evening air.

"What is your theory?" I asked tentatively.

"Robbery," he said. "What else?"

"Things are not always what they seem. Poor Ezra's was not a very happy existence."

"On the contrary, I rarely saw a man more pleased with his lot."

"You think he was contented to see his wife unfaithful to him?"

"He took a great pride in her attractiveness."

"And you are really suggesting that he *enjoyed* her infidelities?"

"There are men like that."

"Are you one of them?"

I heard that gust of laughter. "I wouldn't endure it for a moment."

"Yet you feel it all right for others to?"

"Everyone has a right to act as he pleases. If people don't like something they must find their own way of stopping it."

"Do you think that's what Ezra was trying to do?"

"I think Ezra was trying to stop someone's taking his purse."

"Or his wife?"

"What's on your mind?"

"Just that."

"But it was his purse that was missing."

"That could have been taken as a blind."

"You're becoming quite a sleuth."

"I should very much like to know who killed Ezra Bannock."

"So should we all."

I cried out passionately: "Shall we stop talking round this. I want to know the truth. Did you kill Ezra Bannock?"

"I? Why ever should I?"

"There's a perfectly good motive. You're his wife's lover."

"Then what good would his death be to me? I have a wife.

I'm not free to marry Isa even if she's free to marry."

I didn't answer. I was deeply shocked, for he had not denied being her lover.

I stood up. "I'm going in. I find this conversation distasteful."

He was beside me. "And," he said coldly, "so do I."

I went to my room and sat at the dressing table looking at my reflection without seeing it. He would marry Isa if he were free, I thought. But he is not free because he is married to me.

Then it was as though the room was full of warning shadows. Isa had not been free once, but she was now. He was not free at this moment but why should he not be at some time in the future?

Oh, Ben, I thought, what have you done? How much did you really know your son?

Proud as a peacock, he could not give up what he coveted. He wanted above all to be in control—of the Company, of the town, of everyone. That was how he saw himself, the supreme director of us all. He had two passions in his life—opals and Isa, and it seemed that he was determined to lose neither of them.

But what of me?

I began to see very clearly that I stood in the way.

Several weeks passed. My nights were uneasy. Fears beset me then, but often my fancies of the night would disappear with the light of the day, and when I went into the town I could push them to the back of my mind. I tried to forget my apprehension by concentrating more and more on the business and was able to take part in the discussions round the boardroom table and even make one or two suggestions—not about the actual work, of course, but sometimes about the conditions of the workers. I was aware that my prestige was growing and that the deference shown to me was not only because I was Joss Madden's wife and co-shareholder.

I had great fortune one day, in that room where the sorting was done, of selecting one piece about which I had what I can only call a hunch. I asked that it be worked on next because I just had a feeling that under the potch was something rather special.

I was humored and some work was set aside that the merits of this particular piece might be explored. To my great joy—and I must admit to a crowing delight in the fact—

the experts were more than a little astonished when it turned out that I had picked a winner. There, revealed by the facing wheel. was as fine a piece of opal as had been seen for many months.

"She's got it!" cried Jeremy Dickson excitedly. "Mrs. Madden, you're a real opal woman."

In my triumph I forgot my growing anxieties for a few hours.

But they were soon coming back to me. In the town was the reward notice to remind me. Fifty pounds for anyone who could give information regarding the killer of Ezra Bannock. Then I thought of Isa smiling secretly at Joss and the argument I had overheard and the fact that Ezra had ridden out from Peacocks to his death.

I had to know what was thought and being said in the town and whether there were suspicions that Joss was Ezra's murderer. I made a habit of going into the Trant's Cookshop for a mid-morning cup of coffee. Ethel always left what she was doing to come and chat with me. She had clearly taken a fancy to me. Moreover she was a born gossip and had her finger on the pulse of the town. She would know what was being said and how people felt about everything. When Joss laughed at me for my regular visits I retorted that it was as well to know what people of the town were thinking and there was no better way than chatting with Ethel.

"I can see you're going to bring a new depth to the Company," he said.

"Don't you think that would be good?" I asked.

"Let's wait and see," he parried, and I fancied I saw a shadow of concern on his face. Was he afraid of what I might learn about him? I wondered.

As I sat stirring my coffee and talking with Ethel the topic soon came round to the recent murder.

"I reckon Ezra has the Green Flash," said Ethel. "And I'm not the only one who thinks it. I reckon he stole it for his wife."

"Surely you don't think she has it now?"

"It wouldn't surprise me. There was a regular to-do when she first came out here. Came from Home, she did. An actress, they said. He'd seen her at some theatre and fallen madly in love with her."

"Why do you think she came out here?"

"To marry Ezra. She thought he was going to make a fortune. She was young then. There wasn't a man around who wasn't crazy about her. They hadn't seen anything like Isa Bannock out here in the Bush. They were all ready to be her slaves. Even James's eyes would glitter at the sight of her. That just suited her. Of course Ezra did well. He was one of the top men in the Company under Ben Henniker and your husband, of course. But he never got as far as she wanted him to. Now this Green Flash. Mr. Henniker had hidden it all the time. Ezra was in and out of Peacocks, and well. . . ."

"I can't believe that Ezra was a thief."

"It's not the same stealing the Green Flash. It makes its own spell, that stone. People can't help themselves. It's some evil spirit that takes them over. Possession they call it."

I thought of my father who had loved my mother and promised to marry her. Then he had seen the Green Flash and was ready to forget everything for its sake. Possession! Yes, that was the word.

"I reckon he took it for Isa, and when it was his he got the bad luck it always brings. The bushranger was waiting for the first who came to Grover's Gully and because his luck had turned, that one was Ezra Bannock. People are saying that the Green Flash ought to be found." She was eying me speculatively, and I felt there was more in her mind than she, gossip that she was, would tell me. "All this mystery about its whereabouts makes talk," she added.

"I'm sure you're right," I said.

I left her and went back to the office. At the door I met Joss.

"Well," he asked, "been feeling the public pulse?"

"Yes," I replied. "There's a lot of talk going on."

"Naturally. There always is."

"This is about Ezra and the Green Flash."

"I don't see the connection."

"People evidently think there is one."

"What have you discovered?"

"It's being whispered that Ezra stole the Green Flash because Isa wanted it. It would have been his for a while and because of it the legendary bad luck sent him to Grover's Gully at the precise moment when the bushranger was there."

I saw the tightening of his lips and the steely look I dreaded come into his blue eyes.

"Nonsense," he said. "Absolute nonsense."

"At least," I went on, looking straight at him, "that's one theory."

He shrugged his shoulders impatiently, and I thought: How

far is he involved? Was he the one who had taken the Green Flash from its hiding place that he might give it to his mistress? How far had his infatuation led him?

I felt sick and afraid.

I sat on the terrace as I often did when I returned from town and Mrs. Laud or Lilias would bring me a drink. It was usually Lilias's homemade lemonade.

On this day Mrs. Laud brought it.

"You look disturbed," she said. "Has anything upset you?"

"No, not really. But I wish we could solve this mystery of Ezra Bannock. He was such a genial man."

"Is there really a mystery? Wasn't it a bushranger? His purse was stolen after all."

"Yes, I know."

"You don't seem to think that's what happened."

"It appears obvious of course."

"You're worried. You mustn't let all this upset you, Mrs. Madden. I get quite concerned about you."

"You're always so kind and helpful, Mrs. Laud. You have been ever since I came out here."

"Well, why not? And you the mistress of the house. I think you should put all this out of your mind. That would be the best way."

"I can't. Did you know that some people have an idea that the murder has something to do with the Green Flash?"

"Whoever thought that?"

"There's talk in the town."

"But what could Mr. Bannock's death possibly have to do with the Green Flash? It's missing, isn't it? Mr. Henniker put it somewhere and it's been stolen."

"That's the point—and perhaps we ought to do something about finding it."

"How, Mrs. Madden?"

"Make every effort. The Green Flash was stolen from this house. We should find out how and when it was taken. Mr. Madden's against it. He doesn't want inquiries about the Green Flash and old legends revived. He doesn't want people to think that opals are unlucky, which they always do when the Green Flash is talked of."

"He's right. Jimson says that sort of talk is bad for business."

"We needn't stress whether it's lucky or unlucky. What I

want is to find out the truth. I must know what's happened to it."

"What will you do, Mrs. Madden?"

"I'm not quite sure, but I'm going to start ferreting around."

"By yourself?"

"If I can get help, I will. *You* might be able to help, Mrs. Laud."

"You can be sure I'll do all I can."

"You know who came to the house."

"Well, you saw at the Treasure Hunt—there are hundreds of them. People are in and out of Peacocks all the time."

"The fact remains, Mrs. Laud, that someone came into this house, found the hiding place, and took the Green Flash."

"You really think it could have been Mr. Bannock!"

"I find it hard to believe that of him. I liked him very much, although I had known him such a short time. He seemed such a happy man. It doesn't seem possible that he could have anything on his conscience."

"Yes, that's very hard to believe. So you're going to start making inquiries."

"Discreetly, not openly—because Mr. Madden doesn't want it."

"No, I see he wouldn't. . . ." She stopped suddenly as though she had said more than she had intended to.

"Why?" I asked sharply.

"He . . . er . . . wouldn't want inquiries. . . ." She looked a little distressed.

"It's because of this talk about opals being unlucky," I said firmly.

"Oh yes, of course. That's the sole reason. That's what I meant, of course."

She was protesting too much. I thought I understood what was in her mind. She knew of Joss's infatuation for Isa. Isa was like one of those princesses in the fairy tales of my youth. "To win my favors you must bring me the. . . ." and then would follow the seemingly impossible task which the prince always accomplished in the end.

It was becoming obvious. She loved opals. "I want my collection to be the finest in the world. . . ." How could it be, if it lacked the peer of them all? "You must find it for me, bring it to me and then . . . my hand in marriage. . . ." Wasn't that how it went in the fairy tales?

But they had not been free for marriage. Isa was free now

though. Joss wasn't . . . not yet.

"You're shivering suddenly," said Mrs. Laud. "Are you cold?"

"It's nothing . . . someone walking over my grave, as they say at Home."

She smiled at me strangely, enigmatically. I asked myself then: Are we thinking the same thing?

12

The Spinet Player

A few days later I made an alarming discovery.

During the last weeks the house had seemed to oppress me. I had the uncanny feeling that there was something there from which I must escape. I thought a great deal about Ben because his personality was stamped on Peacocks. Lately, I suppose because I was in a rather nervous state, I had fancied I sensed his presence there. I believed that if there had been a close bond between people it did not necessarily end with death. He was after all the only person who had really loved me. For a short while I had been happy in that love, and when he died I realized how alone and desolate I was. I suppose everyone longs to be loved and those who do so most are those who have missed the good fortune of enjoying that which I have come to believe is the most desirable thing in life. My childhood had been loveless. I was an encumbrance from the first. My own mother had found life intolerable and had left me. I could not say that my childhood had been unhappy because it was not in my nature to be unhappy, and in those days I had not missed what I had never known. In fact, it was having been loved and cherished by Ben that had taught me what I had missed.

Perhaps that was why I felt this special bond between us, and I fancied that his spirit was in the house warning me in some way because I was in danger. Everything had certainly not turned out as he had planned it should. He had bound Joss and me together, but such interference in the lives of other people could be dangerous. Had he really known how far Joss would go to get what he wanted? Had he ever thought that I might be the wife who was in the way of a ruthless man and because of this I could be in a situation of acute peril?

Who was it who crept up to my room at night and would on the last occasion have come in if the door had been unlocked? Why? For what purpose? Was it Joss? I believed

t was. Had he come to plead with me to let us begin a new
life together? No, he was too proud for that. He had always
said he would not force himself on me. Then why? And
what did it mean?

Was I right in thinking that there was some element in
the house which was trying to warn me?

So when I came in and found Peacocks quiet, I often had
the desire to get out of it. Sometimes I sat in the pond garden,
but more often I chose the peace of the orchard. There among
the lemon and orange trees I could relax and think about
my day at the offices and what I had learned. I would then
admonish myself for my foolish fancies, and there among
the oranges, lemons, and guavas I felt a return to common
sense.

I had brought several books from the offices and these
were teaching me a great deal of opal lore. I liked to take
one of them to the orchard, find a shady spot, and sit and
read, as I did so memorizing facts with which I loved to
startle people, in particular Joss. I could see that he was
impressed, though he never said so, but there would be a
certain lifting of the corners of his mouth and twinkle in
his eyes. I found this very gratifying because I knew that I
was arousing his grudging admiration.

It was there in the orchard that I made the discovery.

The grass was coarse and where the earth showed through
it was brown and cracked. I suppose that was why the spot
which had been dug up recently was noticeable.

Looking up from my book, my eyes went straight to it,
and I saw at once that the earth had been turned over and
that something looked as though it was protruding. I studied
it for a few seconds without moving. The sun caught it and
it glittered like gold.

I went over. It *was* gold. As I pulled it out I was limp
with horror, for what I had found was a red leather purse
with a gold band, and I knew at once that it had belonged
to Ezra Bannock, and that he had carried it with him when
he was shot at Grover's Gully.

Who had buried it in the orchard at Peacocks?

I could no longer stay in the orchard. I went to my room
in a haze of horror and indecision.

I could not make up my mind what to do. The theory
that a bushranger had shot Ezra was false. What bushranger

would come to Peacocks and steal into the orchard in order to bury the purse there?

There seemed to be one answer to the mystery. Someone at Peacocks had killed Ezra Bannock and taken his purse to make it look like robbery and then buried the purse in the orchard.

There was only one I knew who had a motive.

With Ezra out of the way, Isa was free. But *Joss* was not. He was married to me, and while I lived he was not free. While I lived. . . .

That was the thought that kept recurring. It was becoming like a nightmare.

I took out the purse and examined it. "He had a red leather purse full of sovereigns. He used to fill it up every morning. . . ." Isa had said something like that.

What was it that Joss had aroused in me? Was it love? I wanted to protect him, whatever he had done. I wanted to go to him and say: "I have found Ezra's purse. You hid it in the orchard . . . not very cleverly. The ground was so parched it was obvious. We must get rid of it. . . ."

But why should he bury the purse in the orchard? Why had he not got rid of it somewhere in the Bush? It seemed like a panic-stricken action. Strangely enough I could believe he might be a murderer, but not that he would ever suffer panic.

He would say to me: "So you believe that of me. Why don't you betray me? Why involve yourself?"

"Because I'm a fool," I would say. "I have the same feeling for you as you have for Isa Bannock. Perhaps now you understand."

But I would say nothing of the sort. I did not know what to do, and being in doubt, I put the purse into a drawer and then was afraid that it might be discovered. It was the perfect clue which would lead to the murderer.

I must tell him. He would lie. He would say he hadn't put it there. But who else, Joss? Who else?

I spent a sleepless night and twice rose to look at the purse in the drawer to assure myself that it was there and I hadn't dreamed the whole thing.

The next day Joss had left when I went down and I rode into the town with Jimson. We talked as we rode, but I don't remember what about. I could think of nothing but that red purse with the pieces of orchard earth staining it.

As soon as I returned to Peacocks I went straight up to

my room and as I entered I knew that something had
changed. One of the drawers was not properly shut and in-
stinct told me that someone had been there looking for
something. I went immediately to the drawer in which I had
put the red purse. It was not there.

I sat down in a chair and thought of what this meant. Whoever had killed Ezra now knew that I had discovered the
purse and taken it from its hiding place.

It was difficult to appear normal. I tried to think what
would be the best line of action. I told myself that as soon
as I saw Joss I should know, because even he must be shaken
by what had happened.

I went to the window and stood there looking out across
the grounds to the arid Bush. I could just make out the
calico tents on the fringe of the town. As I stood there, I
saw Mrs. Laud drive in with the buggy. She often took it
down to the town and brought back provisions which were
carried into the house by the servants. She looked up and
saw me, lifting her hand in acknowledgment.

I went to the hall. I felt an urgent need to get back to
normality.

"It's very hot, isn't it?" I said.

"My goodness, yes."

"You should have taken Lilias with you."

"I think she sees a little too much of Jeremy Dickson."

"He's a very pleasant young man. Why don't you like
him, Mrs. Laud?"

She didn't answer but pressed her lips tightly together.

"You must be worn out," I went on. "Why don't you have
a cup of tea."

"I thought I'd go to my room and make one. Would you
care to join me, Mrs. Madden?"

"Why yes, I'd like to."

We climbed to her room and she put the kettle on the
spirit lamp. It was a very cozy little room with a bunch of
dried leaves in a pot in the fireplace and on the polished
table a runner of red plush. The chairs had tapestry seats,
and I was sure she had made them herself. In the corner
was a whatnot on which were displayed miniature pieces of
china, and there was a cuckoo clock on the wall.

She watched my gaze. "I brought these things out from
England, and when I came here Mr. Henniker let me furnish
my own room. I appreciated that."

"That must have made it seem very homey."

She made the tea. She seemed upset about something and I determined to find out what. It took my mind off that other terrifying matter.

"I hope this is to your taste, Mrs. Madden. Tea doesn't taste right here to me. Not like Home. They say it's the water."

"You were going to tell me about Mr. Dickson," I prompted.

She looked at me in a startled fashion. "Was I?"

"You . . . er . . . don't like this friendship between him and Lilias?"

"I wouldn't go so far as to say that."

"How far would you go?"

"I'm being silly, I suppose. I wouldn't want her to make a mistake. I suppose mothers do feel like that about their daughters."

"Has he done anything to upset you?"

"Oh no . . . not him."

"Someone else . . . then?"

She looked at me in a worried way, and she reminded me of an animal caught in a trap.

"I have been in this house so long," she said, which seemed to me straying from the point. "There I was at my wit's end. . . ."

"I know, and Mr. Henniker offered you the post."

"I brought my children up here. I was treated . . . as though I belonged."

"Mr. Henniker was a wonderfully kind man."

"I couldn't bear anything to go wrong in this house. I just don't like what's being said."

"What was that?" I asked sharply.

She looked at me blankly then she said: "When you think back it's hard to put your finger on it. It's implication . . . or something like that."

"Who implied what?"

She looked over her shoulder as though she were seeking some way of escape.

"You're the last one I should be saying this to."

"Why? Does it concern me?"

"It's a lot of lies . . . plain lies. . . ."

"Now, Mrs. Laud, you have said too much to stop. Someone's been telling lies about me, have they?"

"Oh no, not about you, Mrs. Madden. Everybody's sorry for you."

"Why are they sorry for me?"

"They say it's a pity Mr. Henniker made that will. They say it's forced things. Mrs. Bannock's not liked in the town. She's not liked at all. Oh, Mr. Madden would be angry if he knew. I really mustn't say any more. He'd turn me out. Perhaps I deserve it for talking to you like this."

"I want to know what they're saying."

"If I tell you, will you promise to say nothing to him?"

"To my husband, you mean?"

"Yes, please don't tell him that I talked to you like this. He'd be so angry . . . heaven knows where it would end. It's only talk, that's all, but it upsets me. I told them it was a lot of lies . . . but that doesn't stop them. They wouldn't say anything to you, of course. You're the last one they'd talk to."

"Mrs. Laud, I want to know what this is all about."

"It's not exactly what was said. It's the looks . . . the nods . . . and. . . ."

"Implications," I said. "What was it?"

The words came out in a rush. "They said they'd always known how it was between them. Ezra put up with it for a long time because of his position in the Company. Then he wouldn't have it . . . and that's why he died."

"No!" I cried fiercely, forgetting that it was exactly what I had thought myself. "It's impossible."

"They say she has the Green Flash, that he took it from its hiding place and gave it to her."

"I never heard such nonsense," I cried firmly.

"No more did I, but it upsets me . . . and you just caught me at a bad moment."

"I'm glad you told me, Mrs. Laud. But let's forget it, shall we?"

She hesitated. "Well, I don't believe it, of course, but I think . . . well, I just think you ought to be on your guard. . . ."

I stared at her and she bit her lip in embarrassment and went stammering on: ". . . on your guard against gossip."

"Cuckoo, cuckoo," said the clock on the wall, and went on repeating his silly cry to denote the hour.

When I went into the town, I imagined people watched me furtively. They were sorry for me, asking themselves how much I knew. In a place like this everyone knew everyone else's business. The notices asking for information about Ezra's murder looked out at me from every post.

It was an uneasy town. The cozy theory was that Ezra had been shot by a bushranger who was now miles away, the only other alternative being that we had a murderer in our midst. Murderers had to have motives. I knew that the murderer was someone who came to Peacocks and was such a frequent visitor that no one would notice when he went into the orchard to bury a purse.

When I went into the offices, Jeremy was waiting for me. He wanted to show me the finished product of that opal I had had such a feeling about.

"You can be proud to have your judgment proved correct," he told me.

"Does it really mean I'm learning or was it just good luck?"

"It was pure hunch, and that's what we all wait for."

He said he would make tea, and as he did so I felt a great urge to talk to him about my discovery and my fears, for it occurred to me that he was one of the few people I *could* talk to; but I knew that would be unwise.

I brought the subject around to the Green Flash.

"Have you heard the rumor that Ezra stole it and died as a result?" I asked.

"I never take any notice of rumors like that."

"I suppose there's just a possibility that it might be true."

"In the first place, Ezra's no thief. He would have never stolen anything."

"His wife has a fine collection. Suppose he wanted to add the best of all to it."

Jeremy shook his head.

"If the Green Flash could be found it would be helpful," he said.

"Ah yes. But where is it? I only wish I knew where to start looking for it. You see, it's very awkward because Joss doesn't want to start fussing about it."

Jeremy wrinkled his brows. "It's very strange," he said. "Perhaps he's making secret investigations."

"Since I am a joint owner, I think he would have consulted me. Can you suggest anything that I might do?"

"Well, presumably it was there when Mr. Henniker left. There was obviously no break-in, so it must have been taken by someone who was known to the house. That could have been anyone at the works because they could come or go without much notice being taken. You might start questioning the servants. And you can be sure I'll keep my eyes and ears open and do everything I can."

"Thanks."

The door opened suddenly and Joss looked in.

"Oh," he said, "cozy chat, I see!" and was about to go when Jeremy said: "Did you want me?"

"Later will do," replied Joss and disappeared.

I left the office soon after that and went back to Peacocks. I lay on my bed with the blinds shutting out the heat. I could not concentrate on reading and kept thinking of Joss's burying the purse in the orchard, and the more I thought of it the more absurd it seemed. How simple it would have been to have thrown it away in the Bush, which the suspected bushranger might easily have done.

I was startled suddenly by a gentle pat on my door. It was so light I scarcely heard it. I called "Come in" but there was no answer so I went to the door and looked into the corridor.

"Is anyone there?" I called.

There was still no answer. Then from above I heard the sound of the spinet. It was a Chopin waltz.

I wondered who in the house played the spinet, and my curiosity sent me to the stairs leading to the gallery. When I was halfway up the stairs the music stopped abruptly. I opened the door of the gallery and went in.

There was no one there.

I looked round in dismay. If someone had been in here playing, I must surely have seen whoever it was coming out of the room.

Had I imagined it? No. I had distinctly heard it.

As I came downstairs I heard someone in the hall. It was Mrs. Laud just coming in.

"It's hot in the town," she said.

"Have you been ordering again? You should have gone this morning."

"A few things I had forgotten. You look startled, Mrs. Madden."

"I thought I heard someone playing the spinet, in the gallery."

"Oh no, I don't think so. Nobody's touched it for years. Mr. Henniker used to play it sometimes. He had funny fancies for a man such as he was. He used to say to me: 'Emmeline. . . .' He used to call me Emmeline . . . always my full name

. . . 'Emmeline, when I play this I fancy I'm calling someone from the grave. . . .' He had this strange feeling, you know. She died . . . of a broken heart, he said, and if he had stayed in England he could have saved her. Funny you should have fancied you heard it playing."

"It didn't seem like fancy."

"I can't think what else, Mrs. Madden. I can't really."

"Oh well." I shrugged my shoulders. "It's not important."

But it was, because I was certain I had heard someone there, and I could not understand how that could possibly be the case.

Later that day, after sundown, I went up to the gallery. It looked ghostly in the candlelight for only a few of those on the wall sconces were kept lighted. It could be a blaze of light when there was a party. I could almost make myself believe that I sensed a presence there. Did people really return, people who had taken their lives and could not rest? Perhaps my mother would want to take care of me especially because she had left me to the far from tender care of my grandmother. What was the matter with me? Finding the purse had unnerved me, so that I could really believe that it was my mother who had tapped on the door and that in playing the spinet she was letting me know that she was watching over me.

When I came back to Peacocks the next afternoon, Jeremy Dickson rode with me. "I shall be going away for a short time," he said.

"Really? Where?"

"Mr. Madden spoke to me yesterday after you had left. He wants someone to go to the Sydney office and he suggests that I go."

I felt a mingling of disappointment and exhilaration. I should miss Jeremy, and yet what if Joss was sending him off because he knew that I was rather friendly with him? That could mean that he was not indifferent to that friendship. I had sensed that he was a little piqued by it.

"Are you pleased?" I asked Jeremy.

"I've become too enthusiastic about our plan to track down the Green Flash. Wouldn't it be strange if the answer was in Sydney?"

"I can hardly think that's so."

"Why not? If someone took it would he stay here with it?"

"But we said it had to be someone who lived here . . .

someone who could come in and out without being noticed."

"That may be. However, I'll drop hints about it when I'm in Sydney. It's amazing what comes to light during casual conversations."

I found comfort in talking to him and missed him when two days later he left for Sydney.

Joss was sardonic as we rode into the town.

"I'm sorry to deprive you of your playmate," he said.

"Playmate?" I retorted angrily. "Workmate, you mean."

"You and he always seemed to be enjoying each other's company."

"He treated me like an intelligent being, that's why."

"Oh come, there's not a man in the Company who doesn't salute your intelligence. But you can start looking into other facets of the business now. You've spent too long with the facing wheels."

"Even you had to admit my hunch proved a good one."

"I've never denied it. But you can't live on the glory of one hunch all your opal-working days. You go and look through the books with Jimson Laud. Accounting is a very important part of the business."

"What's happening about Ezra Bannock?" I asked.

His expression changed. "What do you mean?"

"Are you nearer to discovering his murderer?"

"It's hopeless. Quite clearly it was a bushranger. I expect Ezra put up a fight and that was that."

"His purse was taken. I thought it might have been found."

He stared at me in amazement. "His purse! You don't think the thief would keep that, do you? He'd throw it away . . . and quickly. He wouldn't want to keep something that could incriminate him."

"It was a red purse with a gold ring."

"Yes, that came out in the inquiry."

"But it was never found . . . ?"

"Did you expect it would be? There must be hundreds of such purses in this neighborhood."

I wanted to tell him, but I couldn't. It would be like accusing him of murder. He would never forgive me . . . particularly if he were guilty.

It was true that there were hundreds of such purses. Perhaps that one had been lying in the orchard for a long time. But then why had someone later taken it from the drawer in my room?

We reached the office and I went to Jimson's department

but couldn't concentrate. I could think of nothing but Isa and Joss . . . together. I should never forget that moment when she had shown me the Harlequin Opal and blatantly announced that Joss had given it to her.

When I left the offices instead of riding back to Peacocks I decided to go to the Homestead to see Isa.

I left Wattle with one of the grooms and went into the house, where, in the hall, I immediately noticed a big trunk which looked as though it were ready for imminent removal.

A servant took me into the cool, chintzy drawing room, and I had only been there a few moments when Isa came in. She looked beautiful in flowing black chiffon—secret-eyed, I thought, and predatory.

"Jessica, how nice of you to take pity on me."

"I thought I would come and see you. You did invite me."

"Oh please, you mustn't make excuses. Haven't I always told you that I love callers?"

"It must be lonely for you now."

"Oh, people are *so* good. They call often."

A faint smile at the lips. Joss, I thought.

"I'll ring for tea," she said. "Oh, what should we do without tea? It's our refuge from this thirst-parching heat."

She rang for tea and asked how I was getting on with the Company. "I've heard you're something of a genius."

"Whoever told you that?"

"These things get around. I think you're going to be a martinet. You'll make them all keep their noses to the grindstone."

"That's nonsense. I happen to be very interested."

"It's clever of you. Processes and all that. All I can do is enjoy the finished product."

"You said that you would one day show me the rest of your collection."

"Didn't I show you once?"

"Yes, when you had acquired the Harlequin Opal."

"A gem. It *was* good of Joss."

"I'm sure he enjoyed giving it to you."

"He knew it would be in good hands."

"It's not the best in your collection though, is it?"

She looked at me shyly and shook her head.

"What would you say is the finest opal you possess?"

"Ezra used to say: 'You shouldn't talk so much about your collection. One of these days someone will come along and steal it.' "

"But you didn't take his advice."

"I've always found that advice is something always to listen to but only to take when you want to."

"Now that I know a little more about opals I should appreciate your collection so much more."

"Oh yes, you were a novice when you first saw it. But not so much so that you couldn't recognize the qualities of the Harlequin."

"They were rather obvious as I should think others in your collection would be."

"Oh yes, of course. How is Wattle? It was a shock for her to discover Ezra. Isn't it strange, but for that horse his death would have remained a mystery forever. It's rather frightening, isn't it . . . when you think of what can happen in a place like this. I wonder how many bodies have been buried in the Bush with never a faithful Wattle to unearth them. So you saw the groom and the servant who brought you the tea. We might be alone but for them. Did you tell Joss you were coming to see me?"

"I didn't. I may do. Or perhaps you will."

She opened her eyes very wide. "Do you think I shall see him? Is he coming over?"

"Is he?" I asked. "Are you going to show me the rest of your collection?"

"No," she answered.

"Why not?"

"Guess."

"Is there something so valuable that you'd rather not show it?"

"There are certainly valuable stones there." She laughed suddenly. "Oh, I know what you're thinking. The elusive Green Flash. Do you know what they're saying in town? That Ezra stole it and gave it to me and that he died because it brought him bad luck. Do you think I'd want bad luck?"

"You wouldn't believe in the bad luck, would you?"

"I'm very superstitious. And the reason I shall not show you my collection has nothing to do with the Green Flash."

"What then?"

"It's packed away."

"Are you sending it away?"

She nodded. "It's going with me. I shall be leaving for England in a few weeks."

"Leaving for England! Leaving . . . here!"

"For a holiday. I might come back. I need to get away now that Ezra's gone."

"Are you going . . . alone?"

The tiger eyes gleamed. "You ask too many questions," she said.

I wondered what she was hinting at.

I left soon after. I did not want to be out after sundown.

The house was quiet when I arrived at Peacocks. Joss had not yet returned from the town. I was very uneasy because I felt there was something significant about Isa's departure. How would Joss feel about her going? If he were indeed madly in love with her he would certainly be upset. I could not wait to see him.

I mounted the stairs to my room and once again I heard the notes of the spinet. I took the stairs two at a time but when I reached the landing the playing had stopped. I went into the gallery. No one was there.

I looked all around. The only explanation was that unless there was another way out of the gallery the spinet player could only be someone who did not have to take account of walls.

I sat down in one of the chairs and looked around the place. As usual the sound of music had touched me deeply. Perhaps I wanted to believe it was my mother returned from the dead to care for me. But why . . . suddenly? What of all those years I had spent in the Dower House? Surely I had needed her care then.

Ben had given me a temporary stability; he had changed me; helped me to grow up; then he had married me off to Joss whose affections were already engaged and who had agreed to the marriage purely for gain.

The significance of my theories was startling. Only now did my mother think that the time had come for her to protect me. So . . . I was in danger.

Yes, I could sense it. Something evil was here. It was in this gallery. I could easily imagine I could hear a voice warning me. Be careful. You are in danger.

I sat still, my senses strained. Why play the spinet? Why not come to me and talk to me and tell me plainly what threatened me. Supernatural manifestations were never straightforward. They were always implied in some strange and unearthly way.

Then suddenly I heard the sound of hysterical weeping. I

went quickly to the door of the gallery and listened. It was coming from the upstairs quarters. I ran up. The door of Mrs. Laud's room was slightly open and it was from there that the sounds were emerging.

"Is anything wrong?" I cried.

I went into the room. The three Lauds were there, Jimson, Lilias, and their mother. It was Lilias who was half sobbing, half laughing. Jimson had his arm about her.

"What's the matter?" I asked.

Mrs. Laud looked distressed. "Now you've disturbed Mrs. Madden. Oh, I *am* sorry. Poor Lilias was a bit upset. Her brother and I have been trying to comfort her."

"Why? What's wrong?"

Mrs. Laud shook her head and looked at me appealingly as though begging me not to ask questions.

Lilias pulled herself together and said: "I'm all right now, Mrs. Madden. I don't know what came over me." She was obviously trying hard to control herself.

"Just a little personal matter," murmured Jimson.

"I was in the gallery and I heard sounds of crying," I said.

"In the gallery," repeated Lilias, and there was a tremor in her voice.

"I thought I heard the spinet again."

There was a brief silence, then Jimson said: "It must be out of tune. I've heard that spinets have to be tuned frequently."

"Are you sure that everything's all right?" I asked.

"Oh yes, Mrs. Madden," Mrs. Laud assured me. "We can look after Lilias."

"I'm only sorry that we disturbed you," said Jimson.

"Yes," echoed Lilias meekly. "I'm very very sorry, Mrs. Madden."

I went out. There was a great deal that puzzled me about that family.

Mrs. Laud came to my room while I was changing for dinner.

"May I come in for a moment, Mrs. Madden?" she asked. "I wanted to have a word with you and tell you how sorry I am for what happened this afternoon. It was dreadful that we should have disturbed you."

"Oh please, Mrs. Laud, it was nothing. I'm only sorry for Lilias's trouble."

"Well, that's it, Mrs. Madden. She's a little upset. You can guess what it is perhaps."

I looked at her blankly.

"It's this Mr. Dickson. She's upset because he'd been sent to Sydney."

"Oh, I understand."

"She's very taken with him. I've been against her marrying, but perhaps I'm wrong."

"Have they talked of marrying?"

"There's nothing been said officially, you understand, but Lilias was very upset when he went away."

"But he's only gone for a short time."

"She's got some idea that Mr. Madden might want him to stay permanently in Sydney."

"I didn't gather that."

"You would know, of course. I keep forgetting you're one of the directors of the Company. It seems so strange for a lady to be in that position."

"It was Mr. Henniker's idea."

"Oh, I know he was a one for ideas. Well, I thought I'd better explain about Lilias."

"Don't think any more about it, Mrs. Laud."

Lilias seemed to have recovered at dinnertime. The conversation was, as usual, about business. I was able to join in now, and I always enjoyed doing so. But suddenly my pleasure was shattered when Joss said: "I think a trip to England will be necessary in the not too distant future."

I stared at him in amazement. "It seems we have only just arrived here," I said.

"That's how it is in business," he replied easily. "One can never be sure when something is going to arise."

"What is this that has arisen?"

"New markets are opening up in London. There's a growing demand there for black Australian opals. Naturally we want to exploit that."

"So you are proposing to go to England?"

"Nothing definite yet. It's just something that may well be necessary."

I felt deflated and wretched. It was so easy to understand. Isa was going to England, so he would go too. I dare say it would be very discreet. She would leave and then he would discover that he had to go too. He was already paving the way.

I no longer had any appetite, and as soon as we left the table I made an excuse to go to my room. I had noticed the way in which Joss had looked at me when he had made the announcement that he was about to go to England. It seemed as though he were waiting for me to protest.

I won't give him that satisfaction, I thought. But I shall let him know that I am aware that the reason for his sudden desire to leave for England is not due to business but to Isa.

I had made up my mind that when Jeremy Dickson returned I would tell him about my discovery of the red purse. I could talk to him freely. Then I told myself that I could do no such thing because it was an implied accusation against Joss. How could I bring myself to talk about the red purse?

I had never felt so alone in the whole of my life.

I came home one afternoon to a quiet house and went to my room. As I stood there, my hand on the door handle, I heard again that ghostly touch on the spinet keys.

I ran upstairs as fast as I could. It was the same procedure. The music stopped and there was no one seated at the spinet.

Someone was playing tricks on me. And as I looked around the gallery I noticed that there was a difference. One of the curtains which hung at intervals along the walls in the manner of the gallery at Oakland was disarranged. I went to it and drew it right back. I had disclosed a door which I had never known was there before. A light shone through the mist now. Someone had been playing the spinet and stepped behind the curtain and left the gallery before I arrived by way of that door.

This must be the answer, for the door was not quite shut. That time the trickster had had to escape in too much of a hurry to disguise his escape.

I pushed open the door and peered into darkness. I felt with my foot. It was a stair. Cautiously—for I was in complete darkness—I stepped down two steps. Then something shifted under me. There was a clatter and I felt as though I were sailing in mid-air. I clutched at something to save myself. It was a banister, but I couldn't see it. I felt my feet slide from under me and I was seated on something dank and cold.

So shocked was I that I was unable to move for some moments. I was aware of the sound of heavy objects falling, with bumping sounds, as though they were falling downstairs.

I called out: "Help. Help," and tried to stand up. My eyes were growing accustomed to the darkness and I could make out this staircase which seemed to go down into the gloom.

Then I heard someone shouting from below. "What is it? What's wrong?" It was Mrs. Laud's voice.

I called out: "I'm here, Mrs. Laud. I've fallen."

"Did you come from the gallery? I'll come up there . . ."

I sat there waiting. I realized what had happened. I had started down a staircase which was blocked in some way. I had had a narrow escape for I should have had a very bad fall if I had not found the banister in time and been able to save myself.

Mrs. Laud appeared behind me.

"Whatever's happened? Let me help you, Mrs. Madden. Just a moment, I'll get a candle. It's that old staircase."

I stood up gingerly and she half dragged me back into the gallery.

"I saw the door open," I said. "I'd no idea there was a door there."

"It was hidden by that curtain. There's a stairway between this floor and the one below. It hasn't been used for years. Someone must have put boxes in there at some time and used it as a sort of cupboard."

"It's very dangerous," I said.

"I don't remember anyone's using it for years. Just stand up will you, Mrs. Madden. I don't think you've broken anything. How do you feel?"

"Stiff and sore and rather shaken. I thought I'd broken a leg or something."

"You could have done yourself some real damage. Perhaps I should help you to your room. I could get you something. They say a cup of tea with plenty of sugar is good for that sort of shock."

"I just want to sit here for a moment and think. I heard the playing this afternoon."

She looked uneasy. "Did you really, Mrs. Madden?"

"You think I imagined it, don't you?"

"Well, people do imagine things when they're a bit wrought up, don't they?"

"I didn't know I was wrought up."

"Well," she flapped her hand vaguely. "Everything. . . ."

"Everything?" I insisted.

"Well, Mr. Madden talking of going off like that and the way things are."

It was impossible to keep secrets from people who shared one's household. I dare say there was a great deal of talk about my relationship with Joss.

I said: "What I should like to know is why that door was open. No one has used that staircase for years, you say. But someone has been using it lately, I think, someone who has been playing the spinet and escaping that way. I think that today, whoever it was, didn't forget to shut that door but left it open for a purpose."

"Who could have used the staircase with all those things on the stairs?"

"Someone who knew they were there . . . someone who put them there . . . knowing that I should see the open door and investigate."

"Oh no, Mrs. Madden, he wouldn't go as far as that."

"He? Who?"

"Whoever it is who is playing these tricks with the spinet. . . . That's what you said, isn't it? It's someone playing tricks."

"I have got to get to the bottom of this, Mrs. Laud. Don't move anything on that staircase. I'm going to see what is actually there."

"Well, Mrs. Madden, there's a door on the landing below this. It's so unobtrusive you'd hardly notice it's there. I put a curtain over it, since no one uses it as a staircase. As you've seen, it's dark and dangerous. It looks to me as if someone used it as a cupboard and piled boxes on the stairs."

"Anyone would see on opening the door down there that it was a staircase and not a cupboard surely."

"I can't think how it happened," said Mrs. Laud helplessly.

I took a candle, lighted it, and peered down the staircase. I could see the huddle of boxes on the lower stairs.

"We'd better clear it out and open it," I said. "I don't like the idea of these secret places."

And as I was speaking I knew that someone had lured me onto that staircase, had put the boxes there to trap me, someone who had hoped that I would have an accident . . . or perhaps break my neck. I knew it was not the spirit of my mother—or anyone who cared for me—who had lured me to the gallery with the spinet playing.

It was someone who wished me out of the way.

I rode into the town next morning, for I had suffered little physical effect from yesterday's adventure.

I said to Joss: "Did you know there was a staircase connecting the gallery with the corridor on the lower floor?"

I watched him carefully as I asked the question. His expression did not change as he said: "Oh yes, I remember. I used to play hide and seek a lot when I was a boy. It was one of my favorite games, and I remember using that staircase."

"You haven't used it lately?"

"I'd forgotten about it. What made you mention it?"

"I discovered it yesterday."

"We ought to open it and use it."

"That's what I said. Did you ever play the spinet?"

"What makes you ask?"

"Just curiosity."

"As a matter of fact, I did."

I laughed.

"What's amusing?"

"The thought of your sitting at that dainty stool rendering a Chopin nocturne."

"I wasn't bad at it. I'll show you one day."

"Have you played recently?"

"Haven't touched it for years. I expect it's out of tune. We ought to get someone to look at it. I can't think who. Spinet care would hardly be a profitable profession in these parts. I can't think why Ben ever brought it out here."

"For sentimental reasons, I believe."

"And they are rarely sound ones."

How could he be so calm, so matter-of-fact? He didn't want me. I was well aware of that, but would he really play the spinet and try to make me break my neck? Ruthless I knew him to be, in love with Isa and making little secret of it. There were people in the town who suspected him of murdering Ezra—Mrs. Laud had hinted at it—and what was the use of getting rid of Ezra if nothing was to be done to remove the other encumbrance.

I must face the facts. If I did not exist, he could marry Isa. They had been lovers for a long time without contemplating marriage, so why should they suddenly desire it?

I realized that it was not so much that I believed Joss would not dispatch me but that I could not believe he would have used such a method. Why not? Above all my death must appear natural. It would be too much of a coincidence if *I* were supposed to be shot by a bushranger.

In Fancy Town Joss was a great power; people were afraid of him. But even he would have to be careful how he committed murder.

13

In the Haunted Mine

The next morning, when one of the maids came in with my hot water, she brought a letter for me. I was astonished, because we collected our mail from Fancy Town when it came in from Sydney every Wednesday, and for a letter to be delivered at the house was unheard of.

"How did it come?" I asked, turning it over in my hand.

"It was found in the hall, Mrs. Madden. One of the servants saw it lying there and it was addressed to you, so I brought it up."

It had obviously been delivered by hand and the writing on the envelope was vaguely familiar. I opened it.

My dear Mrs. Madden, [I read]

I have made a discovery as I hoped I might. I rode in late last night to drop this letter at Peacocks. I must see you alone and in secret. My inquiries have revealed so much and it would be very unwise for us to meet openly at this stage. You are in danger. So am I. I have something to show you and it is known that I have it. I hope you won't think this is too melodramatic, but I assure you there is something melodramatic about the whole matter and both our lives could be in jeopardy. Therefore I am going to ask you to meet me tomorrow . . . that will be today when you get this letter. I have tried to think of a suitable meeting place, for I assure you it must be very secret, and I have decided that the best would be Grover's Gully. Could you be there at three o'clock? There should be no one about at that time, but we must be very careful. I'm going to suggest that we meet in the underground chambers of the mine. There is nothing to fear and descent is easy by means of the old ladder there.

Please don't show this letter to anyone. That's

very important. You will understand the reason for
this when we meet.

Sincerely,
Jeremy Dickson

The words danced before my eyes. It sounded wildly dramatic, but then everything connected with the Green Flash
was—and I was certain that this was connected with that
stone.

Of course I would do it. I was not afraid, although the
mine was said to be haunted. I had always liked and trusted
Jeremy Dickson.

I could scarcely wait for three o'clock.

I did not want anything to be different, so I went as usual
with Joss in the morning. If I was more silent than usual, so
was he. We left each other at the doors of the offices and I
went into Jimson Laud's department.

I could concentrate on nothing that morning.

I had seen some of the chambers of disused mines, and I
would take a candle with me so that I should be able to find
my way through the passages.

I left just after midday and went back to Peacocks, which
I had to pass on my way to the Gully. In my room I picked
up the candle and matches and set out, confident that no one
had seen me leave.

There was not a touch of wind nor a cloud in the sky.

The day was at its hottest. I rode fast so eager was I to
reach our rendezvous in time.

The sun was high in the sky—a white, blazing light—and
as I rode I left a cloud of dust behind me. The song of
cicadas filled the air, but I was so accustomed to it that I
scarcely noticed it. Away on the horizon a kangaroo leaped
in his ungainly progress among the clumps of mulga. Over-
head the inevitable kookaburras laughed together, and never
before had I felt so conscious of the loneliness of the Bush.

I went through the pass and there was the mine. There
was no sign of anyone there. I looked at my watch. It was
five minutes to three. Shading my eyes, I studied the landscape. I could see no one. Jeremy had said in the underground chambers and he must be there already although I
wondered whether he had hidden his mount. I slipped off
Wattle, who showed no objection and seemed perfectly at
peace. I tethered her to a bush and went to the mine.

I stood at the head of the shaft for some moments, looking

around me. Just utter loneliness. Could it really be that Jeremy had found the Green Flash and had it to show me? If so, where was his horse? Perhaps he had not yet come and in a few moments I should make out his figure riding towards me. But he had stressed the time. Three o'clock, and it was almost that now.

I descended the iron rungs; they were very rusty and looked as though they had not been used for a very long time. I reached the bottom and stepped into a cavern which led into another and from that one several passages had been hewn out of the rock.

I peered into them and could see very little.

I called softly: "I'm here."

There was no answer.

I lighted my candle and started to explore the first chamber, but I had only taken a few steps when the flame flickered. I advanced and as I did so it went out altogether. I relighted it, but it flickered faintly and again went out.

I could not understand what was wrong. The passage had turned at right angles and I was in complete darkness so once more I tried to light the candle. This time there was no flame at all.

A sudden cold fear possessed me. It was as though every sense I possessed was calling out a warning. I did not know what it meant except that I was in acute danger. It was as though a flash of inspiration came to me. Jeremy did not write that letter. But it was in his handwriting. How well did I know his handwriting? I had only glanced casually at it once or twice. Other people would know that handwriting. Would it be so difficult to copy it in order to deceive me?

"Jeremy?" I called.

There was no answer.

Someone had lured me here and it was not Jeremy. I would know very soon. . . . Right at the end I should know.

What a fool I have been to step right into the trap.

"No, Joss," I said aloud. "Oh no, Joss . . . not you."

I had never known fear like this. It was the strangeness of everything . . . the silence . . . the darkness closing in on me . . . and most of all the silence, the terrible silence.

Get out, I commanded myself. Why do you wait here? Why don't you get out? There may still be time to escape.

But an odd lethargy was creeping over me . . . it was something that was completely alien to me. It was as though I were being slowly paralyzed.

I stumbled through the passage out to where I could see a faint shaft of light, but I could scarcely lift my limbs, and slowly, it seemed, for it was as though time had stopped, I sank to the ground.

"Joss?"

Yes, Joss had come. He was holding me in his arms.

"So . . . you came to kill me," I murmured. "So it *was* you. You want Isa. It's all clear now. I guessed. . . ."

Joss did not answer, but I could vaguely hear a lot of shouting voices and I realized that I was no longer in the mine.

I was lying on the ground and Joss was bending over me. I heard him say: "She's got rid of the poison, I think. Give her air . . . don't crowd round. . . . Plenty of air. . . ."

I opened my eyes and I heard him say "Jessica" in a way he had never said my name before, half reproachful, half tender. Something about the way in which he said my name made me feel very happy.

Then I heard him say: "You've got the buggy?"

He lifted me tenderly.

"I'll take her back," he said.

I was lying in the buggy and Joss was driving it. We stopped and he lifted me out.

I seemed to be only half conscious and the voices seemed very far off.

"Trouble at the mine. Mrs. Laud . . . hot bricks, please, and milk."

"Oh, Mr. Madden, how terrible."

"Never mind. She's safe. I got her out in time."

He put me on my bed. My eyes were shut, but I was aware of him. He bent down and kissed my forehead.

When I opened my eyes he was sitting by my bed.

He smiled at me. "It's all right," he said. "I got you out in time."

I closed them again, not wanting to know more just then. I wanted merely to revel in the knowledge that he had saved me and that he cared about what happened to me.

It was dark when I awoke. There were candles in the room, and Joss was still sitting by my bed.

"Still here?" I said.

"I wanted to be here when you woke up."

"What happened?"

"You did a very foolish thing." He was the old Joss again.

"I was going to meet Jeremy Dickson."

"We're going to get him. We're going to find out what he's after."

"I don't think it was Jeremy Dickson."

"I saw his letter. Lilias brought it to me."

"Lilias! Where did she get it from?"

"She found it in your room. Like you, she doesn't believe he wrote it. Thank God she had the sense to bring it to me without too much delay. I went straight to the mine because I guessed he meant you some harm."

"He was not there. It was just that I began to feel so strange."

"You felt strange because you were poisoned. Jeremy Dickson sent you into that mine because he knew just what would happen. Now we've got to find out why he wanted to kill you. People hereabouts know that nobody goes into mines that have been disused for a long period without first expelling the poisonous gases. There are several ways of doing it. You should have seen that your candle didn't stay alight."

"I did."

"That was a warning. It meant . . . get out quickly. There are pockets of poisonous gases down there. We've searched the place now. There's no sign of Dickson. He was never there. No one was there . . . but you."

"So people went down after I came up?"

"We had made it safe by lighting dry bracken and throwing it down. The descending blaze changes the temperature, stirs up the currents of fresh air in the shaft and so drives out the poison. Then we give it the candle test, and if the flame stays we say it's safe to go down. Dickson lured you there for some reason. I'm going to find out what."

"It was something to do with the Green Flash. I had talked to him about it."

"Why not to me?"

"You had other interests."

"What nonsense."

There was silence for a few moments; then he said: "There was something you said when I brought you out. You said: 'So you came to kill me. So it was you, Joss. . . .' That was what you said."

"I spoke my thoughts aloud."

"You really believed *that* of me. Oh my God, this farce has gone on long enough."

"Why shouldn't I believe it? It fitted. You got rid of Ezra. I thought it was my turn. . . ."

He stared at me incredulously. "Don't you understand anything," he said with the old contempt.

"I understand that you hated me . . . you avoided me . . . you humiliated me whenever possible."

"What did you expect me to do? Didn't you avoid *me* . . . humiliate me by your constant assurance that you wanted *me* out of your way."

"Because I didn't fall victim to your virility. . . ."

"I can see you have a lot to learn, and it's not about opals. Get well quickly. I have to start to teach you right away."

I half rose in my bed and he took me by the shoulders and kissed me.

"Joss," I began, "there's so much. . . ."

But neither of us wanted explanations then.

At length he said: "Ben was right. I realized that pretty soon. I was waiting for you to come and tell me."

"Why didn't you say so?"

"Too proud," he replied. "I wanted it to come from you. Many times at night I've come to your bedroom door. Once I almost burst in."

"I know. I heard you. I thought you'd come to murder me."

"You're crazy," he retorted. "I'll have a lot to say to you. Just now you've had a shock. We might have gone on and on like this, but when you asked me if I'd come to kill you that was the end of it. I plot to kill my own wife . . . the only wife I ever wanted!"

"Say that again."

He did, and I cried: "Why didn't you tell me before? Didn't you know it was what I wanted to hear more than anything else?"

"What a deceiver you are! You made me feel you were trying to get away from me all the time. Now you're getting excited. You mustn't. You came very close to death in that old mine. It has its effect. Perhaps you'll wake up tomorrow morning and find you still hate me."

"Don't talk of hate . . . talk of love," I begged.

"I will . . . endlessly . . . when you've rested. Don't forget I'm in command. You've had a great shock and you need to stay here quietly."

"Will you stay with me?"

"I will, but you must lie still and rest. Just lie there thinking of two foolish people who have said good-by to their folly and are now going to wake up and live."

I felt lightheaded, as I had in the underground passages of the mine; but with a difference. This was not the delirium of fear but of joy.

I must have slept a long time, for it was midmorning when I awoke. Joss was sitting by my bed watching me.

"You're better now," he told me. "You've had a good night's sleep. You've cast off the effects of the poison, but you'll have to go quietly for a day or two."

"There's so much we have to say."

"We've a long time to say it."

"Just tell me one thing: Is it really true that you care about me?"

"It's the truest thing that ever happened."

"Yet you were planning to go to England with Isa Bannock."

"When I go to England you're coming with me."

"Why did you pretend . . . ?"

"Because I wanted to goad you. I wanted you to show some feeling for *me*."

"You seemed so involved with her."

"I've only been involved with one woman since I married. The rest was pretense to try to break through her indifference."

"You gave her a magnificent opal."

"Why did you think I did that?"

"Because she wanted it and you were so besotted by her and wanted to please her at all cost. You liked to show her what an important man you were. She only had to express a wish for you to grant it."

"Wrong again. I gave it to her because I knew you'd hate it. I thought it might show you how foolishly you were acting and arouse some feeling in you. I thought it might be a first step towards sanity. . . ."

"Rather an expensive step."

"Anything that brought about that state couldn't have been too expensive." Then he turned to me and kissed me fiercely. "That's what I mean by sanity."

"You have changed . . . changed overnight. Because I go down into a mine. . . ."

"Because I came near to losing you I made up my mind I was going to keep you and make you understand."

"Why didn't we talk before?"

"We did nothing else but talk. In fact I think we got rather fascinated by all those verbal fireworks. Time and time again I was on the point of pushing all that aside and being the primitive male."

"Which I believe you are."

"You'll discover," he replied. "But just now you have to recover from a rather shattering experience. You think you have already, but the shock was great. I want you to stay quietly in the house for the rest of the day."

"Where are you going?"

"To find Jeremy Dickson. He's concerned in this, and I want to know the meaning of that letter."

"Lilias said it wasn't his handwriting."

"Lilias is trying to defend him. He's somewhere in the neighborhood, and I'm sending people out to look for him. I was waiting for you to wake up so that I could tell you this and where I was going."

"I cannot believe this of Jeremy Dickson."

"One can never believe these things of the people who do them. That's why they get away with them . . . up to a point."

"You really believe he sent that letter, don't you? Why should he want me dead? It doesn't make sense."

"That's what we have to find out. I've sent off parties in all directions. I'm going off now and taking Jimson with me."

"Do you think he had anything to do with the purse?"

"What purse?"

"Ezra's. I found it in the orchard . . . buried there."

"You couldn't have."

"I did and later someone took it from my room."

He was puzzled. I had an idea that he thought the poisonous gases had made me a little lightheaded.

He said: "We'll talk about all that later. I just wanted to make sure you were all right before I went." His eyes blazed for a moment. "I can't forget," he went on, "that you might have died in that mine . . . believing that I wanted to kill you."

"It's over now," I answered. "What I'm remembering now is that you risked your life to save me."

He grinned, his old self again. "I just had to," he said. "It was pure selfishness, for what good would the mine have been to me without you?"

I felt then that I had reached the summit of happiness.

Joss became brisk. "You're to have a restful day. I'm going to leave you in the care of Mrs. Laud and I'll be back before sundown."

Then he took me into his arms and held me as though he would never let me go, and I was content to remain there.

He said: "If Ben were looking down . . . or up from wherever he is . . . he'd be pleased with himself. I reckon he's laughing in the way we remember so well and saying: 'I told you so.'"

Then he kissed me again and again.

"Till sundown."

14

The Green Flash

I rose in a leisurely way, washed, and dressed. I was still feeling a little dazed. Mrs. Laud came to my room to see how I was.

"Not at all bad," I answered. "Just a little tired."

"It's to be expected after what happened. What would you like to eat?"

"I'll wait for luncheon."

"Come to my room and I'll make a cup of tea."

"That would be nice," I said.

"Come up when you're ready. I'll go and put the kettle on."

Within five minutes I was knocking at her door.

"Do come in. You look so much better. The tea's all ready. I've poured out."

"What a cozy room this is," I said.

"I always thought so. Mr. Henniker used to like to come in for a cup of tea."

I sat down in the chair she had pulled up to the table with the plush runner. Her workbox was open, and a piece of needlework lay on the table.

"Oh Mrs. Madden, what bad luck you've had lately. First you nearly fall down the stairs and then you get into that mine. It looks like bad luck, doesn't it? People will be saying *you* must have taken the Green Flash and this is the result of it."

I sipped the tea, which was refreshingly warming.

"People will say anything."

"That's a fact, they will. But it was bad luck, wasn't it? . . . first one and then the other. I'd like to know what that Jeremy Dickson thought he was up to. How's the tea?"

"It's very good, thank you."

"Drink it up and I'll give you another cup. I always say there's nothing like a nice cup of tea."

"There's a good deal in that."

"They're regular tea drinkers out here . . . every bit as much as we are at Home. Let me give you that other cup."

"Thank you, Mrs. Laud."

"Do you feel rather sleepy?"

"I feel a little . . . strange."

"I thought you did somehow. The house is quiet now, isn't it? Do you know we're the only ones here. Everybody's out. They've all gone on this wild goose chase. All except two of the girls and I said they could ride into the town and get some goods for me. They're both friendly with gougers there." She chuckled. "I reckon they won't hurry back."

Then I noticed that she was watching me very intently and that there was a strange gleam in her eyes.

"I'm going to show you something before you go," she said.

"Show me something . . . before I go . . . where?"

"It's in my workbox. There's a little secret drawer. You remember that night . . . the Treasure Hunt? That Ezra . . . he knew. I could see the look in his eyes that something had led him to my workbox."

I tried to stand up but I couldn't. My legs seemed as though they were not part of my body.

"Don't try to go yet. You'll want to see this. I had it since he went away. Mr. Henniker couldn't have been far out at sea when I found it. I was always particular about the spring cleaning. You can't trust those servants. There was always a lot I liked to do myself. I was always very fond of that picture. Mr. Henniker used to like it. He said it reminded him of Joss, and he had a way of looking at it and laughing to himself, and it struck me that there was something rather special about it. That was why I paid such special attention to it. I found the spring, and then I knew it was meant. That was how it happened." She leaned forward, her arms on the table. "There's something inside it, something that's alive . . . a living god. Do you remember Aladdin's lamp? Well, it's like that, you see. The genii is there and it does your bidding."

I said: "You're talking about the Green Flash at Sunset, Mrs. Laud."

"Yes," she answered. "That's what I'm talking about."

"Are you telling me that you had it all the time?"

She started to laugh. A change had come over her yet again. It was as though she had been impersonating someone at a masque and now it was the time for the unmasking. I had never known this woman. No wonder I had felt that she was like the chorus in a Greek play—she and her family. She was no longer the mild housekeeper so grateful to have become the master's mistress and found shelter for herself and her family all those years. She was someone else. But perhaps the mild housekeeper was the real person and that it was another which looked out at me from those wild eyes. She was possessed.

She repeated: "You shall see it before you go. I want you to see it. I shall never forget the moment when I found it at the back of that picture and it just burst on me . . . all that brilliance, all that power. 'I'm yours,' it said to me. 'Keep me. I'll work for you. Anything you want will be yours.' I wasn't going to keep it at first. I was just going to have it in my room and look at it. I used to wake up in the night and remember I'd got it. I'd get out of bed and look at it. And then I started to see that I could do anything I wanted because the Green Flash would give it to me."

"Show it to me, Mrs. Laud," I said quietly.

She drew the workbox towards her and fumbled there. I have never seen a miser counting his gold, but I could imagine what he would look like and that was as Mrs. Laud looked at that moment. Her face changed again; her mouth twitched and her eyes blazed. I thought: She really is mad. The Green Flash has driven her mad.

She took out a mass of cotton wool; her fingers shook as she unwrapped it. Then she took something in the palms of her hands and crooned over it as a mother might over a baby.

She leaned across the table and there it lay in all its fabulous glory, the most magnificent opal of all time, the stone which had shaped my destiny, the unlucky one, the most beautiful jewel I had ever or would ever see in my life.

It is impossible to put into words the qualities of that stone. I can say it was large . . . even larger than I had expected it to be; even with my sparse knowledge I knew that it was perfect in every way. I can say that there was the deep blue of a tropical sea and the lighter blue of a cloudless sky, and the glint of red was like shafts of sunlight breaking over the sea. But this does not convey the utter fascination, the aura, the living quality. It had life; it changed as one looked. I was feeling more and more dizzy and hazy and it really seemed to me that I could lose myself in that scintillating color, drown in that deep deep blue sea. It had a power, that stone; a subtle emanation came from it. It was magnetic and I could not stop myself reaching out to take it.

"Oh no you don't," she said. "You think you're going to take it from me, don't you? You think you've found it at last. I tell you this, Mrs. Madden, I'm only showing it to you, that's all. I thought you should see it before you died."

"Before . . . I died . . . ?"

"Feel sleepy, don't you? It won't hurt. You won't know anything. It was something I put in your tea . . . nice, peaceful sleep, that's all. Look at my hands. They're strong. You've got a little neck. I've often looked at it. It'll be easy. I know just where to press. But I'll wait until you're fast asleep. I don't like hurting things . . . so it's better that way. You'll know nothing about it."

I could feel the hair rising on my scalp, and it was because she spoke so quietly in such a matter of fact way that was so sinister. It was only when she mentioned the Green Flash that her hysteria became apparent. I was alone in this house with a mad woman. I had not really taken her seriously until I had seen the Green Flash. Then I knew that she was indeed mad. She had put a sleeping draught into my tea; and I was going to get more and more drowsy under its influence.

I wondered if I could make a dash for the door, but my limbs were already leaden. I kept thinking: Alone in the house . . . everybody gone . . . alone with a woman who is mad.

She was looking down at her hands . . . those hands which were waiting to strangle me . . . but not till I slept, so I must not sleep. I must keep awake. I must find some way of outwitting her.

I said: "You play the spinet well, Mrs. Laud."

It was eerie—the manner in which she slipped from the malevolent personality of the murderess to that of the homely housekeeper.

"Oh yes, I used to play for Mr. Henniker. He told me about this Jessica who was your mother. I didn't like that much, because I was fond of Mr. Henniker myself. He had this fancy about playing and her coming back. So I played for him and he said it reminded him of her."

"And then you played for me?"

"You started to pry, didn't you? As soon as you got back you did. You always had your eyes open and you were looking for the Green Flash. I knew that. I got wonderful ideas from the power that's there. I was there when you looked with Mr. Madden and later with Mr. Dickson. I watched

you take down 'The Pride of the Peacock.' I didn't want
Lilias to marry Jeremy Dickson. I wanted Mr. Madden for
her. That was a fancy of mine. I guessed Mr. Henniker would
leave him the Green Flash and then it would be partly
hers. But no, it was mine. Never mind Lilias . . . because
you'd come then and you'd have to be got rid of. I didn't
want Lilias to have it even. It was mine and I wanted to
keep it."

"You've been getting it to work for you, have you?"

She nodded. "It first came to me when Tom Paling came
over to the house and I went into the stables and meddled
with the wheel of the buggy. Then he had his accident and
Jimson had his job and did very well at it. You see, the
Flash puts the notions into your head and shows you how
to do it."

"So you lured me to the gallery."

"I wanted you to think it was your mother warning you."

"Why did you want me warned?"

"The Flash is clever. It never does anything without reason.
I wanted you to tell people you were afraid . . . because you
thought your husband wanted you out of the way, didn't
you? When wives die mysteriously husbands are the first to
be suspected. I knew how things were . . . separate bedrooms
and Isa Bannock. I thought you'd tell someone. He used to
play the spinet long ago. Ben liked to hear him at it. And
he knew about the stairs, didn't he?"

"So it was you who played, and you escaped by way of
the stairs and then you arranged for me to have an accident,
and if I was killed you would have seen that my husband
was suspected?"

"It was not really the Flash's idea. That was mine. It
wasn't very good. It was hardly likely that a fall down those
stairs would have been the end of you . . . and there was all
that playing to get you up there and I could easily have been
caught at that. But if you'd had a bad accident it would have
stopped your prying for a bit and it would be a sort of
preliminary, if you know what I mean. Lilias spoilt it. She
got hysterical about my playing the spinet and she and Jimson tried to stop me. They were always watching me closely.
They didn't know I had the Flash of course, but they thought
I'd changed and they got frightened."

I must stay awake and keep her talking so I said: "By this
time had you given up the idea of Lilias marrying my
husband?"

"Well, it could have been a good idea, but the main thing was to keep the Flash. When I came into my room that night and saw Ezra Bannock looking into my workbox I knew he had guessed. There was something in his face which told me."

"So you killed him?"

"Yes, I did. I waited for him at Grover's Gully and I shot him and buried him there. He'd have stayed there hidden for years if it hadn't been for that horse. And you were the one who found him. That was it. . . . The idea came to me that you were Danger. The Flash put it into my mind so I knew it was right."

"And the letter from Jeremy Dickson?"

"I spent hours copying his writing on his acceptance to the invitation to the Treasure Hunt. I think I did well. There again it was the Flash. I thought that would have done it. And Lilias . . . my own daughter stopped it. She found that letter. What was she doing prying in your room? She was jealous of you with Jeremy. Well, she found it and she swore it wasn't his writing. She went into the town with the letter and it was all spoiled again. Now of course something's got to be done."

Her face puckered and she looked as though she were going to burst into tears.

"I could see it in Mr. Madden's face. I could see he wasn't going to let it rest. Someone had threatened *you*, and he'll find out too much. He's like Mr. Henniker. He'll go on and on until he gets to the bottom of things . . . and I've got to stop him."

"You will never be able to."

She looked cunning. "The Flash has the answer. The Flash always has the answer. There's no beating the Flash. It's only when I don't let myself listen that I go wrong . . . like burying that purse. That was silly. I took it because I wanted them to think it was for robbery. I should have thrown it away in the Bush somewhere. Then it wouldn't have mattered if it had been found. So then I had to get it back and that was wrong . . . I won't act without the Flash again. The Flash is all powerful. No one can go against it."

"You tried to kill me and you didn't. Twice you've failed."

"I didn't understand what the Flash was telling me."

"And you think you do now?"

"Oh yes. I've got it all clear now."

Oh God, I prayed, help me fight off this overwhelming desire to shut my eyes and escape into oblivion, help me to keep awake. While I'm awake I'm safe. I've got to keep her talking.

"It won't work, Mrs. Laud," I said.

She looked startled.

"You have drugged me. You've got so far and you think you're going to kill me."

She nodded, smiling benignly. She looked down at her hands and stretched her fingers, flexing them.

"Suppose you kill me," I went on. "I shall be in this room. How will you explain what happened to me? You'll be exposed as a murderess. They don't let murderesses live, Mrs. Laud. So what good will it do you?"

"You won't be here," she said. "You'll disappear." She laughed, and it was a demoniacal laughter that sent cold shivers down my spine. It reminded me that I was fighting for my life with a woman who was mad and yet had the strength to kill me. One false step could be the end of me. I could see no way of escape.

In the palm of her hands she still held the Green Flash. She seemed as though she could not put it down, as though she were afraid that if she let it go some power would leave her.

All these months when I had been living in this house with her she had been mad.

I did not speak, because while she forgot my presence, as she appeared to now, I was gaining precious moments. She would not touch me while I was conscious. She was not by nature a violent woman; it was only this thing which had possessed her which could make her capable of perpetrating acts of violence.

I thought of Joss . . . I could not stop thinking of Joss. I was still tingling with memories of our encounter. There was so much explaining to do . . . but one fact surpassed all others. He had come down into the mine to bring me up. He had risked his life to save me. He had come riding to the mine with all speed when he had seen the letter. He loved me. He wanted me. Those steps in the corridor had been his. He had given Isa Bannock the Harlequin to sting me into awareness of my true feelings and he had succeeded, because it was after this that I had realized my need of him. We had both been foolish; we had refused to see the truth. Ben had been wiser than we had. And now when I saw it clearly I was in deadly danger of losing it. Our pride had kept us apart—mine no less than Joss's; and now in his ignorance he had left me alone with the murderess.

Death faced me, and if it was victorious I would never know the life Joss had promised me. I could see two roads stretching out before me—one ended abruptly in death and the other was full of exciting twists and turns which life with Joss would be. I should long ago have started down that road. Why had I been such a fool as to fear it?

Oh where are you now, Joss? I wondered. I want us to start to live . . . now.

Where would it end? He was off on a false trail, hunting for Jeremy Dickson, who was no doubt sitting in his Sydney office discussing the properties of certain stones which had recently been found in the Fancy mines.

Mrs. Laud was remembering.

"Everything is ready. It's in the garden . . . I shall bury you there and no one will think to look. I shall hide your traveling bag and some of your clothes will be missing."

"You couldn't do it, Mrs. Laud. Think what happened to Ezra Bannock's purse. The Flash wasn't very clever about that, was she?"

"I told you that she did not want that. It was where *I* went wrong. I wouldn't mock her, if I were you. She'd never forgive you. She was warning me then. She was saying: 'Bury her deep. No one must find her as she found the purse. . . .'"

"Still you *were* wrong about the purse."

"It was meant as a warning to me. It was a preparation for this. That's how it happens sometimes."

"It seems strange to be sitting here discussing my burial."

"What are you getting at, Mrs. Madden? You've always been one for a joke. But this is no joke. I shall tell them that you have the Green Flash, that you showed it to me, that I tried to persuade you to give it up. That you've gone right away with the Flash."

"It wouldn't be possible. Unless you are going to kill Wattle and bury her too."

"Oh no. You'll have gone away with someone who came for you. He brought horses and you rode away together."

"Jeremy Dickson, I suppose."

"That could do for a start. . . ."

"And when he comes back?"

"The Flash will know. Why don't you go to sleep? It's better if you do. Then we can get it over."

"I'm not going to sleep."

"You must. You can't help it."

She was wildly fanatical. I saw the greed in her eyes and I thought this stone has done this to her. She means to do exactly what she has told me. This stone ruined my mother's life and now I may well die because of it. I have seen it and that is enough, for I understand what it can do. There is evil in it and it has taken possession of this woman.

I gripped the table. Waves and waves of weariness swept over me. I tried not to think of the softness of a feather bed and downy pillows. I thought of death and Joss's coming back and finding me gone. Would he really believe that I had gone off with Jeremy Dickson . . . and later when Jeremy returned . . . with some person unknown . . . taking with me the Green Flash.

Others had been obsessed by that stone. Would he believe that it could happen to me?

I *must* stay awake. I was fighting for my life as I had never fought for anything. I must remind myself that all that stood between Joss and me and our exciting future was a mad woman.

I heard myself saying over and over again: "You could never do it. . . ."

I saw her face as though it floated before me . . . the mask down . . . the madness of the possessed, and I knew that her very madness would give her the powers she needed.

The scene in this room was getting more and more remote. I felt that I was outside looking in on the actions of others: myself limp and lifeless being dragged to a spot in the garden where the sandy loose soil encroached on the cultivated part. It would be easy to bury me quickly there, and later she would make a better job of it. She would give me a deeper grave. She would take my clothes away and hide them. . . .

I saw Joss returning from the hunt for Jeremy Dickson, which would prove fruitless. How could it be otherwise when he was working in Sydney? I could see his anger, his fury, his wounded pride. How he had hated to be repulsed by me! How he had retaliated by wounding me through Isa Bannock!

And now he would believe that I had deceived him. How could he? Her plan could not work. With whom should I have gone off? There was no one who could possibly be suspected.

Yet who would believe that the quiet, unassuming housekeeper could be capable of such diabolical plans. But it was not really this one. It was the evil which possessed her.

I heard myself murmuring: "No . . . no . . . no. . . ."

The minutes were ticking by.

"Cuckoo, cuckoo, cuckoo. . . ." said the silly little bird in her clock. I could hear the cuckoos going on and on in my head, as I felt myself slipping away. But every time I brought myself back.

She was getting worried.

"I don't understand this. You should be off by now."

"My will power is stronger than your drug, Mrs. Laud."

"Why," she said, "anyone would think *you* had the Flash."

"It is mine . . . by right. I share it jointly with my husband. Perhaps it knows that."

I saw the real fear in her eyes.

"Yes," I went on. "It knows. See how it shines for me. It knows it is mine."

"No, no. I've had it all this time. It's not the one who owns it by law. It was meant to be mine. I'd never had anything very much before but with the Flash I had everything. It's possession that counts. All this time it's worked for me."

"But not against *me*, Mrs. Laud. You made an accident for Tom Paling. You killed Ezra Bannock. You lured me to the stairs, but see how I saved myself. Then you tried the mine and I was rescued."

Her face had turned a pale gray.

"You see," I went on, "the Flash won't hurt me because I'm the true owner. It's mine, Mrs. Laud."

"I'll never give her up . . . never," she screamed.

"Look, Mrs. Laud, it's only a piece of opal . . . silica deposited at some time in the rock. How can you attach special powers to that?"

She looked at me as though she did not understand what I was talking about.

"It's done you a great deal of harm," I went on. "Don't you see?"

She stared at me blankly.

Oh, thank you, God, I prayed. I'm fighting off my sleepiness. I'm going to do it. I'm going to live. Keep her talking. Keep remembering that Joss is waiting for you and you are going to start to live as you never have before.

"You've become obsessed by a stone . . . by a legend . . . you've built all this up in your mind, but it doesn't really exist."

"How dare you call it just a stone. *You* haven't lived with it. You haven't held it in your hands. Look now. . . ."

"Yes, let me see it. Let me hold it in *my* hands."

She shook her head craftily. "Oh no. You can see it from where you are. Look at it. It's the sun going down into the sea. If you look closely you might catch a sudden flash of green. That's what the sun does and that's what my Green Flash does too."

I was alert suddenly. I thought I heard sounds from below.

Someone was coming. I looked at her, but she was staring at the opal, absorbed in the wonder of it and her own beliefs.

Waves of relief were sweeping over me. I believed I had won.

The door was flung open. Joss was there. Someone else was with him. It was Jimson.

Jimson cried out in a voice of anguish: "Mother."

She stood up, her eyes on her son. "You've brought him back," she screamed. "Lilias did it before . . . and now you. My own children. . . ."

She stood up clutching the stone. Joss's eyes were on me and I stood up and tottered towards him for now that the need to hold tightly to consciousness was no longer urgent I felt the waves of drowsiness too much to resist.

Joss caught me in his arms. He said my name twice. It was wonderful how much he could express by just that. He held me against him and I was content to stay there.

I heard Jimson's voice, anguished, pleading: "Mother, I had to. I knew something was wrong."

Joss said: "Give me what you're holding in your hand, Mrs. Laud."

Her agonized scream broke into my unconsciousness bringing me back into the room. There was silence which seemed to go on and on.

When I awoke from my drugged sleep I remembered it all vividly—every intonation of her voice, every expression on her face.

Joss told me how she had cried out that she would never give up the Green Flash, and before they could stop her she had dashed onto the terrace.

When they picked her up from the stones below she was dead, but still clutching the Green Flash in her hands.

It was six months later when Joss and I went back to Oakland—a new me, a new Joss.

They had been a wonderful six months of discovery and adventure—the greatest adventure of all, being loved and loving.

Lilias had married Jeremy Dickson before we sailed. She talked to me a great deal and told me how she and Jimson had both realized that their mother was verging on madness, though they had not guessed how far she had gone. They had not been aware of course that she had the Green Flash, but they suspected that something had turned her brain. They had discovered that she played the spinet and this was what had so upset Lilias on that occasion when I had discovered her hysterically crying. Both she and Jimson, while being eager to protect their mother, had wondered what her motive had been. When I had had the accident on the stairs and had been lured to the mine they became very suspicious; and that was why Jimson, when he had heard that I had been left in a weak state with his mother, decided to tell Joss of his anxieties for my safety, which resulted in Joss's speedy return to the house.

Lilias, in great distress, tried to explain to me, but I told her there was no need to. I understood perfectly. They had tried hard to protect their mother who had done everything for them when they had been helpless children. She had come to Peacocks, had worked for Ben, had loved him and hoped to marry him. But Ben did not want marriage and she had to content herself with a home for herself and her children. She had been a very conventional woman, and the situation had worried her a great deal. I could imagine how she grappled with her conscience and how she might have quieted it by telling it she did what she did for her children's sake. But it would have preyed on her mind, I realized, and she would have been constantly trying to make things right. If Lilias had married Joss, she might have felt everything was worth while. That was certainly in her mind, Lilias told me, and it was the reason why she had tried to stop a match between her daughter and Jeremy Dickson.

Then she had discovered the Green Flash and the madness had set in. It had led her to maim Tom Paling, to murder

Ezra, and to attempt to kill me. Still, somewhere at the back of her mind must have been the idea that if I were not there Joss might marry Lilias, but her great fear was that I would find the Green Flash. She had been jealous of my mother and that had meant that she had been against me from the start. But how well she had concealed her animosity with her humility and her constant expressions of her desire to help me. It did not seem possible that she could be so devious, but I had come to the conclusion that there were really two Mrs. Lauds—the housekeeper eager to please and help run the house smoothly, and the mad woman whose mind had become deranged when the fascination of the Green Flash had caught her and made her its prisoner.

I was sorry for Jimson and Lilias, but Jeremy was about to comfort Lilias, and Jimson seemed to find a certain solace in his work.

And when Joss and I decided to go Home, it was due to the Green Flash.

I had talked this out with Joss and it was one of the matters over which we were in disagreement. There were, of course, many matters over which we disagreed and somehow that gave a stimulus to our life together.

Joss used to laugh when we argued fiercely. "Well, I always knew I must expect fireworks from you," he said.

"Fireworks make such a glorious blaze," I retorted. "You must admit they're exciting to watch."

"I always enjoy them," he answered. "And they make the occasions when we do agree extra good."

Of course everyone in the town was waiting for bad luck to strike us.

"There'll always be legend attached to that stone," I said.

"Naturally. It's unique."

Joss liked to take it out and look at it. "You're getting obsessed," I accused him.

"Nonsense. There's only one thing in the world I'm obsessed with."

"And that?"

"You know very well it's you."

"Oh Joss," I cried, "you say such marvelous things sometimes. Obsessions can be momentary though. They often don't last."

"There you are. Never satisfied."

"Well, there was a time when you were obsessed by Isa Bannock."

"That was before you came. Everyone was obsessed by Isa. I fell in love with her when I was sixteen . . . in common with everyone around here."

"But you continued with the affair."

"She seemed to expect it."

"And you gave her the Harlequin Opal."

"Ah, but only to spite you."

"Sometimes I hate you, Joss Madden."

"I know. It makes the times when you love just marvelous." He was serious suddenly. "Forget Isa. It's over. I behaved as I did because you wouldn't have me. You scorned me . . . scorned the peacock. Peacocks don't like that. They get spiteful."

"That was the cruelest thing you did . . . to give her the Harlequin."

"I'm going to make up for it. I'm giving you something more valuable. The Green Flash."

"No, Joss."

"Yes, you'll forget that Harlequin incident then. I'm going to relinquish my share. It's yours. It's a thousand times more valuable than the Harlequin."

"I've been meaning to speak to you about the Green Flash. I'm frightened of it."

"You! Frightened of a stone?"

"Yes, I am. It ruined my mother's life. It changed mine. Ezra died for it. Tom Paling nearly did . . . and so did I."

"You're not going to let all that talk upset *you*."

"I'm not thinking of myself, but my family . . . I won't run risks. There are some things which are too precious to be put in jeopardy."

"Me? The child?"

I nodded.

He was moved, I could see, so he laughed at me half derisive, half tender. "So what do you propose to do?" he asked.

"We're taking the Green Flash to London and we're presenting it to a geological museum there. People will be able to see it and marvel at it and I'll cheat the evil in it because it won't belong to anyone."

"So you're resigning all claim of my gift to you?"

"Your gift to me, Joss, is not a stone. It's much more than that could ever be."

"Do you know," he said "you're getting sentimental as you grow up."

"Do you mind that?"

"How can I when you're making me the same?"

I wanted my baby to be born in Oakland Hall, and it was a whim Joss was ready to humor. I knew Ben would have been pleased. Joss was his son, and there would be a new line to add to the genealogical tree in the hall which always intrigued him. Mr. Wilmot and Mrs. Bucket thought this right and proper.

Oakland had not changed. Why should it because I had been to Australia and fallen in love and come near to death, when it had stood for hundreds of years and had no doubt witnessed as many tragedies and comedies?

Miriam had a child now. "She'll live to rue the day," said my grandmother.

My grandfather was a little bolder than he had been, and the whip with which my grandmother had scourged him had lost some of its sting since I had brought Oakland back to the family in a way, and because Xavier had now married Lady Clara and was managing the Donningham land.

My grandmother was quite respectful to me and most interested in the child who was to be born at Oakland—a gesture with which she entirely agreed. She even took to Joss after the first few skirmishes. I think she recognized some power in him which it would be impossible even for her to subdue.

She used to say: "Well, he received a large part of his education in England," as though that made him acceptable; and the fact that he had brought Oakland back to the family made him most admirable in her eyes.

My son was born on a mellow September day in the vaulted chamber where my ancestors had made their first appearances.

This was the culmination of my happiness. I sat up in the big four-poster bed and looked out on those lawns which had mellowed for hundreds of years, and I had a feeling that I had come home; and yet I was well aware that nothing was half as important to me as the rich and full life I should live with my husband and son.

Joss came and looked at the baby, marveling at the tiny creature as though he couldn't believe he was real. Then he turned to me. "It's good, eh?" he said.

"What?" I asked.

"Life," he answered. "Just life."

"It's good," I agreed, "and going to be better."
"Who can be sure of that?" he asked.
"*I* can," I retorted. "And I will."